The Fo﹏ Winds

Gerd Brantenberg

translated from the Norwegian by

Margaret Hayford O'Leary

WOMEN IN TRANSLATION

English translation copyright © 1994 by Margaret Hayford O'Leary.

Published by arrangement with H. Aschehoug & Co.
Copyright © 1989 by Gerd Brantenberg
Publication of this book was made possible in part with financial support from the National Endowment for the Arts and NORLA (Norwegian Literature Abroad).

Text design by Clare Conrad.
Cover design by Kate Thompson.

Library of Congress Cataloging in Publication Data:

Brantenberg, Gerd, 1941–
  [For alle vinder. English]
  The four winds / Gerd Brantenberg
     Mp.   cm.
  ISBN 1-879679-05-1
  I. Title.
PT8951.12.R34F6713 1996
839.8'2374—dc20 95-43075

First edition, February 1996
Printed in the United States of America
10 9 8 7 6 5 4 3 2 1

Women in Translation
3131 Western Avenue #410
Seattle WA 98121-1041

CONTENTS

Introduction

Gerd Brantenberg, lesbian and active participant in the Norwegian women's movement since the early 1970s, is one of the more outspoken and original feminist novelists in Norway today. Brantenberg's concern with sexual politics figures in everything she has written, though serious topics never seem ponderous thanks to the author's sense of humor. Already in her first book, *What Comes Naturally* (1973), Brantenberg demonstrates that her good natured yet pointed humor is an effective means of bringing readers face to face with their prejudices, sexist attitudes and homophobia.

Language is another weapon Brantenberg has utilized to great advantage in her campaign for sexual equality. In her next book, *Egalia's Daughters* (1977), she set out to create a fictional society in which sex roles are completely reversed, but she soon understood that the patriarchal language of contemporary Western society is itself a subtle form of oppression and as such could not be used in the matriarchal land of Egalia. So she invented a new language for her new social order where the "wim" have all the power and the "menwim" stay at home minding the children and making pretty "pehoes" (penis holders) for their sons to wear to the "Maidmen's ball." This novel, which was to become a major international success, is alluded to towards the end of *The Four Winds*. The idea for this book comes to the main character while she is sitting on the streetcar and she begins to laugh out loud, for the very realization that she can write such a novel is both liberating and exhilarating.

Brantenberg's most ambitious literary project to date has been the three semi-autobiographical novels about Inger Holm. She calls on her own experiences of growing up in the closed milieu of small-town Norway to write *The Song of St. Croix: A Book about a Town (1948-55)* (1979) and its two independent sequels, *The Ferry Landing: Student Lives (1955-60)* (1985) and *The Four Winds: A Novel about a Girl (1960-65)* (1989). As the subtitles would indicate, the first two novels can be considered collective novels, the main character being the school class of which Inger Holm is a member—the class that graduated from Fredrikstad Høyere Almenskole in 1960. The novels follow the students of the class from the time they enter elementary school in 1948, through their years in school and beyond. Although the town of Fredrikstad and the school itself are described in intimate detail, the main focus is on relationships. Brantenberg tells the stories through switching points of view, including an occasional omniscient author comment, signaling the shifts by changes in dialect and language usage.

A major theme of the first of these novels, *The Song of St. Croix*, is the stark contrast between the limitless potential of the little girls beginning their first year in elementary school, and the reality of the dashed hopes and expectations of their mothers. Several unhappy women, unfulfilled in their roles as housewives, are portrayed, including Evelyn Holm, Inger's mother. Although she adores her children, and is in many ways the perfect mother, she regrets the dramatic life of the stage she left behind. She now lives with a difficult husband, Ørnulf, whose short temper and domineering personality are only exacerbated by his drinking. Yet despite the alcoholism and abuse plaguing their marriage, they are bound by love and affection, and Evelyn and Ørnulf cannot live without one other. Their love is put to the ultimate test when their older daughter, Helga, dies of polio at age thirteen. This death is a recurring issue for the whole family, as each family member struggles to deal with feelings of guilt and helplessness.

Another theme is Inger's growing political awareness and

consciousness of class differences. This theme gains importance throughout the trilogy, as Inger struggles to come to grips with her homosexuality and the political implications of her sexual orientation.

In the second novel, *The Ferry Landing*, eleven of the twenty-three girls who had graduated from St. Croix school continue at "The Yellow Institution," their name for the middle school/high school in Fredrikstad. The difficulties of growing up, and questions of identity, religion and sexuality are explored. Again Brantenberg employs a shifting point of view to examine the fates of several of Inger's classmates, both male and female. Inger becomes one of the leaders of the student club, and at the same time as she discovers her leadership abilities and talent for writing, she also becomes conscious of her tendency to fall in love with girls. Her mother and father experience even more severe drinking problems and increased tension in their marriage, and for the first time Inger stands up against her father to protect her mother.

As the children of the town change and develop, so does the town. Bridges are constructed over the Glomma river, replacing two of the ferry crossings. This book ends just as *The Four Winds* begins, with the class of 1960 graduating from high school and preparing to leave Fredrikstad to make their way in the world.

Language and challenges for the translator
There are two official written languages in Norway, *bokmål* and *nynorsk*. The majority language, *bokmål*, is derived from Danish, and in its earlier versions, was called first Dano-Norwegian and then later *riksmål*. Very conservative *bokmål* is still often called *riksmål*. In addition to these written forms, there are hundreds of spoken dialects. Both *nynorsk* and *bokmål* have a range of acceptable usage, which is largely determined by local oral dialect and social class. The "radical" version of *bokmål* (which actually approaches *nynorsk*) was often used deliberately by university students to make a political statement.

Brantenberg is a master at using varying forms of dialects and linguistic register to signal social class and shifts in point of view. She also enjoys word play, pushing the meanings of words to the limit. Language is equated with identity, as demonstrated throughout the novels, but particularly in *The Four Winds*. Inger and her family do not speak the local dialect, and her relationship to the Fredrikstad dialect is reflected in that fact. She finds it difficult to accept that the dialect spoken in Fredrikstad is a legitimate language rather than evidence of lack of education. This difficulty becomes a topic of political debate between Inger and her politically radical English friend, Rose Mary, a fellow student at the University of Oslo, who deliberately employs the above-mentioned radical forms as a political tool, a new experience for Inger.

Brantenberg's use of language is brilliant, but does create challenges for a translator. In some cases I have chosen to leave some Norwegian in the English translation. This was necessary in the scenes set in Edinburgh, where Inger is struggling with her difficulties in expressing herself in a foreign language. In the debate between Inger and Rose Mary, where Inger gives several examples of what she considers improper language use by people in Fredrikstad, I tried to find similar dialectical variations in colloquial American English. Another challenge was to find a way of expressing the difference between the two Norwegian words for "yes." The word *ja* is used to respond to a positive question: "Are you tired," where the word *jo* is a positive response to a negative question: "Aren't you tired?" This is not usually an important differentiation in a translation, but in this case Brantenberg uses this subtle difference to make a point. When in Edinburgh, Inger is greatly frustrated because she yearns for the distinction when she is trying to speak English; another time Rose Mary, who rarely makes errors when speaking Norwegian, misuses the word *jo*, to Inger's amazement and amusement.

The popularity of *Egalia's Daughters* among readers of English demonstrated that Brantenberg's wit and word play can be translated and, moreover, that there is an audience eager to read more of her work. Readers who delighted in the imaginary land of Egalia will find the same exuberance and sense of humor in Brantenberg's story about Inger, but they will also find that *The Four Winds* strikes a deeper chord, underscoring the emotional and psychological range of this versatile and talented writer.

Margaret Hayford O'Leary
St. Olaf College
Northfield, Minnesota

The Four Winds

THE STEPS OF THE PHOENIX CLUB

Inger stood on the steps of the Phoenix Club in Fredrikstad wearing her graduation cap. She'd done well. But within her was a catastrophe. Papa stood beside her, craning his neck to get in the picture. Mama stood watching on the other side, together with the other mothers. Around her stood the whole graduating class in straight rows on the seven steps—each with a sponsor, just like her. Hartvig with Caspar Olesen, Leif Monradsen with his father, Elsa Tøgern with Turid from the Plus artist colony, Lillian with her mother (one of the few mothers in town with a high school diploma), Tove Midtbø with her father. Everyone. This is everyone. This is my world, Inger thought. That was one thing she was sure of. This class has been my whole life, everything I know, and now we'll be split up, and within her was the catastrophe.

No one could see the catastrophe. No one in her world, of all those who knew her so well, for it was invisible. She was a fairly pretty girl (they said), and she was smart, and she was even something as attractive as funny. They said she was pretty, even though they usually qualified the compliment. "You should lose some weight," Jorunn Johansen had said. "If she'd only fix herself up a little—Hell, she'd have been the prettiest girl in the class!" Sigvart Jespersen had said (but not to her). Her hair and flab and sloppiness got in the way of her looks.

Everyone could see that. But that could be changed. She stood there under her student cap and knew that this could be changed—the day she made up her mind. All she had to do was quit sneaking all those caramels and Coca-Colas, fix her hair, stand up straight and put on some nice clothes—she'd be transformed, just like the ugly duckling from Hans Christian Andersen. But the catastrophe would still be within her. And who can spread her wings with a catastrophe inside?

The catastrophe was Tove. The catastrophe was that Tove was standing there, the prettiest, most beautiful person who'd ever set foot on the steps of the Phoenix Club, or strolled down Nygaardsgata, the main street of Fredrikstad, and filled the world. The catastrophe was that when Tove looked at her, talked to her, took her arm, cried or laughed or played bridge with her, she'd achieved her goal in life.

Once—one single time—early in the morning while the birds were singing in Kirkeparken, she'd been on the verge of telling Tove about the whole catastrophe. They were sitting at the outdoor restaurant on the way home from a graduation party, after another all-nighter (marked by one more knot in the tassel of her student cap). But just as she was about to do it, her heart began pounding so hard that her words stuck in her throat. Now they were going their separate ways. Tove had gotten a job in a pub in Wiltshire, pouring beer for the local farmers. It was a mystery how Inger's legs could possibly hold her up when Tove's train left.

My life shouldn't have contained mysteries like this, Inger thought, but they'd always been there. There was always some girl who came along and made her legs unreliable. Her skin came alive and her thoughts flew a hundred times faster than before and stirred up all kinds of crazy ideas. If Tove had been the only one, and there'd been no others, the catastrophe wouldn't have been so big. But that's not how it was. No, a thousand times no! All she had to do was gaze out over all of the new, young, black caps and know that there stood Beate Halvorsen and Elsa Tøgern and even Jorunn Johansen, and

4

they'd all happened, each in their own way, not all as intensely, or as long, they'd happened as differently as their faces, their voices and their laughter. She was just plain incorrigibly *girl crazy*. It was enough to drive you nuts. Yes, *that* was the expression, the one people in Fredrikstad could use for the catastrophe, and that everyone would understand. And if they heard it—if all these people who were her world had heard it—they'd have thrown up.

They'd have thrown up. There was no doubt about it. She herself didn't throw up. She had to live with the beauty of these girls. She had her diploma. She could do whatever she wanted, and there was just one thing to do, and that was to go out into the world and hope that the girls would disappear.

All of them stood on the steps of the Phoenix in Fredrikstad. They stood there hoping and thinking about getting away from the town that had nurtured them. About getting away from the town they owed everything to. But they didn't think about it like that. They didn't think they owed anything to anyone. They hadn't asked to be born, they just were. In Fredrikstad—most of them. Almost all of them had come into the world at St. Joseph's Hospital. And they didn't owe anything to anybody. But they weren't thinking about this or anything else for that matter. They just stood there smiling. That's what you do when you're being photographed.

They stood there hoping that they would look good in the picture. That they would look appealing. That they would look just like themselves—so that everyone could see how good-looking and intelligent they were. "Look over here, everybody!" the photographer said. And everyone looked at him, hoping that good looks and intelligence would shine out in the picture, especially from them.

The picture turned out great. Just as clear and good as all the other pictures taken of graduating classes on the steps of the Phoenix in Fredrikstad. It was on display at Sollem photography studio for everyone to admire who was interested in stopping and looking at it as they walked by. They leaned in towards the window, squinted and said: "There she is!" or: "There he is! Do you see him? On the right, second row from the top! I always knew it—that boy, he's something special."

But for other passersby, who didn't know any of the graduates in this year's class, there was nothing particularly special about anything. It was just another generation of heads under black caps. It's amazing how alike they were, year after year, except that there were boys and girls, of course.

And some people stopped, thinking: That should've been me standing there.

Inger had always known she would stand there. She was just as sure she would be standing there among the graduates as she was that there would be ice at Wiesebanen skating rink in the winter and blue anemones in Rødskogen woods in the spring. And now summer was finally here, with no school waiting at the end. As always she went out to the beach at Tjøme with her parents and her little sister, Ellen. There was the sea and the smooth, sloping rock, and she didn't have any idea what she wanted to be. The reason she didn't was that she wanted to be a writer.

"What are you going to be?" people said. Be, be, be. There'd always been be. "I'm applying for teaching positions in Karasjok and Kautokeino, in northern Norway," she said, for she'd just discovered something called the Norwegian State Employment List, and there they listed openings in Karasjok and Kautokeino. "That'll have to be my military service, since I'm not allowed to defend my country in any other way because of my *sex*." That was ridiculous. Of course the military was also ridiculous, none of the boys wanted to serve. But that didn't make the other any less ridiculous. She didn't get any reply, from either Karasjok or Kautokeino. "Oh well. It's their loss." Or she said: "I'm going to make it big as a pop singer someday." "Hey, Inger?" said Liv Mo. "When you're a famous actress, and I bring you flowers, will you promise to recognize me?"

The funny thing was that they actually expected her to make it big. No matter how. And she joked her way through the future's possibilities. "Maybe I'll be a journalist." Journalist was the word she used for writer. For her hopes were so big that she hid them in her heart, together with the catastrophe.

When she became a writer she would write *Kristin Lavransdatter*. She'd write *Anna Karenina* and *Mutiny on the Bounty*, and she'd also write a book called *A Thousand Kettles*, which she hadn't read yet. She'd also like to write *The Mutiny of the Elsinore* by Jack London and *The Emigrants* and *The Immigrants* by Moberg, especially the part called *Peasants at Sea*. *Peasants at Sea* was the finest of all the books she was going to write.

If she was going to write all these books she had to get away. In Fredrikstad she'd never experienced a single thing you could write about. Either things were so boring that she'd doze off before she got halfway through, or so awful that you couldn't talk about them. The essence of a novel was the exact opposite of everything Fredrikstad was.

Abroad—that's where things were happening. She wanted to travel to other countries, immerse herself, live in them, and become famous. When she became a famous person, she'd have touched life's innermost core, and everything she had experienced up to that point would be transformed. She was absolutely sure of this, and she was absolutely sure that the place for this transformation was called abroad.'

One day something very decisive happened in her life. Solveig, her mother, Evelyn's, oldest sister, came fluttering into the yard in her flapping, red clothes, newspaper in hand. "Look at this!" she commanded, pointing. "Edinburgh family of six wants au pair for a year. Write to: Mrs. Mayfield, 6, Aberdeen Road. Edinburgh 5. £1 a week."

Inger stared at the ad. The "£" was impressive. "But you

7

know I can't stand housework!" she said.

"That doesn't matter!" Solveig said, having worked at the strangest jobs herself, both in Europe and in America, just so she could experience the world. Inger looked skeptically at her aunt. "You'll get away! And you'll never regret it!"

Inger wrote that her name was Inger. She was eighteen years old, and her main interests were playing the guitar and writing and reading, and that she didn't like housework. Yours sincerely, Inger Holm. And then she waited with bated breath for life to begin happening.

Finally a letter arrived. Mrs. Mayfield wrote she was sorry that Inger didn't like housework, but that the post involved only "light housework," and that she could go to the Royal High School three or four evenings a week, and on Sunday evenings she could go to The Scandinavian Church in Leith. (So she thinks I'm going to go to church!) Here's our family.

A small picture of the family was enclosed. There were Mr. and Mrs. Mayfield, Glen, twenty years old, Sheila, eighteen, Duncan, fourteen and Adam, six. It looked like the two youngest boys were wearing some kind of uniform. Sheila was wearing a summer dress and a tiny box-camera smile. Inger hunched over the picture and studied it, and knew at once that this girl—the unknown Scottish girl there in the tiny picture—would be her new catastrophe.

Evelyn and Inger sat on the rocks, the sea gulls scolded and Mama fretted about her leaving. "It's so lively when you're around!" she said. But she also said: "When you live in the same place year after year, one year is just like all the others. But when you're abroad, everything is new, and you'll always have a wealth of experiences to draw from."

They'd been swimming, and their legs were tanned from the sun. Inger had inherited Evelyn's slim legs. The fact that she wasn't slim otherwise was something her mother had never nagged her about. She always said: "You just wait! When you fall in love you'll slim down!" After all, that's what had happened to her, and to her sister Lisa. Thin and in love. Mama talked about other countries. She talked about when she'd been young and in love. Before Papa came along. Inger knew all about her mother's whole life. Mama at fourteen, giggly and shy, when she met her best friend, Ragnhild, under the desks at Ris school, while the teacher wondered where they were. Mama as a five-year-old, a little too chubby, with blond bangs. She could only speak German then, and she couldn't say her st's very well. And that would've come in handy, because she quickly learned that when somebody taunted her with "fatty, fatty, two-by-four!" she was supposed to yell back "sticks and stones may break my bones!" but it always came out, "shticks and shtones!" Mama had always lived in Germany and was homesick when she was a little girl. But her mama, Emilie, had said that every day at twelve o'clock, they'd think about each other. So every day at twelve o'clock Mama thought about Emilie, who might have been in Italy at the moment, or perhaps in Oslo, many miles away, and every day at twelve o'clock Emilie thought about Mama from wherever she was.

Inger knew what it was like to be Mama now, too. She was bound hand and foot. She was nervous. But Papa made her even more nervous. "Nerves?" Mama said when she was young. "What are those?" But then she married Papa. That was in Potsdam in 1937, and it was because Papa had made sure that Helga was on the way. The worst thing that ever happened to Mama was losing Helga. It was the worst thing that'd happened to Inger, too. They shared that, and had shared it many times. Inger didn't know anymore how many times they had gone over the five days starting the Saturday Helga got sick and they thought it was just the summer flu, or maybe mumps, until she died of polio early one Tuesday morning, September 27, 1951.

Helga was in the rock. In its roundness and nowhere else. She was in the screeching sea gulls, and in the rock formations they called "giants' cauldrons" on the other side of the bay. Nowhere was her presence as strong as it was here. Both of them knew that as they sat there. They could talk about it or leave it alone. Do you remember the time she stood over there by the mooring bolt, swinging her hips, singing: "Tarara boom de ay!" And then they laughed. Helga was funny. Maybe it was a little odd that they laughed at her. But Helga didn't know that she'd always be the sister who died.

And now Mama's going to lose me, too, thought Inger. But of course I'm not going to die, exactly. Though you never know. From the time Inger was ten years old she knew that dying was something you could do at any moment. Being a child didn't help. It didn't even occur to her to be afraid of dying. After all, she'd just go to where Helga was, and she'd always trailed along after Helga anyway. But from that moment she'd always been afraid that other people would die.

"Haven't you ever been in love?" Mama asked.

The question came so suddenly. They'd been sitting quietly for such a long time. Mama's question. It was close and warm.

Inger knew, and had always known, that this question would come. Some day. Some moment. The moment was now. It wasn't some other time.

Her heart pounded. I have to answer. The question was here now. The rock was round and smooth, they gazed out at the skerries. Inger looked away from her mother. "Don't you think I have feelings, too?" she answered. "Of course," Evelyn answered quickly. Because she did think so. Absolutely.

But Inger had answered, and she wasn't going to say any more. She could feel Mama's longing, and she thought: Oh, Mama! You should've had Helga! What kind of a daughter am I anyway, who can't answer that question? The worst thing that's going to happen to me, do you know what that is? It's having to say good-bye to Tove. But the words—those incredibly simple words—just wouldn't come out.

August was full of good-byes. Each time someone left, the city became more unreal. Fredrikstad was being drained of life. And here she stood at the train station with a crowd of others who hadn't left yet either, to watch a train depart, and her legs carried her in spite of themselves. When would she ever see her again? When would anybody see anybody again? No one knew when any of them would see each other again, in spite of the assurances that they'd always be friends. Did they realize how big the world really was? But what is the world? And what would it contain, when it wouldn't contain *us*?

No one cried at these good-byes. They were young and they didn't cry. The feet they stood on cried. But no one saw that.

Inger was leaving on September 26th. That extraordinary date was approaching. Any date always does, of course. But this one was thoroughly unreal. "I just can't stand to think about that day," said Evelyn.

But Ørnulf was sure about one thing. As long as he had to send his little girl out into the world, he was going to send her off in style. They had gotten a little brochure from Fred. Olsen lines with a cross-section diagram of the M/S Blenheim. All the cabins were designated by squares of different colors that stood for the classes. First class was red, but even these had different shades, indicating price and quality. They couldn't afford the darkest red. But he didn't want her to travel in the lightest pink, either. That's where everyone traveled who could just barely afford to be fashionable. Inger sat on his lap, studying the brochure with him. He pointed. "Here!" he said. "We'll buy a ticket on the next to the cheapest first class!" "But can you afford that?" "Oh, yes," he nodded genially.

One day he called her into the living room. There was something he wanted to say, and his voice was formal. Evelyn was already there. "Inger?" Papa said. "We've been thinking about something." "Oh? What is it?" "It's just that Mama and I can't imagine you without a typewriter."

Inger was so happy she was speechless. A going-away present? She looked from one to the other. Then she laughed. "Are you crazy?" "I've called the office store," Papa announced proudly. "You can just go down and pick one out."

It was a little Royalite portable typewriter, shiny and light gray—with white keys and a light brown leather case. She picked it up. Carried it over to the customs office. It needed an official seal. It got a small, round seal-thingy. And Inger thought that she had the most wonderful parents in the world. "Have a good trip to Edinburgh!" the customs agent said.

Have a good trip! Have a good trip! everyone said. When she stood in Lillian's apartment, Lillian's tall, thin mother came to the door of the living room to say the same thing. Mrs. Oppegard had always been a little stern. But when she stood there, saying it, tears sprang into her eyes.

It was so strange. They cried. Fredrikstad was crying.

Ørnulf and Evelyn held a going-away party for their daughter. It was held at the Phoenix Club, behind the venerable steps where the photograph had been taken. Even though many of her friends were already gone, there were still enough left to say good-bye to her, too.

Inger thought: This is my party. I can dance with anyone I want to. And I want to dance with Sigvart Jespersen. He's always chasing the girls. The only problem is that he never gets around to chasing me. For in spite of the catastrophe she carried in her heart, even at this going-away party, Inger longed for a boy. She had always longed for a boy, and she knew that when he came, the catastrophe would be wiped out.

She hadn't forgotten Sigvart in the pool. He'd made a bet that if he passed his oral exam in French, he'd jump into the bird fountain at Flora outdoor restaurant, and he'd done it. She hadn't forgotten the time at Grusbanen Fairgrounds either. They were both in the same class, in her first year of high school, and he had a white shirt and came from Trara school. Half of Fredrikstad was gathered at Grusbanen because a daredevil was going to jump into a barrel of flaming water. Then Sigvart arrived on a green bicycle. He stopped right in front of her so hard that his brakes squealed. "Have you done your math homework?" he said.

It surprised her that she should remember this, so long after. But she figured that if she was going to go out in the world longing for boys, it was things like this that she should hope for more of. Later she'd had him, too. They'd lain with their arms around each other in Lykkeberg park on cold fall evenings behind the Blue Grotto movie theater. He was warm and big. They'd lain on the grass along with a whole gang of others from St. Croix and Trara schools, who were together the same fall. And when Sigvart climbed, dripping wet, up from the bird bath with a C in French and had to apologize to Mrs. Olsrud herself, the leader of the whole Flora morals squad, the feelings from Lykkeberg park flared up.

That's how it should be, Inger thought, longing for Sigvart, and there he came across the floor. "One last dance?"

Sigvart and Inger danced. They sang "I could have danced all night" and looked into each other's eyes with all the shared memories in their gaze that no one talked about. Do you remember the daredevil who jumped into the barrel?

But Ørnulf witnessed a completely different scene. He saw Inger in the arms of the class skirt chaser, he saw her merry willingness, and went berserk. He headed straight across the floor, rigid with drunkenness, and put his arm between them. "Cut that out!" he shouted.

"But Papa! We're just dancing!" Although that wasn't completely true. "Come here!" Ørnulf said. "I want to show you something."

He led Inger outside. "There!" he said. And there was the moon. It hung yellow and round over the white wooden building of the Methodist church. Papa stood swaying back and forth. He was dead drunk—a rare sight, since he drank heavily every day. But now he'd managed to get plastered, as he called it himself, and he was showing Inger the moon. And that was all he wanted to show her.

They stood and looked at the moon, and Inger knew that whatever it was that was tearing him apart, he couldn't talk about it. For he was as jealous as a husband. That was the whole truth, and Inger knew that all Papa could say about it was: "Look at the moon!"

She felt sorry for him standing there. Papa loved her so

much, and had loved her ever since the first time he saw her at the Josefine Street Hospital, and he'd gone out with his best friend, Frank, in that dark night during the war, and out there he'd stood looking at Frank's footprints in the snow. What now?

In these footprints was Papa's love for Inger, and in these tracks was Inger's love for Papa, too. She had never forgotten the footprints and what they meant, even though she'd been lying inside the hospital, just born. But now Papa said: "I want you to know that the day you introduce me to a son-in-law I'll make mincemeat out of him."

He had said this many times before, but now he said it to the beautiful moon over the Methodist church. No one could pronounce the word "son-in-law" with greater contempt in the "s" than Papa. And he'd never forgotten the apple core he'd found under the bed when she had a party one time when her parents were gone. She had slept with Mofa there, but of course Papa didn't know anything about that, and how an apple core could come from that was something she had never understood. "Sigvart is no son-in-law," Inger said. "He's a hooligan," Papa answered.

Inger was furious. She could get almost as furious as Papa, so she went right in and kissed Sigvart. Papa didn't own her, damn it! He didn't even know Sigvart, and he knew absolutely nothing about whether he was a hooligan or not, and she didn't give a damn. He'd better not think he was always the boss. No. They found a hiding place behind some drapes where they kissed each other again. It was delicious standing there kissing Sigvart, and it was none of Papa's business, and later they went out onto the floor and danced some more, and Inger was certainly not completely sober herself. No one was sober. But Ørnulf was the least sober of all, and now he was coming over the floor. He grabbed Sigvart by the arm, shoving him roughly away. Sigvart slipped a little, flinching. "Get out of here, you hooligan!" Ørnulf shouted again, and pushed him off the steps.

This was the performance the steps of the Phoenix would witness three months after the historic photograph. The police came. The whole party had come out onto the steps—in their thin party clothes. Sigvart was gone. The policemen came across the street, Ørnulf stood swaying on the curb looking down at them. "We got a call," the officers said. "I am Dr. Holm," Ørnulf said calmly. In that brief interval his manner was completely transformed. "We heard there was a fight," the policemen said. "There's no fight here!" Ørnulf replied.

The officers glanced up at the guests first, then over at Ferry Landing Road, and then down in the gutter. "All right," they said, put their hands to their caps again and disappeared in their squad car.

But then something remarkable happened. Mofa stepped forward. He was quite short, and he stepped right up to Ørnulf in the gutter. He shook his fist right under Ørnulf's chin and hissed: "You apologize to your daughter!"

This was against all the rules. The boys were supposed to yield to the fathers. They were supposed to bow and shake hands, they were supposed to keep quiet when they came. They were supposed to sneak down the kitchen steps and hide in the bushes. Ørnulf looked down at Mofa. He stood there swaying as he looked down at him. "Holm!" Mofa hissed again, red in the face. "You apologize to your daughter!"

Ørnulf looked away. He went away speechless. Up the steps and into the other part of the club, where Evelyn was. She'd gone in a little earlier, and had no idea what had happened. He staggered in. The going-away party was over.

Everyone had seen the horrible scene. But nobody said anything. Now everyone had seen what Papa was really like. She'd always kept quiet about this. Kept quiet about his eternal drinking and nightly quarrelling. Kept quiet about the times he'd been so mean he'd made Mama cry. It was something that belonged indoors. Inside everything that everyone knew went on in Fredrikstad. It didn't belong anywhere. And now it'd come out—out on the steps, out in the fall evening, and the police car had come and disappeared. There's no fight here.

And in a flash, right there, Inger saw what it meant to be Dr.

Holm, rather than Jens Jensen. If it had been Jens Jensen, he'd have been tossed into the drunk tank tonight. Suddenly it was clear to her, and now everyone else knew it, too, that Papa would have been thrown in jail, if he hadn't been Dr. Holm.

Inger was ashamed. Ashamed in front of them and ashamed in front of Sigvart. She wrote a letter to him, apologizing for her father. But afterwards she was ashamed of that, too. They ran into each other outside the Blue Grotto, and held each other tightly. We're adults now, thought Inger. We can stand here in broad daylight and hug each other good-bye. But they didn't talk about what had happened. And she was still ashamed. And the only thing that could wash away the shame inside her were Mofa's words as he stood there: "You apologize to your daughter!"

And Ørnulf did.

They went for a long drive on Kråkerøy island in his new Austin Cambridge. He eagerly showed her how to put it into reverse. First you pull the gear-stick straight out, then press down, close to the steering wheel.

"Try it!" he said eagerly. "Sit right here." Inger got to try the car. "I know I'm not an easy person. But I'm the only father you'll ever have," Papa said.

That was the extent of Papa's apology to Inger. And she wasn't sure if she could accept it. He'd ruined her going-away party. And for the first time her childhood truth was shaken. That she loved her father.

"I don't love him anymore, Mama, when he does things like that!"

Evelyn was startled. "Of course you love him, don't you?"

"But love can be destroyed!" she burst out.

And they were both shocked by her words.

How will Mama manage without me? Inger thought. How will Mama and Papa get along?

Suddenly she saw Ellen's little blue-overalled bottom disappear behind the closet door with a little suitcase. Inside sat Tone, who lived on the third floor, and who came to play every afternoon. Saying good-bye to Ellen would be the hardest thing of all. Ellen had always trailed after Inger, just as Inger had done after Helga. Now she could hear Ellen's voice in the closet: "And then I have to bring stockings, and a nice dress, and I must have my typewriter. Look! This is my pretend typewriter. It won't fit in the suitcase. Bye, bye, Little-Ba! You'll have to take care of the house while I'm away." "Yes, good-bye, Big-Ba! Will you buy a surprise for me when you're away?" asked Tone.

This was the world Inger was leaving behind. She turned nineteen the fall the M/S Blenheim carried her away. It was as big a mystery to her where she'd end up as it was to the farmers who had crossed the ocean a hundred years ago. She was going to do "light housework," and she saw it before her in a cloud. She knew she'd learn. And she knew that she had to get away. And at her feet, there by the railing stood a small, brown typewriter.

The couple on the Fred. Olsen dock got smaller and smaller. He was wearing gray trousers and brown shoes, a jacket in a slightly different gray color, bareheaded. She stood in a short yellow jacket with big pockets, flowered summer dress, high-heeled, white shoes and a comb in her dark brown hair. They were standing close together, apart from the others who stood waving. And Papa's head towered over the others. No one was as bareheaded when he didn't have anything on his head as he was. For the top of his head was shiny, with three black hairs combed over, and a dark fringe around. And now this typical Papa head was getting smaller and smaller, and she wanted to cry.

But she didn't. She forced back the tears when they came. It made her dizzy, fighting the tears. Her head was quivering inside. How small they were! So terribly small.

Another passenger in a six-pence cap and knickers stood beside her. He was watching a girl in a blue pea coat waving. He looked over at Holmenkollen and Akershus Castle, and didn't wave at anyone. The couple on the dock got smaller, soon they were only a black speck. Inger took off her big, colorful silk scarf and waved it over the railing at the tiny speck. She noticed the other passenger, who was just looking and looking. "What does he know?" Inger thought.

FAREWELL

When they said good-bye Evelyn burst into tears. She'd made up her mind that she wouldn't, but it didn't help. Through her tears she saw Inger's face, frightened and bewildered—and in a brief, clear glimpse she saw the same face, nine years before, one early, early fall morning, and the voice that said: "Mama, what's wrong? What's wrong?" And she couldn't answer.

Helene had answered then, Ørnulf's mother. She'd placed her hands on her grandchild's shoulders and said the words Evelyn hadn't been able to force over her lips. "Helga is gone."

Evelyn remembered all this now, and an old grief was awakened and blended with the new. The ship was now so far out that it was no longer possible to distinguish the passengers. They stood there anyway, watching, Ørnulf's body close to hers, his thoughts just as close, almost like something physical.

Evelyn had always been glad that Inger hadn't been a boy. If she had been, she and Ørnulf couldn't have stood to live in the same house, and she'd have left home much sooner. She had inherited his strong temperament. So it was good she hadn't inherited his strong arms, too. She felt them now, as he held her, securely. If only he'd confined himself to using them like this!

But he had a strange need to prove that he was superior. And Evelyn thought that he was—in many different areas. But she had never understood why he felt the need to prove it with his fists. "Well, we can't set up camp here," he said sadly, in an effort to cheer her up. They suddenly discovered that they were the only people left on the dock. Evelyn laughed a little, stretched up on tiptoe and kissed him on the mouth.

They went up to Vinderen, to her family. The house was full of people. Evelyn's cousin, Paula, had finally come from Germany to visit.

But Evelyn couldn't handle any of this now. She escaped to where her sister Lisa was.

Lisa was standing in the kitchen making up a gigantic platter of sandwiches, with crab and smoked salmon and "everything in the book," she muttered, a work of art in bright colors. When Evelyn caught sight of her, she threw her arms around her. And they stood crying.

Lisa held her little sister tightly. Ran her hand through her hair, they were very much alike, the two of them, with their dark brown, round heads, but Lisa was shorter and rounder. "Little Evelyn, little Evelyn," said Lisa. "She'll come back, you know!"

"I know," wept Evelyn.

"And just think of all the letters you'll get! She writes wonderful letters, Evelyn. Now it's your turn to get them!"

For years Inger had carried on a lively correspondence with Lisa, and told her about all the ridiculous things that had gone on in Fredrikstad, and about some secret episodes in the park during the fall, too—and Evelyn hoped that Inger would confide more in her letters than she had in real life, and found comfort in Lisa's words. She let go and dried her tears.

"I'm such a baby!" she said and tried to smile.

"You're my baby," said Lisa.

"But I'm so afraid to go home again!" Evelyn burst out, and she sat down at the kitchen table and lighted a cigarette.

And Lisa knew. She knew what was going on in her little sister's head, and how everything came out at a good-bye. She had kept up on everything in Evelyn's life—from the moment she had been born in a snowstorm in April 1918 in this very house. And she'd always loved her, and she'd never had a child of her own. Because of a stupid act committed in a back alley in Paris when she was eighteen. "My baby," Lisa said when she'd had a few drinks, "my baby's lying in a gutter in Paris."

But there Evelyn sat with moist eyes, and Inger had left, and these were the two who'd always gotten the love the baby in the gutter should've gotten. "She'll come back, Evelyn!"

"But Lisa, I'm afraid," Evelyn whispered. "I'm so scared to be alone with him!"

Lisa knew this, and what could she say? "I'll come and visit," she said. "Will you?" "Yes, I promise. Soon." "But can you stand to be around him?" "He wouldn't dare touch me," said Lisa. Whenever they were in the Gjarm house Emilie wanted Evelyn to come into her room, alone. Evelyn sat by the kitchen table, knowing that her mother was waiting. And she was nervous about it. "Aren't you going to go and talk to her a little before we eat?" asked Lisa. "Yes, of course," replied Evelyn obediently, and went.

Emilie Gjarm had spent most of her old age in a chair on the second floor of her large house at Vinderen, with a view of Oslo fjord. From here she'd kept up on everything that went on in the world, read all the newspapers and carried on an extensive correspondence. She'd had what one would call a rich life. But it had not been without pain, and the greatest pain had been to live to see her two homelands at war with each other. They'd called her a traitor. A traitor? She, who'd given her blood to this country. Borne six children to it! She had written a poem cycle about this and called it "*Zwischen zwei Ländern,*" and had hidden it away in a drawer.

True, she had been a member of the Norwegian Nazi party. Was that against the law? Suddenly it was against the law. It'd cost her a significant portion of her fortune, even though she hadn't done a thing, other than remain in the party when her countrymen arrived. She'd paid for her treason with one of her Munch paintings, "Melancholy," ironically enough. Hans Rudolf had brought it with him from Paris at the turn of the century, because Munch had owed him two hundred kroner. Which he hadn't had. So when Hans Rudolf was about to leave, Munch had said: "But I do have a picture."

Hans Rudolf believed in tempering justice with mercy, he was a magnanimous man when it suited him, and took the picture. When she had the opportunity to pay a fine to avoid prosecution, everyone said: "Just wait! Don't pay the fine. After a while they'll give in. It's just now, when they're drunk with victory, that they're demanding such high fines. But she didn't want to wait. She wanted to settle up and be done with it. So she surrendered the picture and sat waiting to be deported to Bear Island, halfway to the North Pole. She was absolutely certain that she'd be sent there. After all, that's what they'd said. All traitors would be sent to Bear Island.

But no one had come to take her away. Then she fled to a farm in Valdres. And since then only her faith in the Lord had helped her.

Her faith—the only certainty in an absolutely uncertain world—helped her now too, for the world hadn't become any more certain, and anyway she was full of expectations for the future, and had no desire to die.

She sat waiting for Evelyn, her darling. She'd heard them arrive quite a while ago. But Ørnulf was probably keeping her, as always. He had her to himself twenty-four hours a day, and when she finally was in Oslo, he had to have her to himself then, too.

She'd done everything to prevent this marriage. If it'd been up to her, she'd have kept little Evelyn with her forever. But when a new little future was on the way, what can you do? Emilie wrote a frank letter to her husband. And so Evelyn got the man she wanted.

It was a disaster. Emilie had always known it was a disaster— from the first moment she saw him come into the house as a young student, tall, dark and headstrong. Were there any of her children he had not laid a hand on over the years? In terrible quarrels between one-thirty and three-thirty in the morning. If people would just go to bed, the world would have looked different. And this man, her youngest son-in-law, was the one who should have gone to bed first. He was a devil when he was drinking.

When the terrible thing happened, she'd hoped—in the midst of her own pain over losing her grandchild—that the grief would bring Ørnulf and Evelyn together, that the loss of Helga would soften his disposition, ennoble him, even bring him to a sort of faith. That was how it had been for her. Why not for him?

But it hadn't happened like that. Instead he had turned to the bottle. He drank more than ever. And Evelyn was left alone with the burden, and carried a new future under her breast. Emilie had hoped once again. Perhaps with the new little one he could become gentle? And for a time things had looked promising. At times they looked like quite a happy little family when they arrived, once again they were four! And when Emilie looked into little Ellen's beautiful blue eyes for the first time, she knew that this child had come from the Lord. In the radiance from her eyes she saw that this one had just now been sent from His hand.

Inger was cast from a different mold. There'd always been obstinacy in her eyes. She took out the opera glasses and aimed them at the distant blue water that was the Oslo fjord. She knew there was little hope of catching sight of the M/S Blenheim at this distance, but it was the thought that counted, she thought, and focused sharply on the part of the fjord that the ship definitely would not be passing.

Emilie had a feeling that Inger would end up in a strict home, more like her own childhood home in Magdeburg than the free, loving home in Bjørnegården, with a mother who always humored her. Indeed, she'd experience many a shock in the new country, spoiled as she was, more a Holm than a

23

Gjarm with her argumentative and stubborn nature. She'd never been an affectionate child. "Just give yourself more time with her!" Evelyn had said, but Emilie had never been able to forgive the Lord that it was Helga He had taken that time, and not the youngest child—that was pure chance!—though she buried such blasphemous thoughts within her. But now and then thoughts came that one absolutely shouldn't have thought. A short prayer hastened in the direction of the binoculars, toward the white dot she'd decided to tell Evelyn she had seen.

"Dear God! Let Evelyn survive Inger's leaving. And do not let Ørnulf destroy her life. Bless Inger's stay in Scotland and let her come home a new and affectionate grandchild. And, dear Lord, let me live so that I might see your great mercy and that my prayers will be answered."

There was no doubt in her mind that Inger would come back as a student, settle down in Oslo, and have an excellent academic career. So there was no need to pray for this.

Finally—Evelyn was knocking at the door. "Evelyn, my darling!" she cried, and spread out both arms so that she looked like a sitting T. "I saw the boat!" Evelyn rushed over to the window to catch sight of it, too. At the same time as she halfway kneeled in her mother's arms.

"It has just disappeared," explained Emilie. "But not without a blessing. Now, my child, sit here by me."

This was what Evelyn feared. Now they would sit "*und sich haben,*" as their German relatives called it, and she couldn't handle it, anxiety grew inside her, for in Lisa's living room Ørnulf was pacing back and forth, waiting. While he was doing that, she was supposed to be opening her soul to her mother.

"How is he treating you?" Emilie asked.

"He's sweet," Evelyn replied. "Of course he was ... of course he is just as fond of Inger as I .... That is, of course he's always claimed that he loved her *more*, and that I loved Helga most. But I think such claims are absurd."

But Evelyn knew, as she uttered the words, that for Emilie

24

the claim was not absurd. She'd always treated her children differently, and the one she loved the most was sitting with her right now.

"Has he . . . has he quit drinking?"

"No. But we've been talking about trying a new alcohol-free period . . . ."

Evelyn felt the words ebb away as she said them. Because she didn't believe it. His response to a loss was not sobriety.

"But is he treating you well?" Emilie repeated.

"Yes, Mammi, he is kind! You've never understood that he can be kind, too. He's the world's most loving papa, and we *are* happy together."

Evelyn was ashamed over her outburst, as if she were hurting her mother by saying he was good. She didn't think that Emilie had ever known what it was to be happy with a man in that way. She certainly hadn't been with Hans Rudolf. And she hadn't had any others, had she? Although her brothers were always letting their imaginations go on that front.

"Evelyn," said Emilie. "I would like us to pray together."

"But you know I don't believe in God!"

"No, but I can pray for both of us."

Emilie folded her thin hands, full of wrinkles, in front of her forehead. She prayed, whispering, yet audibly, in German. She repeated her prayer that all would go well with Inger in Scotland, and she was about to pray for something else, when her prayer was interrupted by a knock at the door. "Evelyn! Are you planning to sit in there until the next century?"

Everyone was gathered for sandwiches in Lisa's living room. They sat on her enclosed porch, with the big windows facing the city and the fjord, blue, blue over there, where the boat no longer was. In the middle of the veranda door stood Paula. Evelyn let out a yelp. They rushed into each other's arms. They hadn't seen each other since they were fourteen telling secrets under the blankets in her father's strict home in Magdeburg.

25

But they'd written letters, through war and hard times, they'd never completely lost touch, and now all this beamed at them from the other's face. They cried out each other's names in amazement.

Frank was there, too, Ørnulf's old friend from Trondheim; he'd arrived straight from the Caribbean, his boat was in the harbor, a Swedish tanker. "What an incredible coincidence. Old buddy!" he said, slapping Ørnulf on the shoulder, and immediately decorating him with an endless, multicolored garland that he pulled out of his pocket. He also had a little time bomb with a handle. It was a red metal contraption, and when you held it by the handle and spun it around in the air, a small gear would strike against a flap inside of it and make an ungodly racket. He accompanied this racket with a rendition of "Beautiful, Beautiful Brown Eyes," which described his own eyes.

"*Hier ist mein alter Freund Frank,*" Ørnulf introduced him, exhilarated at speaking German again. "*Er ist wahnsinnig. Er ist der einzige Person . . .* " He stopped and suddenly looked uncertainly at Evelyn. "*Die Person,*" Evelyn said. "*Ja, also!*" Ørnulf said with emphasis. "*Er ist die einzige Person, die von Schweden nach Norwegen während des Krieges geflüchtet hat.*"[1] Everyone laughed. "*Ach so?*" Paula said, deeply interested. "That is a long story," Frank replied. "Let's find something more amusing to tell about." "Yes, let's see who can tell the longest story with no point," Evelyn suggested. Everyone laughed again, and they ate Lisa's sandwiches and ended up laughing at everything, and no one wanted to be the first to leave. A strange euphoria had come over them all.

Paula listened in fascination to the family's ancient anecdotes. This was her first trip to Norway, and she planned to visit the family for two weeks. But Ørnulf was anxious to get home. Because as long as he had the drive ahead of him, that meant no booze. He rose, stood in front of Paula: "*Kommst du mit?*" And with five minutes notice Paula decided to pack up her newly unpacked suitcase and go with Ørnulf and Evelyn to Fredrikstad. Everyone was happy over the unexpected outcome. And Frank stuck the noisemaker and the garland back in his pocket, and climbed into the back seat beside Paula. He waved his Panama hat at everyone who might not be interested. An especially cantankerous character glowered at them at a gas station. "We're driving onward through a blaze of joy and glory!" Frank exulted. And at long last it was a merry company that drove over Rådesletta and into the eternal city by the Glomma river. "This is where I've longed to be!" Frank said. And with an even deeper voice he said: "Evelyn, my lovely butterfly!"[2] "Now, now, now!" Ørnulf said. "Ørnulf, my lovely butterfly!" said Frank, as they drove through the hollow by the Seut river.

1. Ørnulf says that Frank is the only person who fled from Sweden to Norway during the war.
2. Reference to Henrik Ibsen's *Brand,* in which Brand says to his wife: "Agnes, my lovely butterfly!"

6, ABERDEEN ROAD

In the bar on the M/S Blenheim was a charming Danish woman who was at least thirty. She had fair, curly hair in a casual style, a cigarette holder and slender silk-stockinged legs, one placed impertinently over the other on the bar stool. On the whole it was simply a matter of bad luck that she hadn't ended up in Hollywood, but instead she had a ruined marriage behind her; she told her whole life history to a young girl on the stool beside her. Straight to the point. The girl also told selected portions of her own: it was clear she'd led a trouble-free life so far. For her part, the girl marveled over how older people can tell the most horrible things to a perfect stranger, but she felt like she'd ended up in the middle of a world adventure already. The bartender poured drinks, and the woman treated. Everything was exciting. But then they neared Horten. Already here the boat was beginning to make some slow sideways movements, back and forth, that made her incapable of following the story of how the lady's ex-husband had tipped over the table on Christmas Eve—with roast pork and everything, she couldn't catch all the details of the menu. "Have a whiskey, honey! It's good for the waves!" the lady said, and the girl believed her. She downed whiskey and drank toasts with the lady, who by now was in the middle of an attempted strangling off the Atlantic coast, and as they rounded Færder Lighthouse, there was only one possibility in the whole world. The toilet.

Inger didn't see anything more of her fellow passengers in the next to the pinkest first class until she stood, dazed and chilled, in a large, gray hall on Tyne Commission Quay a day and a half later.

The new country was flat and gray with unending railroad tracks, chimneys, tiny lawns with laundry hanging out to dry and a dark, flat sky above. And suddenly the sea opened up. "Berwick!" called the conductor with rolled r's unlike any English she'd ever heard before, and that's how it was with everyone who said anything. It was as if they had the language inside their mouths; it wasn't supposed to be pronounced clearly! The industrial revolution.

She walked toward the gate at Waverley Station with the neck of her guitar leading the way. She'd checked the rest of her luggage. Seventeen pieces in all. Why'd she have to bring along her guitar? It seemed completely out of place. A guitar is always out of place until it ends up in your lap at a party. Here there was nothing to indicate a party. A mob of people all hurrying along under the roof of an enormous train station.

"Are you Inger?"

A completely strange lady with gray hair, tweed suit and large, nervous eyes had suddenly stopped her with this question. Inger had a sudden desire to answer "No" and go home right now. She'd never seen complete strangers before. In Fredrikstad there were no completely strange people. Even the ones you'd never seen before, you had seen. Inger stared at her in terror and hostility. I don't have anything to do with this lady. "Yes," she said, intensely unhappy.

"Is this all your luggage?" the lady asked, still in English. But unlike the others she'd heard, she spoke clearly. "No, it . . .*blirsendt-med-reisegods* . . . it, it, it . . . comes, I mean . . . it."

Where was her English?

"Will it be sent separately?" the lady inquired. "Yes," Inger nodded so hard that her head practically came unhinged, in order to make up for the English she'd studied passionately for seven years and always gotten A's in. Mrs. Mayfield took her bag and marched on brisk half-high heels three steps ahead of her in the direction of the taxi stand.

The taxi drove up a hill away from the station and came immediately up into the city. A castle partially obscured by fog rose toward them. They turned to the right into a horde of burgundy-colored busses with white roofs, everything on the wrong side of the street. "This is Princes Street!" She said it as if it were the most famous street in the world. Inger saw it all through a perfectly nightmarish glow. "This is the Scott Monument." She pointed at a dark sort of Eiffel Tower towering up. "Did you have a good trip?"

"No," Inger replied. "I was . . . was . . . *sjøsyk*."

"Were you seasick?"

This was dreadful. Her mouth just wouldn't cooperate! And the workers in the coal mines during the industrial revolution in Anglo-American Reader I, II and III had never been seasick. They had been the subject of the Iron Law of Wages. That wages tend to fall to the lowest level which the most desperate man will accept. Should she say that?

They drove up hill and down on perfectly straight streets, the houses got smaller, they lay in endless rows, in pairs, and all the doors were open. They were green. With a number above. They stopped in front of one with the number 6. They'd arrived! She had reached her goal. Mrs. Mayfield seized her bag and marched ahead of her up the little garden path. Inger had never seen a drearier house.

A chilly and slightly cloying smell confronted her when she came in. She looked in at a long hallway and a staircase. Mrs. Mayfield stopped at the end of the hall, Inger followed her. "Inger, this is your room." And she stood there staring into a closet.

There she saw: a narrow, dark-brown chest of drawers, two straight-back chairs, a bed with a gray-green blanket and a margarine crate for a night stand. Through the window she looked out at a wall where there were two gray garbage cans. The land of her dreams, the Edinburgh of her fantasies, sank down inside her and disappeared in the depths of her soul. A year! she thought.

A year?

She was placed behind a mound of mashed potatoes. Now they were to eat "lunch." In the middle of a smell she had never had in her nose before. The family was sitting around the kitchen table. Sheila stared directly at her from across the table with eyes as big as saucers. She gestured with her fork while she talked at breakneck speed with her mother. "Bt wht kn yu du?" she said. Here they had learned all this time that "but" is pronounced "baht" and not "boot," and then it was only "bt." She listened fascinated. Of all the remarkable things she had seen in this short time Sheila was the most remarkable. She had a prominent mouth, which was red, and small freckles on a nose that was a little bit flat over the root, and didn't look the least bit like any of her classmates who'd stood on the steps of the Phoenix.

Adam was small and picked at his food, and Sheila teased him. Glen was tall and skinny in a military-colored shirt and ate without saying a word. The smell was coming from him. "Eat your food, Adam!" Mrs. Mayfield yelled. "Just wait till your daddy gets home!" The daddy, and the one called Duncan, weren't home. They were at the office and at school, respectively. Mrs. Mayfield addressed her son exclusively in the form of threats. Whatever would happen when his father got home was clearly big and terrible. But he continued to pick anyway. "Mummy?" he said, "This meat is rotten." The little mouth was obviously full of imagination. Mrs. Mayfield exploded. "Adam!" she bellowed. "What do you think Inger thinks of you?"

As if she were doing anything of the kind—having an opinion about his potato eating! "She's not eating either," Adam said. Inger's mashed potatoes were now becoming the center of attention. Crushed, she stared down into the potatoey land-

31

scape. The North Sea undulated through her now, the first time in two days that she was no longer in motion. Not since Rakel Jonassen's blood pudding in seventh grade home ec class had she felt so wretched.

A disgrace. Here she arrived at a strange house, eighteen years old. And the first thing she did was to not eat up her mashed potatoes. But the alternative was to throw up all over her new family. Mrs. Mayfield removed the potatoes with an expression of disapproval. "H!" she heard clearly. Glen put on some bicycle clips with odd staccato movements. "Cheerio!" he called and disappeared out the door. It was the first thing he'd said. Sheila donned a helmet. Then she disappeared on the motorbike with the same strange word for good-bye. Up to Edinburgh University. She sent Inger a quick glance before she disappeared. Maybe she can't stand me, Inger thought suddenly. Such things happened. You could look at a face for half a second and know that you couldn't stand the person. In that case I'm certainly not going to stand her either.

The first thing Inger did in her new job as maid was to burn a hole in some rubber gloves. She was supposed to put them on to remove a red-hot grate in the stove in the kitchen so that she could rake out the old embers and pour on more coal. This was supposed to be done with the poker, not with your hands. But who had ever heard of a poker? Inger didn't even know what it was called in Norwegian, and she was certainly not interested in finding out either. But there was a definite possibility it was called an *ildrake*. At any rate she'd burned a hole, and her forefinger hurt like hell. Mrs. Mayfield stared at the result. "They were brand new!" she exclaimed. The burned finger didn't interest her in the slightest. "Do you know what?" she continued in a threatening way. "We've had eight girls in this house, and none of them have wrecked more than *three* things in a whole year. How is it going to go with you when you already start wrecking things on your first day? If you wreck more than three things, you'll have to pay for them yourself."

Wreck was *ødelegge*. She didn't know what the word for *salve* was. She just stood there smarting.

At six o'clock in the evening supper was to be eaten in the living room. It faced the street, and through the windows you could look out at all the other gray houses, in pairs, mirror images, just like this one. Mrs. Mayfield couldn't stand her next-door neighbors. They had dogs.

The supper table was set—large, dark brown and polished—with blue-flowered cups and plates on a trolley next to the table. The trolley. "Inger, come here!" Inger was not used to tables. Papa would usually eat his dinner standing—with his plate on top of the refrigerator. Mrs. Mayfield showed her how she should put one and a half teaspoons of sugar in the teacups on the trolley, and three spoonfuls in Daddy's cup. Daddy's cup was twice as large as the others and rounder. She looked at it with all the jealousy and irritation it deserved. "How much do you eat for supper?" Mrs. Mayfield inquired. What kind of food? Don't I just help myself? I eat until I am full. Five pieces of rye-krisp with cheese, thanks. And a cola. "Ah . . . I . . . maehhh . . . what?" she said. "Well, Sheila and I eat three half slices of toast for supper and two half slices for breakfast. Inger thought that sounded like much too little. "I will . . . eat . . . yes . . . that . . . thank you, yes, too," she said. "And you can have butter on one of the slices, and margarine on the other two, and if you have jam, you can't have butter, too," Mrs. Mayfield said. "A ha," Inger said. "'A ha' is very bad language in this country, Inger." "A ha? . . . I mean . . . is it that?" "It certainly is." "But, but." "You do want to learn to speak properly, don't you?" "Yes," Inger replied, and missed the Norwegian word *jo*, which she needed to answer a negative. A kind of *jo*-hole appeared. Now she would have to learn to say "yes" through the *jo*-hole.

Daddy Mayfield arrived home. With bowler hat and vest and gold watch and long, contented steps across the floor, he stretched out his hands toward her before he even got through the door. "Aaaaaaaah!" he said. "Here's our new Norwegian girl!" She liked him immediately. He gripped her hand warmly and sat down at the end of the table. "And has she had a good trip?" he asked, to Mrs. Mayfield. "She was seasick, poor thing," says Mrs. Mayfield, to Mr. Mayfield. Then she looked over at Inger. "Isn't that so, Inger?" "Yes," said Inger through her *jo*-hole.

Mrs. Mayfield doled out fried ends of sausage and bacon from her end of the table, and passed them around. Toast wasn't the only thing on the menu. Daddy interrogated his family one by one. What had they done today? They only spoke when he addressed them. Finally he drummed his fingers on the table top. Little Adam hopped down from his chair, ran over to a cupboard in the corner and took out a can. Then he dug out a chocolate biscuit. He ran over to his father with it—with great bashfulness and much squirming. Then he darted back to his mother.

Daddy Mayfield slowly chewed the biscuit in front of the family. It was a chocolate biscuit wrapped in red paper and foil with a tiny jack of clubs diagonally across. Inger used all her strength to keep from looking at the biscuit. Envy crept in from the top of her head to the bottoms of her feet. The biscuit was called "Clubs." Daddy chewed on. No one else got one.

"Well," said Mrs. Mayfield to Inger after they had cleared the table and done the dishes. "You are here as a daughter of the house. That means that the same rules apply to you as they do to Sheila, so I might just as well acquaint you with them right now. You must be home at half past ten at the latest during the week and ten o'clock on Sundays. You must wash your clothes once a week, and you're not allowed to go to the International Club, and you're not allowed to go out with Negroes."

We'll see about that, thought Inger. She doesn't know who she has in her house.

THE LANGUAGE AND THE GIRL

If Inger had known beforehand how awful it was to go abroad, she never would have gone. But now she was here. Abroad one had to vacuum on three stories—with "the sweeper" and "the Hoover," respectively. She surveyed them with deep contempt the first morning when Mrs. Mayfield hauled them out of a broom closet under the stairs. Mrs. Mayfield had a small, round and distinctly low-sitting rear end. The sweeper was a yellow thing-a-ma-jig with roller-thingies underneath. The Hoover was a vacuum cleaner with a brown bag along the handle. "I'm leaving," thought Inger. She was also given the "mopper." The mopper was a long handle with a bristle at the end, the type that until now she had only seen in the movies. So she had labored under the misconception that the tool was a joke. Marilyn Monroe dusting her pink telephone.

There were lots of things she'd thought were a joke that now turned out not to be. She stood in the drawing room upstairs and was filled with a dizzying boredom at the thought of the year ahead of her. The only thing that helped her were the Fredrikstad eyes. They were in the ceiling and in the walls, and everywhere and followed her with unbelieving looks. Then they immediately died laughing.

"Don't you have an apron?" Mrs. Mayfield said. Inger stared stupidly at her. The Fredrikstad eyes eagerly followed along.

"An *apron!*" Mrs. Mayfield repeated more loudly, as if the very sound of the word indicated its meaning. The appalling fact dawned simultaneously on her and the entire population of Fredrikstad: she'd gone out into the world without an apron!

"Dust the house every day," Mrs. Mayfield said. Dust, dust, dust. Dust! If only she could see it! But everywhere she saw nothing but bright, shining surfaces. She was to use the Hoover upstairs on Monday, the sweeper downstairs, the sweeper upstairs on Tuesday, the Hoover downstairs, and the sweeper and the Hoover and the Hoover and the sweeper. But in the attic (a room concealed by a closet door one flight up) she was only to use the sweeper, because the cord on the Hoover wasn't long enough to reach up here.

She always knew what date it was. It was one day less until the day she was going home. She missed Mama and Papa. The longing sank down inside her like something heavy and unbelievable as soon as she was alone in her room. They weren't there. She wanted to go to them and tell them everything. They were waiting. And then they weren't waiting. She couldn't go to them. For the first time in her life there was no living room to go into where Mama and Papa were sitting.

From one day to the next she was reduced to a nobody. It would've been much better for everyone concerned if she'd had a little more training in this. But she had no experience as a nobody. There she had stood with her diploma. She knew that Hargreaves had invented the spinning jenny in 1764, she knew what a turnpike road was and that England and Scotland were united in The Act of Union in 1707. But she had no idea what a clothes pin was called in English. Or a faucet. Or a garbage can. And in point of truth, that was all she had use for when she came.

She dusted the twelve bannister posts from upstairs to downstairs, and it was especially in these posts that infinity lay. From now on my value lies in my ability to remove dust, she thought. What a waste! What a waste of me!

She looked up in amazement. She'd thought her first English

thought.

Rosenkål was called Brussels sprouts. Who would have dreamed that? Cauliflower was also funny. The "caul" came before the flower. She'd come to learn the language. And already after three weeks she had learned a large number of new words and expressions. She knew now that a *klesklype* was called a "clothes peg," *søppelbøtte* a "pig pail," and she knew that an *utslagsvask* was called a "sink"—and every Friday the ash bucket was set out on the sidewalk to be emptied, and this was called "to put the bucket out," (not "to put out the bucket"), and "*vannkran*" was called a "tap," *komfyren* was called the "cooker," *rødbeter* were called "beetroot," and the Hoover and the sweeper, and the sweeper and the Hoover, do the drawing room, do the fireplace, do the potatoes, do, do, do, put, put, put, put the garbage out, put it there, the silver goes in the dining room, thank you Inger, but more than all these things, and beyond them, and from the first moment in this new country, she'd heard one expression, and this expression was: It's not suitable.

It's not suitable. She knew what it meant, and it wasn't because this expression wasn't used in Norway, didn't frequently march triumphantly in all its oppressiveness through Nygaardsgata, but nothing that was said in the small town gossip there by the mouth of the river could measure up to the reprimanding and eternal expression: It's not suitable.

Adam came. He said: "Why, Mummy?" He asked Why about everything, like all children on earth, and his constant protests were a great comfort. "Why do I have to eat up my food, and why is the sky blue?" Mummy heard Adam's questions, and she said, "Because *I* say so. Now, don't be a nuisance! That's the way it is. Wait till your Daddy comes home. Now don't argue. It's not suitable."

Inger learned. She was learning English so fast that it made her head spin. And it sent shivers down her spine.

Glen was sitting there eating. The smell didn't come from him. It was the gas. She knew that now. She just associated it

37

with him. He shouted his messages across the table: "Bread, please! Tea, please!" with a wavering look, and a blush washed over his face. This boy was not like other boys. He never looked his father in the eyes. In the evenings he'd sit sewing on an enormous needlework project. "What's it going to be?" Inger asked. "A rug!" he shouted despairingly into the fireplace. Then he didn't say any more. Inger soon realized that he was backward. That's what it was called if someone acted like that in Fredrikstad. "He's nervous" was all Mrs. Mayfield said. It was not to be discussed. That wouldn't be suitable. Every morning he ate breakfast by himself in the kitchen, because he went to work early. Inger met him every morning on her way to the coal bin. "Where do you work?" she asked. "In Bruntsfield Park!" he answered. But he was a little calmer now. When his father spoke to him his entire face was aflame.

Sheila dashed in. "I'm fed up with this house. Hell's bloody teeth." Entertaining expressions poured out of her mouth. Hell's bloody teeth. Inger laughed enthusiastically. "Stop it, Sheila. It's not suitable," Mrs. Mayfield said. But Inger thought it was awfully suitable. She suddenly needed Sheila to like her face. It was no use that she'd decided from the start that she wasn't going to like Sheila one whit more than Sheila liked her. She liked her. She saw her. She stuck her head with its crash helmet and slightly prominent mouth through the door. She had on long, green stretch pants, or a dark plaid skirt, and a multicolored striped scarf from Edinburgh University behind her. The colors indicated the college. She flung the crash helmet onto the table with a bang.

"Oh bloody hell! I'll freeze to death on that bike one of these days. Look at these legs! They're all purple!" Inger wanted to answer. She was burning to answer: "No wonder your legs turn purple when you drive that bike in silk stockings!" But the sentence hit a dead end at the expression "No wonder." Strange how you could need such a little expression so much. And she suddenly realized that no matter how many English words she might manage to heap up in her mouth, it'd be so clumsy and

38

would take so long that the joke would collapse. She had to face the horrible fact: she was incapable of making her laugh.

Getting girls to laugh at school during recess, boys to howl over their desk tops—that had been life's greatest and most natural pleasure, in the middle of a life where otherwise you were too fat or had no luck with boys. And there she stood, with "No wonder" like a clump of cold mashed potatoes in her throat.

But Sheila didn't let that bother her. She was always full of ideas, and was almost always in a good mood, and she was one of those people who could keep a conversation going indefinitely, asking lots of questions, which she answered herself, you didn't have to contribute a thing. She was tall with reddish curls that she rolled up on curlers every evening, and she had these large, merry, yellow-brown tinderbox eyes that looked straight at Inger, and she said: "Oh, Inger! You're lucky! You get so many letters! You get letters every single day. I never get any!" And Inger said: "That's because I write them."

This was her first decent, witty reply. She was proud and happy. Sheila answered: "Well, then. No wonder you get them."

No wonder! That was how you said it! No wonder! Never again would she be stumped by "No wonder." No wonder, you could say. No wonder.

This was a wonder.

Sheila's words ran incessantly through her head. When she wasn't there, Inger still heard her. It was a remarkable phenomenon, and she looked forward—to the daughter of the house coming home.

It took some time before she realized that was what she was doing. That she was actually doing it all the time. And when the daughter of the house *was* home, she was simply and unexpectedly happy.

One afternoon Sheila couldn't find her gloves. Inger saw them on the desk, and made throwing motions to her, because she was standing in the other end of the kitchen, but since she

39

couldn't think of the right English word for throw, she shouted "*Fakk!*"

Sheila got just as red as she had when Inger had handed her the sanitary napkins the week before. "You must NEVER say that when Mummy is listening, Inger! It's not suitable." "But what's wrong?" "That word!" "*Fakk?*" "Oh, stop it!" "But it's Norwegian! . . . it means . . . to, to, to receive!" "Well it means something entirely different in English." "But what does it mean?" "It means to sleep with someone," Sheila said.

Finally Inger understood that what she had stood there shouting was nothing less than to fuck. "Fuck!" she had yelled, innocently. "So what do you say?" she asked. "Catch!" "Oh, ja," said Inger, "you should hear what the past tense of that word sounds like in Norwegian." "Caught?" Sheila said. "Yes," said Inger, laughing. "But what does it mean? What? What? Don't stand there making fun of me." "It means to . . . to . . . to . . .," Inger said. How could you translate *kåt*? *Kåt* was *kåt* and nothing but *kåt*. "It means to . . . *want* to sleep with someone," Inger said.

Now they both laughed. Stood there not going anywhere. Sheila threw off her jacket. "Ish! I don't feel like going up to the university this afternoon. Let's have some dirty words! What is fuck in Norwegian?" Inger said the word, and Sheila repeated it. It sounded comical in an English mouth. "It's a swear word in English. Fuck off." "Not in Norwegian. You don't fuck off unless you are really fucking off." "What's bloody?" "*Blodig*. But we don't swear with that, either." "But aren't there any dirty words in Norwegian then?" "Sure there are. *Faen i helvete!*" "*Faen i helvete*," repeated Sheila. "What does that mean?" "The devil in hell."

Now they got around to sexual organs. But when they got to the female ones they got quiet. Sheila didn't want to say the English ones, and Inger didn't want to say the Norwegian ones. "*Fitte*," thought Inger. "Cunt," thought Sheila. And they were quiet.

This—the most wonderful place on the whole body, where

all life began, had—on both sides of the North Sea—the worst and most unmentionable name of all. Here there was no difference. The other things you could and couldn't say were ridiculously different in the two languages. But here they merged into a single gigantic linguistic disgrace. Cunt and *fitte*.

The two girls looked at each other. They'd been through everything. And here they stood. They looked down. Then they whispered their words. Sheila and Inger whispered the names of their sexual organs. For that was the worst thing that could be said, so it was amazing that it had any sound at all. And the strange thing was that the word that wasn't their own country's word, they could easily say out loud, without scruples and disgrace.

And this was how Inger managed to hold out at 6, Aberdeen Road.

THE BATTLE AT EL ALAMEIN

But otherwise she was desperate. And she soon made up her mind that she would break all of the house rules on all points that suited her.

She started off immediately with her plans. The first Sunday she went to the Scandinavian Sailors' Church in Leith and discovered that she was the only au pair girl in Edinburgh who had to be home at ten o'clock. They sang number 377, in the Sailors' Mission songbook, *Sing Me Home*:

> In spring when the fjords are like violets blue
> And glaciers in sunshine are golden in hue;[1]

and got tears in their eyes and lumps in their throats. Nothing like that had ever happened before—for such a reason. In one second her whole sense of worth rose back into her body. For there sat Ella Granli from Bergen with upswept hair and laughter. She laughed with Ella and arrived home twenty minutes late. In the darkness of the hallway stood Mrs. Mayfield waiting for her. She looked at her with furious eyes: "Inger! I think we've got different moral standards!"

She explained to her that ten o'clock meant ten o'clock and nothing but ten o'clock.

Moral standards! Here she came to a strange house, and then they throw a bunch of rules at her head. An agreement is an agreement, that's what I've been taught, too, Mrs. Mayfield. But this isn't any agreement, damn it! Who do you think you are, anyway?

She thought. For she was speechless. And she got madder and madder.

She ended up at a party where all the girls were Scandinavian and all the boys were from Jamaica. She danced with them. Again she was in the middle of an adventure. It was the first time she had ever seen a Negro. She'd missed the one who'd walked down Nygaardsgata in 1956. She thought it was idiotic that she'd finally managed to go abroad only to avoid associating with foreign nations. She came home and told Mrs. Mayfield that there'd been only Negroes at the party.

"Only Negroes, Inger?"

Her voice trembled with outrage and horror. "But why don't you like them?" Inger asked. "Fortunately I don't know any of them," Mrs. Mayfield replied. But the strange thing was that it had its effect. She was embarrassed. As if she were a kind of second-rate human being, who couldn't manage to do anything better.

Mrs. Mayfield didn't like gypsies either. She knew one of them. He came to the door every Wednesday and tried to sell onions, and Mrs. Mayfield sent him away with a snort. She couldn't imagine allowing her boys to eat something that he had touched. "Why not?" "Because he is a *gypsy*," Mrs. Mayfield declared. Inger went for a walk with him on The East Breakwater. There they watched the sunset over Forth Bridge, and he proposed to her. But she didn't tell that to Mrs. Mayfield.

Every Tuesday and Thursday Inger ironed shorts from Edinburgh Academy. She ironed in the kitchen while melodies from "Housewives' Choice" gushed out of the radio in the corner and Mrs. Mayfield made food in the scullery.

While they were busy with this and Elvis Presley arrived home from Germany, newly shorn, and sang Mrs. Mayfield's favorite tune, "Wooden Heart," they chatted about lots of

43

things, and it turned out that Mrs. Mayfield didn't like Germans either. She knew four of them—her four previous au pair girls, Hannelore, Heidi, Gisela and Jutta (she pronounced the last one "Dzuhtta"). The Germans had started two world wars, it was their nature. In the bottoms of their hearts all Germans were little dictators. Then Inger quit asking why. She said: "My grandmother is German."

There wasn't a sound from the scullery. Now she realized that she hadn't escaped the dictator blood even though she had gotten someone from Norway, Inger thought. *"Muss i' denn, Muss i' denn,"* Elvis sang. "I didn't mean that your poor grandmother started the Second World War, Inger," it came with a somewhat meeker voice from the depths (the scullery was two steps down). My poor grandmother! thought Inger. If only she'd known about the time Emilie had sent flowers down to the box at the opera house in Berlin. For there sat Adolf Hitler. Hitler received the flowers and looked at the card. And during the intermission came the announcement: "Der Führer calls Frau Emilie Gjarm!" But unfortunately Emilie had just gone to the ladies' room, and didn't come back until the curtain went up, so she never had an audience with the Führer. But Inger decided it was best to keep this unfortunate episode in her family history a secret. Hans Rudolf had once greeted Mussolini, but she also hid this in her heart.

"I just meant that it is the Germans who have started the world wars, and they'll probably start the next one, too. Just you wait and see!" Mrs. Mayfield said.

And Inger folded the shorts and placed them in a neat stack while she waited for the Third World War with bated breath to see if Mrs. Mayfield was right.

One morning Mrs. Mayfield led her into the bathroom next to the scullery. There were two bathrooms in the house, one upstairs, and one downstairs. "Inger," she said, "you use far too much toilet paper."

She took hold of a roll and held it out. "We have always been seven people in this house, and we've never used more than two rolls of toilet paper a week. And now, for the last two weeks we've gone through *three* rolls."

Inger stared at the roll. The paper was thin and transparent and absolutely stiff, and she needed great quantities of the stuff to satisfy her requirements in that department. Mrs. Mayfield pulled out two sheets and showed her. "Here," she said. "This is all you need."

"A ha," said Inger. "I mean . . . ee-oh?" she corrected herself, having learned that "a ha" was unsuitable. She made up her mind to buy her own toilet paper from now on. But no doubt that was also against the moral standard. Was she supposed to walk around with a roll of toilet paper hidden under her jacket all the time?

The household was old-fashioned. They were always scrimping and saving. Mrs. Mayfield had explained that they couldn't afford all sorts of modern contraptions because they had to be able to afford sending the boys to Edinburgh Academy, the best school in the city. The house was ice cold. All the bedrooms had gas fireplaces except Sheila's, which had an electric heater. The fire was to be laid in the fireplace in the living room at seven thirty in the morning. But it wasn't to be lighted until Mr. Mayfield got home. In the maid's room off the kitchen there was no heat.

Inger was constantly cold. She was cold for an entire year. Edinburgh is a cold city. From September to February the ice-cold fog from the Firth of Forth settles over the city, the wind whistles around the old tiled-roof houses, seeping in through all the cracks.

She thought she came from a cold country. But the wind here blew through everything she had on. Her ears hurt. She had an ear ache, especially in her right ear. Every evening the family members went to bed with hot water bottles under their arms. She wasn't offered one, and it didn't occur to her to ask for one. She put her clothes under the covers at night so that she could stand to put them on in the morning. Every morning—after she'd finished the housework—she shut herself into her room. She finished the dusting as quickly as possible so that she could go in here and write. She sat with mittens on, writing, switching from one hand to the other. She wrote to Lillian about the toilet paper. It was ten past twelve. There were still twenty minutes until lunch. Suddenly the door flew open and Mrs. Mayfield came in and turned off the light with a furious motion. "Inger! Here you sit in the middle of the day with the light on! Haven't I told you that electricity is expensive in this country? You haven't washed your hair and you haven't washed your clothes. You said you would and I believed you would. You're supposed to be doing things in the house, not sitting here. And your room looks terrible! Tell me. Are you doing all of this just to annoy me?"

"No," she answered. Just then her ear drum popped, and she sucked in air. Her ear ached and popped. It helped to suck in air. "Don't snarl at me like that!" said Mrs. Mayfield. Then Inger started to cry.

Inger, who never cried when anyone was watching, and who hadn't cried in front of anyone since she was little, cried before the furious, ridiculous and unreasonable Mrs. Mayfield. Snarl? she thought. She wasn't even sure she knew what it was to snarl.

Then Mrs. Mayfield sat down in front of her, leaned over and rested her arms on her knees. "Are you homesick, Inger?" And her tone was completely different.

She didn't get any response. Just new waves of tears.

"You're a good girl, Inger. I'm sure you are," said Mrs. Mayfield.

This touching and unexpected scene resulted in Inger not breaking any rules for several weeks, she washed both her hair and her clothes, and she made up her mind to be *good*.

She even prayed to the God she had probably quit believing in, but who was always there for prayers. "Travel as far as you want—you will never travel from yourself," said Seneca. God is a way to find this "self," that you can't travel from. Help me to hold out! Dear God, help me to stay with the Mayfields.

46

Help me to accept things as they are. Don't let me get so angry, dear God! I only have two wishes for this life. To stay healthy and not get an ear ache and that I will find true love.

Where is true love? Inger was sure that it must exist in Edinburgh. It must exist there, otherwise everything was pointless. She didn't give up.

Every evening Sheila got red patches on her neck. They came when her father asked her about her motor bike. Every Monday the engine would die. She would have to push it up the steep hills to the repair shop. It was a nuisance. She knew why it happened. For every Sunday Daddy would borrow the bike and head off to play golf. He ground the gears and he was too heavy for it. Mrs. Mayfield forbade her to say anything about it to him. The motor bike was the source of constant quarrels between mother and daughter at the lunch table. In the evenings Daddy interrogated her. Sheila got red patches on her neck. And Inger was more and more convinced that if she would get up the nerve to talk back to Mr. Mayfield just once she would be doing everyone in the house an enormous and invaluable favor.

For even though she'd made up her mind to accept the state of affairs, she could not accept Mr. Mayfield's regime. Furthermore she'd fallen in love with Sheila. This last thing she didn't know anything about. She just noticed it all the time. It didn't have a name, either in English or in Norwegian.

Mr. Mayfield was a quite ordinary, friendly man. But everyone was scared to death of him. To Mrs. Mayfield he was a god. She'd met him at Edinburgh University in 1938, where she was studying medicine, he to be a Chartered Accountant—a sort of C.P.A. She immediately gave up her medical studies and started studying home economics. They got married and then she got pregnant. In that order. Then Glen came, and then the War. He was stationed in Israel, and was only home once on leave. That's when they made Sheila. When he came back, he was a stranger. Sheila told her all of this. "When I saw him, I hid behind my mother and said: 'Who is that man?'"

And they hadn't gotten to know him any better since, either. "I never talk to my father about anything," Sheila said.

All of this amazed Inger, and she really wanted to help them break the ice. He couldn't possibly believe he was perfect. But Mrs. Mayfield said that he was. To her amazement, Inger noticed that she was starting to be afraid of him, too. She wasn't used to being afraid of anyone. Not even the principal, not the parish pastor and certainly not Papa. The only person she'd been somewhat afraid of was Mr. Markmo in junior high. He'd managed to drive stupidity into the heads of most of the girls with his mathematical equations. She hadn't dared to talk to him.

And now she didn't dare to talk to Mr. Mayfield. For that matter he didn't talk to her, either. He said to Mrs. Mayfield: "How are things going with her?" "Fine, I think." "And how are things at school?" "I think she's a clever girl. Aren't you, Inger?" said Mrs. Mayfield. And that was the extent of her conversations with Mr. Mayfield.

That particular fall Nixon and Kennedy were battling for power in the U.S. When the election results were about to be announced, something unusual happened. The radio in the dining room was turned on. "Oh, I hope that Kennedy fellow doesn't win!" Mrs. Mayfield said in an agitated tone. For her part Inger hoped that he would win. He was clearly the most handsome. "Why don't you like him?" she asked. "He's a Roman Catholic!"

The word was spat out. "Roman Catholic." Especially "Roman." Of course she already knew that it was possible to spit out Negroes and gypsies and Germans. But she was constantly learning new things. Under the circumstances the election results were encouraging, and when Mr. and Mrs. Mayfield had poured out their disappointment over this, Adam said: "Mummy? Is the U.S. a colony?" "No, dear," said Mrs. Mayfield, "not anymore." It sounded as if the country had just broken away the day before. "But what about Canada? Is Canada a colony?"

"A sort of colony," she replied. "Canada is a dominion."

"What's a dominion? Don't we own it?" he asked.

"Well," said Mrs. Mayfield and looked at her husband. "What exactly is a dominion, Charles?"

Charles took a sip from his tea cup and rubbed his hands together and mumbled: "It governs itself." "But how can it govern itself if we own it?" Adam asked. "It's too hard for you to understand, Adam. Stop arguing. Don't be a nuisance!" Mrs. Mayfield said. "But isn't the Queen the Queen of Canada, too?" He didn't give up.

"The dominions are autonomous communities within the British Empire, equal in status, in no way subordinate one to another in any aspect of their domestic or external affairs, though united by a common allegiance to the Crown and freely associated as members of The British Commonwealth of Nations," Inger said in English.

Everyone stared at her in astonishment. "I say, I say," Sheila cried. "She's a clever girl, Miss H!" "That was very impressive, Inger," Mrs. Mayfield said. Inger basked in the praise. "Where'd you learn that?" "In school."

"Is that what you learn in school?" "Yes, that's what . . . that's what. . ." But she hadn't learned how to say "That's what we *do* learn" and again she stammered out an answer that ground to a halt. But Adam laughed. "Can't you say what you said one more time?"

"It's The Statute of Westminster," Mr. Mayfield said. "It was adopted in 1930." He nodded appreciatively.

"In 1931," Inger said.

Deep silence followed. But that wasn't the worst of it. Oh no. If only she'd left it at that! The indisputable little date. But no. She didn't.

At that very moment her self-confidence had received a boost from an entirely different direction. She'd taken her first exams in English for foreigners, and passed them all. This had never happened before in the history of the house. Hannelore had failed in Lower Cambridge and passed London Stage I and II, and the Norwegian Bjørg had done just the opposite, and Heidi hadn't passed any of them, and soon Inger knew exactly which exams all of the other eight girls in the house had passed and failed, and the evening tea kettle whistled its melancholy whistle through the house and Daddy came home to his tea cup and Clubs. Now the rules for butter and margarine with and without jam didn't apply to Mr. Mayfield of course. He always spread the butter thickly on all of his slices of bread and spread jam on top. But when it was time for his toast with butter and jam on this particular day, his hand paused on its way over the mirrored surface.

They were now in the middle of strawberry jam week. But all that was left in the dish was a pitiful remainder of red pulp with characteristic streaks of strawberry, but no berries. Mr. Mayfield looked at his wife: "Do you mean to say that Inger has been here for two months, and she still doesn't know how to fill up the jam dish?"

Mrs. Mayfield let out a little gasp, deep panic spread over the table, enveloped all of the butter curls and the teapot, Duncan jumped up and rushed out, and came back with the jam jar, which he placed before his father—something that had never happened before in the jar's long history. But Inger got mad.

It was ten to six. That meant that she was permitted to leave the table to go to class. She stood up and went to her room. There she stood. She took out her school things, her coat and mittens. This is enough. Damn it, this is the limit. She trembled with fury. To commit a crime. Jam dish. Jam dish! The hell! She repeated the sentence in her head. It was perfectly clear to her now. Every word. No hesitation. A correct English sentence. That she would serve right at Daddy's head. She marched through the hallway, jerked open the door to the dining room, and stuck her head in: "You don't need to treat me as if I have committed a crime, just because I haven't filled up the JAM DISH!" she screeched. Then she slammed the door shut, and bolted out of the house.

No one spoke to her the next morning. After everyone had left, Inger grabbed hold of the Hoover and took it out. The big brown bag hung down the handle. Dejected she gave it its click. Now everyone is against me, she thought. Now I only have the Hoover. Not even Sheila appreciated my rebellion.

She heard Mrs. Mayfield's step on the stair. She'd already passed by several times. She was going to the hair dresser to-day, and Inger was looking forward to her departure.

"Inger, come here!"

Mrs. Mayfield stood right behind her. She brought her into Daddy's room. The room had not yet been put into use for the winter. The small square room lay in half darkness, the furni-ture was still covered with dust covers, the drapes were drawn. Mrs. Mayfield switched on the lights and stopped in the middle of the room. Inger stopped, too, and looked at her. Mrs. Mayfield was quivering with rage. "Inger, you must not talk to Daddy like that! Daddy is not accustomed to being spoken to like that. He is a prominent businessman. He is a Chartered Accountant. He has been to America twice. He has talked to many people. He's a lieutenant colonel. He fought in the war. He fought with Monty. He won the Battle of El Alamein."

Inger had never heard of the Battle of El Alamein. She stared at the carpet. The pattern was burned into her eyes. Slowly she lifted up her head and looked Mrs. Mayfield straight in the eyes. "All that doesn't mean that he's always right."

Mrs. Mayfield gasped. She let out a short, very audible sigh, and flustered, the words escaped: "Almost always, Inger!" Then she shifted her weight, laid her gloves together in her hands, and said: "You are not of age. We are responsible for you while you're here. And if you cannot comply with the things that we decide, we'll have to send you home."

1. Translation: Sons of Norway songbook.

51

MORALS, BASTING STITCHES AND POTATOES

Evelyn sat at the dining room table in the Bjørnegården apartment building armed with her blue Gyldendal English-Norwegian dictionary. She looked up the word "rude." Impolite, impudent, ill-bred, uncouth. Evelyn stared out into space. She didn't doubt it a minute.

She stared at the letter and felt like a dumb schoolgirl who was caught in the act. She hoped Paula would come home soon. But she was at the hairdresser. Paula always had wise comments on Inger's new life, and Evelyn translated all her letters.

Paula's unexpected arrival had been a blessing. She had arrived with five minutes advance warning, and now—after more than two months—she was still here. The rest of the family was offended. She should have spent some time visiting each of them, and instead she sat in the apartment at Bjørnegården and laughed. Ørnulf was in his element. Because Paula was, as he said, something so uncommon as an intelligent listener. She understood all of his big Points. That was why Evelyn preferred to have her to herself.

Mrs. Mayfield's letter was written in square, clear and fastidious handwriting. Through Inger's numerous letters Evelyn had already formed a picture of her, and she appeared as an incarnation of fear and dread and potted plants. Evelyn had never tolerated housework, and she had imparted her abhorrence of it to Inger with great passion. They'd always had cleaning ladies when Evelyn was growing up, she'd become best friends with several of them, but when she got married, she didn't even know how to cook macaroni.

It wasn't the first time she'd gotten complaints about Inger. There'd been a little bit of everything in the section in the grade book marked "Special reports to the parents" over the years. Once she'd gotten a note from school because she had basted shut the armholes in the blouse they were making in sewing class. "I just couldn't figure that blouse out, Mama!" Inger said. And Evelyn believed her. But Miss Grytum did not. Miss Grytum thought she'd done it to make the class laugh. And that had not been in vain, for the merriment had spread throughout the class, and red and desperate, Miss Grytum had shouted: "You are nonchalant and arrogant! Go to your seat and take out the stitches." "And then what happened?" Evelyn had asked. "Well, I asked what that meant," said Inger. "You'll just have to look it up when you get home," said the teacher. And she ended up with an F in sewing and a note home and no final grade that Christmas. But she did learn two new foreign words.

Evelyn had never managed to do anything but laugh at notes like that. Maybe that had been a big mistake. But she'd always thought: "You can say what you want about Inger, but she is *honest!*" That was the most important thing of all. But now she wasn't laughing. Inger was hurting, and it made Evelyn hurt in the same way. She was cold just like Inger was and slammed the door with her. It was as if all deep morality rested in the basting stitches, dwelled in the jam dish. All of Fredrikstad was permeated with this morality. Evelyn had never forgotten the complaint she had received from the neighbor three weeks after they had moved into the Bjørnegården apartment. The anonymous complaint was that the Holms still hadn't put any plants in the window.

Now Inger had come to such a place. She took hold of paper and pen. She hadn't written a letter in English since she was sixteen years old. All her thoughts had become so childish. Did Mrs. Mayfield think about that? How reduced one became in a foreign language? They'd had nine cleaning girls. Evelyn knew the names of every one of them. Hadn't she learned?

Evelyn tried to imagine Mrs. Mayfield's life. She'd been alone during the War with two children—one of them backward. And maybe Mr. Mayfield hadn't even known about that. Had she been dreading that all those years? Had there been air raids in Edinburgh? Lines of people waiting to buy potatoes? Had she sat in a bomb shelter, holding her oldest son tightly and dreading the day when she'd have to show him? To a man she hardly knew? What was Mrs. Mayfield's life like? Didn't she have a heart somewhere?

Evelyn took hold of the pen, and as she wrote the first hasty words she knew that Mrs. Mayfield had a heart somewhere, and that she would write to this heart.

Ørnulf came through the doorway. He stopped in the middle of the living room. "Where's Paula?" "In town," she said, but she didn't look up right away. She was greatly impressed that she had just remembered that the phrase was: "Yours sincerely Evelyn Holm." "Is she at the hairdresser?" "Yes, Ørnulf, look at this!" Rapidly Ørnulf read Mrs. Mayfield's letter over Evelyn's shoulder. "That's a hell of a note!" he said. Then he began pacing back and forth across the living room floor without saying a word. Finally he stopped and looked at her: "Do you want me to go over there?"

The next day a long letter from Inger arrived with detailed descriptions of the appearance of the strawberry jam, the nature of the jam pot and the door that had slammed. That evening all three of them sat in deep doubt. "Inger is in a very strict home," said Paula. "It reminds me of my own. Isn't it a good idea for Ørnulf to go over and earn some respect?"

"But he can't even speak English!" said Evelyn.

"Yes, I can talk English," Ørnulf replied with a somewhat affected Norwegian accent. "Or I can talk German," he added.

"Are you going to speak German with a man who won the Battle of El Alamein?" Paula said.

"I can talk to him with *this*!" Ørnulf said, and displayed his large hands. "With *these*," Paula corrected him. She was an English teacher. "With *these*," Ørnulf repeated like an obedient school child.

But Evelyn had her doubts. Just imagine Ørnulf on his way down Aberdeen Road to make mincemeat out of Mr. Mayfield. "You should have been born in the time of blood feuds; you'd have been much happier," she said. Paula laughed.

"I understand Mr. Mayfield is quite a tall man," she added.

"Jam dish!" replied Ørnulf. "By God I'll give him a jam dish!"

Evelyn and Paula exchanged quick glances with the strange mixture of uneasiness and desire to laugh that they often felt when he made his pronouncements. "I don't know if that'd be a wise move, Ørnulf," said Evelyn. "The battle of El Alamein!" snorted Ørnulf. "He'll get so much jam that he won't be able to face another berry until way into the next millennium."

"At last Rommel will be avenged," said Paula. Ørnulf glanced gleefully over at her, enjoying himself, even though they weren't living in the age of blood revenge.

"Are you coming with me?" he said.

"What? To Edinburgh?" Paula laughed.

"Yes?" he said. "You're so good at making up your mind in five minutes." He tilted his head. He certainly was handsome.

"Not without Evelyn," replied Paula.

"Ørnulf? Shall we ask her to come home?"

Now they were all silent. Ørnulf's and Evelyn's eyes met: "Let's call."

They said it at the same time, exactly the same words. The rule was that they shouldn't say a word, but hook their little fingers together, move their hands up and down three times and say the name of an author. There was a tacit agreement in the Gjarm family that the author was always Bjørnson or Ibsen. Ørnulf and Evelyn took hold of each other's fingers. One, two, three, silently in step. Then they both shouted: "Bjørnson!"

Now they could make a wish. Evelyn wished that Inger wouldn't have to be so unhappy. Ørnulf wished for a drink. He couldn't think of anything else, the wish just tumbled into his head. Things were going so well for him at the moment.

In the meantime Inger had decided to leave Edinburgh. The family punished her with silence. An amazing weapon. All of them, except Glen, who talked to her when no one was listening. Even Sheila, who swore a blue streak behind her father's back every day, said nothing. She'd probably end up like her mother. She couldn't stay here. Now she'd just have to see as much of this city as possible before it was too late. She hadn't even seen the place where David Rizzio had been murdered. There were plenty of memorials to murders, but she'd only seen the sweeper and the Hoover. And the mopper, too, of course. You mustn't be unfair. She'd seen the mopper, too. And Mrs. Mayfield's sagging rear end.

Rear end, rear end, rear end, thought Inger. She was furious. She made a point of thinking of the worst thing imaginable. Rear end. Her mood improved a little.

Three days later she stood once again in Daddy's Room. But this time with Daddy himself. In the meantime the room had been opened for the winter, the covers had been removed from the chairs and there was a fire in the fireplace. "Inger," Daddy said, and he stood right in front of her with his thumbs hooked in his vest and one foot forward, resting on his heels. "I am convinced that you are an intelligent girl." But? thought Inger. "I also think you have much promise," he continued. But? thought Inger. "But," said Daddy Mayfield, and paused deliberately, "you must learn to control yourself." He looked at her, attentively, raising his slightly pointed eyebrows. "Inger," he said, and shifted his weight slightly, rubbed himself under his chin, "I want you to know that I'd like you to stay." Oh? thought Inger. "We received a letter from your mother today, and she writes—quite correctly, I believe—that in the final analysis it's your decision whether you want to stay or not," said Mr. Mayfield. What makes him think he has the right to decide whether my mother is right about anything? thought Inger. "And I believe that in the event you decide to remain in my house, you will find—at the end of this year—that you have become . . ." He thought a moment, searched for the right words, ". . . a better girl," he said.

And Mr. Mayfield had spoken directly to his au pair girl for the first time since her arrival.

"Yes," she said. She couldn't think of anything more to say. The point was that she dearly hoped that Mr. Mayfield was right. She wanted nothing more than to become a better girl. After all, the reason she'd gone abroad was to be different. And so far she hadn't noticed much of a change. She was the same old person, stood on two feet, and not the least bit thinner. Every time she looked in the mirror, she was the same. She could look and look and stare her eyes out at her eyes, but the face in there didn't change. And she was just as obstinate as before, and didn't give a moment's thought to the family's welfare. She sank down into self-reproach. Getting her in their house was actually pretty bad luck. She tried to make up her mind. Went back and forth. She was homesick. It was awful here. But it was good for her. She needed to experience awfulness. And how would she look back on her experience in Edinburgh for the rest of her life if she broke it off now? Mama telephoned. Her head was full of tears. There was Ellen's little breathing in the phone, too. Far, far away. "Hello, Ellen? Are you looking forward to Christmas?" she tried. But Ellen just kept breathing. Mama took the phone. "I guess she was a little scared." "But what did you write in the letter?" "I wrote that you weren't as awful as she thinks," said Mama.

Saturday morning Mrs. Mayfield came with the weekly pound note. She did this every Saturday at exactly the same time and in the same way. The bill always looked newly washed and ironed, and stuck straight up in her hand. "Here is your pound, Inger." The first time this formal presentation had taken place, Inger was so flustered that she said: "I don't deserve it." This time Mrs. Mayfield added: "And I'd just like to say that I've been completely satisfied with you this week."

These were such strong words that Inger had no idea what to do with herself. She did the only sensible thing under the circumstances. She stared, mouth open.

Satisfied? Mrs. Mayfield was satisfied? How could this be? The words made such an impression that Inger decided to stay in Scotland. She immediately went out and peeled potatoes. She did the potatoes. The potatoes were done in a potato peeling machine. It was a kind of yellow kettle with a lid. There were some metal fingers attached to the inside of the lid and a handle on the outside. Forty-five turns of the handle were required, and the potatoes came out completely deformed and with half of the peel still on. Apparently the inventer of the potato peeling machine must have thought that all potatoes were as round as tennis balls and of equal size. So afterwards she had to go to work with the potato peeler. The potato peeler was a rather normal potato peeler, just a little flatter than the normal Norwegian potato peeler. She cranked and counted. *En, to, tre, fire.* She had to use her strength here. *Fem, seks, syv, åtte.* Crank, crank, crank. *Ni, ti, elleve, tolv*, she counted. For even though her head was beginning to be filled up with English words, she counted: *tretten, fjorten, femten*, for about the last thing to disappear from your head are the numerals of your native land. Everywhere her head was being infiltrated with English words, but the numerals remained. They were only surpassed in steadfastness by swear words in times of need. Interjections—they were the most faithful of all. *Au! æsj! Søren! Pokker!* Here she stood. *Seksten, sytten, atten, nitten.* The potatoes rumbled around in the machine. Struggled against their fate. *Tyve, enogtyve, toogtyve, treogtyve.* Around and around. Today is Friday, November 11th. How many numbers will I have counted before I set foot on mother Norway's soil once more? *Fireogtyve, femogtyve, seksogtyve, syvogtyve.* When I'll be cranking and counting every day? *Åtteogtyve, niogtyve, tredve, enogtredve.* There are 365 days in a year. *Toogtredve, treogtredve, fireogtredve, femogtredve.* Will I really be here that long? *Seksogtredve, syvogtredve, åtteogtredve, niogtredve.* How will I be able to hold out? *Førti, enogførti, toogførti, treogførti.* I can hold out by counting. Time goes faster when I count, it just moves along, *fireogførti, femogførti—SEKSOGFØRTI*—in pure defiance, one last extra crank. Then she went straight into her room and took out a little pad and wrote: 365 x 45 = 16,425.

16,425!

After 16,425 rounds of the potato peeling machine this life would be completed. After 16,425 rounds of the potato peeling machine she'd finally have become a new and better person. She marched out into the scullery and informed Mrs. Mayfield about the results of her calculation. Then—finally—Mrs. Mayfield laughed.

PANTOMIME

There's a stone from Telemark in Leith. It had been brought here as ballast on a ship from Norway. But when the ship went aground and went into dry dock down here, there were some bright folks who took a fancy to the stone. So they brought it on land and placed it outside the Norwegian Seamen's Church. Anyone who was Norwegian and was homesick could sit there. It was an ordinary rock, like you find along the roadside in Norway. Gray and original, just as it had been found, it lay peeking up from the little lawn outside The Scandinavian Church, which itself was gray and small, amidst the large buildings of Edinburgh.

Every Sunday dozens of young people come to this church. There are people who may have no relationship to the god the church was built for, and some come here especially for Him. But all come seeking the church, and to see the stone. The word they are seeking is not simply spoken, but the stone says it in a language that everyone can understand. Here in the area of the unknown harbor town it can say what it wouldn't have been able to say if it had remained on the rocky hillside in Telemark.

This was how it looked, the place where Norwegian au pair girls in Edinburgh, mother's helpers, engineering students, dental students, medical students, and even beer brewing students rediscovered their self-worth. For in the rear of the church with the stone in front was a room, and in the room, shelves, with newspapers from all over Norway, including Fredrikstad. Here there was news from precisely the place they wanted to hear news from. A plump lady was sitting at a piano playing songs from the Seamen's Mission songbook, *Sing Me Home*, there were glazed buns, and Deacon Tønnesen who blessed them—but never went on too long; there was a bustling life, and every now and then a sailor turned up.

Inger went there every Sunday and holiday. But on Christmas Eve Sheila came with her. The Christmas tree stood adorned with small Norwegian flags, and yet another year had passed since the decree had gone out from Caesar Augustus. As they sat beside each other and listened to Deacon Tønnesen's sermon, Sheila's arm happened to press against hers. Through the fabric of her coat. Inger just sat there feeling the pressure. It felt good. How could such a small thing feel so good? How could a touch make me so happy? She listened to the Christmas story and thought: I must sit completely still. If I move as much as a fraction of an inch, the arm might disappear. I can just sit like this. It was Sheila who'd moved her arm. It's not my responsibility to move away. I'm just sitting the same way as I was. And if she'd rather sit the same as she was before, she can just move back.

But Sheila didn't move her arm. Why? Do you know that your arm is pressing against mine? Or was it just a fluke, and "Joy to the World," for that's what they were singing now, and Sheila didn't move her arm. There she sat and was overjoyed through the entire hymn. The whole congregation should have known.

Inger made up her mind to move her arm away. Afterwards she remained sitting in the same position through the whole service.

I'm in love with her, thought Inger. And she was alarmed and terrified. She sat in her little room and tried to think her way out of being in love. She knew that she was the only girl in the world who fell in love with other girls. She knew that there were some women like that somewhere, but it was just as remote as the fact that Nefertiti with the neck had once been alive, and those kind of women didn't exist in her world or anywhere she would ever go.

Through the following days, through all of Christmas, through turkey with stuffing and Christmas cake with six-pence (the six-pence took the place of the almond they always had in Norway! And Adam found it), through all the presents, Inger felt ashamed of the pressure. She shouldn't have felt it.

This is not normal, she thought. It sets me apart from all other human beings in the most vital area of all. Then she began fighting against joy.

She fought against her head, she fought against her body, she fought against her skin when it sensed that Sheila was suddenly coming down the steps. She swept and hoovered and fought against her ears, which were constantly listening for Sheila's voice. She fought against her eyes, which met Sheila's.

The whole family went to The Pantomime. It was tradition, and as soon as they sat down, Inger forgot to fight against thinking all the time that Sheila was sitting beside her. And was beautiful. She laid her arm on half of the armrest and hoped the Sheila would lay hers on the other half. It got dark in the theater. She disappeared. Inger tried to see her in the dark. She noticed that Sheila moved slightly, and happened to bump against her with her knee. That sent a sudden shock of joy through her. Why do I have to be so dumb? thought Inger. Then she felt a hand on her leg, just above the knee. It squeezed her lightly. Then it remained there.

Inger was immediately happy. She sat without moving her leg. A hand-shaped spot of happiness sent wave after wave of pure happiness through her. And she knew that she had only one desire on this earth, and that was that Sheila's hand would stay on her leg to all eternity.

This desire was not fulfilled. For after the first act Sheila took her hand away and used it to applaud. And then for the first time Inger realized that she'd sat through an entire act without fighting against the fact that Sheila was sitting there. She'd forgotten it! She moved her leg. She tried with all her strength not to hope that the hand would come back. But it was all in vain. During the second act the hand came again and Inger sat without moving her leg. And she knew that she had only one desire on this earth, and that was for Sheila's hand to come and go, come and go, come and go on her leg to all eternity.

This desire was fulfilled—if not to all eternity, then at least through the whole performance, and it felt like eternity.

Inger sat with Sheila through an eternal performance. Beforehand she'd thought: Pantomime? How boring. Are you supposed to sit for a whole evening just looking at movements? But here she was wrong. The pantomime was accompanied by song and music and by a prince in a red jacket and black Prince Valiant hair, and was played by a lady. There she was holding her chosen princess around the shoulders, and everyone applauded. "A lady?" Inger said. "Yes, that's how it is," said Mrs. Mayfield. "It's always like that. The prince is supposed to be a lady," she nodded. And all Edinburgh applauded, for that's how it was supposed to be, it was most suitable, and the two were married in the end. A lovely couple.

Indeed, Christmas was full of surprises, and Inger was happy. On the other side of the North Sea Evelyn was packing an enormous cardboard box. She filled it with Christmas comics, stockings, marzipan pigs, 1961 Almanac, with everything she could fit in, including ten rolls of toilet paper. Yes, Evelyn was sending ten rolls of toilet paper across the North Sea this Christmas. "Here, my darling! Now you can use toilet paper until it comes out of your ears! Wish everyone a Merry Christmas from Mrs. Holm. And a special greeting to Sheila. I'm happy you have her. We'll be thinking about you on New Year's Eve, at midnight. Then you can go out, outside the house at 6, Aberdeen Road, and look up at the stars. And know that we will be standing out on the balcony at Bjørnegården apartment looking up at the same sky."

· · ·

But there—on the other side of the sea, more precisely on Nygaardsgata and the adjoining streets by the mouth of the Glomma river—as Christmas approached—a strange rumor had been started. Was it true? Have you heard? But the fact that something might possibly not be true had never prevented anyone from spreading rumors in that town. For what folks claimed, in the middle of the Christmas season and all, was that Doctor Holm's daughter, she'd gone to Scotland and been told to use less toilet paper. "Well, what did I tell you? They'll just have to learn."

THE WORLD AND THE GIRLS

Inger thought about Mama's words. I'm glad you have Sheila. That was *so* true! She longed for Mama to know how true it was. But she'd never in all the world be able to tell her.

Inger had gone out into the world hoping that the girls would disappear. But the world was full of girls. Fat girls, thin girls, girls with broad shoulders and narrow shoulders, girls with a perfect A-shape or H-shape, according to the current fashion, girls with upswept hair and girls with exactly the kind of curls that you supposedly just shook into place. Some girls were so pretty that you couldn't stand to look at them. So you did anyway, and were blinded. Many girls yelled "Nah!" and pulled away and didn't dare to do anything crazy, and some were all gray and pretended that they weren't there, and if you approached that kind of a girl and said something funny and revealed that she actually was there, such a girl might suddenly beam and become pretty. Most girls had faults. Their smile might be a little too wide, or a little too rabbit-like, or their nose actually just a lump, and some were so unlucky that their thighs went all the way down to their shoes, but there wasn't a single girl in the world who couldn't become pretty if you talked to her. Almost none, anyway. Of course there were girls who were completely hopeless, who never got pretty, no matter what you said, but usually these were girls who already were pretty. They thought they were movie stars. Their laughter was movie star laughter, and they didn't want to let their real selves get out. For there was a real self inside every girl, and at the core of them all dwelled a peal of spontaneous laughter that was just waiting to come into its own.

Inger saw girls everywhere. And she knew that it was wrong of her to see all these girls, but see them she did. She could be sitting on the bus and see a girl. She might see her get up and notice that she had slender hands and a red sweater. The girl might get off the bus, and she would never see her again. Even so, the sweater and hands were burned into her memory, and for months she knew—even for a whole year—that she'd seen this girl.

She just couldn't go on like this. But the world was full of girls in Edinburgh, too. There was Ella Granli from Bergen with the laughter and the lipstick, Birgitte from Nakskov with the strawberry mouth and high cheek bones, and Ricarda from Wuppertal, tall and musical, and she couldn't get her out of her head. There was always some girl she couldn't get out of her head, and such was life. The world had always been full of girls, and right now it was full of Sheila F. Mayfield (the F stood for Fiona, but that was a deep secret).

They quarreled quite often. Usually the quarrel was over nothing. Sheila was constantly getting the better of her. Rarely did Inger have the last word, just because she had to limp along in English. That was the whole explanation. She liked her so much because she got the better of her. What kind of reason was that to like someone? It made her furious and happy at the same time. That certainly wasn't any state of mind to base her life on.

Why does my life consist of waiting for her to come? The only thing that matters is that she is nice to me. If she's nice to me in the morning, before she leaves, I have a good day, and I float around with the Hoover. If she's aloof, everything is ruined, and there I sit—while she lives her life at the university and forgets about me, who just goes around lifting up small objects in her room and dusting her hair brushes, hoping she'll talk to me when she gets home.

Inger would deliberately do a sloppy job in Sheila's room. It bothered her a lot that she had to dust this room in particular. The worst was when Sheila stayed home to study. Then she saw her with the Hoover.

They sang together. And sometimes they would fight. Suddenly they would fall on top of each other and lie there wrestling on the floor. I'm too big for this, thought Inger. But she enjoyed it.

The next day they quarreled again. All it took was for Sheila to ask—as Inger passed her with bucket and shovel on her way from the coal bin: "Inger, are you in a bad mood today?" That put her in a bad mood, of course, even if she hadn't been in one before. "No!" she bellowed. "I can tell," said Sheila.

Why can't I just not give a damn about whether she likes me? But that was impossible. But the hand in the middle of the pantomime darkness, she wouldn't have put it there if she hadn't liked me, would she? The pressure through the cloth of her coat on Christmas Eve had been different. That had probably just happened because they'd been crowded so close together. But there was absolutely no chance that she'd been unaware of the hand in the pantomime darkness. I have absolutely no control over Sheila's hand, she thought, and it's not my fault.

But it is my fault that it felt so good to have it there. And how good it felt to lie there wrestling on the kitchen floor, fighting for something or other, an apple core! that is my fault, my fault and my fault alone. Sheila laughed, and I did, too. But if she only knew why I was laughing she'd stop laughing immediately.

How many times is this going to happen, while I pretend it's not happening? How many times will I be happy when I'm with another girl, and pretend that I'm just laughing? How many times will I think about another girl, think and think about her, and hope, when I know there's absolutely nothing to hope for? Will I go through life like this? Will I go through life pretending that the most important thing of all is not happening?

That's it! she thought. I'm going to write down the names of all the girls. I'm going to write down all the names from my whole life—from elementary school, yes all the way back to when I lived on Collettsgate and was just three years old—because that's when it all began, I guess I know that!—it started with Ulla Jespersen on the corner during an air raid. There she sat, laughing, in the bicycle shed with her girl friends, together with the other people who lived in the building. I haven't forgotten that, and how happy it made me to have her sitting there.

And she took her diary and did as she'd been thinking. There was a long list of names of girls who had made her happy in her life. And it ended with: Sheila F. Mayfield, 6, Aberdeen Road, Edinburgh 5. I love you.

Inger stared at her words. This was perverted. But she'd written it anyway. Finally it was written down, the thing that everyone would have thrown up at. She longed for something that wouldn't be completely disgusting to long for. She knew that if her longing ever were to lead to actions, she'd be a criminal. There were laws against that sort of thing, she knew that. But she had no idea exactly what acts were meant. She just longed to wrestle over an apple core one more time. Inger stared at her forbidden words. She'd done something similar once before. That was a long time ago now. She'd told God that she loved Beate. Then she'd torn out the pages and burned them. Now she promised herself that she would never burn these. Because only by looking the truth in the eyes could she fight it.

Then she lay down between her cold sheets and blankets and fought against the truth. But soon her hand found its way to the place between her legs, and after a short time she began to behave just like an animal, there must be something wrong with her head, to carry on like this, every time she had made up her mind that this would be the last time, but it came again, it just came, and she couldn't keep from behaving as if she were completely insane, and there came Sheila and put her hand on her leg in the middle of the pantomime darkness, and the feeling of well-being exploded inside her.

This is ridiculous, she thought afterwards—all warm and sweaty. This is the last time.

Why aren't I a boy? she thought. If I'd only been a boy, there wouldn't have been anything wrong with all these girls. I think and feel like a boy, and here I stand with upswept hair along a wall with twenty-five other girls at the Cavendish Ball Room and try so hard to hope for a boy that my brain creaks. And there comes one of them. He sees me. I can see that he sees me, and I try to look like I see him, too, by looking in a different direction, and maybe he thinks I'm pretty, or pretty enough at any rate, to dance with. But I'm a wolf in sheep's clothing.

The boy came. He was handsome and dark and nice, and his name was Ian MacNeal, and Inger tried to see him. Her body wanted to dance, and it wanted to be close to his. One body was better than none, and it was boys' bodies her body was supposed to be close to, and if she just could get close enough to him, maybe all of these girls would disappear.

He walked her home, and kissed her on the corner. Inger set her sights on the boys of Edinburgh. She set her sights on Ole Yngvarsen, a Norwegian dental student she'd met behind the Fredrikstad newspaper. "Are you from Fredrikstad?" "No, I'm from Halden," said Ole. Then he set his sights on Birgitte from Nakskov. It was the strawberry mouth he was after. How did you set your sights on a boy? She was too fat, that was obvious, and there was nothing more obvious than being too fat. But Ella from Bergen was fat, too. And Tore from Haugesund set his sights on her. How did you set your sights on a boy? "Use your eyes on him!" Unni Tøgersen had said. But she didn't have the kind of eyes that could radiate through the room while they were singing about fjords "like violets blue."

Inger longed for a boy. Where was he? She thought: My body needs a boy, my soul needs a girl. It is just my soul that's in love. Through my eyes. But my body's waiting for a boy. She longed to be held tightly. By strong hands that came straight out of a book. Straight out of *Jane Eyre,* which she was reading now, and which turned out to be even better than *Peasants at Sea.* But where were the hands?

Thornfield Hall, she thought. Where Mr. Rochester came. Everything was much clearer in books. So that if you didn't get the one you loved, you died. The heroine collapsed on the heath, or she threw herself in front of a train. In real life you always kept on living after you'd actually thrown yourself in front of a train.

"Are you reading *Jane Eyre?*" said Mrs. Mayfield. "Yes," said Inger.

"That's a good book, don't you think?"

Inger's dream world immediately collapsed into ruins. Mrs. Mayfield had read *Jane Eyre!* How was it possible to have read *Jane Eyre* and still look like Mrs. Mayfield? "Oh yes," she said. "Ah, Mr. Rochester!" exclaimed Mrs. Mayfield. It was the most passionate thing Inger would ever hear her say.

Inger stood alone in the dining room bent over the Trolley (the Norwegian word had long since been wiped out of her memory) putting sugar in the teacups and thinking about Mrs. Mayfield and Mr. Rochester. Maybe that should be her new novel. Mrs. Mayfield could stand in the leafy grove and see Mr. Rochester fall off his horse, and then she could say: "I think we've got different moral standards!" And Mr. Rochester could clutch her around her distinctively droopy rear end, and exclaim: "Who the Deuce do you think you are?" And then he would kiss her so wildly and fervently that she'd instantly make up her mind that if she couldn't have him, she'd throw herself in front of a train.

That became one of the many novels she started in her head.

It was to be called *Peasants on Land,* and unlike normal books, the title wouldn't have anything to do with anything that happened in the novel. For that's how life was. It would be a thoroughly abnormal book.

She stood bent over the Trolley and thought about it. Then suddenly she felt someone right behind her, who stopped and stood right up against her. For an instant she was startled. It was Sheila. She hadn't heard her come in. She leaned against her, for a moment Inger felt her body against her back, Sheila bent her head toward her and put one hand to Inger's ear and the other around her waist, for a moment she stood there in this sudden embrace, then Sheila whispered: "Two and a half!"

In the next moment Mrs. Mayfield promenaded in with the tea-pot, and Sheila continued around the table and sat down at her place with her arms folded and a sincere expression on her face. But the message was clear enough. Inger didn't doubt for an instant what the message meant. Sheila wanted to have two and a half spoonfuls of sugar in her tea!

Shaken, Inger stood by the trolley. For one thing was totally clear: The extra spoonful would be smuggled in, even if it cost her her honor and her job, and meant she'd be sent home on the first boat.

Disconcerted, she stood holding the sugar bowl, her heart pounding. Because now the others were coming in. It didn't look good. Sheila began to draw attention to herself by telling her mother she had a thread on the back of her skirt. Mrs. Mayfield started turning around in circles to find the thread, and in the general confusion that arose around this, Inger quickly put an extra spoonful of sugar in Sheila's cup.

Then she walked around the table and took her place. Her place was between Sheila and Adam on the one long side of the table. Mr. Mayfield arrived home. It was Friday and fried haddock. Daddy interrogated his family. Everything was as usual. Except for an extra spoonful of sugar in Sheila's teacup. A secret alliance. Finally Mrs. Mayfield said: "And what have you been up to today, Charles?" He drummed on the table and took the first bite of his Clubs. "Fiddling," he said. That was how he always answered, and that was the only insight he ever gave his family into his world. (But he was a stock market speculator.) Then the hand came.

Sheila's hand lay on Inger's leg. Daddy ate his Clubs. She likes me, she thought. Why else would she do such a thing? The hand lay there, quite heavily, and incredibly noticeably. Inger drank her tea and pretended that nothing had happened. But from somewhere beneath the Mayfield family's dark, polished table with butter curls and toast racks and gooseberry jam, a sweet, strong and completely incomprehensible feeling of well-being spread to all parts of her body.

That evening Inger and Sheila sat out in the kitchen talking until 11:30. The stove still gave out a little warmth even though it had been made ready for the next day. (The rubber gloves had never been replaced, so Inger got a sooty finger every day, washed it clean, but of course it got just as dirty again the next day through the hole, and she never had a completely clean index finger again until she got to the other side of the North Sea.) Inger sat in the armchair in the corner, and Sheila sat on the kitchen table with her feet resting under her on a chair. They were in deep conversation. Deep always meant about boys. Whatever you might think about boys, they were always good to have to talk deeply to girls about. Now I'm done for.

The last sentence just floated down into her head. That's the way you thought when you were from Fredrikstad. And in the next instant Inger was possessed with the desire to tell Sheila that she loved her.

She panicked. Very calmly she sat in the armchair and panicked.

"Have you done it?" said Sheila.

Some things about the English language were really amazing. So "done it" was the same in both Norwegian and English.

"No," said Inger. "Have you?"

"No."

Sheila told about all her boys. There was one in her history class who always sent her looks, his name was David. And then there was an Iranian she'd had coffee with once. Don't tell Mum! Now she was going with a Norwegian medical student named Truls. He was from Skjåk, and really wanted to "do it." He was allowed to, a little, when they were in his room, but only on the floor. "I feel beds are naughty," said Sheila. But it was Peter she loved. She had a picture of him in a little locket she wore around her neck. But actually she knew that she'd end up marrying Mr. Alexander, the Sunday School teacher. He looked at her during the prayer every Sunday over the heads of the little boys he was supposed to be teaching, while she taught the little girls.

Inger heard all about Sheila's boys with Sheila's feet in her lap. For Sheila had put them there while she was talking, they were cold, they were always cold, and Inger warmed them. "This is not the land of the purple heather, it's the land of the purple legs," Inger said. She'd gotten to the point where she could be quite funny. Sheila laughed. "Aren't you in love?" she asked.

"Yes," said Inger.

"Who is it?"

You, of course. You, you idiot! Panic rose up in her again. Where was Inger's boy? She had to have a love life, of course. You just couldn't be a nineteen-year-old girl without having a love life. If you didn't have a love life that floated around in the form of a boy you went dancing with, almost slept with on the floor of his room, or had in a picture in a locket, at least you had to have a love life inside of you—in the form of a boy you never got that far with.

That was the solution. She could populate the world with present or absent boys who either didn't want her or whom she didn't want herself. And that's what she did.

She came up with a boy. She decided that she would be in love with Ole Yngvarsen, because she was a hundred percent sure that she couldn't have him; after all, he'd set his sights on

Birgitte from Nakskov. They would take a bus tour to Loch Lomond with Deacon Tønnesen. Inger decided that she would fervently hope that she'd end up next to Ole Yngvarsen on the bus, since she knew that Birgitte from Nakskov wasn't going along to Loch Lomond. But what would happen then? Ole Yngvarsen would sit down next to Reidun from Åndalsnes! He'd just sit there chatting with her all the way across the Highlands, past all the small, shaggy Highland cattle, past the banks of Loch Lomond and Stirling Castle, all the way to Glencoe; and when they'd look at Glencoe, smelling the battle of 1697, Ole Yngvarsen would stand next to Reidun from Åndalsnes then, too, and Inger decided that would ruin her whole experience of the legendary memories of clans and massacres and everything that would otherwise have made life worth living to hear about. "Oh, Reidun from Åndalsnes!" She decided that she could just kill her! "and what is life all about anyway, but taking your life?" she asked Sheila.

And Sheila agreed totally. "You have to fix yourself up!" she said. "I'm going to give you a home perm." "Nobody wants me!" said Inger. "Of course there's someone who wants you!" Sheila exclaimed indignantly. Inger basked in her indignation. Sheila curled Inger's head. Inger pretended that she was nervous that the curls would be a flop. But she wasn't. On the contrary. She hoped they would be a flop. Because if that happened Sheila would—absolutely certainly—come with her hands and give her a new home perm.

Unfortunately the home permanent was a huge success already the first time, Sheila admired her handiwork and Inger headed off to the Cavendish Ball Room where she was standing along the wall with a long row of other girls, trying to hope for a boy.

Such was life. She made her way through it with lies. That was the truth.

What kind of a life would it be? What difference would it make if she learned fluent English, wrote witty stories about life that made everyone laugh, if she could never love someone? She'd have to sneak her way through life. The girls she fell in love with would never find out about it, and then it was as if she were deceiving them, just by being there. They obviously didn't know how happy they made her, and then it was as if she were stealing the happiness. Would she end up living her life as a thief and liar?

Where was the boy who could rescue her from all of this?

Inger was waiting for a feeling she'd never had. She was waiting for a boy who'd come, and when he touched her, her whole life would be changed. She waited for happiness. Almost like a house—with colors no one had ever seen and a sky overhead that was a different blue color. Why did happiness only live in books? Why couldn't it come out? Why did it just live in books, even though all the people in books were unhappy, too? But they were unhappy in a happy way. There was a point to a book.

For one year Inger lived in a house on the north end of Edinburgh. It was a gray, semi-detached house with two stories, of the type found all over the British Isles. Every day she did the dusting here in a fifty-three-hour work week for £1 a week, and she never had a day off. She was one of hundreds of thousands of young foreign girls who worked every day in comparable houses with comparable tasks and for comparable pay. She despised her work. And every day she longed for the day when she would go home.

No, the house she had come to and her life there bore so little resemblance to happiness as she could possibly have imagined when she stood waving on the M/S Blenheim. And in this house she found happiness. She knew it, and she turned her back on it. She knew that Sheila made her life worth living, and that this was at the heart of everything. And she knew that if she were to live in happiness like this, she'd be unhappy the rest of her life.

FEBRUARY 26TH

All year Sheila's hand ended up on Inger's leg. It happened every day during the evening meal, at about the same time Daddy received his Clubs. It was very strange, and Inger often wondered about it. Every time she sat without moving a muscle. She was convinced that if she made even the slightest movement the hand would disappear. The hand was there only on the condition that she didn't notice it. And each time it brought about the sweetest pleasure.

Not once did it occur to her that she could do anything with the hand. For example, lay her own hand over it. What do you do when you get a hand on your leg? What does it mean and why is it there?

They argued and sang their way through the winter. They went to the Coffee Pot at Golden Acre, the nearest shopping center, where the 8, 9, 19, 23 and 27 bus lines went toward the city with white roofs and good advice on the sides: DrinkA PintA MilkA Day, at all of the bus stops in the entire city were waste baskets with a picture of the skyline, £20 fine for littering, This City is Beautiful, they said. Edinburgh is a cold city, a dark city, a historical city. Some say it is the world's most beautiful. Connie Francis' sharply sweet metallic soprano oozed out of the jukebox at the Coffee Pot:

'Cause everybody's somebody's fool
and everybody's somebody's plaything.

That was the scourge of the land that year, and no one sang more truthfully that particular year. Life was wonderful.

Hot days descended over the city. They could go out in the yard and play ball, even though it was only February. It was on such a day that they went out to play badminton, after they had successfully frittered away the afternoon thwarting each other's efforts to read. They tried to smack the birdie so that not even a world champion could have returned it, for example by hitting it right down in the dirt a half yard in front of yourself, and these ridiculous exercises didn't last long before they began to fight over the birdie itself—the shuttle-cock, as it was called in English. As a matter of fact the shuttle-cock ended up way over by the garden wall, and they raced over to see who could reach it first, Sheila got there first, and she served so wildly that it flew in through Inger's open bedroom window and disappeared.

The surprising disappearing act astonished and excited them so much that they immediately rushed after it into the room, it had landed on the bed. Inger threw herself over it, but instead of standing up at once with her trophy, she remained lying on her back for a moment, catching her breath. Then Sheila tumbled on top of her, and she wasn't trying to get hold of the shuttle-cock at all. Instead she pressed herself against Inger with great fervor, they felt each other from their shoulders all the way down to their knees, as one body, one desire and in the next instant melted together in a rhythmic and unmistakable attack of lust.

Sheila and Inger made love in the middle of February. How this could happen was mysterious and unfathomable, and it didn't fit into their conceptual framework that two girls could enjoy each other like that. And besides, they had all their clothes on. But that didn't matter. They made love through their clothes. It was good. Yes, it was so good that after a very short time they sprang away from each other—frightened, breathless and confused.

But Inger knew instantly that if Sheila had stayed there, she'd have given up any resistance. Her entire moral structure, her bulwark against abnormality, the deeply serious decision she'd made in her diary—where the truth had been written down so that she could fight it—she simply wouldn't have given a damn, she'd have just lain there—how long? how long? how long was it possible?—??—yes, she would have thrown herself into it endlessly and without thinking, for could there possibly be anything better?

It had taken one second for this to become obvious.

And it confused her more than anything else had ever confused her. Sheila stood by the edge of the bed, red in the face, looking just as confused. That's where the line went. They knew that—in the look they exchanged. They didn't say anything. They were overcome by the embarrassment of the moment, and quite soon they both mumbled similar excuses to go their own way.

Inger had never imagined that she would make love to a girl. That was not what she was longing for, she longed for closeness, no matter how. What had happened was something completely private, it was more like what she used to do with herself, and every time she decided it would be the last time. She was amazed that it was possible to have this feeling when you were with another person.

So maybe it wasn't so wrong after all? For the weird thing was that she was sure Sheila had felt exactly the same thing. So maybe she wasn't the only one who was going crazy. And no matter whether it was right or wrong, she would have given anything to have been crazy with her a little longer.

And then she thrust the whole new insight down into the depths of her soul.

The next day they flared up into one of their incomprehensible arguments again. It was while they were doing dishes, one word led to another, and it didn't make things any better that Inger was gradually getting better at making swift retorts. The argument ended with Sheila saying that she had absolutely ZERO interest in talking to her unless she were allowed to be rude.

That was going pretty far. Being rude was the worst thing you could be in this house. You could be sent home for that. But Sheila was already home. She couldn't be sent anywhere. Especially not by Inger, who had no other means of power than a dish towel. There they stood doing the dishes in silence.

Inger hated this silence, which Sheila was so good at. She made up her mind to stop allowing herself to be tyrannized by her. She decided to put up with the silence. But she heard it in her ears. It was everywhere, in all the movements she made as she dried the white plates with the gold stars on the edges. The silence stood on the wet lawn she saw through the window over the sink, it was impossible to think of a single thought besides the silence.

It's strange how thoughts can come to a complete standstill. It was Thursday evening. She was supposed to go to a get-together at church. Now she'd have to go the whole evening, the whole next morning with thoughts that had come to a standstill. For an eternity of hours they'd just be waiting for Sheila to come back tomorrow afternoon and perhaps get them going again.

They finished the dishes without a word. Sheila went into the living room where the rest of the family was already sitting. Inger went into her room to get her coat. Now she would have to stick her head in and say good-bye to them. Otherwise she'd be rude. But she had no desire to say good-bye to Sheila. She had no desire to say anything at all to her before she'd taken those words back. But she had to say good-bye to the others. She stood there, torn, with her coat on. Then she went toward the living room and opened the door.

There they sat, the whole family, behind newspapers, books and handwork, as usual, silent, tranquil, with a fire in the fireplace. There were never any conversations in the living room. "Well, good-bye," Inger forced out. Her throat was completely dry. "Good-bye, Inger," they all said. In that moment Sheila stood up. She let her newspaper slip to the floor and went quickly toward the door. She came out into the hallway where Inger was standing, closing the door behind her. Out there in the half-darkness she knelt down in front of Inger. She held her hands flat together in front of herself and looked up at her: "Forgive me!" she said.

A short hesitation followed. Inger stood right in front of her, Sheila's head reaching just above her waist; she looked down at Sheila and those eyes, felt relief flow through her body, and saw the pleading hands toward her. "I love you," she said.

The words hung in the half-dark air of the hallway, they were unmistakable, and there was no chance that Sheila hadn't heard them.

Sheila was still on her knees. She looked at her, and Inger didn't know what to do except to take her head and press it against her. For a moment they stood like that, closely, holding each other's hands, then Inger let go and went quickly out of the house.

The wind was mild. She walked past the green hedges and patches of lawn in the pale dusk, amazed at her words. And she knew they were the truest words she'd ever uttered.

She was glad! Glad that they had come.

At the bus stop on Ferry Road, where bus 21 goes to Leith, she stood looking out. For here she was met with an amazing sight. The whole skyline of Edinburgh was silhouetted against the sky. She'd stood here many times and waited, looking out over the endless athletic fields, but she'd never seen anything but boys playing rugby in the fog.

But there—far away—rose the old, dark towers, beautiful and clear, and behind them, clear and green, Arthur's Seat. The fog had lifted. The city was clean! This was Edinburgh's spring thaw. It came through the sky. And it was Thursday, February 26th.

But later she thought: "I love you" wasn't the same thing in Norwegian and English. "*Elske*" was stronger than "love." And she never would have said "*Jeg elsker deg*" to a Norwegian girl. For some strange reason the word "love" was much weaker. They had such a frivolous association with the word "love" in this country. "I *love* peanuts," they might say. But Sheila couldn't possibly have thought that she loved her like you loved peanuts? She hoped so. She hoped she would forget the whole thing. And she made vigorous efforts to forget it herself.

THE CASTLE

According to an old Edinburgh custom Arthur's Seat is as-
cended the night before the first of May, and a religious service is held up there. The mountain lies treeless, like a green
piece of Highland in the middle of the city, it's a long hike up,
and whoever dips their face in the dew here will have eternal
youth.

With a group of other Scandinavian girls, citizens of the city,
young and old, Inger watched the sun rise red over the Firth
of Forth, and she dipped her face in the grass. For she didn't
believe in the prophecy, and she was glad that she was growing irrevocably older.

Have I become a better girl? What will I become? A girl who
loves girls? The one had replaced the next one. There was no
end to it. And now I love someone. I know it and I see it, for
otherwise the sunrise over the Lowlands would never have
been so beautiful.

Some distant shouts could be heard through the crackling
and static. Inger has twisted and turned the dial and put her ear
right up to the brown radio in the kitchen. Here it comes!
Here come the flags right through the radio. The band is playing its oompa, oompa under the budding trees, all the way

across the North Sea. Now the graduates are bursting out at home in Norway. Now the class of 1961 is yelling its yell throughout Nygaardsgata. Inger pressed her ear against the radio and wept.

Then she headed off with upswept hair to the Carlton Hotel, for it was here the Norwegian colony in Edinburgh was to celebrate the Seventeenth of May, Norwegian Constitution Day. She didn't pick anyone up, and she didn't care. In the early, early spring night she walked through Princes Street with Ella. The birds were chirping from all their invisible places, there was no one in the streets, all was bright and quiet. They sat at the foot of the Scott Monument, in the middle of Princes Street. There they told each other about home. They talked about their fathers and how impossible it was possible to become.

Ella was fun and pretty. She was the best friend Inger had there, of the Norwegians. That time at Christmas, when she made up her mind to leave, Ella said: "Oh, no! Don't leave! I'm staying all the way till June!"

It was so strange to be Norwegian. That was the best thing anyone had said to her this whole year in Edinburgh. Now the city would soon be emptied of its foreign girls and filled with new ones. Ella talked about a boy she'd loved in Bergen, a man, actually, he was twenty-seven years old, after all, and he cheated on her. They remained sitting so long by the monument, Inger suddenly knew that she could tell Ella about everything. She didn't dare to, but she didn't want to let her go, either. They decided to meet the next day. They wanted to go sightseeing at The Castle.

The 18th of May was an incredibly warm day. A brilliantly clear summer day, of the type that seems to contradict the very essence of the city, its dark buildings and ancient towers—and for that very reason it was warmer and clearer than all the other summer days you remembered.

Ella and Inger took bus number 8 from East End over The Bridges to the old part of the city, where Inger wanted to go into Thin's book store before they went up to The Castle. This was actually a rather roundabout route. It would have been shorter to take bus 23 or 27 up The Mound. But Inger had her own special plan with this. A hope that arose as soon as she felt the sun climb up and noticed how it sent its warmth through her body and got stronger and stronger as the afternoon went on. The hope itself was related to the sun, and she couldn't help but reach out in its direction, no matter how completely and incomprehensibly insanely dumb, ridiculous, incredible and unfathomable the hope was. How on earth it could strike her to grasp at such a hope, it was so indescribably dumb that it was pure luck that no one had any idea about it, or would ever find out about it, for the hope was that by taking this particular road to The Castle, and walking along Chambers Street she and Ella would happen by the steps of The Old Quad, where Sheila might perhaps be sitting.

What on earth, she asked herself, causes me to be driven by such an uncontrollable desire to do precisely this? To walk past the place where she might possibly be sitting—in the sun— instead of being somewhere inside the building at a lecture or in a reading room? What is it that makes me go out of my way just so I can see her for five seconds, when I see her every single day—morning, noon and night—see her every single time we do the dishes, see her often in her free time, in the evenings, on weekends, see her, see her, see her, constantly, she always came back, nothing was more certain than that—Sheila would come, she would appear, suddenly her face would be there, and she would say: "Hello, honeybun!" or something else she was in the habit of saying. I always see her, there's no one I see so much, talk with so much, joke with, play with, laugh and sing with, tease, argue and eat with. Why on earth should I go out of my way just so that I can see her even more than that? *I must be crazy.*

Completely crazy and absolutely beside herself with inner

restlessness and increasing hope, Inger took bus number 8 with Ella over The Bridges, went into the bookstore—where there were plenty of things to interest her, for that matter, and it wasn't difficult to find a book you would like to buy—armed with this book, it was a historical map of Scotland, in fact—with humorous pictures of all the battles lost and won—thus, suitably armed, they strode up toward The Castle via Chambers Street, and not down again toward High Street, which *is* shorter, no, not just shorter, but frankly a shortcut by a couple of blocks, but Ella allowed herself to be led, she didn't need any special explanation of why just now they were going to walk through the university campus, but they were walking here, the sun was high in the afternoon sky, the students were swarming everywhere, none with long scarves now, they were carrying their books, sitting, hanging out, standing chatting, some in close embrace, looking deep into each others eyes, hanging intellectually on each other's words, full of knowledge and love, and Inger and Ella strode past them on their way to their sightseeing at The Castle; and as they went past The Old Quad, and the old buildings from the eighteenth century past the colleges and departments there—on the university steps outside Heriot Watts College directly across from The Royal Scottish Museum, they suddenly heard a cheerful shout: "Hey, you two!" and a laugh. There sat Sheila.

She was sitting right outside there with her face turned upward toward the sun and not reading one bit, but trying resolutely to get a tan on her face and arms and legs, she was sitting with her legs outstretched and a summer dress and a notebook in her lap and she saw them at once. In fact, they saw each other almost simultaneously, and in the very instant they caught sight of each other, Inger experienced the strongest and most sudden joy of her nineteen-year-old life.

For the fact was that she was completely caught off guard by this meeting. She was completely unprepared for the fact that Sheila, who was the only reason she was walking here, was actually sitting there. It was the greatest surprise of her young life, and it completely disconcerted her.

That joy, that this joy, could turn out like this, explode, transform and reform all the buildings and steps around them, the sky above, the sidewalk and street, and make them burst into beauty—no, this she had not expected. It came quite abruptly, confused her momentarily and embarrassed her more than a little. But it was unmistakable.

They didn't stop. They just shouted cheerfully at each other. "What're you doing here?" shouted Sheila. "We're sightseeing," Inger shouted back. And one could hardly call that a lie. She was on the most wondrous sightseeing trip of her life. But she added: "We're going to see Edinburgh Castle." Then they walked on by. They continued toward the corner. But when she knew that in a moment Sheila wouldn't be able to see them anymore if she were watching, she turned, couldn't keep from turning to see her just one more time and to see if she was looking, and Sheila was—she was watching them, and when she saw that Inger was watching for it, she lifted her arm, a bare and sunburned arm, and waved, and once again she sent the whole neighborhood into beauty.

It's over. I saw her. And now I can't see her anymore. A peculiar feeling of melancholy, almost nausea, came over her. So brief!

A terrible dizziness enveloped her as soon as they rounded the corner. It was a completely unfamiliar feeling. And the sun, warmer now than before, intensified the feeling that everything she saw around her wasn't real, because it was so terribly clear. Her legs could barely carry her through all of this clarity.

She couldn't speak. Normally they carried on a lively conversation. Before they got to Chambers Street they'd talked nonstop. And now—she was silent. She was ashamed to look at Ella. She had a terrible feeling that she'd deceived her. Misled her—led her astray—on the wrong path—on a perverted and unnatural detour. And she followed unsuspectingly along.

Do you see it, Ella? Do you know what's happening? This dizziness, the light and the dizziness, in everything, don't you feel it too? And know the reason for it? She was overwhelmed by fear. Ella could see it—straight through everything! And against all the laws of nature her legs carried her onward—up The Royal Mile.

This was the road that Mary Queen of Scots took. They could see all the old buildings with the curious shops, pawn brokers one flight down, bustling commerce, all sorts of people, Scots in tartan up on the Esplanade, all this was suddenly more beautiful, clearer, stronger than in any painting or any novel she'd ever read—though nothing was as exquisite as there— but not even the most beautiful dream of castles and towers from fairy tales could measure up to the real tower and castle she now surveyed, the actual old stones. Here was St. Margaret's Chapel, the city's oldest building, quite small, the Banqueting Hall with its polished floor and flurry from balls of times past, crown jewels and canons, the castle itself, as it arched over Princes Street Gardens, which lay far below with its Flower Clock with—it is said—no fewer than 11,000 little flowers forming its face and hands and numbers—yes, far, far below they could see it—the flower clock—and a little group of tourists standing below, checking the time and admiring it in all its colorful subtleties, as if everything there of present, past and future was summarized here—in one single blooming stroke of time.

It's a marvelous work of art, the Edinburgh Flower Clock! And up on the parapet stood two young Norwegian girls gazing out over it all and looking like two young Norwegian girls gazing out over it all. But that was not the case. For one Norwegian girl was standing steadfastly beside another Norwegian girl, who had just discovered love.

THE MAN UNDER THE STARS

For many months Inger had had a book lying on her bedside table. It was a book she'd brought with her from Norway with unclear notions as to why. On the cover was a picture of a man standing alone on the globe under some stars. It was *Philosophy in Antiquity* by Eiliv Skard.

She tried to forget the girl she so shamefully and in deep secrecy went out of her way to see, and looked at the man under the stars. This was a fine picture. Just a man and the sky.

More and more wide-eyed she read about all these men of the past with their completely contradictory views of how everything had come into being, and how they actually moved and why. They all disagreed and knocked holes in the theories of those who'd gone before. And now and then someone emerged who tried to combine all of the viewpoints into a single all-encompassing doctrine. But he was more despised than all the others put together.

The strange thing was that she didn't disagree with any of them. As soon as she'd read that everything originated in the sea and actually *was* water, she thought that a deep truth lay in this. And as soon as she saw that you couldn't presume that something *was* anything at all, for everything was in constant change, everything was flowing, and you didn't step twice into the same river, she thought this was a sudden flash of truth.

Even the man who came and said that the origin of all things was neither earth, air nor water, but fire—and that all things would return to fire in the end—was a crazy man on the one hand, and on the other no one was as right as he was.

This was how Inger pitched and rolled her way through philosophy in antiquity, and the only thing she had difficulty accepting was the guy with the arrow. He said that a flying arrow did not fly and that Achilles never would catch the tortoise in a race, if the tortoise had just a slight head start. This *had to* be wrong? But what a fascinating mistake! For it was amazingly difficult to argue against it.

She dreamed herself through the thoughts of antiquity, she absorbed them just as passionately as she once had absorbed *Peasants at Sea.* What could be more respected and inspiring to occupy yourself with than how all things really were?

She sat in a kind of trance. This book was the origin of all other disciplines. It contained everything, as if the Greek natural philosophers had tried to create a system of thought that contained everything. How was it possible that a person who tried to fathom all these thoughts was the same person who spent her days dusting a strange house?

Resolutely she took hold of a pencil stub. Then she wrote on the last page of the book: Housework will never be my destiny. *Also sprach* the Hoover and the sweeper. I want to study. *Become* a philologist, once and for all. History, Norwegian and English. Amen.

It was like a revelation, and she took it completely literally. She'd *become* a philologist. A lover of words.

She wrote to her old French teacher, Miss Grytum, and asked for advice. She'd argued endlessly with this home economics teacher in junior high, but they'd developed the best relationship as soon as they started on French. Armholes and arrogance were forgotten, and Miss Grytum brought France and the Champs Élysées into the classroom.

Frida Grytum, who in the meantime had begun transporting the Champs Élysées into the classroom of a new group of students, wrote back with plans and a study guide. Welcome to the club!

Welcome to the club! Inger sat holding the letter in her hand. And she was proud that she would be joining Miss Grytum's club.

The morning she was to leave she was completely in a daze. She was going to do something she wanted to do and something she absolutely did not want to do. She wanted to go home, and Sheila would have to be torn out. How could she be torn out? She's become my sister! With both a heavy and a light heart she packed her last things in the little closet-room. Good-bye, dresser, good-bye two gray garbage cans outside the window, good-bye. . . . There was a knock at the door. And there stood Glen.

As the door opened he thrust his arms out to the sides and backed away, the blush spreading over his forehead, and in his hand he held a little package. "Good-bye, Inger!" he shouted, desperate from shyness, and held out the package. The little performance took her by surprise; she took the package. He stood in the doorway, watching her open it. It was a pin. A small, silver-plated pin with a turquoise stone. "It's Scottish!" he shouted, just as desperately. "Oh, Glen!" she shouted back, and hugged him. He put his arms around her, a brief moment. "Thank you so much!" "Oh, it's nothing!" shouted Glen. They just stood there, at a loss.

"I'll miss you in the mornings!" said Glen.

Sheila, Mrs. Mayfield and Adam stood waving on the platform. The platform lay in the little valley just below The Castle, where there had once been a loch. Was this where she had arrived?

Ever since she was little she had noticed this. The place you left was never the same place you came to. When she left the

90

station in Halden, where her grandparents lived, she always had to turn around and walk backwards to realize that it was the same town. And even then it was nearly impossible. "It's strange," she thought. "You have to be able to remember what you were thinking."

After just a short time the three figures were gone. From one moment to the next Sheila was gone. It was dizzying and unreal that she could disappear so suddenly and mercilessly on a platform at a station. Once again everything she saw around her, the houses, the chimneys, the green landscape in the sunshine, became so beautiful. And it hurt.

It troubled her that it was so dizzying to see another person disappear on a platform. It set her apart from all other people. And she didn't want that. She wanted to be within. She desperately wanted to be a normal part of humanity.

Therefore she made a firm decision on the boat home. "I'm giving it one more chance—to not happen again."

The Blenheim's sister ship, the M/S Braemar, skimmed through the waves in a northeasterly direction. In the lounge sat a woman with coal-black curls and a hawk nose, gazing out over the throng of fellow passengers. If she caught the eye of one of them, she didn't look away. She soaked them in and waited for one of them to interest her. Her name was Iona Fairchild, she was from New Orleans, and for many years she had run a school where she'd divided the students up solely according to astrological principles. She had the best results in the whole state of Louisiana.

There was a young girl who caught her eye—for she used only one at a time—and who did not cast her glance down either. "Hello," she said. "My name is Iona Fairchild from New Orleans. May I ask what sign you were born under?"

But the girl didn't know! So that was where things stood. There were no limits to modern ignorance. But it didn't matter in the slightest for her purposes, for naturally the girl knew when she'd been born. "May I buy you a drink?" she said. "I'd love to look into your future." The girl said she could buy and tell fortunes all she wanted, but all she cared for was a Coca-Cola, the trip over to Great Britain was still fresh in her mind—that was a year ago, as a matter of fact—and a Danish lady had deluded her into drinking whiskey for the waves, with the result that she had ended up shuttling back and forth between her berth and the sink the rest of the trip.

The girl spoke good English, with a British accent, and seemed to be skeptical by nature. A good candidate, this one. She didn't like the ones who were too pliable. Iona Fairchild ordered two colas, and without delay took her hand, which she examined closely at the same time as she thought about the foot prints in the fresh snow that had fallen over the Norwegian capital city on October 27, 1941. For the girl was quite willing to talk, and was clearly familiar with her own history. She looked directly at her, still holding her hand. There was something that made her not want to let go. She could always tell. "Your life," she said, "will not be *simple*." She knew that this always made a good impression. "Come on, anybody could say that, and they'd always be right," the girl replied and laughed a little. It was obvious that she didn't for a moment believe in fortune telling, and that she thought it was only a game. "But because of this," Iona Fairchild continued, "precisely because of this, many people will confide in you."

Inger looked back at the half-crazy woman. She was perhaps sixty years old, and very beautiful. What a bunch of nonsense, she thought. I suppose soon she'll start in on the fantasy that a dark-haired man is thinking about me, and that I'll have five children and be very, very happy, just like the gypsies who occasionally set up camp on the Coal & Charcoal-dock in Fredrikstad used to foretell. Confide in me? I'm not the kind of warm, confidence-inspiring person that people flock to in order to confide in. How was that going to happen? Was she going to start up an agency? And besides—how could a person who never dared to tell the truth herself—ever hope to get truth in return?

"You will go through a time of great confusion," said Iona, "but by virtue of your artistic abilities, your fury and your unyielding determination, with time you will become a person many other people will seek out."

The fortune-telling was now clearly over, and Iona Fairchild released her hand. "Isn't it true?" she said eagerly. "Don't people already have a tendency to confide in you?" This was certainly way off base, except for the fury. But Inger didn't want to disappoint the American fortune teller by telling her how far off base she was, and besides it was quite entertaining, so she said, "Oh, sure. Sometimes."

Then she forgot the whole prophecy, and didn't give it another thought until twenty years later.

The next day the southern coast of Norway lay bathed in sunshine. The yellow sloping rocks, the white houses—wood frame houses!—stood in the August sunshine, and the sea gulls scolded. It was so clear! How clear the knolls, how clear the little waves. Could she possibly come from such a pretty country? She wept when she saw Norway. Oh, thank God, the rocks called out. Thank God I'm home again!

Early, early the next morning she got up, and when the M/S Braemar docked at the Fred. Olsen dock, she was the first one to bound on shore.

HOMECOMING

When Ørnulf was little, he was always tormented by the smell of the dinner that was never to be eaten until his father got home. His father was strict with him, and every other month he took him by the ear and shaved his head in order to save money. Mr. Holm, the customs agent at Steinkjer, a small town in Trøndelag, recorded all the household expenses in small, black notebooks, and once he had paced back and forth over the living room floor all night because the accounts didn't balance. There was one *øre* missing, and he couldn't fathom where it could have vanished. It was the first and last time anything like that ever happened. But he never was able to explain it. He was an avid sportsman and hunter, and every Easter vacation he dragged Ørnulf along on interminable ski tours in the mountains.

However, the thing that made the greatest impression on Ørnulf in his childhood was one night when he'd seen his father standing by the sink in the kitchen. He watched him from behind, as he slowly and meticulously opened one bottle after another of fine, old whiskey and emptied the contents in the sink. This was during Prohibition, and the shipment had been confiscated at the border. There stood his father, faithful servant, and poured it all out without a single witness, except for Ørnulf, ten years old, whom he suddenly turned and discovered. "Get out of here, boy!" he thundered.

This scene was and would remain the most idiotic and infuriating thing Ørnulf had seen in his whole life.

Therefore when Ørnulf became his own master—which happened when he turned sixteen—he drank uninhibitedly all the liquor he could afford, he shunned all outdoor activities, he let his hair grow and grew a mustache and sideburns, in the fashion of the time—his hair was luxurious and black as coal —was liberal in his handling of money, and when he established his own home, it was forbidden to sit around a table. "Gathering everyone together!" Ørnulf said. "Gathering everyone together for the sole purpose of stuffing food into a hole in the middle of your face I regard as barbarity."

Now as a matter of fact Evelyn did not miss the dinner table in the slightest. When she was little she and her five older brothers and sisters sat around a large table where her father, Hans Rudolf, presided. He was an authoritative gentleman, and there was nothing between heaven and earth about which he did not possess an exceedingly definite opinion. One was that they should live off the land, procuring what they needed from plants grown in the large garden around the house and fertilized with their own excrement. Whatever ended up on their table was always spartan, and Emilie had a pantry for her own use, which it was forbidden to enter. They were seated around the table according to age, and the serving dishes went around according to the same principle, and Evelyn was always hungry. One time an amazingly large ham appeared on the table, and in an unguarded moment Evelyn's second oldest brother, Borgar, started to call to it: "Here, doggie! Shake!" He figured that it must be so full of worms that it could walk on its own.

Evelyn's oldest brother, Knut, was in the habit of lifting the table perfectly slowly and imperceptibly, and then suddenly letting it go, with a surprised look on his face. One time he made up a story about what would happen if one day the food were poisoned. Their parents would die. He himself would be permanently impaired. Solveig would have convulsions and would just barely survive, Borgar would throw up for days, Lisa would vomit a couple of times, Jan Michael would get a little green around the gills, and Evelyn would run around just as healthy as before.

Unfortunately this hypothetical story was completely realistic, so when she finally met a man who said: "Gathering everyone together! Gathering everyone together for the sole purpose of stuffing food into a hole in the middle of your face I regard as barbarity," she was inclined to agree, and they were compatible, both on this and a number of other points. "You have a difficult husband," Lisa used to say, "but at least he's not *boring!*"

It was true. The world was full of boring husbands and Evelyn had always counted her lucky stars that she wasn't married to one of them. She could stand in the kitchen window and watch Solum, the director of a firm, pass by. He never said a word. Except for the times he would suddenly exclaim: "Fandastic!" he said it like that, with a d, and no hints—either discreet or direct—could budge him from this pronunciation. Or she might see Gokstad, the engineer, disappear around the corner by Sollem's studio. He fell asleep at every party without having contributed a thing. But he always had such a good time that it never occurred to him that he should leave.

These were the thoughts Evelyn had had about Fredrikstad's marriages through her window over the years, but now she wasn't standing there alone anymore. Now Paula was watching, too, and soon Evelyn had given her these and comparable descriptions of all the members of the Phoenix Club and their wives. Paula knew all the names, and it was good to have her in the apartment at Bjørnegården.

Through Paula, Evelyn got her life back, all aspects of it all the way back to the time they were fourteen, lying under the covers in Magdeburg. Paula was with her—through the war and charges of treason after the war, through Ørnulf's mood swings and the children's fairy-tale world. Through Paula, Helga came to life again.

Helga had loved to put on make up. She fastened tight-fitting patent leather belts around her waist and made false teeth of cardboard. "Mama, I'm going to be a world famous prima donna! And when I'm forty, I'll just kill myself!" When she got big she was going to marry a sailor or a doctor. "For if I'm married to a sailor, he'll be gone so much that I'll be left alone. And if I'm married to a doctor, he'll be so intelligent that he'll *let* me be alone."

When Inger was on the way, Evelyn worked at the Carl Johan Theater. She didn't want another child, and had been to two doctors to get an abortion. But Emilie stepped in. And the doctors refused. She had to keep the baby, and both she and Ørnulf were convinced that it was a boy. When the baby arrived at the Josefine Street Hospital one October night during the war, it turned out that she was a girl, and she was covered with red spots and completely bald. The baby was so homely that Ørnulf was filled with an instantaneous love for her and decided that she would end up being almost as intelligent as he was himself. Evelyn's family, who worshipped beauty above intelligence, expressed their consternation—everyone, except for Lisa, who immediately loved the child just as much as she loved Evelyn. From the first moment, Helga had been adored for her striking appearance, her raven-black hair and her entertaining nature—she sang cabaret songs on the steps of the Gjarm family home when she was two, stark naked and with a wreath of flowers around her big tummy—and Emilie had chosen her to be her special pet.

"It's a girl!" Evelyn said that October night at the hospital. "She's going to be Papa's little girl!" said Ørnulf, and since then he always maintained that Evelyn loved Helga the most and he himself loved Inger best.

"That wasn't true," Evelyn said to Paula there by the kitchen window many years later. "How can you measure the love of a child?"

But Ørnulf never gave in on this point. It was one of life's axioms, and he said: "It'd be harder on me if Helga died than

97

if Inger did. My conscience is clear with Inger."

Evelyn couldn't stand to discuss such dreadful issues. He wanted her to say what she thought would be worst. She refused, and he answered for her. She protested. But she thought: It was true that Ørnulf and Helga had some violent confrontations when she was growing up. She had an obstinate side, just like him, and they could stand and scream at each other from opposite ends of the sofa, and then chase each other around it. Sometimes he hit her. "But if you feel guilty about Helga, then tell her!" Evelyn said. Then one day it was too late.

Evelyn talked. "It was a Saturday, and your parents had just arrived on a visit from Germany." Paula had known all about this, from far away. But now she lived through the days with Evelyn, day by day, the longest ones in Evelyn's life. It took five days from the day Helga opened the door of the Gjarm house and said: "Mama, I have such an awful headache!" until she lay in the iron lung in the Østfold County Hospital and said: "Even small flowers must wither . . ."

"That was the last thing she said!"

We were standing on the veranda at Vinderen, Ørnulf and I. The whole family was gathered in the house after the funeral, but we went outside—we couldn't stand to be there. He stood with his arms around me, and we looked at the sky. I wanted to see a star so much. Then a black pillar of smoke rose up over the rooftops in the east. It looked like there might be a fire over there. 'It's the smoke from the crematorium.' Ørnulf said. 'They're burning Helga now.'

"Something shattered inside me then. I cried, he was drunk and repeated his words. That was his way of looking the truth in the face.

"We stood with our arms around each other, and I thought: We have to stay together through this. And I said to him: 'Ørnulf . . . From now on? From now on I never want us to talk about Helga when we've been drinking.' We held each other so tightly then, I felt like it was a pact. But we went home, and he broke it. 'Do you remember what we promised each other that time?' I said. 'I'll decide for myself what I promise,' he said.

"He started going to the Club. I urged him to go, I thought he was so alone. But he'd be gone until late in the evening, and I'd pace back and forth in the apartment with all of my thoughts. If only we'd gone up to Northern Norway that time! I thought. If only I hadn't been so dumb as to be afraid of the darkness, he would have taken the position up there as district physician, and the disease wouldn't have touched us. It came, of course, then and there, just when it came. In Fredrikstad.

"Fredrikstad was an endless coincidence in our life. We had no ties to the city, and didn't know anything about it. We came here because Ørnulf had heard, through a friend, that he could buy a medical practice here. It was only one of hundreds of places we could have gone. And when we arrived, there was only one doctor in town who called to wish us welcome. The rumors about Ørnulf's views during the war had preceded us, and at first there were almost no patients in the office. 'We'll go to Argentina!' Ørnulf said. He couldn't bear to be in this country, where they had executed Quisling. He couldn't bear to be somewhere where stupidity had triumphed, and where he himself was eternally in the wrong. For in his heart of hearts he'd hoped all along that Germany would win the war. In Argentina he had a colleague who had left for similar reasons.

"We bought a Spanish Linguaphone course. Every afternoon for over a year we practiced Spanish, teased each other in Spanish, quizzed each other on vocabulary. But Ørnulf never heard from his friend. And one afternoon Ørnulf came in and said: 'Today there were *seven* patients in the office!'

"We wept with joy, Paula! And we forgot about Argentina. If only we hadn't done that, Helga would be alive today. That's what I kept thinking while I was pacing up and down the living room floor, while Inger slept and Ørnulf was at the Club. Where had the infection come from? We didn't know. It might have come from some fruit she ate. It might have come from other children at school. They said that if you were a particu-

99

larly active person, you were especially hard hit. We had taken a trip over the Swedish border to Strømstad the week before she got sick. On the way home we lay wrestling and kicking each other on a bench on the boat and laughing, and I thought: I never should have done that.

"But Ørnulf remembered a hug. In early September he'd had a patient in the office with headache and vomiting. It was a little boy, and he admitted him to the hospital on suspicion. Later it turned out that the boy had a mild case of polio. But Ørnulf had come straight in from the office, and Helga flew into his arms before he had a chance to wash his hands. She was so happy. She wanted to show him her new school books.

"'We can't spend the rest of our lives blaming ourselves, Ørnulf,' I said. But the grief was his. It changed him. It was as if I felt I was carrying the grief for two people through life. Whenever he came home, he was drunk. 'Helga's dying was worse for me than for you,' he said then. ''Because you were always nice to her!'

"I felt that measuring grief for a child was even more mean-ingless than measuring love. But now I was dragged into this new discussion, more unbearable than the other one.

"Even so I've thought many times: an old grief was stirred up in him. It wasn't that way with me. He had lived with grief since he was fourteen, when he lost his sister, little Hilde."

Evelyn told about little Hilde, whom she had never known. She had died of tuberculosis at Granheim Sanatorium near Lillehammer after two years of illness; she was sixteen. Ørnulf's parents, Thorleif and Helene, spent all their money going down to visit her, and on grapes and other things that might build up her strength, but every time they went there, she was thin-ner. Ørnulf stayed up in Steinkjer and waited, while people in town said that when T.B. came into a house it was because it hadn't been kept clean enough. "It was so unfair!" Evelyn said. "No one kept house better than Helene. But out on the street Ørnulf had it hurled at him: 'Spit wad!'"

The last time Helene saw little Hilde, she was sitting in bed with her knitting. Suddenly she let it sink down into her lap and said: "I don't think I'll ever finish this knitting, mother!"

Ørnulf was fourteen when this happened. He heard about her death at Røros, where they always spent the summers. He went down to the bridge over the Glomma and watched the river flow by.

Evelyn told about Ørnulf on the bridge, fourteen years old. He saw the bright eddies in the water. "The first time I visited Røros, I said: 'Show me where you stood!' So we went there together, I held him close, and he cried.

"But now we both needed comforting. And we couldn't give it to each other! Helene gave it to me. When Helga died, she confronted the death with enormous strength. She put her arms around Inger's shoulders and told her what had happened. She took her to Halden, where she had to be quarantined. Of course she wasn't allowed to play with other children. Ørnulf and I went away. We watched a sunset that flamed over the mountains and we saw our own pain, and forgot the child we still had. But Helene and Inger stood on the city bridge in Halden, and hand in hand they said farewell to Helga against the same sunset.

"Helene always said that Inger reminded her of little Hilde. She had a photo album where Hilde was smiling sweetly in all the pictures, with a narrow face and large front teeth. I've never quite been able to see the resemblance. 'Oh, yes!' Helene said. 'The slightly crooked way she squints into the sun!'

"Maybe it was wishful thinking, maybe they really did look like each other. Suddenly I realized how Helene had searched and searched for comfort. Of all the people who were close to me then, there was no one I felt closer to than her.

"I tried to comfort myself. If Helga had had to sit in a wheelchair the rest of her life she would have been deeply unhappy. Or I thought: It would have been worse if Inger had died, because Helga never would have gotten over it. That's how I consoled myself. But what did I know about what Inger was thinking? She didn't cry, she didn't say anything. She had nightmares for months afterwards. We found her in the middle of the night in the bathroom. 'What were you dreaming about?' we said. 'I was dreaming about red machines!' she said. But she couldn't remember the dream. There were just some red machines that kept grinding and grinding. So we let her sleep between us. Not until half a year later did she cry when she was awake. I sat in her room on the edge of her bed. I asked her what she was crying for. At first she didn't want to say. Finally she said: 'You know why. I'm crying for the same thing we're all crying for.'

"I made up my mind to share my grief with her, and she was my salvation. There was so much life in her! I told her that I couldn't bear the thought of Helga sitting in a wheelchair. 'How could you think that!' she shouted. 'If Helga had sat in a wheel chair, she might have become a famous painter, and I would have pushed her everywhere in her chair!'

"At that instant I made up my mind that Inger would not be alone in life. For the first time in my life I decided to have a baby.

"I got pregnant. It wasn't difficult. All I had to do was stop asking him to pull out in the inside curve, as it's so euphemistically called. And when it was done, all I had to do was wait to tell him until it was too late for him to put me on his examination table and remove the result.

"When he found out, he was against it. He didn't think that my body could survive another pregnancy. But I stuck to my guns. And when I began to be completely sure that it would go well, I told Inger. She came and woke me after my after dinner nap, and came bouncing on top of me, as usual. 'You'd better not bounce on Mama like that,' I said, 'for there just might be a little one inside me.' Then she jumped up from the bed, stood there with her hands on her hips and looked sternly at me: 'If this is a joke, Mama, it's not a *funny* joke!'"

Paula laughed. She laughed and wept her way through Evelyn's life, just like Evelyn herself had laughed and wept her way through it.

102

"I've always protected Inger," Evelyn said. "I so desperately wanted her to be happy, and not like me. . . ."

Evelyn knew that if she'd been stricter, Inger wouldn't have had such a tough time in Edinburgh. It wouldn't have been such torture to sit around a highly polished Daddy-table, and she wouldn't have thought it was so terrible to dust or peel potatoes in a potato peeling machine that required forty-five turns of the handle, and if she'd had a different father, she wouldn't have yelled at Mr. Mayfield about the jam dish.

But good lord! Here I go feeling guilty because I was nice, and if I'd been strict, I know I would have felt even more guilty! My generation has fallen through the cracks. When I was a child, everything revolved around the grown-ups, and when I had children of my own, everything revolved around them.

But that's fine with me! I never wanted to be a strict mother. I don't like the word "mother." I want to be her friend. And I've never understood what it was to spoil a child. How is it possible to spoil a child?

Paula missed Inger, too, for a year shared all Evelyn's thoughts—on morning trips to town, in the afternoons when Ørnulf was at the office, in the early evening hours before he got home—and all year Evelyn had worried that one day Paula would say: "I have to go home now." Paula's presence cheered them up so much, initially they had been full of joy over seeing each other again, yes it had been like falling in love, and they both had felt that way. Yes, I actually was in love with her, Evelyn thought. Strange as that seemed.

Then Ørnulf came home, and there they sat in the living room, and all three of them were in love. Ørnulf and Evelyn hadn't spoken German since their honeymoon in Germany in 1937; their youthful language of love had become a loathsome language of orders and commands everyone hated. Now it blossomed again in the living room at the Bjørnegården apartment.

But there was something that Evelyn absolutely did not like.

That Ellen was pushed aside. There they sat talking German. And every time Ellen came with her small needs, she was shushed. Paula had never learned a word of Norwegian, and both she and Ørnulf thought that Ellen was in the way. "She's so childish," Ørnulf said. "Yes, but she's only six years old!" Evelyn said.

Evelyn spent a long time, every evening, putting her to bed. She slept in their bedroom, for Paula had taken over Inger's room. Now she could finally do what she'd had to give up when Inger and Helga were little: teach her the songs and nursery rhymes she herself had learned from her mother as a child. She'd never forgotten the disgust that spread at breakfast at the little hotel in Lillehammer April 11, 1940, two days after the German invasion. There they sat packed together with the other evacuees after the day of panic in Oslo. Little Helga, three years old, sang with her high, clear voice: "*Hänschen klein/ging allein/in die weite Welt hinein.*" No one would speak to them after that.

Evelyn looked at Ellen. She's still too little for me to tell her this story, she thought. They folded their hands and recited:

Lieber Gott, mach mich fromm
dass ich in den Himmel komm'
Ich bin klein
mein Herz ist rein
Soll niemand d'rin wohnen
als Jesus allein.

And she was so pleased that Ellen managed to pronounce the words perfectly. Then she sang: "*Guten Abend, gut' Nacht,*" and tiptoed quietly out.

In late spring Evelyn got sick. It turned out that she had to have gallstones removed, and Ellen was sent to her grandparents in Halden. Just after this something happened that Evelyn was never able to forgive.

She had just come home from the hospital, and Ellen was still in Halden. Ørnulf had talked Paula into sleeping with them in the big double bed. Evelyn thought it was a good idea, they often had friends stay overnight, and it was always fun to wake up together in the morning. But when they had gone to bed, Ørnulf wanted to make love. It'd been such a long time. Evelyn couldn't imagine doing it—with Paula lying right next to her. "But she's asleep," Ørnulf whispered. Evelyn just couldn't imagine it, even if she was sleeping. Besides she didn't feel well enough yet. Then he took her, lovingly, and promised to be careful, and Paula lay with her back to them, breathing evenly, so she let him do it. Then she noticed that Paula was awake after all, and she pushed him away.

"I think I'll go into my room," Paula said, wide awake. Then Ørnulf took Paula in his arms, which had happened many times before. But before Evelyn had a chance to comprehend what she was seeing, he heaved himself over Paula and made love to her. Evelyn sat up in bed, unbelieving and in a daze. Then he took Evelyn by the wrist and made love to her again, he hopped back and forth, as if it were the same intercourse he was in the middle of, he wanted them both, at the same time, and he kept it up until Paula went into the little bedroom, and Ørnulf finished off between Evelyn's legs. "Get me a beer?" he said gently. "Yes," Evelyn said, and went out, and that was the first thing she had said. Then she went straight into Paula's bedroom and locked the door.

It didn't take more than a couple of minutes before Ørnulf got suspicious. He got up, and started pounding on the door. "Are you in there?" "Yes, we are, and we're going to stay in here!" Evelyn shouted. He rattled the door knob and hammered on the door with his fists. "Open the door, blast it!" But Evelyn and Paula were doing exactly the opposite. They weren't sure he wouldn't be able to get the door open, and they pushed a heavy bookcase in front of it. "What the hell are you two up to?" Ørnulf bellowed. And then he went and got a hammer.

He managed to break through the door paneling in two places before he gave up. And when he gave up, it was because it made such an infernal racket that the neighbors had to be able to hear it, and sure enough, there was the doorbell. Then he went into his room and went to bed.

After that night Evelyn knew there was no limit to what Ørnulf might do to her. He'd hit her many times, going way back to when they were young. One time before the war when Helene had come to visit them when they had lived on Collettsgate, she had bruises on her face. "I ran into a closet door," she said. But each time it was as if the boundary of his disrespect for her was moved. It didn't stand still! And now he'd made love to another woman, right in front of her face. It was as if he wanted to destroy her completely to the bone. That he wouldn't quit until there was nothing left but tiny bits.

It had all happened so quickly that it didn't become real until later. It became more and more real. She had to get away from him! She was forty-three years old. She had a long life ahead of her. She dreaded life. But she had a little child, she couldn't bring herself to leave her, even if she'd attempted it many times in her despair. Every year she got more and more paralyzed.

She was bitter at Paula after this, and closed herself to her. It was a betrayal, for Paula could certainly have gotten up from the bed. But she stayed there. At the same time Evelyn needed her, and she couldn't see how things would go if she were left alone with him one day.

Ørnulf and Paula had been living out their love-life with each other right before her eyes. That was the truth. She could see it now, but she hadn't wanted to put it into words before. When she saw them making love there in the bed, she had a definite feeling that it wasn't the first time they'd done it. They'd taken advantage of the situation while she was in the hospital.

Adultery? Nothing was farther from her life than that. She'd taken it for granted that she didn't want any other man and that he didn't want any other woman. People in Fredrikstad cheated on each other all the time. How often hadn't they sat—after the spring ball at the Phoenix—and laughed at people who jumped into bed with each other's spouses? They were bored, that was it. So they tried to force as much extra excitement out of small town life as they could.

All that year they boozed it up. Evelyn was more and more sick of it. She'd hated liquor when she was young. But he forced her to sit up with him. At first he was cheerful and sweet, then he got melancholy and then he got gloomy, after that he got disagreeable and finally he got dangerous. Evelyn knew that he might have flung that hammer right at her head that night, if he had broken through.

Even so it wasn't the hammer or his violent fists she was most afraid of. It was the slow suffocation he was forcing on her by making her stay up with him.

"Why don't you leave him?" Paula said. "You want it like this!"

The words frightened her. She'd never wanted it like this. But it was just as if there no longer were any way out of the apartment.

"Are you in love with him?" Evelyn asked. "Do you want him?"

"I couldn't imagine him without you," Paula replied.

In many ways Paula was a sphinx.

Ørnulf and Evelyn had sat in an apartment on Meltzer street and boozed it up all night with Frank and his ex-wife, Mona. They'd been in high spirits, where they relived episodes from the past, and how Frank and Mona suddenly, one day thirteen years earlier, had stood outside the door at the Bjørnegården apartment, guitar in hand, newly divorced and happy, and sung: "Happiness comes, happiness, goes," and the year before they'd been flinging Great-Grandmother's dishes at each other's heads. Now Ørnulf and Evelyn stumbled, miserable and exhausted, out to the car after two hour's sleep.

The passenger terminal at the Fred. Olsen dock was already jammed with people when they arrived, but no passengers had come ashore yet. Then a shout rang out through the throng: "Mama!"

And in the next moment a young girl in a white summer dress with green polka-dots came and flung herself into Evelyn's arms. "Inger!"

The reunion was so exuberant that people standing around got tears in their eyes. They smiled and looked at them and the tears just flowed. There was Ørnulf's head, towering above them all. Oddly enough it was Evelyn she had first caught sight of anyway.

"I don't believe it!" he laughed, in disbelief and joy. He had tears in his eyes, too. "I don't believe it!" he said again. "Were *you* the one who saw her first?" And his face shone with love and pride. But Evelyn hurried over to the baggage claim and shouted to the attendant: "The guitar!" and stretched out her arms. She got the guitar, took it in both arms, holding it tight. Then they found all the suitcases and went out to Papa's Austin Cambridge. There he pointed at the speedometer, which oddly enough was showing 10,441 kilometers. That was the license plate number on the old car. "Even *the car* is welcoming you home!" Papa said.

It was the shout! The clearly nervous shout for the guitar with strong r's, the arms that stretched out for the instrument, the swaying, uncertain steps. She was clearly not sober!

But there was something else, too; she was different, as if something had broken to pieces inside her. What had happened? She knew that Mama had been in the hospital for her gallstone operation this spring. But they'd written that she was healthy again. But she wasn't.

Inger recognized this unsteady Mama from the Sunday afternoons of her childhood when she herself came back from a walk, while they'd spent the morning over a drink, and din-

108

ner wasn't ready. Every step she took was unsteady, and she laughed out loud at Papa's jokes. But now she was like that—all the time!

Mixed in with all this was her terrible disappointment that Ellen wasn't there. In her imagination there'd always been three people standing on the dock. But Ellen was at a camp in the country near Toten. Camp! This didn't belong in their life either! Why had they sent Ellen away when she was coming home? There was something dead wrong here.

Inger sat in the back seat of the Cambridge and rode down the highway to Moss. She saw the pretty view of the small boat marina at Ulvøya, the white bridge there and everything she knew so well and in front of her were Mama's and Papa's heads that she'd thought about and longed for every hour of the day for a year. Mama fumbled for a match, looked uncertainly at Papa, as if she expected that he might stop her any second.

"Is it really you?" Inger said.

"What on earth happened here?" Inger said and stared at the door to the little bedroom. It had two round holes in the paneling. "One night Papa was being difficult, and Paula and I locked ourselves in the little bedroom and barricaded the door," Mama answered.

Inger stared at the holes. As soon as she came into the apartment she had noticed a strange atmosphere. Paula came toward her wearing an apron. But she wasn't doing the dishes. It was hard to say what she was using this apron for, because she soon took it off and sat in the living room with Papa. There the two of them sat and talked German in low voices, as if there were a deep secret that occupied them the whole time. Inger went into the living room, and sat in her usual place. Good lord! she thought. They're sitting there *flirting!*

The intensity between them was palpable, and Papa savored every word he said. Of course that was nothing new, but now he spoke German, and his enjoyment was greater. The sentences were long and complicated, and he started every other one with "*tatsächlich*." Paula listened fascinated.

This was not how she'd imagined it would be as she stood with the sweeper and the Hoover. Every day she'd been relieved at the thought that Paula was staying. The hole after her own departure would not be so big or painful. And there she sat as if she were absorbed by "*tatsächlich*."

"I want us to go and get Ellen!" Inger nagged in irritation.

"Not until we celebrate a golden wedding anniversary," Papa said.

"Are you trying to be funny, or something?"

"Well, not our own," Papa said. "I guess there's not much chance we'll ever experience that. But Grandma and Grandpa's."

They went and celebrated a golden anniversary. With grouse shot by Grandpa the year before. He tapped on his glass and announced that he wanted to hold a speech for his wife.

"Marriage," Grandpa said, "is like a wagon. It must be pulled. It's not so easy. You run into bad roads, the wheels get stuck in the mud, but suddenly you're on better roads again. And we've been pulling this wagon," Grandfather said, and his voice broke, he took out an enormous handkerchief, "we've been pulling this wagon, you and I, for fifty years!"

According to Ørnulf Grandma had never loved Grandpa. She'd loved a romantic, young author she had met in Oslo at the turn of the century, and who since had become very famous—for one solitary book. Naturally the author had also loved her, beautiful and intelligent and agreeable as she was, but he was already married. When she met the young customs agent from Trondheim, her entire family thought she'd married beneath her.

In Ørnulf's opinion she was far superior to him both in intelligence and other human qualities, and of course she was the one that he himself took after the most.

"Well, after that speech I think I need a drink!" Grandma said, and they all laughed through their tears, drank toasts to each other and sang, and Grandpa and Papa—who had never been able to stand being under the same roof—started telling old stories about Martin Kvennavika who had such an awfully tough pudding. It was so tough, that pudding, that he had to . . . but here the joke kept disappearing in Papa and Grandpa's tears of laughter, it was so tough! Yes, it was so tough! they laughed and laughed, and the others had to laugh, too, even though they hadn't managed to hear how tough it was yet, but finally they managed to get out that he had to chop at it with a spoon and tug and pull on the pudding, oh, how he tugged and pulled! but now the story disappeared in hiccups again, until Grandpa finally managed to get out that Martin Kvennavika had had to run all the way around Snåsa Lake before it let go.

Papa looked at Inger across the table and cocked his head. "Do you want to?" he said. And she knew perfectly well that the question was whether she wanted to sing "Nidelven." Because Papa could never forget the time they went to Trondheim together, just the two of them, and she was twelve years old.

"And when we got to the old city bridge," Papa narrated, and he got tears in his eyes, and everyone waited expectantly, even though they'd all heard the story before, "I said to Inger: 'There's the old city bridge.' And?" Papa said and peered mischievously at Inger. "What'd you do then?" "No, you tell." "She sang: 'The OLD town bridge is the portal of bliss,'" Papa sang, and his voice was quite high as he sang it. "Sing it? Won't you?"

> Far in the distance
> beyond mountains blue,
> lies a place, lovely and true,

Inger replied, and everyone listened devoutly to her clear, young voice, and suddenly it was as if everything fell into place.

A young girl with long, tanned legs and long, dark hair in a hair ribbon came storming up the hills at Toten, shrieking, as only children can, with joy. "Big sis!" she shouted, and they were in each other's arms. "I saw you in the car all the way down the hill!" Ellen shouted. "But you were just sitting like this!" She stood in profile, with her nose in the air and acted out how a big sister looked when she didn't catch sight of her little sister after a year.

Inger had a big jar of hard candy for her, the kind she herself had dreamed of after the war, and a big, colorful beach ball, which was part of the same dream. They sat looking at each other in the back seat. They were so funny! So awfully funny. Ellen had changed a lot the past year. Her face wasn't round anymore. Now she was going to start school. "Look at the heifers!" she shouted and pointed at some cows in the pasture. She saw heifers everywhere.

During the night Inger dreamed about the little Ellen with short hair she'd left behind, and the new Ellen who was going to be starting school, and who knew what heifers were. It was as if she had two sisters in her dream. Now I have to get to know her all over again, she thought.

Thank goodness Inger is home again, Emilie thought. She's the only one that man listens to.

She called her over. They sat by the window, and Emilie asked her what she thought of the fact that Paula was still in the apartment. "Mama's gotten so nervous!" Inger said. "She's much more nervous than when I left."

Emilie was sure she was right. She understood what was going on, and she was furious at her niece. "And you know it's not exactly good for Ellen," Inger added. "They talk German all the time." Emilie said: "Would you consider telling Ørnulf that he should ask Paula to go home to Germany?"

And Inger did what Emilie asked.

Two weeks later Paula went home to Germany.

THE TRUTH AT SKILLEBEKK

Everyone was gone. They were off studying in Barcelona and in Oxford, and at the Center for Anthroposophy in Stuttgart, on vacation at Torshavn or still working as maids in Brussels and Paris. The boys were in the service on Andøya Island or way over in Fort Worth, Texas, where they'd done something so weird as enlist. She knew that, of course. She written to most of them, or had heard about them, all year. Even so, imaginary graduation capped heads popped up among the flower boxes at Flora. They weren't there! You couldn't just walk out onto Nygaardsgata anymore and find life right there.

Finally she got hold of Jorunn Johansen. But Jorunn was desperately buried in papers. She was supposed to be filling out an application to the teachers' college in Elverum, and couldn't go out. There Inger sat—on her first evening at home. And none of all the people who had been her world could welcome her home.

This was where her friend Lillian had been missing her for the past year. She knew that. It was strange to see the back stairs, the eternal connection between the second floor and the fourth floor, their own private passage. But Lillian didn't come. She didn't hear her step on the stairs—ta-*tam*, ta-*tam*, when she came like Roy Rogers on his horse, Trigger. She didn't ring the bell so that the three on the doorbell box fell down, so

Inger could saddle Topper and gallop out to her as Hopalong Cassidy.

It was a long time now since they'd played that. But when she got home, it was these memories that struck her. Suddenly everything was so terribly long ago. And it was only three weeks since Lillian had left.

She'd heard from her in Edinburgh. One of the first letters. Lillian hadn't been raised to show her feelings. She came from a strict home, almost as strict as the home at 6, Aberdeen Road. But in the first letter she got from her she'd written: "Dear Inger! *Partir c'est mourir—un peu . . . .*" She wrote how Kirkeparken lay there without Inger running around its trees, how the hill lay there without Inger's bicycle on it, how the leaves turned yellow and autumn rained down through her heart.

Fredrikstad was filled with memories. Suddenly it was a city of longing. But she had known that, always. She had to get away from here. Life was somewhere else. But she'd always thought that Fredrikstad would still be there as before. She hadn't thought about it like that. She'd just believed it. And then it wasn't. It had changed.

She missed Sheila. Pulling herself away from her, knowing that she would never again be a part of her life, was unnatural and painful. Even though she knew that the feeling that gave her this feeling also was unnatural. But that didn't help. She grieved.

A new life was beginning. Oslo. Life was named Oslo, and she wasn't coming there like the peasant students in the novels she'd read in high school. She knew Oslo as the strawberry patch of her childhood, but it was made up of puzzle pieces. One piece was long and narrow and went straight up from the train station to the National Theater, and on to Vinderen tram station where they had the best sweet rolls in the world, and on up to her grandmother Gjarm's house with the big garden.

114

Another piece was called Collett street and St. Hanshaugen park and the wall by Bislet Arena, in the sky overhead were airplanes. In a third piece there was a boat. It was full of children eating ice cream. She searched for a long time for this piece, until suddenly one day she found it in the middle of Frogner Park. The pieces were starting to fit together! When she was little, she never knew how to get from one piece to the other, because Mama was always with her. Or Helga. But now she rode around on Helga's old bicycle, and found them again. But there was one piece she never found. In it she'd gotten banana-flavored pop. It was an outdoor restaurant with a view and the weather was so beautiful, shining on the banana-flavored pop. But that piece was disputed. Nothing like banana-flavored pop had ever been produced.

Inger stood in a large, 16 x 20 foot rectangular room on the fourth floor at Skillebekk and felt an enormous sense of freedom. The room had high windows and outside the Jar streetcar scraped by. Finally she had come to a city with streetcars. Here she could think. The ceiling was 14 feet high, a chandelier with a rosette and eight little light bulbs, and halfway up the wall there was a ledge. This would be her first book shelf. The window sill became her pantry. Here she placed a large bottle of beer. Now, she thought, I can finally become an existentialist.

For the first time in her life she'd come to a place where there was no one to boss her around.

The room was located in a large, old-fashioned apartment with a long hallway, and in the middle lived a couple with a baby and baby bottle. They'd never be bohemians. Farthest in was yet another vacant room. The landlady lived on the floor below. She wouldn't be meddling. She came fluttering with flowing hair and said: "Are you really the niece of the charming actors Knut and Solveig Gjarm? They were so delightful when they were young. And so *cultured!* Well, you can do as you like here. Fix up and paint. I rent exclusively to talented people." With that she vanished. But it was a mystery how she knew about this relationship. Because the ad had said only: "Doctor's daughter seeks rental room. Call 60 97 68."

Inger biked off to her first day at the University. She had to get her student I.D. card and go to the Health Service. All students had to have chest x-rays. Two people came walking across the middle of the University square. They stood out from all the others. They had two legs and heads on top, one a little taller than the other, and along their bodies they had arms, four all together. Despite this exceedingly ordinary equipment they stood out, they were carried over the cobblestones, glowing among all the other people walking across the University square then. They had Flora-faces. They were none other than Hartvig Gravdahl who lived on Sportsveien and Elsa Tøgern from Oredalen coming across the plaza.

They let out a roar of laughter. They laughed at the fact that they were standing there. And were trying to find the right line. "So, have you found a place to live?" Elsa said. She was wearing a brown suede Spanish coat without a collar and black leather gloves. Her mouth was red, like Elsa's mouth had always been. "Yeah. How 'bout you?" "No." "Then you can move in at Constance Amalie Høland's at Skillebekk. She still needs one more renter." "Are you trying to be funny or something? Is that really her name?" "Oh yes. But I *am* funny." "Well, ladies!" Hartvig proclaimed and gazed at the statue of Holberg, the great eighteenth century dramatist, breathing in its aura. "Now we shall enter the high halls to receive the baptism of the mind! And what're you going to study, my dears?" He laughed his uninhibited Hartvig-laugh with his head flung back and his hand over his mouth. "We're going to study Russian," Elsa said. "Spanish! French! Serbo-Croatian! Sociology!" "Sociology? Whazzat?" "It's about them there people and how they flounder around, y'know!" "How 'bout you, Gravdahl? I s'pose you're going to study philosophy?" "Intellectual history!" Hartvig corrected her. "And ancient Greek." He straightened up. They paraded past a sea of litter and propaganda toward the basement of the auditorium. Norway out of NATO. Stop the atom bomb on Novaja Semlja. Jesus is the answer. Stop the Treaty of Rome. Ten pieces of advice for new students. Join The Oslo Housing and Savings Association. "Join The Oslo Housing and Savings Association, and you'll have an apartment by 1970!" they said. Then they laughed and no one joined The Oslo Housing and Savings Association. "I think our little globe is the loony bin of the universe," Hartvig proclaimed. "Give it a rest, Gravdahl!"

Once more the world was full.

At last, the three of them were to enter the most venerable of all the halls in the land—the hall where Albert Schweitzer had received the Nobel Peace Prize, where the Comedian Harmonists had played, where Fridtjof Nansen had stood, the hall in the middle of the Central Building of the old university, in the middle of everything. Where "History" hung, the enormous mural by Edvard Munch.

But instead of a gloriously illuminated ballroom with chandeliers and tapestries appropriate for the glory of bygone days, they entered a series of dark, straight rows of seats, dimly lit, not unlike a quite ordinary movie theater, only larger. On the stage stood a thin little man. His white shirt-sleeves were rolled up and his face was eager and shining. And next to him stood a magnetophone.

In the next instant Adolf Hitler's voice thundered out in the University Auditorium.

The monstrous voice shrieked with a hoarse fury that suited neither the magnetophone nor the podium he must have stood at. Only a few words could be distinguished as words. Nonetheless they were soon supplanted by a unanimous roar of jubilation from thousands of voices. It was a miracle that the magnetophone didn't explode in a shower of sparks against Munch's painting of the sunrise. They were sitting in their first psychology lecture.

The man peered attentively out into the auditorium. Rolled

up his shirt-sleeves a bit more, his slightly high forehead glowing with deeper meaning. Abruptly he shut off the tape recording and stared at them.

"This is mass suggestion," he said.

He paged through his papers and talked about mass suggestion. About how the masses could become an undisciplined, deranged animal with only one will. A packed auditorium noted down everything the man said. The pencils flew over the notebook pages. Stopped. Their looks once again focused on the sinewy wizard on the stage. Three hundred students sat spellbound.

Inger and Elsa raced through the university and discovered the world. Elsa was the kind of person it was fun to discover the world with. She always had a sarcastic remark about everything, and you felt part of the group. As long as the sarcasm wasn't directed at oneself. But that happened. Elsa came straight from studying in Barcelona, and she was always on the lookout for interesting people. The first prerequisite for being an interesting person was that you had never had the slightest connection with Fredrikstad. Yes, if you were even from the same county, everything was ruined.

Now she was moving into the other end of the long hallway in the apartment at Skillebekk—in a corner room under a green tower. She cooked coffee in a mystical coffee cooker that took half an hour for the coffee to get done, and made exotic casseroles of which she never revealed the ingredients, then she would tap on her castanets in anticipation of the interesting people who were supposed to appear.

Geneva had been exclusively populated with interesting people. The most interesting had been an absolutely beautiful Negro from Guadeloupe, whom she had met in the park while she was dragging little kids along. But at night she snuck out and had an interesting time with him. She described it in great detail. "What about you? Anything happen with you?" she asked. "No," Inger replied.

Inger sat down at the typewriter and worked on a funny novel. It was about a Norwegian girl, Berit, who went to Edinburgh as an au pair. At first she'd thought about sending her to Newcastle as camouflage, but she quickly realized that it was no use. Berit had gone out into the world to experience freedom, and she ended up in a prison. Berit swept and yearned. That was a good expression. Swept and yearned. Was this her? She who had never done housework at home. Berit was a spoiled child. But now she was going to learn. Ralph appeared. He appeared with a fluttering, striped university scarf, white crash helmet and eyes as big as saucers. "Hello, honeybun!" he said. And then he disappeared. And in her thoughts, Berit followed him up to The Old Quad.

Inger read the first chapter of *Our Norwegian Girl*. Why wasn't it the same? Why couldn't she, for example, simply substitute "Susan" for "Ralph"? Infatuation was infatuation. Why couldn't Berit fall in love with Ralph? This was just a book. She could write whatever she wanted. No one was dictating what she should write.

But she couldn't just invent Berit. She didn't fall in love with Ralph. And if she wrote that Berit had fallen in love with Susan, all of her readers would throw up. Did any publisher exist who would publish a book that caused the readers to throw up? And besides, she would never dare to write it.

But if she defied all this, and wrote the book anyway, the book would be about something other than what she'd intended. It was supposed to be about life as an au pair and all the exasperating dust and what it was like to be in a foreign country. But if Berit fell in love with Susan in the middle of this, it would have to be about that. She couldn't just bring Susan in as a natural part of the dust. Ralph she could bring in like that. He could just come and flit and be charming.

But she'd never write that book. The very thought made her blood boil. How could she manage to write a book while her blood was boiling?

"What are you scribbling on in there?" Elsa said. "Just some stuff," said Inger. "I'm practicing being an interesting person that *you* would like to be around." Elsa looked at her. Then she took out her guitar.

Elsa was unusually musical. She made harmonies for everything, and not just an ordinary, banal harmony, a third above the melody. They imitated Åge Samuelsen, the popular hallelujah-preacher.

> For there was power, power, power so wonderful
> in the blood of the la-a-mb!

In their graduating class they'd made a great career with these Salvation Army songs, and had even managed to be refused service at Flora. This was the way to go. They went to a restaurant. They imitated everything they saw. They laughed. Just seeing a man sitting behind an *Aftenposten* newspaper was enough. "When you and I are together it's just as if we're *flirting,*" Elsa said.

If she thinks we're flirting, she must think we're both doing it, Inger thought. But Elsa thought that flirting was something you only did with a potential lover. Elsa was on the lookout for potential lovers. Inger was on the lookout for Elsa.

For the most part that was unnecessary. They were always together. It was good to have someone you belonged with. Inger didn't think she needed anything more, and was absolutely not on the lookout for a lover. They sat in Elsa's room and practiced on "*Bella figlia del l'amore.*" They'd just been to see their first opera. The main character began singing a passionate song after he found his daughter dead in a sack. It was impressive. But finally it was 1:30 and Elsa wanted to go to bed. "You go ahead and go to bed," Inger said. She didn't want to go just yet. Then Elsa turned to her and said, "Oh, no. We're not going to have any lesbian tendencies here!"

The remark sent her out of the room—after a suitable interval to prove that it hadn't made any impression on her. She got it good there. She should have been labeled: Inger Holm, undergraduate. Special characteristics: lesbian tendencies.

Did she think she wanted to see her naked? Did she think that the lesbian tendencies were a sort of substance that emanated from her entire being, like a sort of viscous pus that enveloped all women regardless of their clothing? What did she think?

Inger sat in her 16 x 20 square foot room and trembled. Her blood rushed with shame. What was she supposed to do with her lesbian tendencies? The word itself was revolting.

But it was true, of course. She liked being with Elsa. She didn't want to leave. She wanted to stay up a little longer. Elsa was fun. Wasn't she always wondering if she was home? Whenever she came down Drammensveien around the curve by the streetcar stop? She knew precisely at what point on the road she could catch sight of Elsa's window—below the tower. Was the light on? For several yards before the point she wondered if the light was on. The lesbian tendencies rushed toward the light. The same thing over and over again. Why couldn't she break herself of the habit?

There was a new film at the Gimle. It was called *The Victim*, and the lead role was played by Dirk Bogarde with his expressive cheekbones. Dirk Bogarde was living in a marriage—with his eyes and expressive cheekbones. But he had a secret. And he had a high position. But his eyes saw a word on the wall. It was written outside his house—with big letters on the side of the garage. He saw the word, and the word was: QUEER.

In the subtitles the word was translated with: HOMO. Like that. And the world caved in.

A young punk came to him. Extorted money, because of this truth, which he knew about. The Dirk Bogarde character paid the money and suffered the worst agony. In the end his wife discovered his secret.

It was a good movie. Inger and Elsa walked down Fredrik Stang Street and had seen a good movie. With an incredibly appropriate title. "Did you see Espen Halvorsen?" Elsa said. "Who's that?" "He was standing outside the theater." "But who is he?" "An actor. He was going in. He's like that, you know." "How do you know?" "Everyone knows." "Well I don't know it." "You really don't know who Espen Halvorsen is? He was standing there waiting for his friend. You can tell he's a homo a mile away. Didn't you see his scarf?" "Well wearing a scarf doesn't make him a homosexual!" "But he is. You can see it." "You can't see it! You've just heard it!" "I've heard it, but I can see it too. He has such a big Adam's apple!"

Inger thought about Espen Halvorsen and his Adam's apple. And she blessed him because he existed. He was standing outside the Gimle movie theater waiting for his friend. And he kept on living anyway.

She threw herself into Harald Schjelderup's *Introduction to Psychology* beneath the eight little light bulbs and finally realized that her whole life consisted of mistakes. You always did something wrong with your experiences. You either repressed them or you idealized them, or you quite simply forgot them, and not even this was accidental. You were totally unreliable. And if you claimed that others were unreliable it was actually just because you were quite unreliable yourself, and this phenomenon was called *projection*.

How was she going to get hold of Espen Halvorsen? There were lots of homosexuals at the theaters. But she certainly couldn't just go in the stage door and ask for them? Elsa knew of a young actress who had attacked a female colleague backstage. Inger ached to get to know the young actress. Elsa said that the homosexuals got together at a restaurant called "The Original Pilsner Beer." Inger imagined a dark place with dark, homosexual faces. There they sat and drank beer and were homosexual. She didn't know where the restaurant was located, but to try to look it up seemed to her about as realistic as trying to step into Sigurd Hoel's *Sinners in Summertime* and lie down on a rock on the beach in the novel.

Espen Halvorsen was a totally unknown actor. She'd never heard of anyone who had ever seen him in a play. But he reminded her a little of Kurt Randeff who had walked down

Nygaardsgata.

It was Mama who once had told her that there was such a thing as homosexual people. She was ten years old and was standing at the kitchen window and saw Kurt Randeff walk past. He had such a strange name. But that wasn't the strangest thing about him. He always wore a kind of skullcap, with his hair long in the back, and he walked like a woman. He talked strangely, too, stopped on street corners and the boys flocked around him, because he was supposedly quite funny, but even though his voice had changed it was as if he hadn't quite gotten over it. At any rate he walked by, and Inger said: "Mama? Why is he so silly?" Then Mama told her that there were some men who fell in love with men and some women who fell in love with women, and they were called homosexuals.

Inger thought this was awfully strange. "You see, he would rather be a woman," Mama said.

Really? she thought then. Does he want that? Then he can *have* my sex, and then I can have his. And every time she passed him on Nygaardsgata after that, she thought: There goes the guy who can have my sex! As far as I'm concerned I have absolutely no use for it. But he just walked unsuspectingly by.

But now Inger thought: If Mama hadn't told me, I wouldn't have found out that it existed when I was a child, and she became more and more convinced that she'd become a homosexual because Mama had told her the truth about Kurt Randeff.

Mama had always been of the opinion that a woman ought to find a man who was more intelligent than herself. Otherwise she'd be bored. Inger thought that sounded quite reasonable. Besides there weren't any boys who could stand it if you beat them. With your head. But if everyone were to follow this principle, there'd be some girls left over at the top who never got anyone, and some boys left over at the bottom who didn't get anyone either.

Inger lived her student life and kept a stubborn eye out for someone of the other sex. She spotted one. He was in her phonetics lecture and was good looking. And he looked quite intelligent, too, because he never said a word. She made up her mind to hope that he would look at her, and that—if he did it—he wouldn't think: "That girl looks intelligent!" But: "She's really pretty!" She hoped so fervently and so resolutely that when he finally did, it sent chills through her. She told Elsa about the chills.

Elsa was intensely interested in chills. They were reading *Lady Chatterley's Lover* and discussing the deeds of the woods. They were reading *Sinners in Summertime*. These were the first books on their shelves, and they were about chills. They were about the forbidden desire that had never been mentioned in high school, popularly called "The Yellow Institution." At The Yellow Institution the sentence "And in the night, he lay wanting her, and she was willing" was censored in Knut Hamsun's *Growth of the Soil*.

There was an incredible lot of freedom in books. They just loved each other. They always found someone to love. And then they fucked. That's how it should be. They loved each other in the fucking, and the sun was high in the sky. There were sea gulls and rocks.

But Inger knew that the real chills in life—they lay in the mailbox down in the entryway. Because every day there might be a thick, blue letter postmarked "Edinburgh."

How could Inger have spent a whole year abroad without experiencing chills? How could she have been so boring? What should she say when girl friends from Fredrikstad, one by one, showed up and asked: "Something happened, right? Did you fall in love or anything?"

She could answer truthfully. She could say "Yes." Then they would say, and they'd always said, "Who is it? Who? Tell me, tell me!" Because everyone else told who and told about it at the top of their lungs. And one thing led to another. That's what the Monkees sang about once in a song.

If you, if you, if you, if you say A
you must, you must, you must also say B
That's why, that's why, that's why I was so glad—dearie!
when you said you'd fallen in love today.

That's how it was. What should Inger answer?

Should she say, "No" so she didn't have to say B? Should she tell the truth and say "Yes" and then change the sex of B? Should she say A so that she didn't have to lie, and then refuse to say anything at all about B? Should she say "None 'a your business," and keep both A and B to herself? What should Inger do with A and B?

She settled on a B she saw in her phonetics class. She settled on him so fervently that she experienced the truth of the peculiar expression: to lie so well that you believe it yourself.

Then she took her final exam in philosophy.

EVELYN'S DECISION

Ørnulf had always been jealous of Evelyn's family. Of the six Gjarm brothers and sisters, all had gone on the stage, except the second oldest brother, Borgar, who wrote poetry. Evelyn and Lisa had left the theater early, both because of their husbands' jealousy, but the other three had done well. Not a week went by in the fifties that you didn't see one or several of their names on the cast lists in the radio schedule, they went on tour and performed in most Norwegian films, and the two brothers were constantly called in every time someone had to bellow out detestable commands in perfect Berlin-German in some war film or other.

But Ørnulf felt that the very essence of acting was humbug. The deep secret in all acting was that the actors didn't understand what they were playing. He never forgot the time at the Theater Café when he had managed to convince Hauk Aabel, the famous Ibsen actor, that he didn't understand *Peer Gynt*. Hauk Aabel agreed with him! Ergo all of Evelyn's siblings were idiots.

There was no doubt that Ørnulf himself was an intelligent man. "If he'd only just stop saying so many dumb things," Evelyn said. But there he sat with his genius in a small town, and looked after a practice that bored him more and more as the years passed. They came to him with a sore finger and talked about their terrible marriages. Half the population of Fredrikstad wanted to commit suicide. He had a large clientele and as time went on he had become a respected physician. But in the evenings he was gloomy.

The result was that Evelyn was cut off from the rest of her family. In the long run no one would put up with being berated every time they came, except Lisa. She was quite simply fond of him. So there was no doubt that the day Evelyn decided to leave him all her siblings would welcome her with open arms.

It was 6:30 in the morning, and she lay in Inger's bed in the little bedroom. She'd tiptoed in here after a sleepless night. Drinking never made her sleep, the way it did him. So she got up again and took sleeping pills and nerve pills, and the more of them she took, the more nervous she got. She missed Paula. But as soon as she was gone, she saw her life more clearly.

"Tom'ere!" Ørnulf said in his childish sweet talk that he adopted when he was in an affectionate mood. "Linnelinn tom'ere!" "Linnelinn" was what she had called herself when she was little, and when Helga was in the playpen she had said "Tom-tom!" and accordingly he had picked up sweet baby talk from their lives and snuggled up to her with one leg over her stomach and fell asleep instantly. At first the leg felt good, then unbearably heavy. She called his legs logs, but they came anyway. "Does Linnelinn love itty bitty Nulfenulf?" Ørnulf said. And then he fell asleep—in a sort of remarkable—almost innocent—belief that she'd forgotten what he had done.

The morning melodies came out of Inger's green radio on the bedside table. How often she had envied her this radio; as she lay listening to Radio Luxembourg and Top Twenty and everything they were listening to. "Sugar in the morning/ sugar in the evening/ sugar at supper-time!" Evelyn thought. Not everything was that nice. But as long as it wasn't Louis Armstrong it was okay. It was incomprehensible that a man with such an ugly voice could become world famous.

And now she missed him. She missed Louis Armstrong! Dear

Inger! I miss you so much! I even miss the points of irritation. All the life! Your girlfriends. She'd been missing her for a year. Then she came home, and was home for three weeks. But of course I knew that! Did I imagine that she would remain living at the Bjørnegården apartment?

It felt good to lie under the comforter. Her hives had been a nuisance for a long time, but until now they only came when she'd been swimming at Tjøme. She was covered with red blisters. But swimming was the last thing she wanted to give up, so she swam anyway. But lately the least irritation brought on the itching, she couldn't tolerate changes in temperature, and soon there wouldn't be a single piece of clothing she could stand to wear. Everything itched. Soon I'll itch just because I'm alive, Evelyn thought.

The itching was worst on her calves. They were full of small sores, she peered down at them. Once upon a time these had been the most beautiful legs in Fredrikstad, she thought. That's what Ørnulf had always said. She had to get to a dermatologist. But there weren't any doctors in Fredrikstad who could treat her. If she wanted to get well she'd have to see a dermatologist in Oslo.

"I have to get away!" she thought. Hell? Why did the church think up hell? Was it necessary when you had life?

"Are you afraid of *dying!?*" Ørnulf had inquired.

No. She was afraid of living. The anxiety, what was she supposed to do with that? If she got away from him, she'd get away from the anxiety. Clearly he *was* the anxiety. And with this thought an even greater anxiety opened up. Life without Ørnulf. Life without Ørnulf?

That afternoon she went to see Rita.

Her old girlfriend from her Berlin days. Rita Kvanbæk still lived in her little studio apartment on the other side of the river near the old fort in Kongsten Haveby. They went for a long walk through the straight streets, the quiet streets, where folks lived peacefully. There was peace in each of the white and yellow, square houses, the sun hung at an angle over them and cast

128

long, narrow shadows of Rita and Evelyn as they strolled on the embankment out toward Vaterland.

"I want to run away," Evelyn said. "He mustn't know where I am." "Where will you go? To Vinderen?" "No, that'd be the first place he'd look." "Where?" "I don't know. I've been thinking about Ragnhild." "Your childhood friend?" "Yes."

They thought. Shiny chestnuts lay on the ground. Evelyn picked one up and put it in her pocket. Felt the smooth surface as they walked. "Have you been in touch with her?" Rita asked. "No. I haven't seen her in fifteen years."

She held on to the smooth, little chestnut as if it were a token of a pledge. Just as surely as it lay in her pocket, Ragnhild would take her in.

She heard Rita's secure, trudging steps beside her. Rita always had solid walking shoes. Now she told Rita about her plan.

She'd go into Oslo on the pretext of going to see a dermatologist. And indeed she would see a dermatologist. But then she would disappear.

Ragnhild Østen lived in a large house at Nordberg in Oslo. She wouldn't write to her beforehand. She'd just show up and ring the doorbell, like the refugee she was. From here she would inform Ørnulf that she wasn't coming home. But no one must know where she was. "Just you." "He'll throttle me," Rita replied.

They'd reached the small, low wood-frame houses in the outskirts of Vaterland. The Sunday stillness lay over the roofs. The folks here were not well off. They passed the low windows where you could look right in between luxuriant potted plants. A fat, solid woman peered out at them, ready with her watering can. If only I were her! Evelyn thought.

"What about Ellen?" Rita asked.

"I'll send her to Halden. Then we'll see . . ."

Gradually the plan came into being—through the narrow streets in Vaterland, where people lived, in poverty, but free of fear, Evelyn thought. They stood waiting for the ferry. It started out from the Kråkerøy side and came chugging over to the wooden dock, slowly, through the swift black current, free of fear.

The ferryman squinted at them under the brim of his black cap, said hello and shoved off with his boat hook. They were the only two passengers. He set out again through the current, peered over the Glomma river, which he owned. "Nice weather!" Rita shouted to him, she had a way with everyone she met. "Yup. Can't complain today!" the ferryman replied, let his head take a swing over toward the railing and spat into an eddy. Evelyn looked at his back. Safe, safe. If only one were from Fredrikstad!

"What'll we do afterwards?" Rita said. "What should I say to him?"

They looked down into the black eddies. They were standing all the way back in the stern of the ferry, watching the wake. Out of earshot. They saw how the water constantly drowned itself, came up and was pulled down again, came up, around and around. "Tell him I want a divorce," Evelyn replied.

FLIGHT

As Evelyn came up the walk to the house at Nordberg, Ragnhild's head appeared over some comforters that were hanging out of a second-story window to be aired. Ragnhild leaned out over the comforters looking every bit as young as the time she met her under the desk at Ris Elementary School. "Evelyn! I dreamed about you last night!"

For a moment they stood absolutely still and looked at each other. Then a pillow tumbled down and landed at Evelyn's feet. "Let's have a pillow fight!" shouted Evelyn. Ragnhild ran down and opened the door. They just stood there in the doorway and stared at each other. Ragnhild took Evelyn's coat, they went through the usual rituals. Then they stared again.

Ragnhild's husband was on a business trip. They had the whole night to themselves.

When Ragnhild was young she always said: "I would rather marry for money than for love!" And that was what she'd done. She had an elegant house with a garden and a view, expensive clothes, and was just as beautiful as ever—with a recently acquired tan from the Mediterranean sun and eyes so blue that Evelyn had once worried that she'd take Ørnulf away." "Are you happy?" Evelyn said. "No," Ragnhild said. Then she told Evelyn about her marriage.

Most of the time she told him she was having her period.

"Aren't you done with that business pretty soon?" he said. So she gave in whenever she realized that he could figure out that she was lying. "He never calls me by name," Ragnhild said. "'Hey, you,' he says. 'You, you, you.' It drives me crazy."

"What about you? You got the man you loved," Ragnhild said. "Yes, I did," Evelyn said, "and now I've run away from him." "Run away? Does he hit you?" "No . . . no, that is to say, he has. But he controls everything I do. I can't even go to the hairdresser without him deciding when I should be home." "But he's always been like that, Evelyn!"

Finally she fell asleep in a large, soft bed in her own room. Had it stood ready for her for twenty-five years? And she thought: He's always been like that. Jealous. Jealous of everything. Jealous of the theater. Jealous of the hairdresser. When she woke up she felt frantically uneasy. Where was Ørnulf?

It struck her that she could just get up. She could go over to the window and look at the view. And no one would say: "Are you standing there? Haven't you made the beds yet?" She could take a book down from the bookshelf over there, sit down, have a smoke, go to the bathroom, wash up and brush her teeth and make the bed. And nobody would come and say that she should have done all this in the opposite order.

She got ready and went down to Ragnhild. "Tea or coffee?" Ragnhild asked, already standing there with both, and everything else. "I'd rather have tea. Coffee gives me heart palpitations. This is a regular hotel!" She sat down and looked out over the quiet road. "When I was little I was told that God could see everything," she said. "Even when I was alone. So one day when I was walking down Blindernveien on my way to town, I turned right at the intersection up towards the woods instead, just to trick God." Ragnhild laughed. "You were always full of notions!" she said.

Evelyn walked up Karl Johansgate, in downtown Oslo, and felt a terrible uneasiness. In her purse she had a salve she had gotten at the hospital for her hives. But it won't help, she thought. The hives came from inside her. Her skin was the answer to her uneasiness. "You were always full of notions."

She cut through Studenterlunden park, and it occurred to her that she could just go right into the Theater Café and have a glass of wine. But when she passed the large plate-glass windows and saw all the people sitting at the tables chatting beneath the high ceiling in there, she knew she'd never get up the nerve to go in. The uneasiness inside her grew and spread and filled the whole café beneath its enormous chandeliers. She saw herself sitting in there, laughing, with her brothers and sisters, with other actors. She'd become an adult in there. A lady out on the town—with Lisa. Proudly she'd taken out her pack of Medina cigarettes. "Allow me to offer you a cigarette!" What had become of that person now, who'd dared to stand on the stage of the Carl Johan Theater and debut with Tore Gregers?

She: Shall I ask him to light the lamp?

He: Oh, no, he's not a tramp!

she recalled. But one night she misspoke:

She: Shall I ask him to lamp the light?

But Tore Gregers sang unwaveringly:

He: Oh, no, that won't be right!

She nearly collapsed, right on the middle of the stage.

She laughed now, too. He was so fun to act with. Today he was a popular cabaret actor.

With swift steps she walked past the entrance to the Theater Café. Today I don't even dare to trick God, she thought. Did I just walk right in that time? But she knew perfectly well she did. Ørnulf! she thought. How will I manage to find my way out of this when I don't know what to do with myself after half a day? She didn't even know how she was going to find the Jar streetcar.

She found the Jar streetcar. She felt the hangover in her head, they'd gone through more than one bottle of wine during the night. I have to go somewhere they don't drink, she thought. Where don't they drink? Everyone drinks to escape from the mess they're in. And if they're not in a mess, they drink to escape from that. Who has ever managed to drink themselves away from drinking?

Borgar had managed it. He almost never drank anymore. When he was young he had always wanted to kill himself. "The potential suicide was a faithful companion," he said. When she was little, she would lie in bed and pray for him when he didn't come home at night. He didn't want to be anything, and he never got the girls he fell in love with. They all fell in love with his brothers, who were taller and more handsome than he. Even his youngest brother, Jan Michael, had grown taller, and once Lisa had gotten a letter from him while she was in Germany. "Jan Michael looks in the mirror and measures himself daily. I hope he grows six more feet, then maybe he'll stop doing that."

Borgar had a special talent for making good stories out of life's indignities, and that was how he'd survived. Admittedly there were few who read his stories, he had published them himself, printing twenty copies, of which his father had bought nineteen. So Borgar went around for several years speculating about who had bought the twentieth. So he made a story out of that, and finally he became a popular versifier under various pseudonyms.

The Jar streetcar arrived, and Evelyn rode along past Abelhaugen and longed for Borgar. When all was said and done, it was his faith that had helped him escape from alcohol and thoughts of suicide. "If only someone had told me about salvation then!" he said. Evelyn didn't understand his faith and didn't comprehend what it consisted of. But it made him strong, and even if she couldn't share it, it was this strength she needed.

Here's where Inger rides every day, Evelyn thought. If only I were her instead! Riding back and forth to the university and studying and learning and living alone in a room with a girl friend at the other end of the hallway!

Evelyn wished she were Inger. She'd often wished she were

Inger. Inger lived her own life, Evelyn tried to imagine it and yearned for it. She got off at Skillebekk and pretended she was Inger. Immediately she felt greater freedom in her legs, lightness in her thoughts. Cogito ergo sum, Evelyn thought as she walked by the mailboxes and up the four flights to Inger's room.

She'd called Inger from Ragnhild's house, and Inger had become frightened. Evelyn didn't say where she was. But when she got to Inger's, she told her anyway. Inger wouldn't tell. She said: "Mama! If only I were older! Then I'd earn money and support both you and Ellen!"

Evelyn was touched by her outburst. But she thought: A man can feed nine children. But nine children can't feed one father. That was a sort of saying she'd heard once upon a time. Suddenly her whole plan seemed so unreal.

For a week Evelyn stayed in hiding at Ragnhild's house. Only Lisa, Borgar and Inger knew where she was. And Rita. Ørnulf called. No one told him. He went over to Kongsten Haveby where he practically throttled Rita. He showed up at Vinderen, first threatening and then pleading. He begged Lisa to send for Evelyn. He called Borgar. But no one told him where she was. He berated them all, he berated Rita over the telephone, he was convinced that she was behind it all. Then he implored them again.

Finally she agreed to meet him at Lisa's. "Evelyn?" He put his arms around her, laid his head in her lap and cried. "Shall we go to Germany?" he said. "Shall we go to Germany and Italy? We can go to Meran and see the place where Helga was born? We can look up all the places we were? We can walk in the Palm Garden in Frankfurt? I'll be nice, Evelyn! If you just come home I promise I'll be a new person!"

She placed her hands around his head. "I need time, Ørnulf." "Can't you take the time at home?" "No. I want to stay with Borgar." "But when are you coming home? Do you promise to come home? Does little Linnelin promise to come home to

135

little Nulfenulf? Nulfenulf is so lonesome without Linnelinn. And this spring it's our silver wedding anniversary!"

"Will you quit drinking?" Evelyn said.

"Yes," Ørnulf replied sadly. "We'll have to try . . ."

"Can I depend on that?"

"My word of honor, cross my heart. Do you love me?"

"Which one of you?" Evelyn said.

They agreed that Evelyn would stay with Borgar for a few weeks while Ørnulf went home to Ellen. She managed to convince him that she needed this time for the sake of her nerves. He went home and called her every day, and was the one she loved.

On the peaceful residential streets at Stabekk, Evelyn and Borgar went for long walks every day. They were close, as they always had been, there was an extraordinary calm over all conversations with Borgar. They talked about everything and always got deeper. But when they got to her marriage Borgar was strangely inflexible.

"When you get married you make a promise before God."

"I didn't get married before God," Evelyn said. "It was a civil ceremony." But Borgar didn't think that made any difference. A promise was a promise and the marital promise was of a religious nature. Borgar helped Evelyn stop drinking. He was better equipped to help her than many others. But his faith told him that she should stay with her husband.

His faith told him that, even though he—like his four other siblings—could clearly see where it was leading. But at the same time he thought that an almost noble quality had come over her, as if she were made of a different nature—yes, she'd become a very nearly unselfish human being. And he felt that it was precisely because of her difficult marriage that she'd become like this. This touched him more than anything, and he advised her to go back to Ørnulf.

They took their long walks at Stabekk, and here—beside her big brother—Evelyn finally found peace. And she believed what he said, even if she didn't share his faith.

What possibilities did she have for standing on her own two feet? She'd never had any education. "Never be economically dependent on a man!" Hans Rudolf had said to his daughters. So he sent them abroad to learn languages. "Languages are more important than degrees!" he said, and took them out of school time and again. Even though she finally finished junior high, Evelyn figured out that all together she'd only gone to school for seven years. She'd learned languages. But the very thought of using them to stand in front of a classroom filled her with fear. "You can live here with me!" Emilie said. But this filled her with fear, too. She belonged with Ørnulf, and she longed for him, and during this time—with the long walks and Borgar's soothing, warm voice—Evelyn got a new faith in her life, and she longed for the Ørnulf who was warm and funny and loving, and who furthermore was the only man she'd ever wanted, and he came. "Do you love me?" Ørnulf said. "Yes," Evelyn replied.

They returned to Fredrikstad and tried to begin a new life. They read. Two years earlier new volumes of Moberg's *The Emigrants* had come out in Norwegian translation. They bought the whole series and read about Karl Oscar and Kristina by Ki-Chi-Saga. But several times during the winter Evelyn went back to Borgar to get peace. And he always gave her the same advice. And Evelyn followed it. But Ørnulf's alcohol-free periods never lasted longer than the time it took to read a book.

In the spring, invitations went out to a silver wedding anniversary party at the Bjørnegården apartment. Ørnulf and Evelyn sent out an invitation full of corny jokes like: "Welcome to the Waldorf Victoria!," but none of Evelyn's siblings laughed. And none of them came. The only one who would have come was Lisa, but she was sick. Emilie could use her advanced age as an excuse, but Evelyn knew that under happier circumstances she would have come, despite her eighty-seven years. The day before the silver wedding Evelyn said to Ørnulf: "Well, now at least it'll last till *tomorrow*, I suppose!"

Ørnulf repeated this observation in his silver bridegroom

speech the next day amidst great merriment from those present, who consisted nearly exclusively of his old friends and their wives, and his parents. "I've called my speech: 'The Long Leap from Potsdam to Fredrikstad,'" Ørnulf said. "As a matter of fact not a single person who was present then is here today. And I hasten to add that we don't have any papers to prove that we're married. They were bombed in Berlin."

Then he told about how they'd quarreled their way through the marriage from the first moment, and how they'd walked down the road on the outskirts of Freiburg im Breiskau fighting so the fur flew, past some road construction workers, and Evelyn turned on her heel and walked back toward town. But after a couple of kilometers she turned, again, and passed the workers for the third time. Then they raised their heads and said: "*Schon wieder bereut?*" "Which means," Ørnulf said: "Already sorry?" And that's how it's been ever since. So anyone could see what he had to contend with, and it was a miracle that she'd held up, and he raised his glass and extolled her youth and beauty.

For her part she told a fairy tale about a prince who was the handsomest and wisest in the world, who proposed to a princess who was neither the most beautiful in the world, nor the wisest, for she said: "Yes."

Then she presented him with three vases she'd had made—in three different sizes. They symbolized herself and their two children, and she threw her arms around his neck. "I love you!"

And Inger stood up and said that many a time she'd sat in her room and heard such a frightful racket out in the living room, that she had to go out and see what was going on. Besides the potatoes, which were always on. And then she found her parents, in loving embrace, as they sang the Swedish serenade: "Behold the Wind Dancing!"

Her friends, she said, had never understood why she would choose to stay home on a Saturday night, instead of going out with them. "You can't pick your parents," her father used to say. "But if I'd been able to, there's no doubt whom I would have chosen," she concluded.

And that was true, in spite of everything. And everyone cried. And everyone laughed. They laughed and cried all at the same time. For behind the laughter and the tears everyone knew the truth about Ørnulf and Evelyn. They were close friends, and the silver wedding anniversary was full of warmth, despite the truth, or because of it. "A friendly fate brought you to this town," said Gudmundsen from Kråkerøy, Ørnulf's old friend from his student days, "and if it hadn't, we wouldn't have our three children today!"

Ørnulf and Evelyn received love on their silver wedding anniversary. Because even though everyone knew that the love actually being celebrated had withstood more trials than in most marriages, Ørnulf and Evelyn had—perhaps with precisely this love—enriched their lives.

But before the meal was over Grandpa took his glass and toasted those who were not present.

On a silver wedding trip through Europe with their two daughters, Ørnulf and Evelyn retraced their steps. And they didn't recognize a single building. The journey went from Fredrikshavn to Firenze and through all the German cities where they'd traveled as newlyweds along the Rhine—Cologne, Koblenz, Wiesbaden, Frankfurt am Main. They searched high and low for the places they'd stayed; the streets had the same names, the neighborhoods, too, and the Palm Garden was there, with swans now, too. But everything they had in their mind's eye was gone.

But when they got to Freiburg, Evelyn saw a tree. "The tree, Ørnulf!" she shouted, pointing. And there was a thick, old leafy tree, right by the downtown, that had survived all devastation.

A SUMMER NIGHT

When they arrived at Tjøme Ørnulf sat down in a chair. "On the table!" he said. With a clear pronunciation of all the consonants in the word "table." This was his beer command, and it was good-natured and high-spirited. But the good nature disappeared in the glass, and after a few days he was his old self. "You're wandering around in a daze!" he said. Now the truth was going to be nailed down. It was going to be hammered in and nailed down, and it was going to be printed in black, irrefutable letters in the air between them. Their marriage.

Their marriage would never work if she didn't admit that she wandered around in a daze. Wandering in a daze were the words, and if she wouldn't admit that what she did was wander in a daze, then he demanded a divorce.

Divorce! He could talk for hours about the divorce they had to get. "There's no way around it," he said.

"But you begged me to come back!" Evelyn said.

"You'll do as I decide," Ørnulf said.

Inger sat between them and listened.

"I decide!" he said.

"I decide!" Evelyn mimicked his Trønder accent. The accent was always more pronounced when he was drunk. "How can Inger stand to be home, when she's forced to sit and listen to drivel?"

"I decide," Ørnulf said.

"You certainly do not," Inger said. But that wasn't true. He decided that they would all sit and argue about the statement "I decide."

"I don't understand how you could have sided with the Germans during the war! *You* of all people would have suffered under a regime like that!" Evelyn shouted and she slammed her fist into the palm of her hand.

"Churchill is the greatest war criminal in the history of the world," Ørnulf said slowly, pronouncing each consonant clearly. "Yeah, and what about Hitler, then?" Inger said.

"I think . . ." Evelyn said.

"Your opinion interests me exactly as much as birds farting on the island of Svalbard," Ørnulf said.

"Why are you talking to us, then, if you don't care what we think?"

"What you think is about as interesting as a fart on the horizon," Ørnulf said.

"Ohhhhh! Cut it out!" Evelyn shouted.

"And I am the strongest man in the world."

He held out his fists as proof.

"So you're going to decide everything just because you're strong?" Inger said. Then he got up from the chair and came slowly toward her with a nasty expression on his face and his fists in front of him, ready to grasp. He took aim at her leg, and in the next instant he grabbed it. Inger stood up abruptly and tore herself away. "Good God, you . . . !" she shouted.

"Speak properly," he said.

Evelyn had stood up to get between them. He turned to face her, threateningly, with his pincers toward her. "Stop it," she said. "I'll never stop!" he shouted. Then he sat down again and lit a cigarette.

"I am the most intelligent person in the world."

"If you really were you wouldn't be so dumb as to say it," Inger said.

Papa peered at her with his papa-expression. One eyebrow

raised mirthfully. "And you are the second most intelligent person in the world," he said. "How 'bout a little Twenty Questions?"

Now Inger and Evelyn had a choice between a meaningless discussion the rest of the evening or Twenty Questions. They chose Twenty Questions.

One night Evelyn disappeared. In the middle of an argument, when he thought she'd just gone down to the cellar for a beer. But this night, when she opened the door to the fresh morning air, where it'd been light for a long time, she didn't go down in the cellar for the ninth time. She took her robe and disappeared.

She walked through the green ravine, past the strawberry patch and heard the birds through the leaves. Nothing is as invisible as birds. She could think here. And what she thought was: "He didn't become a new man."

Many times they'd thought: "If only we died together in an accident!" Neither of them could bear the thought of living without the other. And one night, when Inger and Helga were little, they'd carried out their plan. They took an overdose of sleeping pills and went to sleep up on the hillside. That was just after the liberation from the Germans and the treason trials determined black and white for all time. But when the first rays of sun reached them they woke up. The stuff hadn't worked! By some incomprehensible mix-up Ørnulf had gotten hold of the wrong pills.

She didn't go to the usual beach; he might follow her there; she took the road to the beach on the north side of the property, and there she began to swim.

Evelyn was a good swimmer. In her youth she swam all the way to Ormelet for cigarettes. She put them in her swimming cap, climbed up on a skerry on the return trip, had a smoke and swam home again. She'd jumped from the highest knoll on Revøy, and she'd taught herself to crawl so that she looked like a torpedo. As a child she finally managed to attract the attention of her older siblings by putting on a demonstration where she parodied everyone's distinctive swimming styles. Emilie lay with half her chest above the surface and floated splendidly, while she exclaimed: "*Wunderbar! Wunderschön!*" And Olga, the maid, had a curious ability to heave her rear end out of the water at each stroke. When she was little, Knut had made a pool in Vinderen Creek. That's where she taught herself to swim. But it was precisely here that she also acquired her first perplexing knowledge about human nature. All the children came to the pool, and they all threw themselves into the water and shouted: "Look at me! Look at me!" And Evelyn suddenly realized that no one was looking at anyone at all.

Evelyn was in the middle of Grimestad Bay. She thought about all these things as she swam. The water cleared her head, as if she saw her entire life in a single wave. The sun rose over the Mågerø peninsula, and the horizon became yellow there above the dark hills, it was like swimming toward a chamber of gold.

"Where's Mama?"

Papa's voice intruded into her dream. For a moment it was part of it, but then she woke up and saw his dark figure, swaying in the rectangle of the door.

"Where's Mama?"

As if she might have dreamed where she was.

But Inger had not. She'd been dreaming about Sheila. Sheila had taken her by the hand and was just about to show her something. "But aren't you in Edinburgh?" Inger asked. "Yes, I am. This is Edinburgh," Sheila replied. But it was the basement of the University auditorium in Oslo.

"Where's Mama?"

Inger woke up. There he stood, drunk.

"Is she gone?"

"Yes. She's nowhere to be found."

"I'm sure she'll be back. Maybe she's just taken a little swim."

"She has to come *now!*" Ørnulf said.

"It's no wonder she doesn't come now, with you standing like that bellowing that she has to come now."

"She can't hear that," Ørnulf said.

"But she's heard it before. Why don't you just go to bed? I want to sleep, Papa. Mama'll come back when she's ready to, you know."

"She's supposed to come when *I'm* ready."

"No one wants to come just when other people want them to. They want to go where *they* want to go, too. Even Mama."

"No. Mama's supposed to do what I want. To the letter. Otherwise there'll be a divorce."

"Divorce! You wouldn't last a day without her. Because then you couldn't sit there and talk about divorce."

He left. She lay down on the pillow again and tried to find the dream. She tried to summon up the touch, but it wouldn't take anymore. It was Mama who took hold of her thoughts and wouldn't let go.

"Inger!"

Inger was immediately awake. But she must have been sleeping anyway, because there stood Mama in the middle of the room. She was naked, with only her blue-striped robe around her, shivering. "Where on earth have you been?"

"I swam over to Mågerø peninsula," Evelyn said. Her teeth were chattering, and she showed Inger her body. It was full of red patches of hives. Inger got up, patted her carefully on the back with the robe, she was frozen stiff, but full of life.

"Mågerø!" Inger said. She knew what that meant. Mama didn't want to go on.

"Do you have a smoke?" Mama said. Then she sat down on the edge of the bed and lit a cigarette and told Inger about the trip to Mågerø. It had taken five hours. For five hours Mama had swum in solitude. With just herself and the depths. Inger wrapped the comforter around her back. She was proud of her.

Yes, she was proud—that Mama had accomplished such a swim, in the middle of hell.

"Can I lie down here a little?" Mama said. "Yes, come here. I'll make a chair for you." The back of the chair was her chest, the seat was her thighs, the chair legs were her calves, and that was how Inger had sat on a chair in Mama's bed many times, and now Mama sat on Inger's chair, and that was how they fell asleep.

M/S GUSTAV BARCON

Two days later Frank stood in the yard at Ekekjær wearing a light khaki suit and carrying a suitcase full of presents. Beside him stood Captain Lasse Svendsson in full regalia. His ship had docked at Slagentangen Oil Refinery Quay.

"This is my home," he said, and placed a gigantic white straw bag with a red rose in Evelyn's lap. "It's from Tut-Ankh-Amon's grave. And here, old boy. . . ." "That must be from Tut-Ankh-Amon's wine cellar?" Ørnulf said. And when the reunion was behind them and Lasse Svendsson had been properly introduced and thereupon had made himself scarce, Frank walked over the hills with Inger. "Inger, you're a lovely girl," Frank said. "Would you like to come to Paris with me?"

But Ørnulf sat in the living room with the bottle from Tut-Ankh-Amon's wine cellar in front of him and watched them. "He's flirting with her!" "But you know how Frank is. That's just his way," Evelyn said. "Are you speaking from experience?" "Good Lord! There's nothing wrong with him being a little nice to her!" "Nice, my foot. His sexuality is completely warped." "What kind of nonsense is that? Do you really think he'd try to seduce her?" "I'll be damned if I'll let him touch her!" "It takes two to tango! He wouldn't dream of doing anything she didn't want him to do." "Nonsense. A man always gets his way." "*You*, yes!" "I, and all other men." "I can't stand listening to you. I'm going down for a swim." "Are you going to kill yourself again now?" Ørnulf said.

And so their dialogue continued in the days that followed, every time Frank and Inger walked over the hills, while Frank said to Inger: "Day by day you're eating yourself to greater beauty!"

He must be in love, Inger thought.

They went home to Fredrikstad and Inger sat in the living room and said: "I'm going with Frank." "*What!?*" "I'm going with Frank on the Gustav Barcon. The captain has given him permission." "Well, he doesn't have my permission. Inger, you'd better get one thing straight. All girls who go to sea are whores." "???" "And everywhere in all the harbors there are girls lining up, ready to welcome the sailors. They're all whores, every one of them!" "Not me." "YES, YOU ARE! If you go you'll be a whore, too." "What rubbish," Evelyn said. "But I want to!" Inger said. "If you go," Ørnulf said, "then you're not my daughter anymore."

He'd never said anything like that before. Not be his daughter anymore? How could anything happen that would make her not be his daughter? It was almost a quarter past one. Her overnight bag was ready and packed in the little bedroom. The Gustav Barcon tanker lay at Slagentangen and was departing at five o'clock. The bus to Lervik left Brochsgate at 1:30, and connected with the ferry to Tønsberg, which took an hour and a quarter. It was a ten minute walk from Bjørnegården to Brochsgate. Ørnulf explained about the whores. He explained about the sailors' non-stop fucking and how any woman who was with them was a fallen woman. For always. It was eighteen minutes past one.

"I'm leaving!" Inger shouted, grabbing her bag and rushing out the door. She raced down Nygaardsgata, arriving just in time to see the Lervik bus pulling out. She waved to the bus driver in the middle of the traffic, even though there definitely was no bus-stop there, and the bus driver, who had no idea that she was running away from her father, whose daughter she no

147

longer was, stopped with his calm and all-powerful movements, and let her on the bus.

Three hours later a young figure with a blue overnight bag ran out onto the long docks at Slagentangen toward the Gustav Barcon. She went up the gang plank, and there—out on the deck—Frank came toward her, and with an overwhelmed expression he took her in his arms. She signed on with a little red paper as documentation, where it was written: "Rank: Secretary," and then Inger and Frank headed out into the world.

And that was how Inger became a whore, and that was how she quit being her father's daughter. No one who had known her up until now would have thought it would go like this, but this was how it went:

M/S Gustav Barcon, a 17,000-ton tanker, chartered by Esso in Bremerhaven, steamed toward Nyborg on the island of Fyn, Denmark. The radio station was located behind the bridge and next to that was Frank's cabin with a bunk at one end and a cot at the other. The first night Frank said, pointing at the cot: "I'll sleep here, and you can have the bunk. And when you want me to come to you, you can just tell me."

And that's how they did it. Frank slept on the cot and Inger lay in the bunk at the opposite end, and Inger never told him to come.

Of course no one on board imagined anything like that, they'd probably never even heard of it before, but every morning Frank brought her a pommac soda pop and a piece of ryekrisp with cheese to the edge of her bunk, but he never for a moment tried to cross over.

This was how Inger became a whore.

It was a wonderful trip. If this was what it was like to be a whore, it was to be highly recommended for all. As long as they just found a Frank.

A Frank who had a taxi drive them from the inn in Odense across the landscape of Fyn, through the land of the ugly duckling with windmills and roofs—the black roofs of Fyn!—while they planned how they would buy a windmill like that and live a totally picturesque life; a Frank who performed his duties with the sailors in every harbor they came to with a good natured groan, because the only thing he was waiting for was to get to the point, and that was to take his girlfriend by the arm and take her by train to Paris, where Sacré-Coeur lay ready to receive them, and the nightclubs with obligatory champagne flourished along Montparnasse, and the ladies who danced the can-can in Toulouse-Lautrec's pictures, they're still to be found at the Moulin Rouge.

But in the living room in Bjørnegården, Ørnulf was furious. And he vented his fury on Evelyn. This time he felt that his fury was so justified that he even phoned and complained to his mother. "She should've had a whipping!" Helene declared. It wasn't usually her habit to express herself harshly, quite the opposite. But this time she felt her son was right. And for that matter it never happened that she did not.

"That's the end of that friendship!" Ørnulf said.

"But Ørnulf! The relationship between Frank and Inger is a *friendship!*" Evelyn said.

But it didn't help no matter how often she said it. How could she know that? How in deepest, hottest hell could she know that?

"Because I'm wondering if she's not more interested in her girlfriends," Evelyn said.

That put an abrupt halt to Ørnulf's rage. He sat a long time and stared out into the living room. Then he said: "Well, of course it's usually the androgynous transitional types who are the most intelligent."

At the Moulin Rouge a remark was made. While they watched the assembling of the ladies from Lautrec's picture. Inger watched the ladies and Frank watched Inger.

"A woman could become bisexual from watching those girls."

Inger felt like she had been caught in the act. Was that how it was? Could you become bisexual from watching the can-can? But *bi?* If you became something, wouldn't it be homosexual you became? Surely the girls on the stage were not hermaphrodites. But maybe he just said that in order to use a more charitable word?

Did he understand the whole business? Because it was true that the ladies were gorgeous. Should she have thought they were a little less gorgeous? And was it so that the more she looked at them, the more bisexual she became?

Inger was sure Frank knew about this. He knew all kinds of people, even the prostitutes in Amsterdam. But she didn't dare to ask. She let him make his remark in peace, and was afraid there'd be more.

The M/S Gustav Barcon glided through a grain field. Out of Amsterdam—out toward the Atlantic. It was here that Frank's hopes were raised. Because the Morse code signals from Bremen announced: Venezuela. Frank came storming into the cabin, danced around the floor, took her in his arms: "Inger! We're heading to Venezuela!"

Venezuela, Venezuela, no name was so full of geography, of the distant geography you'd always longed for there on the world map of your childhood. Inger couldn't imagine this at all. But Frank could. Because now the journey had begun. And he knew it was a long trip. She was young. She was twenty-five years younger than he. He'd just have to be patient. But he said: "Inger! I really want to have a baby! And you'll be its mother!"

"But I want to go to school!"

"I'll take care of the baby and give it a bottle and fry steaks while you're at the university."

"But what would we live on?"

> —*Du hast Diamanten und Perlen*
> *Und alles was Menschen begehrt!*
> *Du hast auch die schönste Augen—*
> *Mein Liebste, was willst du denn mehr?*

Frank replied.

It was a brief escape. A counter-order from Bremen announced Gävle, Sweden.

Frank swore a blue streak. No sound could be more damnable to him right now. Gävle! When you were hoping for Caracas. "I'll show you the salons of Bern!" he said, and the ship set course for Skagen.

It was late in August now and the fall term would be starting soon, so actually this suited Inger well. But Frank was dejected. He dreaded the loneliness.

"I'll write to you," Inger said.

"Inger, you write marvelous letters!"

Now they were at sea for a longer period than ever before, but finally there it lay—the skerries outside of Stockholm in the late-summer sun, so much like Norway that it almost didn't matter that it wasn't Norway. The ship was supposed to dock there before it went on to Gävle. In the Stockholm harbor there was a message from Papa.

Papa? Inger thought. Reluctantly she went toward the office where the telephone was, and soon she had him on the line.

"Inger?" Papa's voice said. "Are you coming . . . Are you coming home?"

"So am I your daughter again now?"

"Inger," Papa said. "Word has come that you've gotten into student housing at Sogn!"

ENTRANCE 13

The dormitories at Sogn are a beautiful complex. The red brick buildings are set into the green hillsides at the edge of Gaustad Woods, and out of them, small, slanting roofs stick out where you can go and lie in the sun in the summer. Sognsveien curves by, peaceful and narrow, and on the other side the spray can be heard from the hoses watering the flower beds at the vocational school. The lower buildings were built for the 1952 Winter Olympics, and the famous art collector Rolf Stenersen donated a significant portion of his Munch lithographs for the rooms where the young people would live. "Man is not made for everyday life," Rolf Stenersen said, for he knew—and remembered—that even in the so-called springtime of youth there was everyday life.

As new and more modern buildings were constructed up along the hillside—with larger kitchens and a better view—the original buildings gradually became known as "The Slum." This was the best place to live. At least that was what the slum-dwellers retorted, because down here there was still *soul*. And soul was, of course, what they'd all come to Oslo for, and they never gave up searching.

Inger sat in room 1314. She'd unpacked all her cardboard boxes and now she sat and listened. The room was about ten by thirteen and faced out on Sognsveien. It was furnished with a reddish brown sofa, two book shelves, and a straight-backed chair, an armchair and a desk. From the wall an erect, dark lady with upswept hair stared out into the room. For the time being she was the only person Inger had seen in the apartment. But on the entrance door she'd seen a sign.

HERE LIVE:

		Ring:
1310	Frida Røyseth	. .
1311	Mina Thorsen	– .
1312	Lidia Galgocsi	– – –
1313	Rose Mary Fernhill	– –
1314	Elisabeth Falck	. –
	No one in particular	.

Inger was just wondering if she should go out and replace "Elisabeth Falck" with herself on the sign, when she heard a key in the door. There were footsteps outside, and a door was opened across the hall. It must be 1310 or 1311 coming home. She went out to ask if she could change the sign, but too late. 1310 or 1311 had vanished. A bit later there were footsteps out in the hall again. This time it sounded like 1312 coming home. Immediately the door to what must be 1310 or 1311 was opened, there was a knock at 1312's door, and a rather loud Trondheim voice said:

"He was here yesterday. And I'm *not* letting him in again!" She then heard a pithy answer in broken Norwegian that she couldn't make out, doors were slammed shut and once again it was quiet.

Inger got up abruptly, threw on her pea coat and went right up to Building 7. Elsa had moved in here. Elsa had ended up in an apartment with physical education majors and paragons of virtue. Now they were all sitting in the large modern kitchen in the new building 7, laughing. "And who'd you end up with?" "I ended up with 1310, 1311, 1312 and 1313," Inger replied. "How exciting. Are they virgins?" "I can't imagine they are. Half of them are foreigners." "Don't tease, who are they?"

153

Elsa asked. But Inger knew she was envious. She hadn't ended up with a single foreigner. On the contrary. She'd even ended up with someone named Marit Heimstad from Lisleby, right outside of Fredrikstad. Marit had graduated with them, but when they came to the point when everyone had to decide whether they were wild or born again, Marit had kept to the born again. The split between the Bethel-gang and the sinners was absolute, and neither Inger nor Elsa had exchanged a word with Marit when they went to The Yellow Institution.

But now when she suddenly appeared at the Sogn dormitory complex, it was as if they knew each other inside and out, and a liberating Fredrikstad laugh resounded from Building 7. Seeing a Fredrikstad face was always like coming home. You didn't need an excuse to talk to a person from Fredrikstad, no pretext to knock on her door. And as the fall went on, when the loneliness behind the closed doors in Building 1 became too great, Inger always sought refuge up here.

When she got back to Building 1, a rather lady-like person stood in the corridor over a scrub-bucket, wringing out a rag. "It's not that we have a housewife obsession in this apartment, but we take turns cleaning once a week. I can't shake your hand, I'm all wet, but my name is Frida Røyseth." Both 1311 and 1312 came out of their rooms now. 1312 was very beautiful. She came straight toward Inger with dark hair and a voluptuous shape and was absolutely and without a doubt the kind of person who belonged to the extremely rare phenomena in this world who go by the name of woman. Inger was so nonplussed that she immediately stuck out her hand and said: "Inger Holm." "Lidia Galgocsi," the woman replied.

1311, on the other hand, was rather skinny. When she said "Mina Thorsen," it was obvious that she had to be the voice who did *not* want to let him in. Whoever he was. Now Frida led Inger out to the bathroom. "This must be washed with ammonia. *Down* inside the toilet bowl, also. I may as well orient you while I'm at it. All the tiles in the bathroom have to be washed, the stools in the kitchen, cupboard doors, and all

154

the floors, of course. The housekeeper comes and inspects. And Rose Mary's coming in a week." "C. . . Can I change the sign on the door?" Inger asked, overwhelmed.

"I have a typewriter," she added. "You have a typewriter!? Do you think I could borrow it sometime for some work for the committee on Spain?" Of course she could, and Inger was about to ask to hear more about this committee, but before she knew what was happening, the efficient 1310 without the housewife obsession had disappeared into 1310, the thin 1311 into 1311 and the beautiful 1312 into 1312. Inger went into 1314 and was 1314.

Rose Mary arrived. And she limped. She had a rather full head of hair that swung from one side to the other when she walked, and there was a creaking sound from the brace she had on her leg that Inger avoided looking at with all her strength. They introduced themselves, and Rose Mary limped onward to 1313 while Inger stared uninhibitedly at her brace from behind. The leg was so small and thin. It was impossible to keep from thinking about it. Rose Mary turned around suddenly, and Inger's glance flew guiltily toward her eyes. They were blue. Rose Mary stood looking at her, as if she were in doubt about something. "Inger?. . . I have a suitcase that's a little heavy . . ." Inger ran down the steps, elated at being of such unexpected use. What had happened to the leg?

"Thank you very much," Rose Mary said in English, and closed the door to 1313.

Apartment 1310–1314 was what you could call a well-established apartment. Those living there had lived together for years, and once it had been a fine apartment to live in. Now there was war.

Frida and Rose Mary were socialists, atheists, feminists, existentialists and intellectuals, and they used all of these designations frankly about themselves, and they'd each had several lovers, Frida as many as eight—a bouquet, as she said—from six different countries. She stood out in the hallway and reeled them off. "The Israeli was the most aesthetic," she said, "because he was circumcised." "What?" Inger said. Frida explained objectively—with her round, cheerful face, as if she might have been talking about a recipe, and Inger pretended that she understood the explanation. "You've heard the water glass theory, haven't you?" Rose Mary said. "Alexandra Kollantaj says that for a woman, intercourse is like drinking a glass of water." "Yes," Frida said, "so remember, little Inger: First work, then love."

Mina was the daughter of a factory owner in Trondheim, was active in the conservative student association, and studied economics, because—as she said—that was a pretty good marriage market. Marriage market was the phrase, and in fact she'd found one for herself, to whom she was engaged, and beyond this she thought it was meaningless to mention sex-life.

Lidia was a refugee from Hungary, and an ardent anti-communist. She'd come in 1956, and was a Catholic and studied the history of religion, and she had a lover. Lidia's lover was always referred to as the Lover, and he always came—totally plastered, as a rule—with his drinking buddies, referred to as the Drinker and the Author, and raised a ruckus, until they were thrown out again. When this had happened often enough, the other girls refused to open the door for them or take messages, and when they ran into the Lover out on the street, they didn't say hello to him. On this basis Lidia felt that Frida and Rose Mary had a perverted sex-life, and she informed Inger of this early on, and according to her the perversion was because of—in Rose Mary's case—her leg. In Frida's case it was due to a forced attempt to be intellectual and liberated. But Frida dragged Inger into her room already on the third day and said: "You should know that any girl who's seen in the Lover's room is *branded*." Later, when Inger met the Lover over a beer in the coffee bar in the Tower building, he confided in her that Frida was frigid. The reason for her attitude toward him was that she actually wanted to have him as a lover. "But if she's frigid, she wouldn't be interested in that, would she?" Inger said.

I believe in the desire of the flesh
and the soul's irredeemable loneliness![1]

the Lover quoted in Swedish.

"Sentimental baloney," Rose Mary said.

This was the war Inger had come to, and she was deeply impressed and the conclusion she came to was that she should stop being a virgin.

She sat in her room and paged through *The College Survey of English Literature*. She thought about the leg. Rose Mary had had polio when she was four years old. She'd had to lie in the hospital for several months, quite still, because that was what you were supposed to do, and there was a war. Inger was full of pity. When she was little, and she fell down and hurt herself, and someone said: "Poor thing!" she hissed: "It's not *nice* to say poor thing!"

She didn't know where she got that from and why she always got so mad. She just knew that she'd never been able to stand this everlasting pity, and now she was sitting here in her room, paging through the books on the English reading list and had to realize that no matter what she did or thought about, she felt perpetually sorry for this girl.

Rose Mary told her about her illness, and she used the word "polio." In Norwegian the illness was called "*poliomyelitt*" and in Fredrikstad dialect they said "*pollmelitt*" with the accent on the first syllable. And over the years Inger had discovered, to her horror, that she was unable to say this word.

But situations had arisen when she'd had to say it anyway. They were completely unexpected situations she just suddenly stumbled into. "Do you have two bikes?" for example. A girl she hadn't known in elementary school might suddenly ask about this. Then suddenly her heart began pounding wildly and her ears rang. "One of them used to be my sister's." "Oh? Do you have another sister?" "No. She died."

Silence.

Silence!

The silence was in everything, it was in her ears—it made the whole park, or wherever they were standing, vibrate, and it was terrible to be alive.

"But why'd she die?" they finally asked. But only maybe. There might not be anything more at all. She had to walk with the silence—on through the park. But now and then came the question: "But why'd she die?"

And when she answered this, nothing more was said. It was rare that someone came along who realized that once you said this you had to say something more! Mrs. Mayfield had. Yes, she actually had. When it came—while she was standing ironing in the kitchen at 6, Aberdeen Road, and she told about Helga, at first there was no sound from the scullery. Then: "It must have been terrible for you, Inger."

It helped. These words helped unbelievably. And she was deeply grateful that they had come.

"Yes," she said.

That was all. It didn't take anything more. But because almost nobody could bring themselves to do something as simple as say that a terrible thing was terrible, unmentionableness closed itself around the word "*poliomyelitt.*"

But Rose Mary had said it. She had no choice. "People ask! And it's my most conspicuous feature." She waved her arms. "'Does your leg 'hurt'?' they say. But it doesn't hurt! It's like they just want to make it sound better. 'No, I had polio,' I say. Then they don't know what to say."

The most common conception about her leg was that there must be something wrong with her head. She had to go around constantly and prove that her intelligence was normal, because before she opened her mouth to strangers they always assumed that she was deficient, and when she said something, and furthermore something with meaning, for example: "Excuse me, sir, but did you forget this package of butter?" they were shocked. "And that's so unfair!" she said and looked at Inger: "Because obviously I'm terribly smart!" And then she laughed.

What hurt the most were people's attitudes, Rose Mary told

158

her. As if it weren't enough that she had the leg, and had to walk slowly. Early on she had to get used to the fact that her leg was a kind of odd taboo. She might pass a mother with a child on the street, and the child would shout in a loud voice: "Mummy? What's wrong with that girl?" And the mother would answer: "Shush, child!"

Shush child, for crying out loud! She had to walk through a forest of Shush. And the worst word in the English language was the word "cripple." That was what they used, the ones who didn't say "Shush!"

"But actually," Rose Mary said, "it might be the opposite of what they think. Maybe my leg has made me smarter than I would have been otherwise. I know what it's like to be an outsider."

Inger bent over *The College Survey of English Literature*. It was a thick, red book with thin Bible pages. She marked off the pieces that were required reading for an English major. "Shush, child!" she thought. How can I ever make it up to her?

Soviet warships were heading toward Cuba. The Lover, the Author and the Drinker came storming toward entrance 13, and staggered enthusiastically in. They could just as well whore and drink and have a hell of a time while there was still a chance! The great and final Bang that would soon strike Building 1 and everything that lived and bloomed was an excellent argument for the erection that was now clearing the way for itself toward the citadel. The girls didn't agree. The three were immediately tossed out on their ears. But they didn't disappear the same way they'd come. They stood there hammering on the door. "The Third World War is coming! Lidia! Let me in!" Three long rings followed. Lidia rushed out and shouted at him through the door. "If the Third World War comes, you can just as well stay out in the hall." "Lidia! You're crruuuuel!" "You promised you wouldn't drink, Jesper!" "But the bomb's coming!" he sobbed and pounded on the door. "Come on, Jesper.

The hell with them." That was the Author's somewhat calmer voice. "Yes," the Drinker said in his velvety voice. "We'll try the second floor. They're much nicer there." The Lover kept on knocking and ringing. "I will not go through the Third World War with you if you're not sober," Lidia hissed through the door. "Oh, what a fate," a voice moaned from outside the door. "The Russians are coming!" the Drinker shouted. Frida had now positioned herself in front of the door with one hand on her hip as if she were looking straight at them. "We would rather have the Russians than you three, Jesper." "Frida! You're heartless! You're frigid." "Come on!" They stormed up the steps. From above you could soon hear a female voice ring out in Stavanger dialect: "Get out of here! I'm rooting for Nikita!"

The next day Rose Mary and Frida stood ready in the hall-way wearing their winter coats. "We're going out to demonstrate now," Frida said when Inger came out. "Demonstrate?" "Yes, in front of the American embassy, of course."

Inger was very impressed. Obviously the U.S. was not at fault here. It just sat there and was threatened. It was the Soviet Union that was sending the weapons. But Frida and Rose Mary had already disappeared down the steps in their winter coats on their way to march against the most powerful country in the world.

"They're screwy!" Mina said, as she and Inger stood at the kitchen window watching after them. Rose Mary leaned on Frida's arm. "She'll never get a man!" Mina sighed. "What a catastrophe!" Inger exclaimed.

"What's with you? Are you one of those, too?"

And suddenly Inger knew that she had chosen sides in the war.

1. Quote from famous Swedish novelist, Hjalmar Söderberg (1869–1941).

LANGUAGE AND STUPIDITY

While the bricks were still new and smooth and red, and the cement so fresh that it still smelled, the auditoriums in Sophus Bugge Hall were already filled with young people. At this time most of the buildings on the Blindern campus were under construction and in the planning stages. But the buildings for the College of Liberal Arts were in place, along with the Administration Building and the so-called student welfare building, which contained a cafeteria so immense that it was difficult to see from one end to the other. Everything was brand-new, and arranged in such a way as to make one as nervous as possible. Thousands of people came here, they found a place among boiled potatoes and cabbage rolls and a sea of unfamiliar faces, they walked with rapid steps and notebooks under their arms on their way between the buildings, purposefully, and without saying hello to anyone, and if they were female, they disappeared straight down a stairway in Sophus Bugge Hall, and into a gigantic room with eight stall doors, and here they lined up before an enormous mirror. Ten to fifteen in a row, they stared at their reflections, and applied their lipstick. Then they grabbed their notebooks and continued on rapid, high-heeled shoes into the lecture hall. Here they sat in rows sloping up the enormous auditoriums where the very thought of opening your mouth sent shock waves through your body. They kept their mouths shut. They listened and took notes. Then they went back to their rooms without having talked to anyone.

When they went home to where they came from people said: "Oh, are you studying philology? Then maybe you know Fridtjof Svendsen?" Then they laughed a sardonic laugh inside, while they politely answered: "No. What does he look like?" or something else that one might suitably answer in a home-town.

Of the fifty-three graduates of the Fredrikstad class of 1960 there were now seven who were studying in Oslo, three girls and four boys. The seven were spread out in various buildings on the Blindern campus, the downtown campus and Halling School. It was pure luck if you ran into them. The rest of the class were at similar schools spread out over the entire Western world, from California in the west to Berlin in the east, most of them boys. The girls went to Teachers' Colleges in Norway, to the College of Orthopedics, to school to be a nursery school teacher or a nurse. A handful of them had just finished a horrible year of child care and dusting and stammering in a foreign language in various legendary European capitals. Of the twenty-five girls who graduated from St. Croix elementary school in 1955 there was only one who currently spent her days going from one building to another at Blindern and to her horror and dread discovered the rows of fellow students in front of the mirror in Sophus Bugge Hall. No, there was no one here to say: "Hi ya!" to. And she fled home to the Sogn Dormitories. She saw the beautiful complex on the hillside, where she came on her black bicycle—Arrow brand—which she had inherited from an unmentionable older sister, and she thought: When I get older, I'll miss this place. I'll think about this time as a good time, and see it in a rose-colored light. And she promised herself that she'd never forget how lonely she was here.

. . .

Everyone in apartment 1310-14 was much older than Inger, and soon she was nicknamed the Child. The Child proclaimed that she didn't want to go to lectures and that she was going to finish her English major in two semesters and speed up her whole course of study. Frida said: "Listen here, little Inger. You'll never manage to finish your English major without going to lectures. You'll be asked about everything from Lord Nelson's lovers to Lady Godiva who ran naked through the streets of Coventry, and you only have your lecture notes to go by, because if Professor Simonsen published a textbook about this, he'd be unemployed."

And Inger did as she was told, because in a very short time she'd managed to get the impression that Frida and Rose Mary were right about everything they said, even though she protested vehemently, and in a few weeks she had—without realizing it herself—turned them into the center of her life. She was constantly figuring out ways to do small favors for Rose Mary. All Rose Mary had to say was: "Oh shit! I forgot to buy the *Guardian* at Narvesen's!" and she'd bike down and buy it for her, and she said to Frida: "Actually good deeds are egotism." But she used the man who always stood down in the subway playing the harmonica as an example. "Every time I give him a *krone* I feel good," she said. "I think thoughts like that are meaningless," Frida said. "If you do something good, then you do something good."

Inger had never met so many objections to her viewpoints. She liked to philosophize about everything imaginable, and often arrived at the notion that something was the opposite of what it really was. Not so with Frida and Rose Mary. They took a position on the most uncertain things. And now Inger began longing fiercely to do the same.

But there was one area where they absolutely held the wrong position. And that was in the language controversy. Rose Mary spoke good Norwegian and rarely made mistakes, but she used radical forms like "*løyve*" and "*vansker,*" which middle-class Norwegian students would only use to make a political statement. It was completely appalling for a foreigner to launch into such forms. Inger immediately brought Rose Mary's radical Norwegian to earth with a parody. "If you say 'vansker,' I'll say 'difs,'" she said, and proclaimed: "The world is full of difs!" Rose Mary laughed, but she didn't give in. On the contrary she began to justify her language politically. Justify her language politically! The very expression opened new and unexpected perspectives, and as the fall progressed they clashed again and again on the most amazing points.

Inger had always been convinced that when she herself was old enough to vote, the Labor Party would be toppled. The reason for this would be that she herself and most people she knew would vote Conservative. This was not because she was familiar with the Conservative platform. (She was. But that wasn't why.) It was because she knew that the Conservative party was the most sensible party.

Until she came to the Sogn dormitory complex in the fall of 1962 and watched Frida and Rose Mary head out against the world's most powerful nation—maligned by Mina Thorsen—she had practically what one could call a farcical attitude toward life. Political events, human escapades, personalities and authority figures, bridge building and the State Liquor Monopoly—not a single thing existed before her eyes that didn't, in its innermost being—deserve a parody. The most appropriate motto one could find for the class there on the steps of the Phoenix in Fredrikstad, if one wanted to find something, would undoubtedly have been: "Everything is ridiculous." And with this deep realization, they were scattered to the four winds.

Over the course of a half year Inger changed her views on everything. Well, it's actually not completely correct to say it like that. What happened was that she went from thinking that it was impossible to have a definite opinion on anything at all, to thinking that it wasn't. She thought about people, politics, morals, war, post-war treason trials, everything that had happened in human history, as stupid or smart.

The Labor Party typically was stupid. Just the fact that they'd been in something as stupid as Power for their entire lifetime, was proof enough. Except from their very first baby years, when Quisling made a ridiculous attempt to take it over, something he never should have been shot for. That was stupid, too.

Stupidity in peacetime meant that it took two years too long to finish the Kråkerøy Island bridge. When the workers took cover at the least little rain shower and stood there discussing wages, it was the result of a slightly comical stupidity that clung to every municipal laborer.

It would've been impossible to grow up in the Bjørnegården Apartment in Fredrikstad in the 50s without seeing poverty. There were old shacks right next door—down by the river, where the Glomma river flowed into the yard in the spring— and people actually lived here. They didn't have toys and they didn't have boots. They didn't even have money, and had to buy on credit. And when they charged a loaf of white bread, they'd eaten up half the insides before they got home. She'd been in and out of houses like that her whole childhood. And she'd thought of this misery as a result of lack of innate ability. You could hear it. Because people who lived in such places spoke incorrectly. She believed—when you came right down to it— that if they only learned to speak correctly, all of these old shacks would mysteriously dissolve into the air and food would appear on the table.

The Conservatives spoke correctly. They kept to the dictionary and got ahead. And even so they had to sit, quite powerless, and witness all kinds of municipal comedies. For example that in Fredrikstad it was against the law to sell beer after one o'clock on Saturday.

In everything Inger said, she exposed her view of the ridiculousness of everything, it was her primary driving force, and this was how she—over the years—had managed that which was the foremost meaning of life: to make other people laugh.

But now she was thwarted. "You are profoundly apolitical!" Rose Mary said. Apolitical? Rose Mary spoke very good Norwegian. She knew a lot of words in this language that Inger had never heard before. For example this. "*Riksmål* is an upper-class language," Rose Mary said. "The upper classes in the cities have determined what is correct and what is incorrect language." "That are a red house! Isn't that wrong?" "Where in Norway do you find a large group of people who say 'that are a red house'?" "Well, but that proves that there's such a thing as incorrect language! In Fredrikstad, do you know what they say in Fredrikstad? 'He laid outside for forty days,' they say, about the kind of people who live under an old boat at Peterstomta dump. If that's not wrong, I'll eat my hat."

"Eat away!" Rose Mary said. She certainly was terribly stubborn, too. "If a whole group of people in Fredrikstad say 'laid' there, then it's correct there. "That's the stupidest thing I've ever heard!" Inger said. "Can anyone just say whatever they want?" "Yes."

The debate halted abruptly at that point, because in a short time it had become very heated. "But just listen to how they talk!" Inger said. "In Fredrikstad they say: 'Aw, getottahere, you' around their chewing gum. That doesn't exactly sound intelligent."

"You speak as you've been taught. It's not a matter of intelligence."

"Isn't it a matter of intelligence? What's it a matter of then? And besides, it's ugly! 'Hey you! Whatcha talkin' 'bout!' Is that ugly, or what?"

"Who's decided that it's ugly?"

"Well, do you think it's pretty?"

She had her now. Now she had her. She couldn't insist on this.

"Maybe not. But that's completely irrelevant."

Once again a new and deadly word sailed into the discussion. Irrelevant. Here they were, discussing a clearly defined issue, and suddenly what she said had nothing to do with the matter. A fancy word, this was. She made up her mind to put it to use at the first opportunity.

"I don't see that it is 'irrelevant,' as you call it. Clearly they're speaking incorrectly! Isn't that a sign of stupidity? Do you know what they say? They say: 'I should have went,' they say. When they mean 'gone.' So isn't that wrong?"

"Who decided that it's wrong?"

"Yeah, but it just *is* wrong. No one decided it!"

"That's where you're wrong. The upper classes have always decided what kind of language is wrong and what is correct; what is so-called pretty and what is ugly. They've always said that the working class's language was wrong. But if you take a person's language, you take his thoughts, his independence, everything!"

Inger was silent. Because she knew this was true. She'd never forget how she'd stood stammering and fumbling in Edinburgh, and felt that her entire personality crumbled, just because she couldn't manage to say: "No wonder you get purple legs when you drive your motorbike in silk stockings." She got annoyed and sullen. "Should I change my language, then?" she said. "Change my laa-nguage!" she mimicked.

"You should stop thinking that the language you speak is more correct than the language of the municipal workers under the bridge you told me about," Rose Mary said. "Well, at least I'm glad I don't talk like that." "That's pretty arrogant." "Arrogant? But they just stand there talking about wages! and then they go and vote Labor, just because they're laborers. How are we going to keep laborers from voting for the Labor Party?" she exclaimed, and it was just meant as a revelation of one of life's many obvious stupidities. "There's no reason laborers shouldn't vote Labor," Rose Mary said. "But they do it without thinking!" "It's not a matter of intelligence." "Isn't that a matter of intelligence either?" "In a democracy everyone has a right to an opinion." "Even if they don't have any insight?"

But not even this totally logical argument was allowed to stand. Rose Mary said: "No political insight is required to understand that you work hard and get very little in return."

Here Inger ran out of arguments. Because this was a completely new thought for her. Despite this she said after a while: "Do you really think that one is entitled to an opinion without any form of intelligence?"

"The justification of an issue cannot be measured by the intelligence of those who support it," Rose Mary said. "Because it's a matter of living! Of food, shelter and work. If you're poor, you understand it."

"But obviously you have to understand *why* you're poor, too! Otherwise you can't do anything about it."

"But you're operating under the assumption that they don't have any insight into this. That's a common upper-class prejudice!"

Upper-class prejudice! There was another one of those expressions. She thought what she thought because it was logical, and for no other reason. "I think about things, too, you know," she said, hurt.

"Yeah, so do you think you are the only one who does?"

"No, I can tell that you make valiant efforts as well."

But this remark irritated Rose Mary a little, and in a somewhat raised voice she said: "Inger, the things you say I've heard a hundred times before. You're just reproducing the thoughts of the privileged class you come from."

"Privileged class! As far as I know privileges were abolished during the French Revolution."

"Not the economic ones. Do you deny that there are class differences in Norway?"

Inger didn't answer. Because she didn't want to deny this. But she couldn't see that it had anything to do with her thoughts. It took some time before she arrived at this answer. "No, but my ideas certainly aren't connected with the fact that we had enough money at home!" she said.

"Are you sure about that?"

No, she certainly was not. She wasn't sure about anything anymore. Because as soon as she was sure about something, it might turn out that she was completely wrong; that had happened several times now.

They were in the kitchen, and Rose Mary sat behind the *Guardian* while Inger made pea soup. Since Inger didn't answer, she disappeared behind the newspaper again. It was good arguing with her. But suddenly she would disappear. Or she sat, like now, unapproachable behind her reading material. Was the discussion ended? Rose Mary had a distinct talent for seeming to be completely in her own world, whether she was sitting or walking. A distinct talent for having her own opinions and not giving a damn. Inger admired this. Wished she were like that herself. But suddenly she might burst out, shout or laugh—often in indignation over something she had read. She was reading now. Inger looked at her. She was sitting with one leg crossed over the other. Suddenly Inger noticed that this other leg was actually unusually beautiful. So she kept looking at it. Longer than one usually would casually look at a leg. Rose Mary picked up her cigarette from the ash-tray. Inger saw that she was looking at her. "You have a beautiful leg!" she said.

She said it before she had a chance to regret it. That was really something to say to another person. "You have a beautiful leg!" But Rose Mary was immediately full of life. She slung the leg in question up on the kitchen counter, and cried excitedly: "Yes, it's really not bad, is it?"

Inger was tremendously relieved. She sat down at the other side of the table while the pea soup cooked. "You're so quiet," Rose Mary said. "Don't you believe you're influenced by your home?" "Yes, of course," Inger said. But she didn't say any more. And Rose Mary began to explain Lenin's ideas, and Inger listened and didn't say anything more for a long while. Because she'd just discovered that it wasn't just this one leg that was beautiful, it was the whole girl.

THE LAST OF THE MOHICANS

She realized it while she was home in Bjørnegården. And it was Christmas. That the terrible thing—that she'd given one more chance not to happen again—had happened. As long as she saw her every day, she'd seen her every day, and not understood a thing. But now it was vacation, Rose Mary had gone to England, she herself sat between Mama and Papa and played a quiz game from Kåre Kapp's quiz book, and she discovered it in herself like a heavy and incessant absence.

She didn't understand how it could have happened. Of course she'd felt sorry for her. And completely imperceptibly and without her being able to prevent it, the misplaced sympathy had been transformed into the terrible thing.

"When was Napoleon born?" Papa read.

"1769," she said.

And there was no meaning in it. Because the absence was in the birth date, in just opening her mouth to say something, breathing, lifting her little finger, taking a rye-krisp, the absence was there.

How could she miss her so much?

Christmas moved at a snail's pace like no other Christmas before had done. Each hour was endless, a day was unthinkable. Three weeks of longing, and fear of what would happen when her eyes met hers again. It was not Rose Mary's fault, clearly. She hadn't done anything at all, except be Rose Mary. And when the day arrived, the hour, the minute, the second, when she saw her again—there in the hallway it was, she came in, with her dark blue winter coat on—she was filled with fear.

Inger went into 1314 and lived with the fear. Then she began to display enormous energy to cater to Rose Mary, be useful to her, please her, amuse her, impress her, listen to her and absorb everything that came out of her mouth as the absolute truth. What else could she do with her fear? She obviously couldn't stay in a room with a view of Gaustad woods and tremble the rest of her life?

She trembled. But she didn't give a damn about it. She had to give a damn about it. She just had to. Oh, God, how incredibly in love she was with her.

Rose Mary went around as always. She limped. She spoke Norwegian with an English accent. She was a socialist, feminist, existentialist and intellectual. And she was the most wonderful person in the world.

And she had no idea. Was it really possible that Rose Mary didn't know that she was the most wonderful person in the world? How was it possible to go around like that and not have any idea? It just radiated from her—it wasn't just inside her, and around her, only as far as her body and head reached, just the outline and no further. It surrounded her in a gigantic outline that radiated wherever she set her foot, encircled all her words and movements—as soon as she did anything at all, she became a hundred times larger than herself. And the same thing happened when she sat still, too.

Or the streetcar she took. Didn't she notice how the Sognsvann streetcar line lit up with the exact car that she caught? Didn't she notice how she spread happiness around her—to all the people who at any given moment were blessed by being in her presence?

It was possible that she had no idea about it. She did her things, just as before. Did the dishes. Read the paper. Made her indignant outbursts. Laughed. Was mad. Just as before. It was unbelievable.

Inger began the spring term of 1962 and pretended that life was not totally changed.

"You should go to Planned Parenthood," Frida said. She and Rose Mary and Inger were on their way home from Tonsenhagen where they had begun instructing housewives in English for the League for Workers' Education. "You can get a diaphragm there."

She described in completely concrete detail what a diaphragm was, as if she assumed that Inger didn't know this. And she was right about that.

A diaphragm was a round thingamajig made of rubber, sort of bowl-shaped, that you were supposed to put *inside* yourself. And it said stop. To any sperm that might happen by. Inger couldn't understand how there could be room for the diaphragm. There was so little there.

"Sure, sure, but think about the fact that a whole baby has to come out there," Frida said. "Yes, but that hurts." "The diaphragm doesn't hurt," Frida said. "you just squeeze it in."

But Inger was not convinced. And besides she had no desire for one of those diaphragms, in there.

"I don't need a diaphragm," she finally said, when they came to the entrance door. "You see, I'm a virgin."

Then Frida and Rose Mary laughed so hard they practically fell down on the sidewalk. Now it had always been Inger's fervent hope in life to make other people laugh, but this particular time she didn't think she'd been the least bit funny. It was true! She *was* a virgin. And how was she supposed to get the diaphragm in?

Nonetheless Frida showed her her diaphragm as soon as they got inside. It lay in a plastic box and was gray with a ring around it. No way am I going to press in a pancake like that, Inger thought.

But she was sick and tired of being a virgin. She ended up

in bed with the Author. Rolf Johansen was his name, and he'd written four books. "You've really never heard of me?" he said. She read them immediately, and one of them mentioned Vestgrensa. She was impressed that a place right around the corner could be in a book. "I've thought about living off my writing, too," she confided in him. Then he burst out in howls of laughter. "Not even Hamsun could live off his writing," he said. He played Rachmaninoff's second piano concerto. "Listen! Listen to this!" It was good to make love to. Momentous, slow and compelling, so that there was a meaning in lying there. "What're you thinking about?" he said, and pressed her into himself. "I'm thinking about the music," Inger answered. It was a complete lie. She was thinking about Rose Mary. Why did it happen over and over again? I don't want this! I don't want it. Such a long time had gone by now, I thought I was rid of it. And then it comes tumbling down over my head, worse than ever before. Rolf Johansen kissed her. "I can never understand what a woman is thinking," he said. "What does a woman think, Inger?"

But Inger had absolutely no idea what a woman thought. She thought about Rose Mary, and if she slept with him now, at least she'd have something interesting to tell her. "What?" Rolf said, and squeezed her arm a little. "That's a big problem for a writer. That he doesn't know how a woman thinks. A man can't describe a woman. But a woman can describe a man. *There's* a job for you, Inger."

She was flattered and exhilarated and began immediately to invent a man she would describe. He lay in a bed with a woman. And he loved her. He didn't know if she loved him, but he loved her. He'd loved her for ten years before they got to this point. And he had suffered the most horrible torment because he didn't know if his feelings were reciprocated. And he didn't dare tell her about them. She was too lovely for that. Then suddenly one day she took him in her arms.

"You have gorgeous breasts," Rolf said. "You should be proud of your breasts. Are you a virgin?"

She was so flustered by this question, right in the middle of her novel, that she immediately replied: "Yes."

"What!!? A virgin at Sogn!" He sat up in bed. She felt like she was The Last of the Mohicans, or something like that.

"Shit!" he said.

"What's the matter?"

"It's against my principles to sleep with virgins."

Hm, thought Inger. The piano concerto, which had now come to a more sparkling section, reverberated just as doggedly romantically as before. "Why not?"

"They just scream and wail and carry on," he said.

"Not me."

"Oh, yes you will. You, too," he sighed. "Do you want to bet?"

"How can we bet on it when your principles prevent us from settling the bet?"

"I think you're too smart for me, by gosh!" he laughed.

"But how would that work, then? If all boys had a principle like that? Then no one would be able to sleep with anyone at all."

"You're right," he said, "but luckily not all boys have this principle, so I prefer that one of them does the job."

"The job!?"

"It's a strain listening to all that racket."

"Is it that unpleasant?"

"For you, yes. Not for us."

"But!" Inger said, and now it was she who sat up.

"Would you like it if I slept with, slept with . . . Jesper? And then afterwards came here to you?"

"I *never* take over women from Jesper," Rolf said.

"You sure have a lot of principles!"

Just then there was a knock at the door, and without waiting for a "Come in!" the aforementioned Jesper came into the room.

"Oh, excuse me!" he said with emphasis. But he sat down.

"Can't you see I'm busy?" Rolf said.

174

"Sure, sure ... I'll leave right away," Jesper said, and remained seated.

That was the end of this promising beginning, and Inger was even more sick of being a virgin than before. Of all the girls she knew at Sogn, Lill-Ann from Larvik was the only one who was a virgin, too. They made up their minds to see who would manage to lose her virginity first.

One day Jacob came by. He was dark and handsome and she'd met him through Hartvig once when he dragged her along to the Anthroposophic Center. And when he ended up in her room, she said that she'd decided that she wanted to have him for her lover. They sat for hours and talked about whether or not they should sleep with each other.

"I'm a virgin, too," Jacob said. "And I'm probably impotent." "That doesn't matter!" Inger reassured him. They lay down beside each other with nothing on above the waist. There they continued the same discussion. And finally he took out her copy of the Bible and read the Song of Solomon. And Inger thought about Rose Mary in the lines and longed for the moment when she would go out in the kitchen and it was morning so she could make tea, and maybe Rose Mary would come.

One evening some guy climbed up the drain spout and in through her open window. When she came back from the bathroom there he stood in her room. "What's your name?" he said. "Inger," she said. "Inger, I love you!" he said and fell down on his knees. "How do you know that?" she said. Well, he could see it in her eyes. She asked him to leave. "Oh beat me!" he shouted. "Please beat me!" He begged her to beat him, and stretched out on a pile of newspapers in the corner. "Oh, Inger! Please let me stay here! I just want to hear you breathe!" "Breathe," she said, "I don't know if I feel like breathing for you." She ended up having to throw him out in a tremendous scuffle.

There was a party at Elsa's apartment. She ended up next to Marit Heimstad on the sofa in the kitchen. It was not coincidental, because Marit was the only one of the girls who wasn't sitting flirting with a boy. She was a sweet and quite shy girl. But she wasn't the kind of person you could talk about being a virgin with. You discussed politics. And Marit was a staunch nationalist and supporter of the Liberal Party. "Relations between Denmark and Norway will never be good until we get Tordenskiold's body back,[1]" Marit said. Inger had never missed this body, and she was soon entangled in a complicated discussion about the Treaty of Brømsebro from 1645. But then she pulled herself together.

Resolutely she emptied her glass of gin and Coca-Cola. Then she did something she never believed she would end up doing. She used her eyes on a boy.

She didn't know him, but he was tall and handsome. And he was a bit smashed, too. Per was his name, and he was studying math, and when she figured that she had gotten the so-called hook in him, she left the party. And Per followed her. They walked down together. What could you talk to a math student about? She couldn't keep saying $pi\textsc{r}^2$ all the time, and she didn't think he was interested in Tordenskiold's body, and she didn't know anything about integrals, so they didn't exactly have much to talk about, but they went to bed when they got to 1314 and did what Inger assumed was screw a little. It didn't hurt enough to be much to scream about, just a little, so there wasn't much point in doing it so terribly long, so after a few thrusts she said:

"Do you think I'm a virgin now?"

"No," he said.

"Then you can leave," she said.

And he did.

Inger was no longer a virgin. The mysterious transformation had occurred. And she thought that she'd never experienced anything so unmysterious. It was embarrassing. Here she should have reached into some inner core of something, a secret room, and then it was as unsecret as calisthenics in Vesla Jørgensen's gym class. She hoped she never saw him again. What in the world would she say?

She calculated when she should get her period. This was something she'd never done before. Could she get pregnant from something so brief? She was overjoyed at this new, unexpected element of suspense. Now she was a member of the club.

The first thing she did the next morning was run up to Elsa. This was the prize. And Elsa didn't let her down. She listened attentively, and when Inger got her period some time later, they went to the Theater Café and celebrated the event with a fancy dinner.

But in the apartment not a word was spoken. The days passed and Inger hoped that they'd ask her a question, so she'd be able to say she wasn't a virgin anymore. But no natural opportunity arose. Now fourteen days had passed, and they hadn't asked.

It had all been a waste. Here she was, no longer a virgin, and they didn't have a clue about it. She stood out in the kitchen and boiled water. Rose Mary sat behind the *Encounter*. Frida washed the tiles in the bathroom. Inger brewed tea in a mug. Lidia came out to check on the rice she was cooking. In the middle of the steam she said: "Well, Inger? Been seduced lately?"

At last, at last. Lidia must have a sixth sense. Rose Mary was still sitting behind the *Encounter*. "I won't answer that question until Rose Mary asks me," Inger said. "Rose Mary," Lidia said, "you have to ask Inger if she's been seduced lately!" Rose Mary glanced up from the *Encounter*. "Have you been seduced lately, Inger?" "Yes," Inger said. Then Rose Mary went back to her reading.

"Go to Planned Parenthood!" chirped Frida, and soon they all disappeared into their rooms.

Inger felt cheated. They could have asked a few questions. But what would she have said? It was nothing. She thought about the water glass theory. But this wasn't even as significant as drinking a glass of water! She'd have to launch a new theory. The air theory. What would they say about that? It would probably entertain them.

Inger was confused. What had she been cheated of? The prize. The only thing that interested them in the matter was the diaphragm. For the first time in her life she'd met two girls who didn't have boys at the center of all their talk. And she was deeply ashamed at her own humbug.

No one knew anything about her humbug. She had only one person in the whole world to be ashamed for. Herself. And she was ashamed for the whole world. She loved another girl more terribly than she'd ever loved anyone. And then she didn't let herself be taken in! She sat behind the *Encounter*. How was this going to go? Everything was getting so mixed up. She threw herself into escapades to impress her. And she didn't succeed!

It was embarrassing. Everything was embarrassing. The world was embarrassing and terrible.

"A man exists to serve my purposes," Frida said.

Frida and Rose Mary had an island. It had risen from the sea and was just called The Island. Here they would establish a ménage à trois, and have a baby that they would raise completely in common. Frida would be the First Lady and Rose Mary would be Minister of Foreign Affairs, and foreign policy would consist of fighting against NATO and Harold MacMillan, and spreading diaphragms over the French countryside. In order to have the baby, they'd also have to have a man. They'd located him a long time ago, that is Rose Mary had found him—for Frida. Frida hadn't met him herself, but she trusted Rose Mary. He was intelligent and socialist and Spanish. As long as he stuck to the rules, he'd be permitted to be the President of The Island. From here they would plan the fall of Franco.

Deeply impressed, Inger listened to Frida and Rose Mary's talk, which got worse and worse. "But what about love?" she said desperately.

"Love is just propaganda," Frida said.

"Not if you love someone," Inger said.

"Perhaps we should appoint Inger Minister of Propaganda. She'd be excellent for the job, as soon as we indoctrinate her a little more," Rose Mary said.

Inger felt honored. She received the accolade in joy and silence.

"Loving someone is nothing for a woman to base her life on," Frida said. "But what if you do even though you don't want to?" "Work is the only remedy against life," Frida said.

---

1. Tordenskiold was a famous 18th century Norwegian naval hero who won many sea battles against the Swedes for the then unified Denmark–Norway. When he fell, the Danes took his body, buried him in Denmark, and called him a Danish hero.

THE ULTIMATUM

Later in the winter Frida began watching a boy in Building 2 as she stood making rice curry. She'd seen him undress and reveal an absolutely Hermes-like body, it was simply such an aesthetic pleasure that it was a shame he didn't hear about it. And besides, she'd like to have some more performances.

"Inger," she said, "since you're the youngest in this apartment, I have a command for you. You are to call up the boy across the way and ask him to take off his clothes in front of the window one more time."

Finally, a chance to impress them, Inger thought and immediately obeyed the order. She counted the windows in entrance 22, and through the internal telephone book she figured out that the boy's name had to be Hans Bekk Hansen. Then she got on the phone and repeated Frida's message.

And she was not disappointed. Frida and Rose Mary practically fell off their stools with laughter and appreciation of her courage, and Inger stood ready to receive additional commands. Frida was somewhat displeased that Inger had neglected to emphasize the aesthetic aspect, and after the rice curry they drank coffee with whiskey and were soon rather tipsy, and in this state they drafted a letter:

"Young man! We repeat the request for more strip-tease performances in front of the window. Greetings from the Aesthetics Club."

The letter was created in such a way that they each wrote one letter—in disguised handwriting. It went from Frida to Rose Mary to Inger and back to Frida, and when Rose Mary finally handed Inger the letter so she could write the final b, their eyes met. With amazement she felt the look go through her, her hands, skin and movements, I love her, she thought, the words just flew right into her head, it was the first time they came like this, as words, just like a sentence you read one time, that sticks in you head—"Tomorrow is another day," Scarlett O'Hara thought, it was nailed down, even though wings had brought the words down and there was absolutely nothing else to do about it than to go and mail the letter.

Two days later the curtains in the room of the one who had to be Hans Bekk Hansen were drawn. Inger had never seen him, and it was a mystery to her how Frida could see him like that through a window and admire him, though she pretended that she understood it, but now Frida couldn't do it anymore either, admire him, and they drank more whiskey and wrote a new letter that went from hand to hand, and as Rose Mary was about to give Inger the letter, their hands happened to collide, and Rose Mary did absolutely nothing to prevent it, she just looked at her with the prettiest blue eyes anyone could possibly look at anyone with, and that seemed to be created for something much more in this world than just looking, and said: "Your turn, mate!" as if she didn't have any blue color at all and the letter went on, and they complained letter by letter about the unfortunate development of the matter. They begged Hans Bekk Hansen to throw the drapes aside once more, yes they demanded as their crystal-clear right to be apportioned just a small glimpse of his beauty. Grant us this small pleasure in our humdrum existence! Inger proposed as a closing sentence. "Brilliant, brilliant," Frida and Rose Mary said. "Greetings from the U.N.," they wrote. ("Unsatisfied Nymphomaniacs"), and there was nothing to do this time either, but go up and mail the letter.

But to little avail. Hans Bekk Hansen held his own behind the curtains with his beauty. But that wasn't all. Now all the other curtains in his corridor were drawn, too. Then Rose Mary grabbed the telephone receiver and got the telephone number, and without introducing herself or asking who had answered the phone, she shouted: "You're all a bunch of cowards!" Then she slammed down the receiver.

They were in the mood for a beer. But not Frida. After all, she was studying for her French exams. Inger and Rose Mary went up to the coffee bar in the Tower Building. The hill was slippery, and Rose Mary said: "Come here! I have to hold your arm." Inger felt her hand at her side, quite light, they walked slowly up the hill and over them was the winter sky and Inger knew that she could keep on walking like that for the rest of her life, and she said:

"What's your greatest wish?"

God knew where that came from, but that was what she asked about.

"To not have to be in England when Churchill dies," Rose Mary said.

The coffee bar was full of people, and Inger was in a completely meaningless and silly state of euphoria that just grew and grew as the level of beer in her glass sank, and Rose Mary peered at her over her beer glass and talked eagerly about de Gaulle's "No," and now she explained what the Bahama Agreement was about, and Inger had never heard anything so interesting in her whole life, and two hours passed in about five minutes. The bar was closing. With two newly purchased half-liters hidden under their coats—something the bartender always pretended that he didn't see—they wandered out.

There was fresh snow outside. They walked as before, each with their own beer, down the hill, and a large, new blanket was spread between Buildings 1 and 2. As they came in, the evening was over. Rose Mary said good night. Inger couldn't sleep. She just lay thinking about the fresh snow and how they'd walked through it and how infinitely short time was. In the middle of the night she got up. She got dressed again and went outside. There she stood looking out over the snow. It was the most beautiful snow she'd ever seen. How could it be so soft and white?

And she jumped out into it. She headed out, foot by foot, down the long-side of a gigantic U, hopped carefully over to the top of an L several yards long, on down and back and forth in steady style on an equally large T, there she made the leap over to an I, and from here to a large and powerful M, back and forth in her own tracks to an A, and from there with undiminished strength to a new T, she maintained her style, now forcing her way down the long side of a new U, where she finally and without a false step made it through the last turn, she kept the edges sharp, and giving all she had she jumped over to a last, gigantic M.

She did it! She was at the finish. And she got her reward. Because in the morning Frida and Rose Mary came out and admired the ultimatum through the kitchen window, where it stood upside down in the snow. They laughed and celebrated: "Now that Hans Bekk Hansen and company will finally have to realize this is serious!"

It was serious. And Inger thought: I gave it one chance to not happen again. And I promised myself that if it did happen, I would take the consequences.

LOVE FROM A TO Z

In January Frida arrived with a book. It was a thick, unbound book, and she stood out in the hall and paged through it as soon as she got inside the door. It was *Love From A to Z* by Inge and Sten Hegeler, and here was something about the clitoris. "Clitoris?" Inger said. "Yes, clitoris!" Frida said, as if she'd known about it since she was a child. Inger wasn't sure that she should believe in it. Where was it? And if it really was somewhere, why should it have such an peculiar name? "It's a little bump," Frida said, and explained where it was located. But Inger didn't think there was anything that could be called anything at all where she said it was located, and she never quite understood what it looked like down there, you never really got a good look, either, and since the time she and Helga had looked at their bottoms in the mirror when they were children, she had never studied these regions. "It's the center of desire," Frida said. "You can get a clitoral orgasm, too, not just a vaginal orgasm."

They pored over the book and read about clitoral orgasms. It was a *myth* that a penis absolutely had to be inserted for a woman to have an orgasm. A myth! what an appropriate word for something that had absolutely nothing to do with mythology.

The book soon became the reason the war in the apartment

flared up again. Mina Thorsen thought that it was a typical example of absolutely unnecessary reading.

"It's supposed to be a mystery," Mina said, and matters did not improve when she arrived home right when the A to Z lay open on the kitchen table under the heading "Erection." Because this heading was illustrated, and Mina walked right in and saw the illustration. "Look at this, Mina!" Lidia shouted and pointed enthusiastically, and at that Mina walked right into 1311 and slammed the door. And Frida got mad at Lidia because she had been so direct, now the book was branded—as far as Mina was concerned—for all eternity.

Not a day went by in the apartment that they didn't talk about the clitoris. Soon not a day went by that they didn't talk about homosexuality either. Frida and Rose Mary talked about it as though it were a completely natural phenomenon. They thought that the condemnation of homosexuality was the result of prejudice, and that people who had these prejudices were the same people who supported racial discrimination, the oppression of women, the death penalty and Franco's Spain.

This was an enormously sensational speech. Everything Inger had heard until then about homosexuality from her own generation had been full of contempt and laughter. It wasn't true that the word hadn't been mentioned. It was mentioned. And the word was homo. It was a kind of vomit. A glob of fake vomit purchased at a novelty store, that flew through the air and fell to the floor with a plop—to folk's general amusement at parties. To then be danced over in a flat tango.— Tsjam-ta-RAM, you aren't one of them! tsja-RAM? they howled, and: "Do you know him?" and: "Did you see him?" And: "Buy 'The Friend'!" And "You can recognize them by their Adam's apples!" "Oh, I'm swooning, ha, ha, ha!" And in the middle of this atmosphere Frida suddenly sat there one day and said: "It would have been much more practical if you could make love to your girl friends." "Oh!" Inger said. "I couldn't conceive of that! Not even if I were on a desert island. With only women!"

She said that, admittedly ill at ease, for there was probably nothing she could conceive of more than being on such an island, but exactly how she could manage to make love with those present was just as remote to her as the island. It wasn't necessary either. All love was in the eyes.

Why would you want to make love to each other when your eyes could meet? It'd happened, too, on a rare occasion, that love had dwelled in a hand. To feel love in such a touch was higher than any intercourse she was capable of imagining. What would one want with more than looks and touches?

Words, perhaps. You needed words. To say—in some incomprehensible way—that the glances and the touch were there. If not to others, then at any rate to yourself.

But when you had these three things—glances, touch and words—why would you need anything else?

An arm, perhaps? An arm around a body? Yes.

Yes. Precisely that. If she ever got there, she knew she would have arrived in a kind of heaven. But she had no wish for more than this. Once you were in heaven, there'd be no more wishes, and you could finally, finally have peace.

One time—one single time—she'd been on the verge of getting to this heaven—and for a brief second she'd seen that there was a heaven over this one, too. They'd been playing badminton out in the garden in Edinburgh, and the shuttlecock had landed in her room, and suddenly Sheila was lying over her with her whole self. But Inger wasn't thinking about this as she sat by the kitchen table. She'd forgotten that. She'd shoved it down into the deepest darkness inside her, to the place where no living memory comes, and now she sat there and said: "I couldn't imagine that!"

Even so she knew she was lying.

"Homosexuality is quite common where there's only one sex," Rose Mary said. "Simone writes that female homosexuality is a conscious choice in a hopeless situation," Frida said. "A choice!" Inger exclaimed. "No one would choose that if they could avoid it!" "All human actions are a matter of choice," Frida said. "You are what you choose, according to Sartre," Rose Mary said. "But you're something before, too! I mean, I mean . . . You don't choose . . . your *gender*, for example. You don't choose your gender." "Your gender is not an action, but what you do with your gender." "Yes but, yes but . . . how do we know that homosexual people aren't a kind of gender?" "In order to be a homosexual person you must commit homosexual acts," Frida said. "No," Inger said. "You don't."

No one said a word.

As soon as Inger was alone with *Love From A to Z*, she looked up under H. Hair, Hatred, Harems, Hermaphrodite, Heterosexuality, Homoeroticism, Homophilia, Homosexuality.

Here it said that homosexuality among women was very rare. It could be caused by the fact that they had a domineering father. Homosexuality among men could be due to the fact that they had a domineering mother. In addition homosexuality could develop in places where there were only people of the same sex, for example in the trenches in wartime, and it could also be caused by the fact that a young person had identified with the sex he or she did not belong to, and in addition it said that there were many transitional stages: there were few people who were *solely* one or the other.

I'm one of those few people, Inger thought. Why me? And one word—in this otherwise unsatisfactory explanation— struck her with full force. The word *identified*. I've identified with the wrong person! That's the whole explanation. Haven't I always wished I was a boy? I bought *Texas*. And in it there was a sheriff named Buck Jones. He wore a dark sweater with a sheriff's star, and there were always some bandits who came to his little western town and kidnapped the bank director's daughter and took her up into the mountains. Here they bound and gagged her and placed her on the edge of a cliff, and in the picture she had fear in her eyes. Then they demanded a ransom from the bank director. But then Buck Jones came. He came with his star and his six-shooter and up to the cliff by way of a secret path, freed Diana, for that was her name, and Diana was happy, and Buck Jones rode back to his western town and delivered her to the bank.

This was where the big mistake was hidden.

Because she knew now that when she read all these stories, she never imagined for a moment that she was Diana, lying bound and gagged in the mountains. She thought she was Buck Jones. Instead of thinking that she found the secret path on her thoroughbred horse, she should have lain hoping to be rescued.

How come she hadn't understood this before? And now it was too late. Because she knew she would go through fire and water to rescue Rose Mary from the cliff.

They saw a movie called *The Children's Hour*. Two teachers, played by Shirley MacLaine and Audrey Hepburn, ran a girls' school. Rumors flew that the two teachers had a lesbian relationship. In the end the parents took their children out of the school. Audrey Hepburn was shaken. How could anything so untrue be whispered about? she asked. They certainly didn't have any relationship! "I love you," Shirley MacLaine replied.

Nothing on earth could have mirrored the shock at this remark better than Audrey Hepburn's terrified eyes. She had been completely unsuspecting! But the audience knew that Shirley MacLaine had been secretly spying on her for months from behind the drapes, when she went out with her fiancé. Stunned, Audrey Hepburn rushed out when this kernel of truth in the rumor about them was revealed, and when she came back, Shirley MacLaine had hanged herself in the closet.

A body dangles there. It's the end of January 1963. And Norwegian movie audiences had seen their first lesbian woman.

Rose Mary had a book. It was called *The Bell* by Iris Murdoch. Both Frida and Rose Mary had read it, and they talked about Iris whenever they weren't talking about Simone. Rose Mary, who was working on her master's in English, had decided to write her thesis on Iris. Inger borrowed the book.

For the first time she read about her own fate. She'd plowed through the world's love novels, descriptions of ocean voyages, emigrant books and great Russian novels; she'd read the Norwegian classics and now was in the middle of the English ones. In the books she'd met her own inner life, and books were what she secretly hoped she herself would write one day. But never anywhere had she met the feelings, thoughts and agony she was now reading about in Michael Meade.

Michael Meade! She loved Michael Meade. She suffered with him, trembled with him and had his nightmares. He loved Toby. The young, beautiful Toby who came to the community in Gloucestershire where Michael had sought refuge from his perversities, to live a pure life. It was a religious community—and Michael was seeking God. He had to give up the clergy because of his nature; he also had to give up teaching, and now he sought to live out his life here, in service to goodness. But then came Toby.

Toby just came. That was all he did. But that was enough. More than enough, and Michael saw him. He saw him, and one evening he got him drunk on West Country cider. Toby was sitting in the car next to Michael, who was driving. Michael felt his presence every second, and Toby dozed off. As he did, he halfway slumped against Michael and lay pressed against his arm. Michael felt the arm. He felt Toby's arm, and he wished the drive would never end.

But it did. They came to the gates of Imber Court, where they were living. Michael lifted Toby gently and went out and opened the gate. When he came back, and saw Toby there, so young and beautiful, still asleep, he bent down and kissed him.

This was the first kiss in world literature. Not even Scarlett O'Hara in Rhett Butler's arms or Erlend and Kristin Lavransdatter at Gerdarud could measure up to Michael when he kissed Toby at the gate in the car by Imber Court.

And Frida and Rose Mary had read this book! Everyone who had read the book had seen the kiss. And a lady in England, Iris Murdoch, had written about it. Where did she get it from?

One evening Jacob came. He said that he'd find it difficult

to play the role of lover, as they had discussed. "Because I'm not in love with you," he said. "I'm just sexually attracted to you, and then I would be exploiting you!"

She was startled at his honesty. If you only knew, Jacob, how well it suits me that you're not! she thought. Then she performed a scene that couldn't be interpreted in any other way than that the lack of infatuation definitely was not reciprocal. And when she'd done that, he left. As soon as he was gone, she made up her mind. "I've lied about my love life for the last time!" she thought. Then she went toward Rose Mary's door.

It was so quiet in there. Rose Mary was lying on the sofa with her brace on the floor and *The Spanish Civil War* in her lap, a thick, white book. Inger closed the door behind her and remained standing. "Do you want to come in?" Rose Mary said, and snapped her book shut. "Rose Mary," she said. "I've come to tell you something I will regret the rest of my life that I told you."

Then she went over to the window and looked out on Sogn Road as if there was something there she absolutely had to see. It was so awfully quiet in the room.

"Do you want to sit down?" Rose Mary said and indicated the edge of the bed. "It . . . it . . . it . . . ," Inger said. She walked a few steps back again, toward the door. Rose Mary sat up a little and patted the edge of the bed. "Come here!" Inger came, and Rose Mary stretched over for her pack of Teddy cigarettes and offered Inger one first, an English custom that she stuck to. She took one, Rose Mary lighted both it and her own. "What is it?"

"It is, it is, I can't say it," Inger said.

"Is it so terrible?"

She kept this up for a long time. For several minutes she only managed to get out some half sentences, back and forth.

"You just have to quit beating around the bush!"

But then she got completely mute. Rose Mary stretched her

hand out toward her. "Do you think it would be easier to say it if you held my hand?" Inger took it. "Will you promise not to let me down?" she finally said.

"Yes."

"Will you promise not to tell anyone?"

"Yes."

"But I'm so afraid that you'll stop liking me!"

"But I do like you!"

"Yes, but what if I've committed a murder?"

It got quiet. A murder? Rose Mary cleared her throat.

"But it can't be that bad, can it?"

"Oh yes!"

"Well, what is it then?"

"I think I'm homosexual," Inger said.

That wasn't what I came to say, Inger thought. I came to say: "I love you."

Rose Mary thought: She's young. She's four years younger than I am.

Inger thought: Now she knows! I've said it, and yet I'm still sitting here, the ceiling didn't fall in, there's still traffic on Sogn Road, and there was a civil war in Spain.

Rose Mary thought: How can I help her?

Inger thought: Her hand! Her slim, warm hand—is in mine. In every single spot in my hand I feel all her spots.

Rose Mary thought: She's hurting. What can I do? What would Simone say? What would Iris say? What would Frida say?

Inger thought: I'm happy now.

Rose Mary thought: What does she want? Does she want me?

Inger thought: I want you! Don't you see that?

Rose Mary thought: I've got to talk to Frida!

Inger thought: Oh, Lord, it's so good to find words for the worst thing!

Rose Mary thought: What do I say? What do I know about homosexuality? Is she going to keep sitting there, and what should I tell her to do?

Inger thought: But I did come to tell the truth. I have to tell her I love her. I have to do it now!

Rose Mary said: "You're young . . ."

Inger said: " . . . ?"

Rose Mary said: "If it's any comfort, I'm twenty-six and I still haven't found a man."

Inger said: "But I'd rather find a woman!"

Inger thought: But I've already found her.

Rose Mary said: "There's no way for you to know when some man'll come along that you'll fall in love with."

Inger said: "But then why hasn't he turned up already?"

Rose Mary said: "I think you should wait."

"Wait!" Inger said. "I've been waiting all my life!"

THE WORD IN GAUSTAD WOODS

Inger didn't want to give up. She didn't want to give up until she'd said: I love you. That's the only thing she wanted to say, and if she didn't get that out, her whole life, everything she had hoped for, her high school education at The Yellow Institution and her studies at the university were superfluous. "I love you" was inside everything that was the driving force behind whatever she did otherwise, even though she wanted to do many things and had an extremely eager and impatient drive to do them.

The words had come once before. In a half-dark hallway with Sheila on her knees. And even though Sheila hadn't answered, Inger knew that it was the rightest thing she'd ever said.

Then she sat down and wrote the first love letter of her life. She read through it.

Rose Mary is going to see this. Her beautiful eyes are going to meet my letters. They'll see: "Rose Mary, I love you! I love you and desire you!" And that's the only meeting I can ever hope for.

Inger looked at her words on the page and felt an intense joy at the thought of this meeting. That a blue ball-point pen on a white sheet of paper could bring about the meeting was a miracle just as great as the best books she'd read—yes, she was in the book now, at last she was in the book, in *Jane Eyre* and

Peasants at Sea, and she stood up abruptly and went straight through the books and into the woman that dwelled deep inside them, and delivered the letter.

Rose Mary Fernhill had spent her whole life reading. She'd passed all her exams with distinction, and finally she stood there with a Bachelor of Arts degree from Durham University and thought: I haven't learned enough. I want to learn something no one else can. So she ended up in Norway, and soon sat there with new rows of books behind her, and a Norwegian university education. In addition she'd been politically active through all her years of study and had read a number of books about all the important social issues that she absolutely did not need in order to pass her exams, but which she felt one was morally obligated to familiarize oneself with in order to be an aware and responsible human being. And she didn't know a thing about homosexuality.

Now she sat with a love letter from another woman in her hand.

Like all the others in the apartment, except for Mina Thorsen, Rose Mary had also plowed through *Love From A to Z.* And she had not skipped over "homosexuality" either. But she wasn't able to remember well enough what it said there. She'd been far more interested in the article on "Erogenous zones." Now she looked it up again, and what she noted was the word "few."

Homosexuals were in the minority. If Inger were homosexual, what kind of life would that be? She'd be relegated to a minority for the rest of her life. Maybe she wouldn't even want them?

What if she still had the slightest chance to escape? Shouldn't she try that instead? Or am I just being merciless and prejudiced now? Why should I ask her to wait when she doesn't want to? Maybe the only right thing would be to seduce her? Oh, shit! Rose Mary thought. If only I could talk to Frida!

But she couldn't talk to Frida. Never in her life had she needed advice so badly. And now she couldn't have it! She'd promised not to tell anyone, and she'd given her promise without reservations. She'd never had a hard time keeping her mouth shut. But she did now.

Frida was cheerfully curious. "What're you two talking about until one-thirty in the morning?" she asked. But she didn't get any answer. Through the door to 1314 the incessant clatter of Inger's typewriter could be heard. "What're you writing?" Frida asked. "Letters to Agamemnon," Inger replied. "He's dead, of course, and made-up, besides. I couldn't find a safer person to confide in."

They'd been to see *Electra*, and now they were practicing looking like Irene Papas in the hallway. The look consisted of walking down the hall, and suddenly turning, very slowly, but just with your head, and staring at the person behind you with murderous and beautiful eyes.

Frida and Rose Mary practiced the Electra look. And Inger stared at the fatal glances, and Frida put two and two together. And unlike most people of her generation, she got four.

"Rose Mary," she said one day, as they sat drinking coffee without the Child. "Did Inger tell you that she thinks she's homosexual?" Rose Mary didn't answer. Frida said: "You don't have to tell me."

"No! But I can't keep from being honest either!"

Frida looked at her. Sat with her legs tucked under her in the corner of the sofa and gestured. "Is she in love with you?" "That's what she says." "Is that so strange? She has good taste," Frida said objectively. "And what's the difference anyway? Is there that big a difference between being homosexual and being heterosexual?" For what Frida had noted in Inge and Sten's article was the expression "transitional stages."

"I'm wondering about that, too," Rose Mary said. "For example, I've often wondered why you and I don't go to bed together. I like you more than many of the boys I've slept with."

"Maybe we don't have the *desire* to?"

"How can we know that we don't have the desire if we haven't tried it?"

"But you can feel the desire before you try it!"

"Yes, but when you do something about it, you get more desire."

"Or less."

They laughed a little.

There actually were rumors around Sogn dormitories that Rose Mary Fernhill and Frida Røyseth were lesbians. They were started by one of their many political enemies to malign them in the worst possible way. They didn't lower themselves to deny it, which strengthened the theory further.

"But if *we* tried it, somehow it wouldn't be serious. You don't become a homosexual by discovering each other's erogenous zones, I don't believe that."

"But if someone did it, that is to say we, then we'd be homosexual. You are what you do."

"I don't feel that's true, in this case."

Suddenly they'd arrived at a point where Sartre could not help them. No one could help them. The only person who traveled around the country with advice in this area was a Swedish doctor by the name of Lars Ullerstam. He'd given lectures in a jam-packed Dovre Hall Student Union about "The Erotic Minorities," and introduced the idea of the erotic Samaritan. The erotic Samaritan helped the sexual deviants by satisfying their urges, yes, they ought to set up clinics and aid stations at state expense, and consider it all a natural part of health care. Everyone listened with bated breath. No one had ever said anything so strange in Norway before.

"But could you see yourself, Rose Mary, being a sort of erotic Samaritan?"

"It certainly wouldn't hurt me. But would it help her?"

"Maybe it would help her to become homosexual?"

"She says she already is."

"Do you accept that? Maybe she has a spark of heterosexuality that she just hasn't discovered yet."

"That's what I said to her, too."

"What did she say to that?"

"'Wait!' she said. 'I've been waiting all my life.'"

"But Rose Mary—you know it's not your responsibility!"

"Yes it is! I feel that it is. I can't just wash my hands of it. I have to know if the advice I'm giving her is right."

"According to Sartre, when someone asks for advice they are really just looking for confirmation of a choice they've already made. Because when you choose the adviser, you've already made a choice."

"And what had Inger chosen then, by choosing me?"

"You."

The conversation went on for a long time. And they were deeply uncertain of their conclusion.

"Maybe we're not so liberated when it comes right down to it," Frida said.

"No, maybe we're not. But I don't know if it has anything to do with being liberated. I accept what she says, and even so I think: I don't want to take the responsibility of leading her in the wrong direction."

"Wrong direction? Why do you say that, when we don't think there's anything morally wrong with it?"

"People do not tolerate differentness," Rose Mary said. "They can only stand for it in small quantities and with a good explanation. They have to constantly make sure that they are above whatever isn't as it should be. When I was little, I always thought I could never stand to marry someone who hadn't listened to 'The Goon Show.' Many times I think, I have to get back to England, because I can't handle all these Norwegians, and in any case they have not heard 'The Goon Show.' Other times I think: I can't stand other handicapped people. What are they doing here? I can't stand to look at them. And in any event I can't stand the thought that I might have something in common with them, just because they limp—or whatever they do. Then there are other times when I can't stand people who aren't exactly like *me!* Where will Inger fit in? Among people she maybe can't stand?"

"But Rose Mary, you're contradicting yourself now! You're saying that people want to have someone who is like themselves, but at the same time they can't stand them."

"Yes! That's exactly what I'm saying. But that's not really a contradiction. I'm just saying: If what Simone de Beauvoir says is correct, that homosexuality in women is a choice in an impossible life situation, then I don't know if I want to help her to choose it."

"But why not?"

"Because it is the hardest path to take!"

Finally.

Finally she'd managed to say the thing she feared most of all. Finally she'd managed to say the thing she'd always known would have caused the whole Phoenix steps to collapse and the world to fall down onto everyone's heads. And there wouldn't have been any picture. Finally she'd said the thing that everyone would have thrown up at, if they somehow survived the catastrophe. And she was in worse shape than ever. For the only thing she wanted was to come to her.

She hadn't foreseen this. By listening to her words and not throwing up, Rose Mary had become a miracle. Before this she'd just loved her. Now she loved her as one can only love a miracle, when you know that the only thing preventing the earth from collapsing is that she is walking on its surface.

And with this completely new thing that came into her life she knew, too, that she'd come to her with a terrible hope that Rose Mary would say: "Come!"

She received a reply to her love letter. It was written in blue ink, a fountain pen, she followed all the loops, curves, lines, ovals, all these remarkable shapes that are the alphabet, and never had she seen a more beautiful letter. She'd been in all these loops. Her hand, the one that had held the pen, had moved through every single little mark, page after page, and as she did that, she thought all the myriads of thoughts that were required to assemble the alphabet in exactly this order. She read the letter again and again. She read it, looked at it, put it back in the envelope, took it out again, read it again, finally she knew it by heart. She lay down on the sofa and thought about the letter.

In the letter it said that Rose Mary had wondered if she should seduce her. She liked the word. She looked at this particular word for many seconds before she read on. That wouldn't be difficult. "But I don't want to lead you afield," it said after that. "Lead afield?" Inger thought. Strictly speaking the expression should be: "Lead astray." She took pleasure in the little mistake.

Lead me afield? Afield? Afield? But that's what I've been for a long time, every minute of the day, every time I see you I'm afield, it doesn't matter what you do!

Oh! What should I do? How can I quit being afield when I have eyes? But she had to quit. She would just have to make up her mind to quit having eyes. There was no other solution.

But she had eyes. There was nothing she could do about that. And with these she saw the most beautiful person in the world every day. She saw her morning, noon and night, and that's why she wasn't as unhappy as she was.

She was unhappy. She longed more than she'd ever longed. But there was also a life inside her she'd never known before. What should she do with this life? She used it to go straight into Rose Mary's room and thank her for the letter. Then they discussed whether it was possible to discuss politics with one's parents. Rose Mary thought it was impossible.

When Inger went into her room again after this conversation, she felt like she'd been beaten black and blue. She'd had to leave with her mission unaccomplished. What was her mission? That she didn't get to hold her hand once more? She smoked a cigarette. Then she went back. Rose Mary had gone to bed and turned off the light. She stood in the dark room.

I'm forcing myself on her, she thought. This is wrong. But she didn't turn away.

"I'm left with an intense feeling that my feelings don't matter to you," she said.

"Why do you say that? Was there something else you wanted to say?"

Suddenly she went blank. She'd spent the whole day writing a letter to her. What more was there to say? Inger couldn't fathom what else there was to say. And now she was here. That was all she wanted. She sat down. She stammered out some words. "Since I told you, it's gotten so much more real."

"But what do you really want?"

"Actually I just want to sit here and talk to you."

Rose Mary found a Teddy cigarette for each of them.

"Inger, does your difficulty now consist of figuring out which way you want to go?"

Then there was a long silence. Then she answered: "My difficulty now consists of the fact that I want you."

They smoked in the dark. Rose Mary said: "Do you think it's so terribly necessary to tell people that you love them?"

Inger had no idea what she should answer. Did this mean that the most important of all words in life were completely unnecessary? Here she'd spent her whole youth not saying some words that now may turn out to be superfluous—and not at all in line with either Iris or Simone.

"I don't like the word 'to love,'" Rose Mary said. "I prefer 'to like.' It seems to me that when someone says: 'I love you,' they're really saying: 'I own you.'"

Inger was completely confused. She felt like she'd screwed up. What did owning have to do with loving? Did you own the sunset? But the statement ignited a spark of joy. Because if Rose Mary used the word "to like" in the meaning of "to love," then she loved her. "Inger," Rose Mary said, "if it's true you want me, then I'll regard you the same way I would have regarded a boy I liked, but didn't want to go to bed with."

"But I'm not a boy!" she burst out. For in the same instant

her hopes burst.

"You'll just have to accept the situation as it is," Rose Mary said. "How would things have been for me if I'd just sat down and cried over my leg?"

"But your leg shows!"

"Yes, well maybe that's not a good comparison."

"Yes, it is a good comparison. I've often wished that homosexuality showed on the outside. Then I wouldn't have to lie! Just think if your leg had been invisible. You were really limping, but no one saw it. You walked more slowly, but no one waited, they thought you were walking next to them, they didn't pay any attention, but you were really far behind, you didn't make the streetcar, you never made the streetcar, you. . . ."

"Don't get hotheaded!"

"Hotheaded? Why shouldn't I be hotheaded? When I have to be ashamed of the best thing in life, that everybody else just enjoys like the most natural thing in the world!?"

"Do you have to be angry at me?"

"I don't have anyone else to take it out on!"

"But what would it mean to consider your needs? Then I'd always have to watch you out of the corner of my eye! I don't want that! You said when you came that you hoped my attitude toward you wouldn't change. Now it seems like you want it to change. I don't know what you want."

"I want to sleep with you."

Rose Mary was silent for a while. "But what would you get out of it? You wouldn't get any pleasure from me lying there completely passive, would you?" "I didn't imagine that you would be passive." "But I couldn't be any other way. That is, I probably couldn't even do that." "Why not? After all I've spent my entire youth returning caresses that were completely incomprehensible and of no interest to me. Why shouldn't you just tolerate it one single time?" "Of course I'd tolerate it. But it wouldn't be right towards you." "But I assure you that I'm totally prepared to take the consequences!" "Have you given any thought at all to the consequences? It wouldn't help you the least bit. You wouldn't be satisfied with the one time. And I'd still be around you all the time, while you'd be tortured, wanting me . . . I don't know how you feel now, but I'm positive it would be a thousand times worse." "I know that. Why should you care about that?" "Because I care about you."

The words sank down in her like the blessing they were. She was speechless. She could have died on the spot, and she would have attained her goal. She mumbled some unintelligible babble.

"Yes, but you're not unimportant to me!" Rose Mary replied. "Just sexually. I'm not a homosexual . . . unfortunately. And I don't want to be the reason that you go around suffering!"

"You are anyway!"

Rose Mary sighed. "Don't be dumb! If I am now, then it's completely undeserved. But if I were to actively seduce you, then I'd have to begin to assume a certain responsibility."

"That certainly sounds humanitarian," Inger said sarcastically. "It's not the least bit humanitarian. It's thoroughly and completely selfish." "It is, is it? So actually it's just out of consideration to yourself that you say no. Not to avoid leading me afield? Or to spare me? But to spare yourself?" "When you get right down to it perhaps it is. Maybe I'd simply think it was unpleasant." "Old prejudices. Women don't have anything to do with each other, like that." "You're underestimating me." "No, actually I think I'll take a rain check on that."

"Inger, I think this conversation is starting to get rather meaningless."

"Yes." She stood up. "Sleep well."

"You, too."

"Rose Mary?"

"Yes?"

"I do care for you."

She said it with emphasis on the do. And she'd seldom uttered a more superfluous sentence.

After that was said, she went out. She went straight into her room. And there she wrote down the whole conversation. There was something about it that made her want to remember it. She knew that after a while you forgot even the most important conversations, even though you didn't think so while they were going on, because nothing was more important then than it.

But words flow. They're said. They mean everything. And they disappear again. And you are left not knowing why you did what you did or felt the way you felt.

Few conversations in this world are such that they make any of this clear. But sometimes it happens. That a conversation comes—and you answer quite nakedly in it. And she knew, as she wrote, that this was the most honest conversation she'd ever had with another human being.

The spring that came was more beautiful than all other springs, and it consisted of controlling the urge to go into Rose Mary's room. The streams trickled and the birds chirped so clearly, but she mustn't go in. She'd forced herself on her—with a knowledge Rose Mary absolutely did not want, and could absolutely not do anything with. She didn't want her. She'd just have to get that into her head.

But it was no good. She'd been searching all her life—for a person who was worthy of her confidence. She'd found her. And the only person she could go to had become the only person she could *not* go to.

She did go. She sat in her room, and for hours they could sit like that and avoid talking about homosexuality. There wasn't any more to say about it either, for that matter. Rose Mary had a party. They played *The Weavers in Carnegie Hall*. It was a great record, full of folk songs and freedom songs from many countries, they drank beer and the night was light, there were a lot of people in the room, they got intoxicated, the beer keg was emptied, gradually the room was emptied of people, finally only Rose Mary and Inger were left, and Inger thought:

I have to go. I have to go.

Rose Mary was lying on the sofa close by. A Hebrew song of greeting was hurled out into the room, sung in a round. *Shalom chaverim!* First in unison, just broken by small banjo tones, *lehitraot, lehitraot, Shalom, Shalom,* then the same again. The song rose—one-part, two-part, three-part, four-part, until finally it was gathered into a new Shalom. But here the banjo began reverberating fully. The song went up a half pitch, and in a new minor key the message was brought forth, and Inger was lifted up by the music, noticed how its four-part harmony raised her up from the chair she was sitting on and straight into Rose Mary's arms: "I love you," she said.

From the point where "Shalom Chaverim," sung by The Weavers in Carnegie Hall, goes up a half pitch on: "Great tidings we bring, and peace on earth!" and until the song ends on a unison "Shalom," no more than fifty seconds have gone by. When it was over, Inger had experienced everything she'd come for in this world.

Rose Mary sat as before. She'd neither pushed her away nor pulled her toward her. She'd allowed her to be there, and held her. When the song was over, she sat up in bed, and they let go. "I don't know what to say," Rose Mary said. "I feel so small compared to you."

Small? Inger thought. How can you be small when I'm small? I'm the one who's small. How can I make you small by loving you?

One evening, soon after this, Rose Mary didn't come home at night. Inger listened in vain for her footsteps and lay awake. In the morning she saw her coming out of a doorway in Building 2, with one of the leaders of the Spain committee, Søren Haug. They stood there on the step and hesitated a little in the sunshine, then they each went their own way.

According to a medieval theory jealousy dwells in the eye. It's a perfectly concrete bodily substance that flows from the pupil and strikes the object of jealousy in the same way that other bodily fluids find their natural way out, and it's just as impossible for you to stop the flow as it would be for the sun to prevent itself from shining.

Now Inger's eye shone on Søren Haug. A few days later he was there again. Rose Mary took him into her room. Music and voices could be heard through the door. Regardless of what medieval theories said, jealousy dwelled in the ear. A stream that knew what was going on, and hated it. And she fervently wished that she were Søren Haug.

If you were just a boy, it was okay. You didn't have to know each other. You could just fuck.

For several minutes she sat in a sort of trance-like state at the thought of being Søren Haug. She couldn't go in. He was there. The whole spring consisted of not going in. But now she couldn't. She marched out into the kitchen and got a beer. She went back, and drank it, quickly. She grabbed a piece of paper. Without a plan she began digging out everything she had written. She pulled out of drawers and cupboards, from bookshelves and notebooks, from an old, brown folder, and scattered it out over the floor. Soon the whole floor was covered with white papers. There lay all the Beginnings, the letters to Agamemnon, rejected articles for *Dagbladet*, the conversation, the two chapters about the Norwegian au pair girl Berit, who longed for Ralph, and a number of other things she'd written during the nearly two years she'd been a student. She stared at it. She grabbed a paper and read. She only had to read one line, then she knew the whole thing, and it made her sick to look at it.

"Myself!" she thought, and crumpled it up and flung it into the wastebasket. She snatched sheet after sheet. Myself, myself, myself. Soon the whole wastebasket was full. And half of the sheets still lay on the floor. She flattened them out so there'd be room for more. Finally all her words were in the basket. They filled it to the brim. It was a large, gray wastebasket. She embraced it and carried it out into the night.

The night was warm. It was late in May, and during the past few days summer had arrived. She walked up the path between the little houses in Solvang Garden Colony. The tiny, pale green leaves had just come out, they stood ready to burst in the light night. She came to a clearing. Here she emptied the basket and put a match to it.

In the light of the flames she saw a word. She'd made up her mind not to see. Because then she would regret it. But she saw. And the word that came to view inside a brown scorched edge of paper was: Helga.

This was Papa's poem to Helga, written the first midsummer night she wasn't alive. It was a poem full of Papa's grief, and his eyes saw the glowworms shining in the heather. Papa had given her this poem, and now it had—purely by mistake— ended up in a bonfire.

It was too late to rescue the poem. She saw the words in the fire. Helga? she thought. Was it a message? Do you see me? Do you see me standing here, burning everything I've written?

And Helga saw her sister through the night, she saw her from wherever she might be, over the edge of the forest on the little meadow, through the view of Oslo, and she held her close with her eyes.

"Papa," she said. "There's something I have to tell you!"

"What is it?"

"Well, you see. There was one night at the dormitory. And I was feeling sad."

"What were you sad about?"

"Well, I was . . . just sad. So I took everything I'd written and took it up into Gaustad Woods and burned it. And as I stood there I saw your poem was there, the one you wrote to Helga the first Midsummer Eve . . ." Inger and Papa sat and remembered

Midsummer night—the first one you weren't alive—is over.
The sun has turned tonight
for the first time without your glance toward the sky.
The bonfires have burned. You couldn't see them.
Some glowworms still shine in the brown heather
where your foot trod and stumbled.
All the happy shouts that echo in the night remind us of you.
There is something suspended in *our* being—your existence!
Grief? What do we know of grief and joy?
Hold me
and protect my soul.
Let the flowers on your grave
sing their song
like you—and we
—my child!

But they didn't know if they remembered the whole poem, just lines. "Inger, why were you sad?" Papa asked again. And he was very near. But he didn't get an answer. The answer had gone up in smoke over Oslo, and it'd never be given again.

HORMONES AND SILENCE

Suddenly there was a title. *Homosexuality* by D.J. West. It was listed in the *New Stateman*'s catalog of new Pelican Books. And it was quite likely that the book could be purchased at Cammermeyer's Bookstore on Karl Johans gate.

One didn't dare do that.

How was one supposed to get hold of the book?

The situation of homosexuals in Norway in the 1960s has later been compared to the situation of the Norwegian Resistance workers during World War II. The leaders of the Home Front had meetings with sacks over their heads. No one knew who the others were. The enemy was so overwhelming, and had such gruesome methods, that no one must know the others' identities. The 1960s passed into history with the designation "the golden '60s"—with the year 1968 as the banner year. This was a falsification. In most areas the 1960s were dark years—as far as revolt was concerned. The event that shook people's souls most at the Blindern campus in 1968 was the announcement that Crown Prince Harald was going to marry Sonja Haraldsen. That even surpassed the report of Martin Luther King's death, and people in the various departments sat with cheeks aglow, confiding to each other that they once upon a time had attended a lecture for preparatory exams in Latin with the future Crown Princess, and one professor after another remembered well and with absolute clarity Miss Haraldsen in particular, of all of his thousands of students.

It was in the 1970s that the rebellion began. "1968" was a date imported from the streets of Paris, whose cobblestones were once again torn up. And the homosexuals were the last in line to cast their stones.

Inger's back in 1963. She can't escape it. There was no way she could jump ten years ahead in time to the year when the first book on homosexuality written by a homosexual under the author's true name would come out in her country. She didn't know a thing about the revolt that would come. She didn't know what it was to rebel. She looked at herself in the same way, she realized many years later, that the Danish novelist, Herman Bang, looked at himself. A man's soul in a woman's body. (He, naturally: A woman's soul in a man's body.) It was a trick of nature. An error in construction that is *no one's* fault. That was why there was no one to rebel against either.

So she read D.J. West. She did manage to get hold of the book, even though actually purchasing it was impossible. But she sent the woman she loved and couldn't have down to Cammermeyer's Bookstore. The woman she loved and couldn't have was safe—even though the rumor said otherwise—and besides, life had taught her not to give a damn.

Here she read about science's hunt for hormones. For years they'd been studying identical twins, hermaphrodites and homosexuals of both sexes, done tests and performed analyses, followed developmental histories and proposed hypotheses. And it had not been possible for them to find a single, little tiny hormone that caused homosexuality.

The most interesting cases were the hermaphrodites. Small babies who were born with the foundation for both male and female sexual organs. Here the surgeons had to make a quick and arbitrary choice, and remove the foundations of the sex they decided the baby did not belong to. One would think that they'd often be wrong, and that there would as a result be more homosexuals among hermaphrodites than in the population as a whole. But that was not the case. Most of them became heterosexuals, completely in line with the sexual organ the surgeons had allowed them to keep. In other words: the hermaphrodites were raised to be heterosexual. They quite simply went along.

And some did not go along. Just like in the population as a whole. Why some went along and others didn't, consequently became the object of countless studies. All with equally inconclusive results. Homosexuality was and would remain a mystery. Perhaps it wasn't supposed to be explained at all? One should leave well enough alone!

The conclusion lifted Inger several feet off the ground. Why this crusade against homosexuality? Why all these efforts to find out why, when there wasn't any why—other than the same why one could ask when blue anemones bloomed in the woods at Rødskogen in the spring and ice formed in the town moats. She was the object of an injustice! She had reason to be indignant!

The book helped her move a good many miles ahead in her thoughts, even if it didn't help her rush through time.

Papa had always said: "Remember this, Inger, that if there's anything you need, you can always come to me." In a way that was true. He was there. Without her knowing it, he was an enormous security in her life, despite all his unreasonableness and outbursts of anger. She knew he felt more connected to her than to any other person, and that he wanted her to go where he hadn't been able to go. He was always afraid that foolish philanderers and potential sons-in-law would prevent her from doing that. Suddenly it struck her that there was nothing that would have suited Papa more than her coming to tell him that she was a homosexual. Then there'd no longer be anyone he'd need to shove down the steps.

Even so she was silent. First of all for the same reason she was silent with everyone. She was ashamed. But next because she knew he would say: "That's because you're too fond of me."

In no time at all he'd make her emotional life revolve around himself. But it wasn't about him. That she loved another woman had nothing to do with Papa, with her love for him or her attachment, anger, admiration and powerlessness towards him, or anything that she felt or could feel for him. Wasn't there room for several people in a heart? And why should the experience of beauty and wisdom in another person have a cause anyway?

She sat there in silence, because she didn't want to sit and listen to reasons. She was who she was and felt what she felt, and Papa never got an explanation for what he called her lonely *auto da fé* in the night.

The result was that he brooded. Because the story made a remarkable impression on him, he saw it like a symbol, and it didn't let go. There was someone exploiting her. She was under some strong influence or other that she couldn't escape. And even though he'd often wondered where the woman in her was, he still saw this influence in the shape of a male. So one day he had a horrible suspicion, and he immediately aired it with Evelyn: "Tell me, is Inger sleeping with Negroes?"

The fact was that Ellen had gone to visit Inger during a vacation, and there she'd met Martin Robinson from Jamaica. This was the first time she'd ever seen a Negro, and she came home all excited and told them.

Ørnulf couldn't get the question out of his head, and he confronted Inger with it every time she was home. When she wasn't there he pestered Evelyn with it every evening.

"She's sleeping with Negroes," he said, and looked gloomily out into the room.

"When are you going to cut out that rubbish!?" Evelyn said.

"Good lord!" Inger said when she was home. "I'm with whomever I like, as far as you're concerned." "So it is a Negro, then?" "Oh come on, Papa, if you have that attitude, then I guess it was true what that anti-Nazi mob said to you that night!"

But she immediately regretted her remark. Because he hadn't done anything wrong. Not then.

211

BJØRNEGÅRD APARTMENT
BUILDING AND LONGING

One evening during the war Ørnulf had been to a dance at the Ormelet Hotel. It was in the middle of the summer, but Evelyn was pregnant and didn't go along. So he was bored and decided to walk home along the shore. But when he came to a grove of trees he noticed three figures following him. They came closer and shouted at him: "You double-crossing pig! You goddamn sympathizer!" And before he knew what was happening, they were on top of him. Just then they'd come to a steep cliff by a ravine—of the type that criss-crosses all of Tjøme—and he took up the fight there. Naturally it was hopeless and they were able to beat him to a pulp before he finally managed to turn to his only possibility for escape, namely down the slope. He hurt himself badly and ran all the way home, and his face was so battered that when Evelyn saw him, she almost didn't recognize him.

From that day on a vengeance festered inside Ørnulf that he was never able to carry out. He didn't know the men, though he suspected that one of them was the son of a ship-owner from Tønsberg, and there was no way to get revenge. Besides, history had proved the three men right.

When he took his pathology exam in 1942 he was given a patient that he couldn't manage to diagnose. Professor of Medicine Kjartan Mikkelsen and Assistant Professor Lødrup hated him. He always received the best grades and had gotten an A+ in Latin. But that was before the war. "The man with the photographic memory," his fellow students called him. But when the war came, and it turned out that the man with the photographic memory chose the wrong side, they'd tried to finish him off. How did one finish off a man with a photographic memory when he was going to take a final exam in pathology? Well, one has the ingenious idea of giving him a healthy patient. What, one said then, what is wrong with this patient? And then one laughed in one's quiet professor mind, cast a secret glance at one's associate, full of gleeful irony, and then one began waiting for the answer. And the answer came. Hesitatingly, fumblingly. The man with the photographic memory examined his patient from top to bottom. In his head, equipped with this remarkable photo album, were recorded all the diseases on heaven and earth. He listened and tapped, peeked and poked at his healthy patient. But he didn't find any of the hundreds of diseases he'd amassed in his head for seven years. What the hell could it be? The professor and the assistant professor waited. They had plenty of time. One shouldn't make a diagnosis too hastily. Diagnosis was the most important art in all of medicine. How far could you get if you didn't master that? No. Take your time, my boy. You damn nazi-swine. You German-loving devil. What's wrong with this patient? Medical student Ørnulf Holm cleared his throat and speculated. He had now examined the patient from all angles and there was obviously not a thing to be found. That was damn bad luck, he thought. What illness could he have forgotten? What symptoms had he forgotten to explore? The clock was ticking. Soon he would have to say something. He shifted his weight a little, shot a quick look at the professor, back to the patient. "There might possibly be an early sinusitis," he said. "But I can't find much." The professor nodded. The assistant professor nodded. Shortly thereafter they withdrew. Pretended that they were consulting in the side room. Ørnulf waited nervously, confused. Something had gone wrong this time, he knew that, he could barely say anything sensible at all about the patient. Now he would end up ruining his degree just because something had gone right by him. And in pathology! His best subject since anatomy.

Professor Mikkelsen and Assistant Professor Lødrup came out again. They looked at him with poorly feigned regret in their eyes. Shook their heads. "That will be a C minus," Lødrup said. The professor nodded. "C minus, yes," he repeated, as if it were an exquisite vintage wine he was tasting.

C minus! No human being could have uttered a more detestable phrase to Ørnulf's ears. It was as if the heavens tumbled down over his head, over all of his photographic thoughts and all his dreams. All his hopes of becoming—something big. Becoming—what he was. C minus! What disgrace and dishonor. Ørnulf looked away. Felt their eyes on him. The professor exclaimed: "There was nothing wrong with the patient you had, Holm. You should have realized that." "Yes," the assistant professor said eagerly, the stupid louse, "it's not unheard of that one is consulted by a patient who would *like* to be sick, but who isn't in the slightest. One must be capable of seeing through that." What nonsense! Ørnulf thought. He'd better watch that mediocre mouth of his, or I'll diagnose him frontwards and backwards. Just wait! But it wouldn't be now. Now all he could do was stand there and accept their ridiculous and unfair judgement.

And forever after, too, of course. Inger knew this, and she regretted her remark. She wondered if that was how the war really ruined Papa. But did he have to ruin Mama because of that?

And Ørnulf sat in his apartment in Bjørnegården. It'd been twenty-one years since this event took place at the University of Oslo. But here he sat during the late night hours telling this story to Evelyn. She was hearing it for the fiftieth time. Perhaps the seventy-fifth time. And for the fiftieth, or perhaps the seventy-fifth time, she nodded and agreed with him. She nodded and followed his story in every detail, said "yes" and "no," and "yes, that was unfair." But she could no longer manage to bring any fervor to her indignation.

He was dissatisfied. Because the fervor in his own resentment was undiminished. Yes, didn't it even increase a little each time he told the story? Evelyn almost thought so.

But now he was dissatisfied with her. "You don't understand anything," he said. She was listening. But finally she didn't say anything more, and then she concluded that there "wasn't anything more to say!"

"But you have to admit that it was a boorish prank!" Ørnulf said, looking at her. And Evelyn thought that the episode was just as outrageous now as then. But all the strength was pumped out of her towards this old wrong, and besides she didn't know if she thought that "boorish" was the right word.

"It was a terrible thing to do," she said. "Terrible thing!" he repeated. No. Clearly this expression wasn't good enough.

"They should be shot slowly," he said.

"Ørnulf? I think I'm going to go to bed."

"You're going to bed *now*?"

"It's one-thirty."

When Inger got home, this was what she came to. Their whole history was in the walls. She knew it, and it never changed. Every time she came home Papa was still being attacked by three upper-class anti-Nazis and he still was getting a C minus in pathology. But each time Mama had become more sick of hearing about it.

Mama and Papa were sitting in the living room, they were arguing, and they still had gotten married in Potsdam in 1937. Their history was their history. But she wasn't in it anymore. She had her own, that they didn't know. Maybe they thought she was a part of their history, and she was, too, of course, but she was making herself a new one. How was she going to get Mama and Papa to see her history?

She couldn't do it. She neither dared to nor wanted to.

. . .

215

Evelyn realized that her health was broken. And she blamed herself. Her ruined state had come so slowly, and for a long time she thought of it as a result of nerves. The hives were a reaction to psychological anxiety. But tests showed that she had protein in her urine and that she needed another gallstone operation. Her liver wasn't functioning as it should. Her body hadn't tolerated all her attempts at suicide.

It was several years since the last attempt. Ørnulf and the children were sleeping, and she emptied a box of sleeping pills. Then she had gone into Ørnulf's office and slashed her wrist.

She'd sat in the chair where she usually sat, leaned on the desk with the bleeding arm before her. When she saw the blood, she began to cry. Inside the weeping was new life. She grabbed the telephone and called Rita and told her what she had done. Then she passed out and woke up in the hospital.

Inger had come to visit her then. She was seventeen, and when Evelyn saw her, she felt terribly sorry. Inger came over to the bed, and with an arm that was so weak that she could barely lift it, she pressed her hand out from under the blanket and took hold of Inger's. She so dearly wanted to ask for forgiveness.

But Ørnulf hadn't read these signals. The same thing was repeated time and again. He promised to change, and did for fourteen days. He couldn't do it! Not even her attempted flight a year and a half ago had given him the shock he needed. He demanded, just as he'd done since they were young, that she sit up and drink with him until one-thirty. Then they went to bed, and he fell asleep. And Evelyn got up again and took a sleeping pill.

Now her body was protesting against her behavior. For years she'd been campaigning for them to lead a healthier life. But after her flight it was as if there weren't any protest left in her. The swim over Grimestad Bay was the last straw. At least that was a healthier way to end it all, Evelyn thought.

But the water had had the same effect as the blood. When she had gotten far enough out, she wanted to live after all. Not because she wanted to live. She didn't want to live. It was just that she didn't die. But she wasn't going to do it herself.

Now she was living on without wanting to live, because it was wrong to take your life when you had children who needed you. She longed to die. Whenever she heard about someone who had died, she envied them.

Every time Inger was home she was homesick for the dormitory. Bjørnegården had become so strange. The dormitories at Sogn did not exist here, and Bjørnegården didn't exist at Sogn. Her life had always been connected before. It was right outside the door, up the kitchen stair to Lillian, out into Kirkeparken, down the hill. Everyone she knew, knew each other, and she longed to get away from everyone so that she could become a new person. Now she'd become a new person, but where was everyone?

They lived lives like she did, spread all over, she saw them occasionally, but they weren't right outside anymore, and life disappeared from Fredrikstad. She could come to the station and walk down the familiar streets, where every street corner and every rooftop reminded her of games she'd played and thoughts she'd thought, and yet the streets had gotten narrow and the houses small, and the road from the station to Bjørnegården so strangely short to walk, as if she suddenly had put on seven-league boots. Then she let herself into the apartment and everything was as before.

Time stood still. She sought refuge in the little bedroom. In here, where she could sit and write, time started moving again. The only place where life was connected was on paper. She wrote, and felt regret. Burning everything she had written, what was the point of that? The conversation she'd had—she longed for it—no matter how futile it had been. All her love was futile. But then she'd had the conversation. A presence was in it. She could read it over and over. Now it was gone. She missed it, missed her words, and realized that she didn't know them by heart at all, as she'd believed that night, and every time she came across something she'd overlooked then, she read it immediately, full of joy at the reunion. If she wiped out her tracks, then her life would never hang together.

She sat down and wrote for hours, as if to make up for her foolish act. Life flowed on. In the middle of it all came Mama's knock on the door of the little bedroom. "Come in!" she shouted, disappointed. Mama wanted her. All her thoughts immediately disintegrated. "Inger! You have to come in and help me. Now he's saying that woman is man's slave." "Ohhhh!" groaned Inger. "What do you think, is she?" Evelyn asked.

It was a question. A completely sincere question. Mama wanted to know the answer!

"No," Inger said.

She marched into the living room. It was ten-thirty. She felt the urge—which she got now and then—to go right up to him, without a word, and slap his face.

Papa sat in the corner, as always. With his opinions. And a tense, glowering look. It was the devil's hour in the living room. "What delusions are you laboring under?" Inger said.

"Woman is man's slave," he answered.

"There, you hear!" Evelyn said.

"Shut up!" he bellowed.

"You shut up!" Inger shouted.

"Speak properly," he said.

"Thanks, the same to you."

They sat down and shut up. Waited. Both Inger and Evelyn waited in silence. Papa's silence. Evelyn drew a breath.

"Don't interrupt!" he shouted.

"She was just breathing," Inger said.

"No! That's a lie. She was going to say something."

Inger and Evelyn looked at each other. The look made them feel like laughing. In the middle of the weirdness. The weirdness was so enormous that there was nothing else to do about it.

218

"We should have gotten you on tape," Evelyn said.

"There! Did you say something or didn't you?"

"I said . . ."

"Answer! Did you say something or didn't you?"

"Oh, Papa! She has to be allowed to say something, doesn't she? Have you gone off your rocker?"

"She claimed that she wasn't about to say something. Didn't she claim that?"

Silence.

"Answer!"

"No, Papa. *I'm* the one who claimed she was only breathing. Mama didn't say anything."

"Didn't Mama say anything? She just said we should have gotten me on tape!"

"But that was later, you know that. That was after you had said: 'Don't interrupt!' just because she was breathing."

"But she was thinking about saying something!"

"Yes, just imagine, I actually was," Evelyn said.

"It's forbidden to interrupt when I'm talking."

"You weren't talking," Inger said. "There wasn't anybody saying anything."

"Yes there was!" he bellowed. "I was thinking. It's forbidden to interrupt when I'm thinking."

"Then nobody can ever say anything," Evelyn said.

"No!" Ørnulf said, lighting a cigarette. "That is quite correct. Not as long as there's more talk than substance, as with you two."

"And what's the substance of what *you're* saying, then?" asked Inger.

"My substance," he said, and took a long pause. Now both Evelyn and Inger sat absolutely quietly, barely breathing. "My substance," he said and took a long, unruffled drag on his cigarette.

A long time passed. At least half a minute.

"My substance . . . is *substance,*" Ørnulf said.

"What substance?" Evelyn asked.

219

"You'll never understand that, you idiot!" he said calmly. "With the substance you inherited from the Gjarms, you'll never be capable of comprehending my substance."

"And that is that woman is man's slave?" Inger asked.

Ørnulf looked straight ahead across the room. Without looking at either of them. Then he said:

"Woman . . ."

And took a long pause. They waited. They barely moved. He still stared out into the room.

"Woman is a hole," he said.

This was Ørnulf's substance. That was his conclusion that evening. They had to sit there and listen to it. The words couldn't ever be stuffed back inside his mouth. They'd been articulated. Right out in the open air. It was one of the grossest things they'd ever heard. But they had heard it. They couldn't cut off their ears, which had already gotten the sound into their heads. And Inger was intensely ashamed of her father.

In the night—in the middle of a dream—Evelyn suddenly heard Ørnulf's voice, loudly, through her dream. "Beer!" She pretended she was sleeping. "Beer!" she heard again. She tried to pretend she hadn't heard it. "Beer!" he shouted louder, and for the third time. Evelyn lay completely still and thought: Now I have the choice of going obediently out and getting the beer for him, or getting hell the rest of the night. She went out and got the beer.

When Inger was home, Evelyn told her stories about Papa. "I'm glad it's impossible to go to the bathroom for another person," she said, "because then I'd have had to do that for him, too."

At one time Evelyn had made many girl friends in Fredrikstad, and she'd made a popular entry into the ladies' bridge club. The ladies of the city still called her when they needed a fourth, even though it'd been several years since the last time she played. Ladies' bridge took place in the banquet room at the Bjørnen Restaurant, on the lower level. But she didn't dare. In spite of the fact that she'd never been met with anything but praise and warmth, loved to play and was good at it, too, she trembled at the very thought. As time went on, fewer and fewer visitors came to Bjørnegården. Friends couldn't stand to sit and listen to arguing, and they couldn't stand to see the slow transformation that was taking place in the sweet, young doctor's wife who'd come to their city once upon a time.

Evelyn was filled with Ørnulf. Soon there was nothing left in her head but what Ørnulf did. But now that she had Inger as a witness, she wanted to call him on the carpet. In the middle of an argument he'd gotten going late in the evening, she suddenly shouted at him: "And there you were—in our bed! There you were—alternating between me and Paula!"

As she shouted, her voice broke. Shaken, she walked back and forth across the floor as she related what had happened, she struck her fist into the palm of her hand. The tears flowed.

"That," Papa said, calmly and slowly while he watched her performance, "that's something you're making up."

"Do you deny it?" Mama shouted.

"Reliability," Papa said with exaggerated pronunciation, "has never been a strong suit in the Gjarm family."

Inger listened like the buffer she was between her parents, and for once she was speechless. She was incapable of imagining the marital darkness that was being exposed here. A cornerstone of her conception of Mama and Papa—through all the arguments, scenes, threats and unreasonableness—had always been that they loved each other and were never unfaithful. Unfaithfulness? That Papa was infatuated with Paula was something she'd realized the minute she walked through the door, and she'd been outraged on Mama's behalf. But she'd thought that it was something that just happened in the *air*. Something he couldn't help. Good Lord, who knew better than she how hopeless it was to fight the air? And then it turns out it's not like that at all.

221

Now he said that this truth, which had been hurled in his face, was malarkey. If there was anything in this world that Mama was, it was reliable. He sat there talking malarkey! He was lying, pure and simple. He'd betrayed her, right to her face. And Inger confirmed objectively, almost coldly: Now there was nothing left of all the things a man could do to his wife, that Papa had not done to Mama.

The next day she was supposed to leave, and she was looking forward to the train leaving. Mama and she stood and looked out the living room window. The backyard lay with the sandbox and the green, untidy lawn, as before. The elm tree was standing with all its memories in the branches. Mama had always been so fond of this tree—the only one in Bjørnegården, and it was just as tall as the building. "What would I have done in this life without trees?" Mama said. On the fourth floor on the balcony over at the Tøgersen's, was a baby carriage. That meant that Tullik, Unni's big sister, was home. It was a high baby carriage, dark blue and modern, that suited her tall, model-like figure as she walked through town. She'd gotten married several years ago, and lived over on Nygaardsgata.

"Sometimes when I see that baby carriage," Mama said, "I think: Why isn't Inger married, and living over on Nygaardsgata and coming home to visit me with a baby carriage?"

Inger turned toward her in disbelief. "Do you *mean* that, Mama?"

"NO!" Mama said.

But Inger felt Mama's longing like an ache in her side. What should she do with Mama's longing? Mama telephoned her at the dormitory. "Are you coming home soon?" And she came.

If only I could tell her, she thought. Tell her about my life at Sogn, just like it is!

TWO GRANDMOTHERS AND A PICTURE

Two days before Evelyn was to be admitted to the hospital, Helene walked down Storgaten in Halden. She would be staying with Ørnulf and Ellen while Evelyn was in the hospital. In her purse she had an old picture. She had been looking for it all day. Now she wanted to go to Tronsart Photography Studio and get it framed. Then she was going to give it to Ørnulf.

In the picture he was standing, ten years old, on the croquet course at Apothecary Sound in Røros. Next to him was her brother, her sister and herself, all with mallets, while they merrily waited for Thorleif, Ørnulf's father, to miss.

At this point in her life Helene was still healthy and active. She was seventy-seven and walked briskly into the photographer's. She'd just had cataract surgery that she was very pleased with, she depended on her good vision to get through all the mending from Fredrikstad, which she still received gladly, and if there was a break in the work, she crocheted on Thorleif's afghan.

Helene was as kind as the day was long, but she didn't think of it that way herself. During the difficult time when Ørnulf had moved away from home, she'd always gone between him and Thorleif, and later she sent newly pressed shirts and macaroon cakes to him in the mail every two weeks for many years, and money, now and then. Thorleif didn't know about this last thing. For years she'd received interest from her mother's estate in Røros, and this fell outside of his domain. The principle —20,000 kroner—was solid as a rock in the bank and had been there since 1932 when her mother died, and it wasn't to be touched, but go undiminished to Ørnulf when she herself passed on. There was nothing to indicate that this would happen any time soon, and she hoped—for Thorleif's sake—that he would go first.

She passed a house on the left, and right here—by the curb —she always had to think about one time when she'd been walking here, a fall day more than eleven years ago, just after Helga had died. A window opened up on the third floor, a neighbor lady stuck her head out and shouted to her so that it resounded down the roadway: "Mrs. Holm. Are you in mourning?"

Helene still didn't know whether she should laugh or cry when she thought about this. She hadn't answered, but hurried on, naturally, but a while later she related this episode to Evelyn. Evelyn told her, several years later: "You know, Helene? After what happened, you were the first one who made me laugh."

That was probably the greatest declaration of love she'd ever received from her daughter-in-law. Declarations of love had otherwise been unnecessary between them. They loved each other through Ørnulf. But from the first they'd also felt an enormous kinship. Now it was true, of course, that they actually were related. Helene was her father's cousin, and naturally that strengthened the bond. But Helene had come to love the young Oslo girl from the first moment, pretty and lovable as she was. She was sure of the most important thing of all: Ørnulf was in the best of hands.

When the most terrible thing that can happen, happened, they'd gotten close to each other in a way that made words superfluous. Helene had felt, in the middle of her own pain, that here, finally, her own senseless loss would come to good use. She stepped in, while they themselves were powerless, and tried to protect the child that remained.

She didn't know whether she had succeeded. In many ways little Inger was a reserved type—even though she talked very eagerly. But her thoughts were amusing, and she'd likely become a writer. Helene felt quite certain of that as she walked along, and she was also quite certain that little Ellen would be a mother and carry on the family line.

She couldn't know this for sure, of course. It was just something she felt. She wished she could follow them far into the future, and it was strange to think about the fact that she wouldn't be able to. She would have loved to have been a great-grandma and great-great-grandma and great-great-great-grandma and sewn pajamas for the dolls of all the great-grandchildren and great-great-grandchildren who might come, if only the Creator—whose existence she strongly doubted—had made things so that was possible.

In the meantime there was just this picture, which she could give to Ørnulf to take along his path. The boy was so troubled. She couldn't understand how he'd become the way he was. As a child, he'd always been kind. But now he wasn't always kind anymore. No, he wasn't, she knew that, even though she didn't want to know it.

She delivered the picture to Tronsart, and then she went over to the grocery store to do her shopping. She never came empty-handed to Fredrikstad. She hadn't actually planned to buy so much, because their housekeeper, Bodil, would take care of Thorleif while she was away, but when she'd made her purchases, she had two large shopping bags in her hands. The door was heavy, the kind that opened in, and she struggled to open it. The store was full of people, but no one saw her dilemma. They were busy with their own things. Then she managed to pull it open herself, but as she was going out, the door slammed shut behind her and struck her in the back with its full weight. So she fell and broke her hip.

Everyone who hadn't noticed her as she stood struggling with the door, came rushing over now, the ambulance was called, and she was taken to Halden Hospital.

Helene never made it to Fredrikstad. She remained in the hospital bed, and the efforts to get her on her feet again were in vain. She knew where things were headed, and she wasn't afraid to die. The only thing she was afraid of was how it would go with those left behind.

A white casket stood before the altar, covered with flowers. Inside it was Grandma. It was a nice casket, and very white, and the flowers were also prettier than flowers usually are. But it had nothing to do with Grandma.

This was the first time Inger had ever seen a coffin. It amazed her, because it had a lid. Somehow she'd imagined that Grandma would be there. And then she definitely was not.

She ought to have seen a coffin before. She'd longed to go to the funeral, that time when she was ten years old, and ever since had wished she'd gone. But obviously funerals were not for children. Children were much too childish for funerals. Therefore she'd formed her own very sharp picture of what a funeral was.

Helga had lain in a dark casket surrounded by red roses. She couldn't move anymore and she couldn't say that she was Helga anymore, but she'd had her black hair and her own special Helga-face that no one else had, and which no one—for all the future—would have, and Mama had kissed her.

Inger had always longed for this. She'd always longed for this last farewell, which she never got. And now she was sitting here looking at a white casket with a lid. And if there was any person this didn't have anything to do with, it was Grandma.

Pastor Blåstad came in, stood by the beautiful casket, and read some words from the Bible. He spoke about Helene Holm, whom he had not known. He painted a picture of her, which was a quite sketchy picture of an old and kind lady, who always did her duty as wife and mother, and even though that was entirely true—and that was exactly what Grandma had done—he

226

managed to make his sermon about something entirely different. He said: "And He had given His life, so that whosoever
believes in Him shall not perish, but have everlasting life." That
was what he said, quite unostentatiously and unctuously and
with a smooth brow and all canonicals, despite the fact that as
recently as the week before he'd been thrown out of the sickroom on his ear by the sweet, old deceased lady, who now lay
in the casket.

Here he'd come—with The New Testament in his noble and
gentle hand, to give her some words to take with her on her
journey into the hereafter. Because both he and she realized
that she would die. Grandma clearly realized that she was dying, and she looked at the figure that came in to her deathbed,
she looked him right in the eye and said: "Is it the pastor?"

No. She didn't *say* it. She hissed it. And her accent was genu-
ine Røros. "Yes, it is, Mrs. Holm," Pastor Blåstad answered, as
was the fact. "Get out of here!" Grandma shouted, still in the
clear dialect of her youth. "I will not listen to such foolishness,
no! Out with you! Out with you!"

And that was that. The pastor had to go. He had to depart
from the room, probably in an attempt to be just as unctuous
and noble as when he had arrived, but he had to leave. And
now he was standing there condemning her to eternal damnation. For how could he believe that the furious old lady in the
sickroom would rise again?

Inger pinched her lips together. What incredible nerve! Can
you hear him, Grandma? There he stands making a farce of
your funeral. If you'd been here now, you'd have *laughed!*

The thought saved her from crying. Oh, Grandma. Listen to
him now! You! Who came to me that time, and held your hands
around my shoulders when I was standing looking at the elm
tree. And said what Mama couldn't bear to say. You, who held
my hand on the city bridge in Halden, as we watched the sunset. Do you remember that sunset, Grandma? Now you are
there.

Evelyn sat on Inger's right side, and struggled with tears. She pressed her arm, lightly, against Ørnulf's, and felt the struggle in him, too. When he got the news, he'd wept like a child. Helene was the last of the old people they thought they would lose. With the casket standing there Evelyn could not rid herself of the thought. Suddenly she felt an intense longing for her own mother.

She had to see her—before it was too late! She had to talk to her! She had to tell her how much she loved her. She sobbed aloud, and felt Ørnulf's large hand placed over hers. He was holding her. In the touch she could tell that he knew what she was thinking.

Pastor Blåstad took the shovel. Ørnulf regarded him with grim, shrewd humor. That one there, he thought, will never set the world on fire. And actually he was relieved. He managed to think what was supposed to be thought at this time. "With you," he thought, "with you, Mother, my little sister, Hilde, has died once again!"

The spadefuls of earth were cast, and the pastor completed his ceremony.

As they were about to leave, Grandpa remained standing. During the entire ceremony he'd sat with his cane right in front of him, holding it tightly, one fist over the other. How alone he was! Never had they seen a man so thin and alone. Finally he stood up and walked two steps forward. There he stood staring at the casket, he stood as if nailed to the floor, as if he never wanted to leave, just look and look—how could she not be anymore?

People in Halden knew this figure. He'd walked through the city for years, over the city bridge to the customs house, long walks every Sunday, they knew his cane, which he thrust cheerfully up in the air, as one did when one absolutely didn't need a cane. And he hadn't become any less vigorous with the years. Now he walked down the aisle like an old, old man.

When they got to Fredrikstad, Papa took Inger out to his office. There was something he wanted to show her. There he took out a picture, old and brown. "It was taken behind

Tuftbakken at Apothecary Sound," Papa said, and his Trønder accent had suddenly become so strong. "I got it from Grandma while she was in the hospital. She said: 'Think of the *good* memories, Ørnulf!'"

Then he hid his face in his hands.

"Was it a beautiful funeral?" Emilie asked.

She lay in bed in her favorite room, a small chamber with a writing desk and an old cupboard and pictures of family members hanging symmetrically on the wall, where she usually wrote her diaries. But now she was lying on the sofa because she had the flu.

"Yes," Inger said. Because it had been beautiful, of course, and one of the bouquets on the casket had been from Emilie. "But the minister was dumb."

"Oh?" Emilie said. "Perhaps he didn't know her?"

"No. Grandma didn't believe in God, you know. But he didn't pay any attention to that."

Emilie folded her hands. It was as if she were holding her own little devotions for Helene there on the sofa. Now she wanted to know what hymns they had sung. They conversed about the ceremony, and Emilie said that faith didn't need to be the faith the church stood for. She was about to say more, but suddenly her head fell back on the pillow, and she said in a hoarse voice: "*Ich kann nicht mehr sprechen!*"

The ambulance came. The men in white coats took her away. Her eyes were filled with fear. She was going home to her loved ones, she'd always known that, to her departed sister and brother, her parents, her husband, to Helga, she knew that, and had found great peace in this thought, but as the men in the white coats tried to get her on her feet to get her over to the stretcher, her eyes were filled with fear.

Lisa and Inger stood at the window with the view of the fjord. Down in the garden they saw the stretcher being carried out through the white gate. Then Lisa burst into tears and threw her arms around Inger: "She's never coming back!"

Emilie was one of those people who'd lived so long that she'd achieved a sort of immortality. Even though she was eighty-nine years old now, none of her children ever really thought she would do such a thing as die.

Pastor Lindholm came to the Red Cross Hospital, where she lay. She saw him, and her eyes brightened. The reason the light came into her eyes was simple enough. She loved him. She'd loved him from the moment he took over as resident chaplain in her congregation, she always sat in the first pew and listened to every word he said, yes, since the age of eighty-two she'd quite simply been in love like a young girl, dressed up for him, put rouge on her cheeks, and this was how she greeted him when he came to tend her soul.

Now he stood there—without a Bible, without admonitions of any sort—and her eyes shone. Then they were extinguished forever.

But even though her eyes were extinguished and her mouth was silent and the doctor told them that all the white blood cells had left her body, she was still breathing. She lay breathing, while her oldest daughter, Solveig, gave her red wine mixed with sugar and water, in small spoonful into the gasping mouth.

This happened ten days after Helene's death. In the meantime Evelyn had been admitted for her operation. Now she came from Fredrikstad, newly operated, straight from the hospital. She ran down Fredrik Stang Street and up the steps of the Red Cross Hospital. Inside she put her arms around her mother, lay her head over her on the blanket, and shouted: "Mammi! Can you hear me?" But Emilie didn't answer. Evelyn shouted and shouted, but didn't get a reply. "It's Evelyn!" she said. "Can you hear me? It's Evelyn!" And she wept over her, held her tightly and laid her head against her breast. All her brothers and sisters stood around her. "Is there any hope?" they said. But Solveig stood with the spoon and said: "Hush! We don't know what she can hear!" And they all were quiet. All that could be heard were the quick gasps of this woman who had given birth to them all, and who now heard—or perhaps didn't hear—the notes of the song she'd always rocked them to sleep by, and that Solveig sang for her, very softly:

> *Guten Abend, gut' Nacht*
> *mit Röslein bedacht . . .*

And so Emilie passed away.

But Evelyn regretted that she'd arrived too late at her mother's deathbed. She regretted all the times she'd refused to go in to see her when she'd been in Oslo. She regretted that she'd been nervous because Ørnulf was waiting. It struck her that all these years she'd had a mother who had been waiting. And she longed for her in a way she hadn't longed since she was a child in Germany and they thought about each other every day at twelve o'clock. Now there is no twelve o'clock anymore, Evelyn thought.

THE INHERITANCE

When Emilie died she didn't leave a will. But that was about the only thing she didn't leave behind. She owned the Gjarm family home by Gaustad Creek in Oslo, a large two-story villa with a view of the fjord and more than an acre of land around it and an avenue lined with chestnut trees, Ekekjær farm at Tjøme with fifty acres of fields and several hundred feet of shoreline, with a burned-down barn, to be sure, but on the other hand a newly built bungalow on the other side of the farm yard and a gazebo on the highest point of the property, and at Majorstuen in Oslo she had an apartment building from the turn of the century, from which she had her income. In addition to this came all kinds of personal property, naturally, Munch lithographs, Frisian Renaissance cupboards, ancient glasses, statuettes and other things, and everything in this estate she'd retained undivided since her husband's death before the war. Now it would be divided six ways.

The biggest problem was Ekekjær. Dividing fifty acres of seaside property with pine forests, flower meadows and knolls, high and low, small muddy tide flats, small inlets with deep water and swaying seaweed, hills with a view of the sunset, small bays with a view of the sunrise, a pine forest with no afternoon sun at all, sea gulls and heather, blueberries and whortleberries, pastures with meadowsweet and hazelnut bushes with mosquitoes, small porcupines, a Bambi that suddenly hops over the stone fence, a building site with a view of Færder lighthouse, an abandoned farm, a cabin, a bungalow with no view—dividing all this by six—and fairly! is a job they all despaired over—one by one.

One of them had gotten an island as a wedding present in 1941, another two acres of shoreline for Christmas in one of Hans Rudolf's generous moments, and they now demanded that these be excluded from the inheritance. The others protested. Quite unsystematically they'd already begun picking out lots while Emilie was still alive. Now they began selling parts of these behind each other's backs. "That was mine, you know!" they said. Without anyone ever making a survey with even an attempt at a fair distribution. Everything was distributed—quite unreasonably and completely unequally. And soon the whole property was one big tangle of overlapping and unclear parcels and new claimants with options to buy that no one knew about, and Emilie's signature appeared on the most contradictory documents.

The six brothers and sisters all showed up with their own attorneys to try to obtain some valid deeds. The meetings at the lawyer's office became a perfect nightmare of spoken and unspoken affronts. One by one they were offended by nearly everything the other five said. They left the meetings in tears.

Afterwards they went to the Theater Café. Here they sat and had a grand time, as long as one word was not mentioned. Namely the word "lot."

As long as Emilie was alive, they each deluded themselves into thinking they owned everything. Now they had to buy each other out. And each time one of them succeeded in this, the other five said to each other: "He got that much too cheaply!" And thus it came about that Evelyn bought the house at Ekekjær with one acre of land around it, clearly too cheaply! from the estate, and her greatest wish now was that Lisa would buy the bungalow, because then she would have her nearby when the August nights came. "I can't afford it," Lisa said, because she was also planning to buy the apartment in the Gjarm villa, where she lived. "You can have it free, as far as I'm concerned! If you buy the bungalow, you won't have to pay my sixth anyway," Evelyn said. But her other siblings did not say that, and there the matter stood.

They held a personal property meeting. So that this could be conducted in a fair and congenial way, Knut, as the oldest, had bought champagne. Solveig, as the second oldest, had made up a meticulous list of all the lithographs, paintings, hundred-year-old glasses, antique music boxes and candelabra. They met in Emilie's parlor where the view over the fjord was just as beautiful as before, but no Emilie anymore to feel *Mutterschmerz* for them all. That was also why she couldn't bear to draw up a will. Knut filled the glasses, everyone had a copy of the list, and they were each supposed to select an item, one by one, according to age, just like when they had sat around the dinner table in their childhood, in as many rounds as the number of objects required, so Knut began. He wanted the seventeenth century Frisian sideboard, Solveig wanted Oma's china, Borgar wanted an old oil painting, Lisa wanted a corner cupboard and Jan Michael wanted the refrigerator. "Refrigerator!" Solveig shouted. "I'm supposed to get that!" Everyone knew that Solveig had wanted the refrigerator, she was the only one of them who didn't have a refrigerator, so she hadn't figured on it disappearing in the first round. "Can't you pick something else?" said Knut. "Can't we choose what we want?" Jan Michael said. Now he met a storm of attempts to persuade him. He already had a refrigerator. What would he do with two? Don't be so bullheaded now. Was it his wife, Wanda, who was behind it? He shouldn't let himself be ruled by that. All the Gjarm siblings had a tendency to be henpecked spouses. Think of something else, Jan Michael. "If I'm not allowed to choose what I want, I won't participate in this meeting!" Jan Michael said. And then he left and didn't come back.

There they sat. Usually they never met, all six of them, except for the dreadful meetings with their lawyers where they discussed bigger things. This was a historic event. The things had to be distributed now, and they agreed that each time it was Jan Michael's turn, they would choose something they thought he would want. They continued, and now it was Evelyn's turn. "Well, I hadn't planned to pick the refrigerator," Evelyn said. The remark brought on a certain restrained merriment. "I'd like to have 'The Magic Treasure Box.'"

"The Magic Treasure Box" was an old oak box that held miniature versions of almost everything on the list. Here were tiny stemmed wedding glasses, a doll-sized sewing table with a mirror, an elegant carriage drawn by two white horses, a pale blue teapot with matching cups and plates, white turtle doves, all wrapped in pink cotton and old tissue paper. Emilie had opened all this and unwrapped it for them, individually, when they were small, and spread it out on the big dining table, and there was a story for each of the objects.

This box was the only thing of all the things on the list that Evelyn desired. When she died one of her children would inherit it, and they would pass it on to their children, perhaps they would place their own small things in it and add new stories to the box, and in this way all the tiny objects would live on down through the generations.

When the personal property meeting was over, a pile of things lay outside Jan Michael's door on the first floor. "What's all this garbage lying here?" he said. Later he maintained that he hadn't gotten a single thing of his mother's effects.

"During a battle over earthly goods man reveals his true self," commented Borgar, and the incident became the origin of at least twenty-seven new verses from his pen.

Evelyn left for Fredrikstad with her share of the personal property in her car, of which the most valuable—besides the box—was an old alabaster lamp and a plaster bust of Aunt Irmtraut, Emilie's sister, whom no one had liked.

"If they'd just put me in charge of this estate, there would have been some order in the bric-a-brac," Ørnulf said. "But they are of the opinion that anything connected to in-laws

235

poisons their decisions—me more than anyone. As if there were any decisions at all to be poisoned in that crowd. Swindle and deceit!—they're masters of that, if they'd only restricted themselves to doing it on stage." Then he took Evelyn's siblings one by one and characterized them in the crudest possible way.

Evelyn didn't know how she'd ever find the strength to go in to Oslo for all the meetings. She wasn't well enough, and she didn't have the nerves for it either. If she didn't get better, Inger would have to represent her at the settling of the estate. But Inger's head was full of other things. The past year she hadn't been home much, Evelyn thought. She was absorbed in her studies and her new life at the dormitory, and when she was home, Evelyn got a detailed report on at least three new books she'd read—as long as Ørnulf was at the Club. They put on Chopin's fourteen waltzes and did the dishes, and she was thinner each time she came home. Evelyn thought she'd never seen her so pretty.

When they did errands in town, she walked through a forest of compliments. People oohed and aahhed and carried on indiscriminately; my goodness, how thin she's gotten! how fat and plump she'd been, they stuck their heads out the windows and shouted: "Have you been on a diet!"

"No," Inger said.

No, Evelyn thought. She probably hasn't. She's in love. But she didn't dare ask. On this point her mouth had always been sealed with seven seals.

She bought a pair of leopard pants. She would wear these hitchhiking through Europe with Elsa. "Well, you won't get a penny from me for such a plan!" Ørnulf proclaimed, but she hadn't thought she would, either. She'd taken a conductor's training course at Schøyen Bus Company, and now was a trained conductor with a week's course behind her. "Conductor!" Ørnulf said. "I have a daughter who is a conductor on a bus!"

"What do you make at that job?" Evelyn said, when they were alone. "Can't I just pay you the money instead, so that I can have you at home a little?"

But Inger said it wasn't just the money. It was the job, too. Getting to know more of life than books.

"My whole life is just *words* now!"

Evelyn tried to conceal her disappointment. She didn't begrudge her this trip. Elsa and Inger were going to show each other their au pair cities—Edinburgh and Geneva. They were going to visit Sheila and Rose Mary, they were going to Paris. Since the time Inger had stood there with her student cap on the steps of the Phoenix Club, and she'd seen them all as they were photographed, it was as if she were torn in two. One part of her wanted to go along with Inger and be happy for everything she would experience. The other part was bound fast to having the pretty student picture as a memento on the entryway table. And for the first time Evelyn dreaded summer.

She hadn't gotten better after the operation. She suffered from edema, and in the hospital they'd installed a tube to drain the fluid. But her stomach swelled up, and the wound from the tube on the side of her stomach wouldn't heal. It oozed, and she had to put new compresses on it every evening. She stood in front of the big mirror in the bedroom and saw her body in it. Then she burst into tears.

Every day after work Ørnulf stood holding her.

"Are you itty Bitty who loves big Big?"

"Itty Bitty loves big Big when he's nice."

"He's as gentle as a lamb."

"Will you be gentle as a lamb when you come back home, then?"

"When I come back home, I'll come back home."

"But why can't you be as sweet when you come home as when you go?" To which he replied: "Gimme a little kiss?"

They gave each other a little kiss. And then they kissed each other again. Then he left. But when he got home, he was morose.

Ørnulf always maintained that Evelyn hadn't tolerated her last pregnancy. But Evelyn didn't believe that explanation. True, she had gotten varicose veins, but except for that she'd never been as healthy as then. "Self-perception," Evelyn said, "that's what you lack! You accuse my brothers and sisters of deceit. That may be. But you refuse to look the truth about you and me in the eyes." "And who's the physician in this house?" Ørnulf said. "The last pregnancy was unhealthy!"

"You should have been a lawyer instead of a doctor," Evelyn said. And Ørnulf agreed, in many ways. "Because then you would have gotten the arguing out of your system away from home. Now you have gotten the healing out of your system away from home," she added.

Then she sat down in front of the television and watched "The Lucy Show." Television! Ørnulf was furious. True, he was the one who had bought it, because there was hardly a single conversation at the Club without some reference to a television program, so he thought: it wouldn't hurt anything if it was there. But he hadn't imagined that they'd watch it.

But there sat Evelyn delighting in Lucy. "She is the world champion at being clumsy," she exclaimed enthusiastically. Suddenly he'd been replaced as the center of attention in the living room. "One fine day I'm going to throw that television set off the balcony," Ørnulf said.

Besides, sometimes there were Negroes on television. But then he just went right over and turned it off.

One night Evelyn got up and wrote a letter. She tiptoed out into the living room while Ørnulf slept. Dear Ørnulf! When you are sweet, it's as if we were in a fairy tale world, where everything is small. Little Nulfenulf and little Linnelinn play with each other, just like in the song we have sung so often: "Is there a little boy, who wants to play with a little girl?" But I miss the love that's in the song when things get serious! Why isn't there ever a *serious* Ørnulf who loves me? The serious Ørnulf always yells at me. Can you understand this? I can't be satisfied with a game?

Evelyn spent a long time on the letter. It was a despairing letter, as if she were writing to him from the outermost island where only the sea gulls screamed. She cried as she wrote it, and she never gave it to him.

When Inger arrived in Geneva there was a letter waiting for her at poste restante. It was from Mama, and in it were 200 Swiss francs. Inger knew immediately that Mama had drawn it from the estate behind Papa's back. And she needed it badly, despite her assurances. In the letter there was first a long and humorous account of how for the second time she had sat down at the dining table with Gyldendal's Blue Norwegian-English Dictionary. She'd written a letter to Mrs. Fernhill and thanked her for the wonderful reception Inger had gotten in London. At the end she added just a few words: Inger! I need your help! Do you think you have a little time for me? In between everything you have to do? It has to do with your future. Yours and Ellen's.

She went for a long walk along the shore and came to the point where the uppermost little section of the Rhone runs into Lake Geneva. How green it was! Completely clear and green. She watched the river as it rushed by and saw Ellen's face in the current. Future?

But Evelyn sat at Bjørnegården full of new thoughts. She finally realized why Inger had gotten thin. Finally everything fit, when she started thinking back on everything Inger had talked about, all the letters from Edinburgh, the last letter from London, where she described the reunion with Sheila, how they flew into each other's arms and laughed, and how she and Elsa hitch-hiked on, all around England, down to London, where Rose Mary and her mother had served them tea in bed. Evelyn lit a cigarette and stared out into the room. Because she'd suddenly realized that Rose Mary and Inger were having an affair.

Evelyn thought about this, quite simply. Inger had always

been most interested in her girl friends. Now she had finally found one who was older and wiser. Every time she was home she told about new things Rose Mary had said. She opened her eyes and showed her the world in a new light, just like Helga had done once upon a time. She'd found a new big sister, Evelyn thought. And she was happy for Inger.

It went as Inger had thought it would. The year she was old enough to vote, the Labor Party lost. But it didn't happen at all the way she thought it would. The little party she'd voted for helped the non-Socialist parties topple the Gerhardsen government. The news reached Elsa and Inger in the form of a tiny notice in a Dutch newspaper, as they came hitch-hiking northwards. A lady they met told them in German: "*Die Regierung in Norwegen ist gefallen.*"

They hitch-hiked onward up through Jutland—toward a strange country where the Prime Minister was named John Lyng. Was it still there? Were there sea gulls? Were there rocky shores with little houses, wood houses, white and red? Did they speak Norwegian there? And what about Galdhøpiggen Mountain? What about Totak, Bandak, Kviteseid and Flåvann Lakes? It was the greatest political shakeup in their young lives.

On the trip they'd managed to have a falling out. It happened on a street corner in Soho. "There are lesbians all over the place here," Elsa said. "How the heck can you *see* that?" Inger said, irritated. "I notice that they're coming on to me," Elsa said. "You can't tell by looking at people whether they are homosexual," Inger said. "You don't say 'homosexual' about women," Elsa said. "You do too!!" "No, they're called lesbians."

There it was again. That revolting word. She thought it was taking homosexual women's existence away from them—that they weren't permitted to have the general name. No. She wouldn't accept that. They repeated themselves several times. Neither of them would give in. No way in hell. "I'm leaving!" Inger said.

And she did. She left Elsa there on the street corner in Soho, and went right into a pub where she allowed an Italian to buy her drinks, and later she went for a walk with him in Russell Square, and before she knew what was happening she was in the middle of an attempted rape. Then she threatened to use the only body part she had that was his equal in strength and rage, namely her vocal cords. Then she took off running through the trees.

That's how it always was later, too. Every time she was subjected to an attempted rape—three times all together during her time at the university—it was because she'd just quarreled with a girl friend. And every time it happened it was because she felt so bad that she didn't give a damn and went along with some guy or other to do whatever, and she knew that afterwards the whole world would say that she had only herself to thank for it.

That was why she never said anything about it. But she never agreed with the remarks that therefore were never made.

When she got home she said to Mama: "I suppose you're happy *now?*" She was referring to Gerhardsen's fall. Mama looked out the kitchen window and thought a little. Then she said—to Inger's great surprise: "No. I thought it was sad . . ."

But when the local election came Ørnulf said: "Here I've sat all day and told my patients: 'Well, of course a doctor should not advise his patients to vote for any particular party, but no matter what you do, do not vote for the Socialist People's Party!' And then I have a *daughter* who does!"

Then he laughed.

Yes, 1963 was full of shocks, as everyone knows, and suddenly a shot was heard in Dallas. And no matter where they were, and no matter who they were, an Italian who missed out on sex in Russell Square, a Norwegian girl who thought she attracted lesbians, a doctor who didn't give political advice to his patients, a doctor's wife who'd always voted Conservative and thought wistfully about Gerhardsen, a Scottish lady who thought that a Roman Catholic should never have become president, a Scottish girl who drove a motor bike in silk stockings, an English girl whose greatest desire was to not be in England when Churchill died, an engineering student who once upon a time was shoved down the stairs or a Norwegian girl who still loved the English girl with Churchill, they stopped, and heard the shot. For an instant the whole world stopped. Then they went on again—in their individual situations.

BRAHMS' VIOLIN CONCERTO

The fall of 1963 consisted of completing her English major.

The English curriculum at the time consisted of a large reading list that extended over many centuries—from *Beowulf* to Dylan Thomas. Everywhere in the books was love, suffering and suppression. People who loved and held the most important things hidden from each other. If people didn't conceal things from each other there'd never be any books. She read about Philip Wakem's forbidden love for Maggie Tulliver in George Eliot's *The Mill on the Floss*, she read about the Lady of Shalott's forbidden attraction to Sir Lancelot as he rode along the river bank, she read about Hamlet's secret, and everywhere in the lines she listened for Rose Mary's step on the stairs. Soon she'll be home, and I can go out and see her. The whole English curriculum was about this. It was incredible how George Eliot, Alfred Lord Tennyson and William Shakespeare, the anonymous author of *Beowulf* and Dylan Thomas had seen this very thing so clearly. "Listen! Soon her steps will be on the stair!" Shakespeare wrote. "She's approaching!" Lord Tennyson wrote. "Is it possible you told her—last semester—that you loved her?" George Eliot wrote. "She doesn't look like it," the anonymous author of Beowulf wrote. "But what does a person look like whom one told last semester that one loved?" Dylan Thomas wrote. "Let's not talk about it again," George

Eliot wrote. "And thus and only thus! can I keep it in check," Shakespeare wrote. "If I mention it again, the tempest will begin."

Consequently Inger was highly doubtful that she would pass her exam.

She passed her exam. And then she collapsed. It happened during a telephone conversation, when Lisa had called her.

"How'd it go?" Lisa's deep, warm voice came through the receiver. Then suddenly Inger began to cry, and Lisa thought she'd failed. But she was unable to explain herself, and dropped the receiver and rushed into her room. Rose Mary grabbed the phone. "No, I think it went fine," she said. Then she followed Inger into the room and put her arms around her. "Why are you crying, Inger?" she said.

But she wasn't crying anymore. She'd sailed into the harbor where she must never moor. With that the tempest broke loose. As long as she had silence around her, she could hang on—convulsively—to an inner peace. The lines had unfolded before her eyes with their quiet and insight. But when Rose Mary's hand came around her shoulder, stroked her head, she knew again what she hoped she'd stopped wanting. She wanted to go to her, and nothing else, just as before, and she went. The life in her drove her to her, she fell on her knees before her, embraced her against her will and knew: This is the worst thing you could do to another person.

The next day she wrote a letter. Last semester I told you I loved you and I said I thought I was homosexual. But you mustn't think this is troubling me anymore. Maybe you do think that, when I act like I did. But I'm just fine!

When she was finished with the letter, it occurred to her that Rose Mary wasn't expecting it. It was better to talk to her about it instead, she thought. But if I start talking about it, there's the risk I might attack her again. That's why I have to get it over with immediately.

So when Rose Mary got home she said: "I have to talk to you! Do you have time?" "Yes," Rose Mary said and let the door to her room stand open as an indication. But when Inger came in a bit later she was sitting on a chair by the window reading a book. She never sat there! She always lay on her bed. She was sitting there so that I wouldn't make a pass at her!

The thought overwhelmed her so that she forgot what she'd come to say. It was as if the whole letter she'd spent a day writing were blown away, and all that was left was one question: "Why are you sitting there?"

"What are you reading?" she said. Rose Mary told a rather long story about Heinrich Heine. "What was it you wanted to say?"

The question came quite unexpectedly. Because all Inger wished was for her to keep on and keep on—with these words that came out so vividly. About Heinrich Heine, or the Bahama Agreement or Lenin's ideas, or anything at all. She was here! "Ohh! I feel so dumb!" she said. "I don't think you're dumb! And I don't think you have anything to be ashamed of either!"

But when she got back to her own room her memory returned. I came to say that I was fine. I'm not troubled anymore, even though you might think so, because I came in to you last night. But I don't walk around day in and day out speculating about my possible homosexuality. No, I don't. I'm studying for my oral exam in English.

She wrote a letter explaining everything. But as she wrote she was filled with one single question: Why were you sitting on that chair? It's more difficult to make a pass at another person when she's sitting on a chair. Was that why? And the question filled her whole body and head, all of 1314 and the dormitory, and nothing existed but a terrible restlessness, that had to have an answer. And it drove her back.

Now she blurted right out: "Rose Mary? When I came in here a bit ago, were you sitting there by the window to avoid any more advances?" Rose Mary looked at her: "That didn't even occur to me!"

She was crushed by this answer. The thing she'd come to say the whole time—that she wasn't troubled anymore—but never

245

got a chance to say, wasn't true! She discovered that in the middle of everything. Here she was driven round and round by one single question. And then it hadn't even occurred to Rose Mary!

She was exasperated. Here I am, tossed back and forth all day long in scruples and agony and longing, and she hasn't even given it a thought! I don't mean a thing to her! There's no room for deviations here. They're just an extra burden! To take those into consideration would just mean delays! Why didn't I say that? That should hit close to home! She wanted to go in again. She wanted to shout at her: "Are we doomed forever to shout at each other? Will we never understand each other's suffering?"

Brahms' Violin Concerto in D-Major, third movement, thundered out of 1314. Its passionate, nearly SOS-like eruption of notes wept out into the room, while Inger energetically started in on a large bottle of beer. I must not go in to her, I must not go in! Next she attacked the bookshelves. First she just pulled down three books. But the ones that had been leaning on them toppled over, and she became absolutely furious at them, and tore them down too, more fell. Then she took her whole arm and pulled down the rest of the series of books, Penguin books, Lantern books, paperbacks from Gyldendal, *Sinners in Summertime*, there went *Lady Chatterley's Lover,* there went *Homosexuality* by D.J. West, there went *The Mill on the Floss*. What the hell was that doing there? There went *Jane Eyre* with Mr. Rochester and his horse, there went *Peasants at Sea*. She stared at them as they flew. There they lay. She started in on the next shelf. *The Collected Works of William Shakespeare* flew across the room—in an edition purchased for thirteen kroner. Thirteen kroner—for one book. A black book with the author's obscure portrait on the cover. Everything was here. It hit the floor of 1314, and the silent lady—virgin, housewife or wife—with upswept hair, dark and proud, stood there in quiet Munchian and long since deceased calm, and was the only witness to her insanity.

246

A girl in the dormitory had torn all her books off the shelves. They were books she'd read and loved, or books she was eagerly waiting to start on. There they lay, half torn to pieces, on the floor. She'd done it to keep herself from going over and embracing another person against her will. How many times hadn't she herself been the object of advances against her will? Did the boys who'd come like that tear down all their books to keep themselves from coming again? Did they drown themselves in self-reproach over the transgressions they had committed?

Inger didn't know, and she wasn't asking this question. That was something quite different, too, of course. She was absolutely certain of that. And consequently it didn't occur to her to construct such an artificial analogy.

THE STATE CHURCH

She doesn't want me. I just have to get that into my head. And
I already knew that. I just have to push it away. If she doesn't
want me, then I'll have to do something else she likes. She
seized a piece of paper. She put it into the typewriter. To the
minister of Vestre Fredrikstad Parish! This is to inform you that
I wish to resign my membership. Sincerely, Inger Holm.

Time and again Rose Mary had said: "I don't understand
you're being a member of the State Church. Would you remain
a member of any other organization whose views you didn't
share?"

But she'd never thought of the church as an organization. She
looked at it as a kind of holy place—above other things—like
the high dome in the church building itself. But of course Rose
Mary was right.

Even so, she thought it was difficult to come to the point
where God didn't exist. It was easier to think that he existed,
but that you didn't believe he existed. But to say straight out
that he absolutely did not exist was somehow being much too
hard. You weren't like that!—that God didn't exist. Of course
he didn't exist. That had become apparent. He was gone when
Helga was lying in the respirator.

Who had helped her then? Grandma. Grandma came to her.
And now she was in hell, according to the pastor.

During the fall—she was right in the middle of studying for her exams—Grandpa died, too. He had believed in God. He'd pointed toward heaven with his finger and said: "And that's why I believe in a Creator!" But she hadn't quite grasped why. Just the fact itself—that he believed.

Grandpa died of grief. She hadn't known before that this was possible and had always wondered about it. Because that's what it had said in *The Journey to the Christmas Star*. The princess disappeared and when all efforts to find her were in vain, the queen died of grief, it said. And the king went out and cursed the star so that it went out.

But now she'd seen that this was possible. It was possible to die of grief. And now Grandpa was in heaven. And there he must have died of grief over not finding Grandma?

Oh, no. She didn't believe that. Grandma and Grandpa— they were together now. They were lying in a grave in Fredrikstad. Together with Helga. And Mama and Papa and Ellen and she would go there and plant flowers in the spring.

"You have to take a stand!" Rose Mary said to her.

She mailed the letter.

That afternoon she said casually: "Well. I've resigned my membership in the State Church." Rose Mary peered at her with those eyes that Inger had every day, no matter how much she couldn't have her.

"I'm proud of you!" she said.

Then Inger was in heaven, and a week later she got a letter from Vestre Fredrikstad Church stating that the pastor was in India at the moment and unfortunately it was impossible to accept any resignations in his absence.

A few days later she was standing in her pajamas in Bjørnegården. It was 11:15 and she'd woken up ten minutes before. Ellen had come in and placed a cup of tea under her nose, hoping that she would wake up. When she finally did, she went straight to the telephone and called the pastor's office.

"Hello," said Pastor Sundbro. "This is Pastor Sundbro."

"This is Inger Holm. I sent a letter stating that I am withdrawing from the State Church, I would like confirmation of this."

"Withdrawing from the State Church is not something you can do by mail," the pastor said.

"Oh? Well, then I'll do it now."

"You can't withdraw by telephone either," the pastor said.

"Wha . . . what does it take, then?"

"You'd have to come to the pastor's office for a conference."

"All right, then I'll come over now," Inger said.

"Oh no, that would be a bit difficult. The pastor's office is closing in fifteen minutes."

"I can be there in two minutes."

"Oh? Well, you'd better come then."

Five minutes later when Inger opened the tall door to the pastor's office in Vestre Church, the pastor turned slowly toward her and looked at her searchingly. "So, this is the young lady who wants to resign from the church!" he said. "Yes," Inger said, already dejected, because she couldn't make herself older. "You had better sit down," Pastor Sundbro said.

She sat down—increasingly nervous. This was quite terrible. "Man is by nature religious," Pastor Sundbro said. "By nature fearful, perhaps," Inger said.

"Is everything going so well with you, then?" the pastor said.

Well! What a sneak attack! No, God knows that things were not going well with her. Things were going miserably, especially right now. "Oh yes!" she answered. "So you don't need any help?"

Help? Yes, of course she needed help. It was a long time since she had felt so helpless. "No," she said. "Not from the church, at any rate," she added, even though she knew that this was one of the usual obstinacies she always found herself in.

Pastor Sundbro stood up. He was a tall man with magnificent gray pastor's hair and eyebrows, and he went over to the window and peered out into Kirkeparken. "I've just been in India," he said. "By the *thousands* they throw themselves to the ground down there. By the thousands they throw themselves down before their idols!" The pastor stood and peered and saw all the thousands of prostrate Indians who prayed to their idols out there in Kirkeparken. "How do you think you will manage without God?"

He had turned toward her.

"I am sure God means a lot to you," Inger said, "but he doesn't mean anything to me."

"God means something for all human beings," the pastor said.

"But when I can't feel his presence?"

"Life often seems black and empty," the pastor said, "and one often asks oneself where God is . . ."

"I have asked myself where God is many times, but he's never there."

"God is always there," the pastor said. "Even Job, who lost everything, had to yield to God in the end."

Inger had no desire to discuss Job with Pastor Sundbro. That was a terrible story. And then it pretended that it wasn't.

Inger thought about the boils on Job's body and the fact that all his children died, and all his cows and everything he had, and he was naked, too, and she didn't look at the pastor anymore when she said: "He shouldn't have done that." "You certainly have a lot to learn," said Pastor Sundbro. "You are definitely a very confident young lady."

He said it as if it were supposed to be an immense flaw, and with deliberate movements he went into an adjoining room and came back with an enormous ledger. Finally, there it was! This book of God she'd always heard about, deposited in Vestre Fredrikstad Parish. Here he found her name. He dipped the pen into the ink and crossed it out with long, scratchy strokes. Next he filled out a small printed form. "Certificate of Resignation from The Norwegian Church." But as she was about to leave, she thought of something. "What if later I decide I wanted to rejoin, would I have to be baptized again?"

The pastor straightened up and looked sadly at her:

"Once baptized, always baptized! But going in and out of the church is not something one does every day!"

"No, no, I hadn't exactly planned to come back tomorrow!" Inger said.

Then she left.

"Well," Inger said to Mama, "I've resigned from the State Church."

"What did he say?"

"He asked if things were going well with me," Inger said. And then Evelyn got an detailed account of the strange conversation.

This was Inger's first morning home during Christmas vacation. When Papa got home, he asked Inger to come with him out to his office. There was something he wanted to talk to her about. Privately. Out there he told her Evelyn was suffering from an incurable liver disease, and that she was dying.

IN THE OFFICE

Ørnulf hadn't expected Inger to believe him. But she knew immediately that he was telling the truth. "So often I give the worst case scenario," Papa said.

But the words were superfluous. She had no thoughts. She saw Papa. He had black hair in a wreath around his head. He said: "So you'll believe me, I want to call the hospital, so you can talk to Dr. Erlandsen, who's been treating her." He took the receiver. She had no thoughts. Just eyes, and she saw Papa's white doctor's coat arm and his hand that dialed the number.

Dr. Erlandsen's voice was in the receiver. It confirmed what Papa had said. "Yes, I'm sorry to have to tell you how things stand, Miss Holm," Dr. Erlandsen said.

As if it were possible to talk about it.

It was possible to talk about it. Dr. Erlandsen talked about liver test results and that there was no cure. Without a functioning liver one cannot live. "Yes," Inger said.

Yes and yes.

She sat in the patient's chair, Papa in the doctor's chair behind the big desk, just like they always sat. On the wall was a little instrument cabinet with a window. The instruments in there were disinfected. Next to that was the scale with its height measurer. She'd grown alongside this. By the window was the glass table with bandages and gauze. Everything was here. The eye chart over the bench with a gigantic E at the top. Who on earth couldn't see that E? Were there people who were so near-sighted? Papa sat there with his arm. It reached over for the receiver, which he took and said good-bye. He turned toward her: "In two years she won't be alive."

Then a deep stillness sank down inside her. The life went out of her body. There was no more movement left in it.

And that was how Inger found out—in deep secret—that her mother was going to die. She loved her. There was no doubt that she did, and there was no reason, either, for her not to. Evelyn was a completely unselfish person.

It was strange, how some people were made so that this could actually be said about them. Goodness, quite simply. Evelyn was goodness. Who could comprehend goodness?

From the time Inger was tiny this was what she had seen. A mother who took her in her arms and ran down the stairs when there was an air raid. And so she wouldn't be afraid, she made a little, sweet melody to the air raid. "Airy raid, airy raid, airy, airy, airy raid!" they sang on their way down to the basement.

What else could she do?

In Germany she had girl friends who were living in houses with three walls. She sent packages. She was always seeing someone she had to help. She was always seeing fates she had to empathize with. And now she was going to die. In deep secret she was going to approach death. Who was going to empathize with her while she did it?

But Inger wasn't thinking this, and she wasn't asking this question. When she began to think again, it was like this: "The law of change," Rose Mary said. "Everything is subject to the law of change." But here there was no change. Here it was: "You're wandering around in a daze!" for 26 years. Here it was: "If you won't admit that you're wandering around in a daze, then divorce is the only solution," for 26 years. For 26 years divorce had been the only solution. At any rate as many of them as she could remember. Where was the law of change here?

Yes. Inger was questioning. But she knew the answer. Because the law of change applied here just like everywhere else. Things got worse. It wasn't a static condition. Because every time you said: "You're wandering around in a daze!" it was worse that you said it, and she had gotten a little worse than the last time. "You're wandering around in a daze!" Ørnulf said. "Admit you're an idiot!"

Admit you're an idiot!

Admit you're an idiot!

How often had she heard this sentence? 3456 times? 34,560 times? And even so it wasn't the same every time. Because every time he said it, Evelyn had come closer to death. That was the law of change as it applied in Bjørnegården, in her parents' marriage.

Papa had gotten the woman he loved. Mama. And then he destroyed her. This was the truth that Inger, twenty-two years old, knew as she sat there in the office.

From the moment Ørnulf found out that Evelyn was going to die, he drank like a madman. He'd drunk a lot his whole adult life. But now he put away such enormous quantities that it was beyond belief that a human body could even accommodate it. He drank morning, noon and night; export beer, wine, port wine and whiskey. He distributed his beer purchases among six different stores in town, because he drank a case of export beer a day. There were only two Liquor Outlets. He managed, in a variety of ways, to have delivered every day: a large bottle of cognac, a large bottle of fine old port wine and one or two bottles of white wine. In addition he drank an undetermined number of drinks every evening at the Phoenix Club. This was what he drank every day—from the time he got up until he went to bed at 1:30 in the morning. It was as if it were a race he was trying to win.

Inger saw all this, and the life in her wanted to get away from it. The life in her wanted to go to the dormitory at Sogn.

Ørnulf sat in the corner and drank. They played Twenty Questions. In a conscious desire to spite him, Inger had just thought of Louis Armstrong. While Ørnulf spewed out his contempt of this phenomenon on the earth's surface, Evelyn went to the bathroom. As she closed the door behind her, Ørnulf said: "She's dying!"

He said it with emphasis on "she" as if she were somehow guilty of some incalculable foolishness. "She's dying!" he said. As if he were flicking away a piece of lint.

Inger sat there without saying a word. But at night she heard Mama weeping in the living room. She'd heard this weeping many times, was awakened by it, was awakened by it when it wasn't even there. But what the voice was crying now was: "I'm rotting! I'm rotting inside!"

It was the truth she cried out. But during the day she peeled her oranges.

Her face was yellow. And the whites of her eyes were also yellow. Her legs were swollen. "How will I manage to give a birthday party for Ellen?" she said. "I'll do it," Inger said. "I can have a miniature theater!" Still, Mama said: "How will I manage to give that birthday party?"

It was as if she hadn't heard her. And as if she hadn't heard herself ask the same question a moment earlier.

It was over a month until Ellen's birthday. "But Mama, you mustn't worry about that! I'll come home and organize the birthday party!" Inger said. "And I can have a New Year's party for her. Now. Before we take the Christmas tree down?"

Mama was grateful and relieved. Still it was as if that didn't help. "Ellen doesn't have a real mother," she said.

She'd always been so full of ideas! Hats and crepe paper, and games. Movie stars you had to try and guess. Songs from musical reviews and Iversen's dog in a laundry basket, that Helga had played. Woof, woof. Songs sung at the table, based on popular hits. All her talent from her brief time on the stage she poured out over her two oldest children. Some of the birthday songs she had written became local hits for long periods of time. "The Song of St. Croix," for example. To "Wonderful Copenhagen." She was the mother everyone would have liked to have had. That's what Inger had often heard. She created a theater in Bjørnegården Apt., to raise money for the refugees—under the slogan We're Knocking on the Door, that was on the "Children's Hour" radio program.

Hush—I hear a strange cry
Can it be children's tears—why?
So many they are! Infinitely many
behind barbed wire they live
who never a real Christmas have seen
like a mother or father could give.

We have Christmas—with songs and with cheer
with children's delight in their homes so dear.
But how will it be for the children there?
Will Christmas come? Does anyone care?

Oh no, little ones in foreign lands,
They live in pain and in sorrow!
So you who are able, reach out your hands
and give them a fairer tomorrow!

She'd written this simple little poem, and Inger had recited it—dressed like an angel. Lillian, Unni and Eva had stood around her—holding candles. She'd written this entire play. She'd worked with them on it for months, every afternoon, made Napoleon uniforms and clown suits and angel costumes, decorated the baby carriage with crepe paper—that was "The Circus Wagon," as the play was called.

And now she stood there, trapped in her sick body.

257

THE DAY AFTER CHRISTMAS

It was the day after Christmas. The buffet had been moved out of the living room to make room for the Christmas tree, as they'd always done. Over the door to the entryway hung a round Christmas decoration with little bells, Santa Clauses and pine needles. It was Ellen's favorite decoration.

Inger and Ellen sat at the dining table getting things ready for Ellen's party. Evelyn went back and forth, she was busy making a fish casserole. The good smell permeated the apartment. Everyone liked fish casserole. Ørnulf was at the club. Inger and Ellen were making up riddles to be on the packages from Santa Claus. You had to guess the riddle before you could open it:

> Oh, you tiny, wrinkled, brown . . .
> zip, to my mouth you'll chase in!

And inside was a little package of Sunmaid Raisins. How's that? Oh yes, Ellen thought that was great. But naturally she didn't want to know anything about the riddle that she'd get herself. Inger wrote out all the riddles on a piece of paper. Ellen cut out little pictures for each package. This year Santa Claus would come by tape recording. Absolutely everyone, big and small, would sit out in the hall, and all the Santa Claus sounds would be recorded ahead of time on the magnetophone that would be hidden under the sofa. Then no one would know where Santa Claus came from or who he was, because of course they'd stopped believing in him a long time ago. "Then they'll probably start believing in him again," Ellen said, pleased.

They'd also have a miniature theater. In the bedroom doorway. The play about "Åse, the Bear and the Prince" was the best one. It had such a wonderful red throne-room set. They rehearsed the roles and changed their voices. "Oh, I can't wait!" Ellen said. "It seems like a hundred years to go. And it's just eleven days! What riddle should we have for the marzipan pig?"

> You, too, are somehow pretty and big,
> you, my lovely, and fat little . . .

"How's that?" "That's good," Ellen said. "I can't wait to see what you'll figure out for me." "You're getting a nail," Inger said. "Wrapped in a gigantic shoe box with red, cellophane paper."

> Ellen loves to get me in the mail.
> I'm such a beautiful, long, thin . . .

"How do you like that one?" "That was just *awful*," Ellen said. "Yes, madam, Christmas certainly is a busy time!" she added, with the word "madam" in an elegant falsetto. "Oh hello! How do you do? How lovely!" Inger answered, in a genteel voice. "Do you really have time to go to the Tea Room in the Christmas rush, madam?" Sonja Munch-Olsen and Josefine Hansen met at the Tea Room in Lilleby. There's no telling how they got there, they just appeared out of nothing. Then they bragged about their husbands and all their fabulous inventions, and about their children who once again had made tremendous progress and were always two years ahead of their peers in achievement and maturity, and then they gossiped about the other two members of the sewing club. Mrs.

Bollerud had always had so many mishaps, and got fatter and fatter each time, and Yvonne Bjerkedal's escapades with strange men got worse and worse. Now she was on Majorca with Mr. Bollerud. "Oh, you know . . ." Ellen sighed, "one needs a breather, of course. And do you know what my husband gave me for Christmas?" "No, do tell!" "A mink stole with ostrich feathers!" "My, how lovely!" "Yeeeehs! And a built-in tape recorder sewn into the fur. That's his latest invention. Then I can listen to all the Christmas carols, you see, as I walk along Storgaten in Lilleby. Yes, indeed!" "How fantastic!" "And what did you get, madam?" "Well, I got a new red sports car. I was tired of the old one. It has built-in water and sewer." "How practical!" Ellen smiled with her stiff how-do-you-do smile. "And how is Anne-Marie?" "Oh, you know she is so brilliantly intelligent! But she always wears pants." "Pants! How dreadful. Couldn't you just sew a skirt for her?" "Oh, I've sewn countless skirts for her," Inger sighed as Josefine Hansen, "but she just throws them onto the floor of her closet. And in the evenings she just lies there listening to Louis Armstrong." "That's just awful. My little boy, of course he's still too little for Negro music. *Fortunately*, I should say. Fortunately. It can make you deaf, of c . . ."

At that moment she stopped, because she heard a key in the lock, and no one must hear their game. Papa was coming home. They could immediately tell by looking at him that he was in a black mood. He nearly always was when he came home from the club. That was where his drinking brought out the devil in him.

He went into the bedroom and changed his socks and put on his smoking jacket. Then he sat down in the chair and took out a bottle of cognac. "Is there any seltzer?" he shouted. Evelyn brought the seltzer water. His foul mood spread over the entire apartment and mixed in with the smell of fish casserole from the kitchen.

"It's not permitted to work in the living room," he said. "Put those papers away!" He couldn't see them from where he was sitting, but it annoyed him anyway.

"But we're making riddles for Ellen's party."

"Put those papers away!" Ørnulf repeated. "It's forbidden to write in the living room."

"Yes, sir! In the living room we're just supposed to sit and listen to your monologues!" Inger said.

"Yes," Ørnulf said. "That is correct."

"How can we enjoy ourselves, if we're just supposed to sit and listen to you?"

"I decide," Ørnulf answered.

They didn't pay any attention to him, and continued making up riddles. Mama came in from the kitchen. "Dinner's ready," she said.

"It's *forbidden* to say that dinner's ready," Ørnulf said.

"Come on, Papa! Can't we eat dinner together for once?"

"I *refuse* to eat if I'm told that dinner is ready."

"Well. Then Inger and Ellen will have to eat first," Evelyn sighed.

"How many times do I have to say that I will not eat if you say that dinner's ready?" Ørnulf asked.

"But it *is* ready."

"It spoils my appetite to hear that dinner's ready."

"When are you going to eat if you're not going to eat when it's ready?" Evelyn asked. Ørnulf made a long pause.

"I'll eat when it suits me!" he said finally.

"Then you'll just have to eat when it suits you," Evelyn said.

"But you said that dinner was ready. Did you or did you not say that dinner was ready?"

"Yes, I said that."

"Good Lord, Papa. She has to be allowed to say that dinner's ready!"

"No!" Ørnulf bellowed. And in the next instant he was across the floor and grabbed hold of the papers Inger was writing riddles on, held the tablet over his head with both hands and in a violent motion hurled it to the floor.

As he did so, the tablet happened to strike the Christmas decoration over the hall door, it fell to the floor and the bells broke into a thousand pieces.

Ellen started to cry.

Then Evelyn came into view in the hallway. She saw the papers on the floor and she saw the Christmas decoration. She stood—with her swollen body and yellow face, and she was only two feet from Ørnulf. Then she slapped him in the face.

This was the first time Inger had ever seen Mama hit Papa. He had threatened her countless times. But now he'd gotten a blow, and he stood there, with a blank expression on his face. It was as if, in a fraction of a second, he realized that he couldn't strike back. So he turned toward Inger and hit her instead.

Then she threw herself at him. He was unsteady, he fell over, she lay on top of him, they were lying next to the Christmas tree, and she grabbed his head, and banged it against the floor. "Now go over to your chair and sit down!" she shrieked. She banged and shrieked. She was beside herself with fury. "Go over to your chair and sit down and shut up!"

Ellen sobbed aloud over her. The Christmas tree swayed.

"Stop it!" Evelyn shouted.

She released him. Pointed at his corner. "Go sit down in your chair!" she repeated and stood up from the floor.

Papa stood up. He went over to his chair and sat down. And he didn't say anything.

They went and picked up the Christmas decoration.

"We'll buy a new one," Evelyn said.

But they all knew that was impossible.

You could always buy a new Christmas decoration, but what had been smashed with it was a ruined childhood, a dream, a hope—that what had happened never would have happened.

Do you see the little bells on the Christmas wreath, Papa? Do you see them? Do you hear them? Do you know what you're doing? Why do you do it? What is it with you? Oh, God—why did you have to behave so that what happened never, never could be fixed?

Was there a prayer? Was there a prayer to pray—that something that already had happened would not have happened? Dear God—let it not be true! Let the Christmas decoration come back to its place over the door! Please don't let Ellen cry like that in the living room! Don't let Papa come and throw sheets of riddles to the floor. And let me never have pounded his head against the floor boards! Oh dear God—bring Papa back to his lamb!

Inger didn't believe in God. Even so she prayed to him. His heavenly darkness had revealed itself to her for the first time when Helga lay in the respirator. Even so she prayed to him. She'd prayed to him from her loneliness in Edinburgh. Let me cope! Let me cope!

Now she had no prayer left—except the one that what had already happened, might not have happened. Mama was going to die. She was alive, but there was no hope.

Dear God! How will I cope! How will I cope when he creates havoc like that? And how will I cope when I'm sick with longing for a girl who doesn't want me?

"Ellen," Inger said. "what has become of Krøllegull O. Muffesen? I haven't seen her in such a long time!"

"Krøllegull O. Muffesen is right here!" Ellen said and dug her out from beneath a jumble. She was a large paper doll made out of cardboard with brown hair and a muff. "And now she's got a best friend!"

Ellen held up the best friend. She had blond curls that exactly matched Krøllegull's.

"I just got her, so she doesn't have a name yet. What do you think her name should be?"

"Solgull Svendsen," Inger said.

"I baptize you with juice, and you shall be called Solgull Svendsen," Ellen said. Then she placed the two cardboard dolls up on the table for all to admire—she called them "cardboard dolls," they were made of cardboard, after all—then she opened her eyes wide and stared hard at Inger with raised eyebrows. "Well, how do you do, madam!" she said. "How lovely!"

Then she clapped her hands together in delighted small town joy.

THE SILENCE

When Rose Mary came back from London after this Christmas vacation, with whiskey in her baggage, as always, she said that when she went home to London this summer, it'd probably be for good. Then Inger realized that she imagined she'd live with Rose Mary the rest of her life.

She knew she felt something for Rose Mary that she'd never felt before—for any person. She realized that was a cliché, and she finally understood how clichés and pop-song lyrics came into being. They were true!

> There'll never be anyone else but you—for me
> never ever be, just couldn't be
> anyone else but you.

All the banal hits in the world could not eradicate the truth. But when you were young, you didn't know that the truth had been true before, and the simplest sentences became the deepest expressions of it.

Inger peered at the cliché she'd just written down, and for the first time she tried to look ahead. For a year Rose Mary had put her life on hold. No, she hadn't. But I've let her do it. When she leaves, my life will be nothing.

> Do the chairs in your parlor
> seem empty and bare?

265

Do you gaze at your door-step
and picture me there?

We'll lose each other. Maybe we'll see each other, every now and then. But it'll never be like it is now. There's no answer for me. My love will always be unrequited. Unrequited love is the greatest and worse absurdity, and there's no help for it.

This was Inger's perspective on the future the day she found out that Rose Mary was leaving. And she found no pop-song lyrics for these.

Doomed to Destruction was the name of a book on the shelf at home. Mama said it was about homosexuality. Inger hadn't read it. The title was too gloomy. But now she understood why it was called that. She was doomed to destruction—not in everything—but in the most significant area of all.

Around this time a debate appeared in *Dagbladet* newspaper. Now there wasn't anything unique about that; all it took was for someone to write: "what is the point of the sixth commandment when half of the population breaks it?" and the newspaper would overflow with letters to the editor. But this time the debate was on homosexuality.

The word "homosexuality" was completely unaccustomed to being in print. People stared at it and read it three times to make sure they'd read the letters in the right order. Then they secretly followed the debate.

The well-known psychiatrist Jan Greve, and the anonymous author of the book *We Who Feel Differently,* Finn Grodal, were debating. The title had passed into the special sarcastic language that raised hell at parties. "You don't feel differently, do you?" people said, with feigned affectation followed by laughter. All references to homosexuality were laughed at, as if it were an extraordinary form of clowning around.

Inger had always been taken aback at the title. It wasn't the feelings that were different. It was just their circumstances. Any homosexual who read *Kristin Lavransdatter* knew that. But there was no homosexual version of *Kristin Lavransdatter,* so that heterosexual readers could understand the same thing. Kristin

266

meets Kristin at Gerdarud, and breaks the engagement to Simon Darre. And if she did that, the calamities surrounding that would be far more extensive than the ones Lavrans brought about, yes, they would be so great that the book would have to be about the calamities and not about the meeting at Gerdarud.

But the debate was not about these existential problems.

Greve wrote—to Inger's enormous amazement—about the homosexual man as "woman-hater" and the homosexual woman as "man-hater." What was further from hatred of the other sex than the homosexual's feelings? If you did anything like hating at all, then of course it *also* had to be a person of the same sex! All feelings, good and bad, were stronger for one's own sex! Even feelings of loathing and disgust! You were bitter and angry, you loved and worshipped, laughed and got lightheaded. This was what homosexuality was. And consequently it was rather one-sided, too, to call it "homophilia"— a word that now had suddenly begun to pop up.

She took hold of her typewriter. She wrote: This is a terrible misunderstanding. How can a lack of desire be confused with hate? Do heterosexual people hate people of the same sex? Does a man hate another man because he doesn't want to sleep with him? Does a woman hate a woman if she doesn't? Signed Inger Holm, student.

The article was returned. The debate was not about hate, either, as claimed by the writer. It was about whether homosexuality was a disease. Jan Greve's main thesis was this: Homosexuality was a result of diseased human development, unknown—as far as he knew—in animals. But, he wrote, one ought not for that reason prevent the contact that homosexuals can have with each other, because this is *the only thing that keeps the homosexual from insanity.*

This was the message. There homosexual readers sat by the thousands all around the country, hidden from each other, reading in the least sexually hostile newspaper in the country that they were insane.

The pseudonymous Finn Grodal wrote that homosexuality was not a disease, but a natural variant of love life. Dr. Greve wrote a long rebuttal where he said that in his statement Finn Grodal had proven the opposite of what he claimed, because if homosexuality had not been a disease, Finn Grodal wouldn't have written under a pseudonym.

Stand up, Finn Grodal! Jan Greve wrote. We want to know who you are!

Yes, stand up! Stand up to the vomit and puke! Why don't you stand up, so you can get the vomit right in your face, instead of having it land pointlessly on the floor? Why don't you do that, Finn Grodal? Here we've gone and bought this fake vomit in a novelty store. Made a special trip and paid for it and everything. And then you're not coming to the party!

Once again a small, brown typewriter was lifted off the floor in Building 1 at Sogn. The discussion is about whether homosexuality is sick. Homosexuality is nothing more or less than feelings one has for people of the same sex. If homosexuals are sick because of their homosexuality, it's society that's made them that way! Inger Holm, student.

This letter was published. There it was. She'd longed for this. Always longed to see her own name in print. She always dove into the newspaper the day after she sent something in, even though she knew they couldn't possibly have had time to print it. For days she waited in an ecstatic and giddy mood, until a small, light green envelope arrived in the mail with the pre-printed card:

> We thank you for your interest
> but unfortunately we are unable
> to use your letter, which we enclose.
> Sincerely, *Dagbladet*

But sometimes her letter was published. Then she was filled with happiness and pride and got comments wherever she went for weeks afterwards. She'd written about everything from the 50 megaton bomb over Novaja Semlja to the view from

Arthur's Seat, and regardless of whether people agreed or disagreed (there were people who disagreed over a view), she always won praise for her pen.

The happiness this produced made up for everything else. Now her name was in the paper again. And she was deeply ashamed.

She was afraid. She hoped nobody out of everyone she knew would read *Dagbladet* on that particular day. Yes, she hoped that in some mysterious way the whole edition would disappear from the newspaper stands in the whole city of Oslo, dissolve into thin air and vanish forever, so that nobody would ever find out that she—Inger Holm, student—had wasted thoughts and letters on a topic like that.

True, she had been careful to write "homophiles" through the whole letter, as if it were a subject that interested her as a socially committed seeker of truth. But it didn't help. It absolutely did not help.

She never found out whether everyone she knew actually had missed reading *Dagbladet* that day. Because, unlike all the other times she'd gotten an article published, no one said a word about this one.

They'd gone blind! On this exact day all of her acquaintances had gone blind.

And it came to pass in those days, that a decree went out from the State Film Censorship Board that 105 feet should be cut from Ingmar Bergman's *The Silence*. This was the first masturbation scene on film during the time Gerhardsen was Prime Minister of Norway. And all went to see the film, each one into his own city. People came flocking, chartered busses were arranged, and people from eastern Norway went across the border and down to Strømstad, Sweden to watch Ingrid Thulin masturbate. And Inger also went down from the Dormitory, from entrance 13, and down to Frogner, unto the movie theater there, which is called the Gimle, to see the film with Rose

Mary, her beloved, being heterosexual. And so it was while they were there, and sat next to each other, the time came that a woman said to another woman: "I love you."

And lo, an intense silence spread in the audience out in the theater, and they were sore afraid. But in Inger the melody welled up of the song from the night she herself had uttered these words and the American folk singing group The Weavers sang in Carnegie Hall: Great tidings we bring! And peace on earth! and she thought that everyone sitting in the rows of seats and the woman who sat beside her now finally would have to hear this message and understand its beauty, and she was filled with awe. Because this was the most powerful scene that ever had come to her on a screen. And she returned home, and praised and lauded Ingmar Bergman for everything she had heard and seen, as it had never been told before.

"Tell me, can you explain that film to me?" Rose Mary said, and immediately added: "I thought it was really dumb. Except for some good photography."

Rose Mary hadn't seen it! Didn't it make any impression at all—seeing a woman sitting on the edge of another woman's bed and begging for her love! That's you and me, Rose Mary. How could it be possible that you didn't see it?

But then—the fact that she didn't see it—was exactly what the film was about!

They walked up Fredrik Stang Street without saying anything—with the crowd of other movie-goers quite a ways ahead of them. It was slippery and Rose Mary's hand hung onto her arm. It was the forbidden blessing of winter—that they had to walk like that, and she felt her hand against her. It was wrong that this brought her pleasure. She walked along feeling the wrong pleasure, and waited for Rose Mary to say something more. She always did. But not now. She just said: "Why don't you tell me what you think?"

But Inger was crushed by the word "dumb." She thought that

finally her own message had been presented. Finally the truth had been told—in a completely public place—without the woman who said it immediately going and hanging herself. Oh, Good God, what a long time it had taken! She'd seen hundreds of films. And in nine out of ten of them there was a person who told another person: "I love you." A man to a woman, a woman to a man. A film just wasn't a film—without these words. Except for *Twelve Angry Men*, which was good despite this flaw. But here it was. A woman sits on the edge of another woman's bed, and she wants her, she is refused, and they are silent.

These thoughts flew through her as they neared Frognerveien to catch the streetcar. But she didn't dare say them. She was afraid to think something different than Rose Mary!

"I feel insecure when you don't say anything, except 'dumb,'" she finally said.

"I'm not an automaton, you know!" Rose Mary exclaimed.

"But I'd like to know what you think first!"

"Are you going to be my disciple?"

They didn't say another word to each other the rest of the way up to the Frogner streetcar. Rose Mary was irritated and Inger was unhappy. It was true, of course! She was throwing herself at her feet. She didn't have an independent will anymore. She was a spineless wimp. It must be terribly irritating to have a spineless wimp by your side. She said: "Actually I'm the sporty type, and I would have preferred to walk to Majorstuen instead of taking the streetcar."

But she remained standing there. And all the way home they said nothing but the necessary civilities.

The next day Rose Mary came into her room, went straight over to where she was sitting at the desk, and stuck out her hand. "I have to apologize," she said. "Why?" "Because I asked you if you wanted to be my disciple." Inger took her hand. "I should apologize myself." "Why?" "Because I said I was the

sporty type and wanted to walk. That was inconsiderate." "But
you certainly could have walked!" "Yes, but I didn't want to
walk!"

Rose Mary remained standing a moment. Inger looked at
her.

"I'm never going to be able to say good-bye to you!" she
said.

That evening they sat talking for a long time. Rose Mary told
about herself—that she couldn't stand thinking about the fact
that she was leaving, either. She'd lived in Norway for five years
and had all her friends here. When she went home she didn't
know what she'd be going to.

"But why do you have to leave?" Inger wanted to know.

"I'll always be an outsider here," Rose Mary said.

When Inger went into her own room again, late that night,
she'd told Rose Mary about her Christmas. She'd told her
about the most painful news she'd received in her whole life
since the time Grandma came and stood by the window. It felt
good to get it out. But suddenly it also had become much more
real. Mama was going to die. She didn't know when. She didn't
know how long she'd still have her. But now she was trapped
inside herself, in her illness. But she was there! She was still
there. In a while she wouldn't be there any more. And that's
all the difference there was in this world. "Dear Mama!" she
wrote. Dear Mama! There's something I must tell you that I
should have said a long time ago. Do you remember your question on the shore? That I didn't answer? The reason was, Inger
wrote, that I only fall in love with girls! I don't know what to
do about it. I love Rose Mary. I'm sitting here longing for her
right now. Can you understand that? I really want you to know
it. That's all there is. She doesn't love me back, but I love her
anyway.

It was a short letter. Just like that. And she didn't mail it.

Why? you might ask. Why didn't she mail this letter—which

was the only right thing for her to write? When she knew that her mother—that Mama—did not condemn homosexual love? Mama didn't share the world's opinion of homosexuality. She'd told her that many years ago. On the contrary. She viewed it with the compassion that she viewed everything that crossed her path. And she didn't classify people according to the degree of reprehensibleness of their behavior, but only according to destinies.

Inger knew all this. She sat there with the little piece of paper with the truth on it. And when her eyes saw the rightest letter she'd ever written to another person, everything went black.

WOMEN'S RIGHTS SOCIETY

"Hello? Does anybody live here?" a loud female voice said in the distance. Inger woke up. It was late in the day. "Hello?" she heard again, still halfway inside the dream she'd been having, which unfortunately was a dream. She got up and went out in her pajamas. A lady in a nurse's uniform stood in the hallway. "Hello. I'm from the Board of Health. Are there really *ladies* living here?" she said, when she caught sight of Inger. The floor was unwashed, there was a sea of dirty dishes in the kitchen, in the corner by the heater in the hall, there were some old cardboard boxes, some coats had fallen off a hook. "No, students do!" Inger said crankily, and marched out to the bathroom.

But that wasn't all. The week before, she and Rose Mary had painted the drab pale yellow cupboard doors in the kitchen an intense revolutionary red. When she came out of the bathroom, the nurse was standing looking at them. "This is the property of the Student Welfare Association!" she said. "This will be reported. I assume you realize that vandalism is grounds for eviction!"

With that she left. Inger went back to bed and tried to retrieve the dream. She'd been dreaming that Rose Mary had come and kissed her in an old fashioned apartment at Frogner. This is completely reprehensible, she thought. Here I lie not making the least effort to prevent it. I just let the kiss come.

She got up, completely contemptuous of her struggles. Why do I dream like that? she thought. I never think about kissing her in reality. It wasn't fair.

She went out into the kitchen, and Rose Mary came back from the store. Inger repeated the exchange in the hallway. "So, we're going to be evicted!" Rose Mary shouted, as if it were especially encouraging news. "Where shall we live, then?" "Oh, I guess we'll have to move to that island." Frida had already left. That is, she'd left the dormitory the previous summer and married the man Rose Mary had found for her. Now she was in full swing spreading diaphragms over the French countryside.

They were out in the kitchen and the conversation went quickly and ironically, back and forth, while Rose Mary read the newspaper. Then Inger saw her hand, and she didn't look away. She looked at it as it took the cup, lifted it to her mouth and put it down again. It was a slender hand, and she savored its fingers and its skin and its movements. She went over and put a kettle of water on, and she looked at the arm holding the newspaper. She looked at it all the way—from the shoulder down to the hand. She looked at the profile of her face, behind the newspaper. It was a beautiful face.

This was the first time she'd ever done anything like this. Without looking away. She knew it was reprehensible and that it was precisely what she must not do. She'd never stop being homosexual, she knew that. But to actually practice it! When she was alone, she made a solemn promise that she would never look at her like that again.

At night when she'd gone to bed, Rose Mary came and lay down beside her. They held each other. They lay like that—next to each other—and held each other until they fell asleep.

Inger fell asleep like that every night. Rose Mary came. She'd made up her mind that she mustn't come. But she did anyway. And how could she stop her? She just did. She just lay there and let her come. It was good. It was good that it was possible for another person to be so wonderful, and just come. And she began to fathom what it meant—this thing she'd always heard about, and which—according to all reports—was supposed to be the highest and most beautiful of everything in life. She began to fathom what it meant for two people to love each other.

That winter something totally momentous happened in Norwegian cultural life. And not just Norwegian, but in Western cultural life as a whole. The thoughts in Betty Friedan's *The Feminine Mystique* were spread all over the world. In Norway they were seized by Birgit Gaarder and deposited in a two-part feature article in *Morgenposten* that appeared February 4th and 5th with the title: "The American Woman in Decline." They were seized by a number of women who'd been thinking these thoughts for a long time and who had discussed them in a rather small circle in Oslo—almost secretly and absolutely against the mainstream for many years. The sensational thing about these thoughts was precisely what Birgit Gaarder had expressed in the title of her article. Things were not moving ahead!

Here for years they'd imagined that everything moved forward. Things moved in different ways, but they did move ahead, nothing was as certain as that, but here it said: the percentage of female students in the U.S. had declined! There were women in America who were qualified and got good grades, and were offered scholarships. And then they turned them down, according to Birgit Gaarder—who was herself in America at that time—because: it reduced their chances of getting married.

It reduced their chances of getting married!

No thank you, replied the qualified and very intelligent women. No thank you, they said. And then they started studying diet pills, curtains and potty training, and American cultural life never saw them again.

Why? one had to inquire. How? and What in the name of hell? one had to ask, was the reason for this? What lay behind the American woman's self-destruction? What forces were driving it? Because that was the word that sprang out of this sensational two-part article. Self-destruction was the word.

Tremendous wrath emanated from this article. Controlled but clear. And in entrance 13 at Sogn a hand took hold of a telephone receiver, a number was dialed and a voice said: "Yes, hello. This is Rose Mary Fernhill. Now I've had enough! Now I want to come home to where I belong. Now I want to come home to where I should have been all along, and fought. Now I'm announcing my arrival in the little arena which for eighty years has been fighting to make it possible for one to stand like this, as an independent girl in a dorm hallway, take the phone and enroll oneself and one's girlfriend in an organization." And that was how Inger was enrolled as a member of the Norwegian Women's Rights Society by the woman she loved.

"Women's Rights Society?" Lill-Ann from Larvik said. They were sitting at The Eternity, as some people had now begun to call the Hangar. "Don't you want the boys to open the door for you? Hold your coat and light your cigarette?"

Inger had nothing against these things. Quite the opposite. "No," she said. "Such ridiculous gestures!"

"Then nothing will be any fun anymore!" Lill-Ann said. "What's so fun about that?" Inger asked. "There has to be a bit of difference. Vive la différence! *I* say!" Lill-Ann said and laughed as she raised her glass in a toast.

Inger had always been irritated at this toast. It sort of implied that girls would put up with anything. Followed by a little laugh. It was a false laugh. The false girl-laugh. She went home and quoted Lill-Ann. "That's completely irrelevant," Rose Mary said. "We're not opposed to common courtesy."

The next day, when they'd partaken of cabbage rolls with eight additional boiled potatoes at The Eternity, around the Larvik table, and had finally arrived at the heart of the matter, namely a South State cigarette, Jakob's match flared against

Inger's unlighted cigarette. "Just save it, Jakob," Lill-Ann said. "Inger can light her own cigarette. You see, she has just joined the Norwegian Women's Rights Society!" "That's completely irrelevant," Inger said. "I'm not opposed to common courtesy." "That's what you said before!" Lill-Ann said. "What are so you opposed to then?" "The fact that women get paid less than men." "*What!?*" Lill-Ann shouted, and got a piece of Danish caught in her throat. "Is that true? Where'd you hear that?" "In the Norwegian Women's Rights Society," Inger said.

The little meeting room at 62 Parkveien was filled with women. They were certainly all what one would call ladies, in that they had nice dresses and firmly permanented hairdos and were of a high and established age—thirty-five and up. But how they talked! It was in the walls, it was among them; a striking determination. These ladies knew what they were talking about!

The innate and apparently natural female indecisiveness—it wasn't there! The women moved their arms as they talked, and their arms emphasized the words, they walked across the floor, sat down on the chairs, and they knew where they were going. They sat down. They were waiting for Eva Kolstad.

This was the gathering that Rose Mary and Inger had ended up at, so strikingly young. They were welcomed—exchanging hand-shakes—as if they were in someone's living room. "How wonderful!" said the woman who had answered the phone, "to get some young members!" It was said seriously and earnestly, like an intimate and intense confidence from many centuries; so that they had to believe they were a sort of historical phenomenon as they entered the room. You are the ones we have been waiting for!

And in came Eva Kolstad.

She was tall and elegant. She was going to give a talk on the topic: "What is Feminism?" She walked through the room and was greeted and applauded in a concentrated mood of appreciation and expectation. Everyone knew that what everyone knew was coming now. This is what they'd come to hear. They'd come to hear what they knew. And they knew it was *this* woman who could say it. Eva Kolstad nodded to the left and to the right, and walked right up in front of the gathering, and there she sat down on the table.

She sat there—on top of a table—and completely without a manuscript. "Well, what is feminism?" She sighed fervently and cheerfully and looked meaningfully and rhetorically out over the assembly. And then—a very, very short laugh. "We might rather ask what feminism is not."

That was what she said. Then she took out her hands.

"As I was walking here today, I thought about the fact that just during this one day I have noticed what feminism was eight times." She listed the eight times on her fingers, the whole talk became a journey through Eva Kolstad's day, as she moved from meeting to meeting, as the politically active person she was, and was the only woman on a committee.

Here sat the only woman on a committee. "It's a kind of sacrificial lamb stage!" Eva Kolstad said. "And if you go deeper into this subject, it's not even possible to reel it off on a few fingers!"

"Reel!" she said—with the singular rolled r that gave her viewpoints an additionally persuasive character, it was a virtuoso lecture, and the applause from the gathering was tremendous and happy. Indignation welled up in the room, shared by all women, but concentrated here in the little room of forty-year-olds and two very young, new ones.

After the lecture there was supposed to be discussion. But what was there to discuss here? No one disagreed with a word of what Eva Kolstad had said. Women had to get involved with the running of things outside the home, and men had to get involved with the running of things inside the home.

The discussion came. How to mobilize? they asked. How to get more women involved in the fight for women's rights? Why didn't they come? When all women—at the bottom of their hearts—were feminists? To be a woman was to be a feminist. To admit it was just a matter of courage. Oh, yes, here were some new thoughts! A slightly older lady stood up: "The struggle for women's rights must never become a mass-movement," she said. "It must be a movement of the elite, that's what it has always been, and that is precisely where its strength lies."

A clicking sound came from a brace. Rose Mary stood up. This was an extremely bold act, but there she stood, and she said in a somewhat agitated and quite nervous tone: "I disagree totally!" Just the accent alone and the agitation in it produced deep silence. "Eva Kolstad's lecture has just shown that women's rights concern us all. I am totally against the mentality that the cause should just be run by a few chosen ones. I think that is . . . quite snobbish!"

Then she sat down again. Confusion. Murmuring. "Yes," Eva Kolstad said. "History has shown that feminism goes in waves. Sometimes there have been few, sometimes there have been many." "But how can we get them with us?" Mobilization? No, they didn't believe in mobilization. Women's suffrage had mobilized people. The days were over when you had an issue that captured everyone's interest.

Many women took the floor on precisely this issue, it clearly captured everyone's interest; ardently they stood up and gestured and said what they thought, and Inger was very uneasy. Because never before had she seen so many elegant women at one time. Women who took the floor and spoke without a manuscript and with great insight. She saw and heard! And she knew that they never, never must learn the truth. That she liked seeing them! Was excited by it, by the energy, the beauty, the self-confidence, by the fairness of their demands, yes, that she quite simply sat there and fell in love with them all, and was happy! And that, of course, was the opposite of what feminism was about!

Inger was sitting at her first meeting of the Norwegian Women's Rights Society. She was deeply impressed and she was twenty-two years old. And she knew that she was hurting the cause by her very presence. Never would she be able to be like them. Never would she have any right to say: Men should take more responsibility in the home. Women should have equal pay. No, never would she be able to stand up anywhere, and say such things, because of course she would never want a man at all. And these hard-working and intelligent and courageous feminists must never find out about this terrible fact.

A few days later a delegation arrived at the Parliament and delivered a proclamation from 129,000 women against sex-education in the schools, honoring the memory of the fore-fathers at Eidsvoll in 1814, who wrote the constitution.

PAPA

Ørnulf had a toothache. He went to the dentist with it, had the tooth pulled, but it wouldn't stop bleeding. He had to go to the hospital. But he knew perfectly well that there'd be no wine there. He took along a bottle of white wine. He spoke with his colleague in internal medicine about this, and he put the wine bottle in the closet in his room. He was admitted at around three in the afternoon, and they expected he'd be released the next day. But about six Evelyn got a phone call from the hospital, and was asked to come immediately. Dr. Holm had had a crisis.

Inger had arrived home the same afternoon, and together they went up to the hospital. Dr. Heyden met them in the corridor and took them into his office. He told them that Dr. Holm had been out to the bathroom and had struck his head against the edge of something (he'd been alone), and the bleeding would not stop. Immediately afterwards he'd passed out, and at the moment he was having convulsions, and they weren't sure he'd come through it.

Therefore he advised them to remain at the hospital.

Evelyn and Inger went to the waiting room and played chess. Evelyn drew white and chose an Italian opening. "No," she suddenly said, a ways into the game. "If you castle now you'll lose your queen." "How so?" Evelyn explained how she'd lose her queen in two moves. "Mama, you're just too nice to play chess." For an hour and a half they sat and moved their chess pieces across the board. While Ørnulf lay in the room next door and might be dying.

At nine o'clock they were allowed to go in. He was lying on his back in the bed, tied down, with a tray on the one side, and his whole body was shaking violently. He peered at them with an empty look. "No, no, no!" he shouted, desperately, and he didn't see them, he waved his arms violently, there was something right in front of him that was attacking him, he shoved it away, it came back. "No, no, no!" A nurse stood beside the bed and took care of him, and talked to him as if he were three years old. "Papa?" Inger said, and went over. She so wanted to know what he was fighting against. But Papa was gone.

When they were out in the corridor again, Evelyn turned to the doctor: "Is it delirium tremens?"

"Oh, no, Mrs. Holm. That's out of the question. Delirium tremens doesn't occur until a couple of days after interruption of alcohol consumption."

They walked down Dronningens gate, the steep hill down from the hospital toward the park. Mama was totally disoriented. Inger noticed her uncertain steps beside her on the hill. She took her by the arm. Papa wasn't there to straighten her out! There was no one by her side to say she was an idiot! Now I'll have to be Papa for her. Otherwise she'll die of anxiety, Inger thought.

"I don't believe it's not delirium tremens," Evelyn said. They telephoned Lisa, who would come as soon as she was able.

This was a Wednesday. On Thursday morning they went up to the hospital again. Dr. Axelsen met them in the corridor with a very serious expression on his face. He opened the door to his office. Evelyn went in, but when Inger was about to follow her, he blocked the way. "No, I think you should stay out here, miss," he said.

But she needs me! Dr. Axelsen, don't you see how ill she is? She can't be without me. But she said nothing. She stood outside and waited while the director of internal medicine at Fredrikstad Regional Hospital gave her dying mother an unknown report about her dying father.

The report he gave was that Dr. Holm had delirium tremens. He'd been at death's door, but now they thought that they had "gotten him through the worst of it." That was the message the head of internal medicine had not found appropriate to deliver in front of the patient's daughter.

Ørnulf was still tied to the bed, and he struggled frantically, as before. Two nurses had to watch him, and it was impossible to get through to him. In the afternoon Inger had to go into Oslo to teach English to a group of housewives, and it didn't occur to her to cancel. What had happened was secret. No one must know. Not even she herself. But she wanted to see him before she left.

When she came in, he was sitting half upright in the bed. "I have to go into Oslo," she said, "but I'll be back on Saturday." "What're you going to do there?" he mumbled, unclearly. "Are you going to the university?" He almost didn't get the last word out. And he asked as if he didn't know the answer. "I'm going to study, you know," she answered. "But Lisa's here." "But isn't the brewery coming soon?" he asked, puzzled. "The brewery isn't coming here." He looked uncomprehendingly at her. "Say," he said. "Can't you run out and get me a beer?"

She had never refused him this before. "No," she said. "There isn't any beer here. And nothing else alcoholic, either." "But Inger?" he said earnestly, and leaned forward a little. "Isn't the brewery coming soon?" "Papa! You're in the hospital!" He looked around. Leaned forward again. "My wallet. It's in my jacket. Can't you run out and get some beerie-poo?" He said it like that. Beerie-poo. "It's against the rules, Papa. You can have some juice." "Where're my glasses?" he asked. She gave them to him, and he wiped them long and energetically with a clean handkerchief he had. Then he handed them back to her without having put them on. "Beerie-poo is good," he said. She took the glasses. "How are you feeling now?" she asked.

"One hundred two," he said.

She called Evelyn from the station and said she thought he'd make it. But she didn't tell her what he'd said. When she got back to Fredrikstad on Saturday, she went straight from the train station and up to the hospital. When she got there, she couldn't get in. In the meantime they'd put him in isolation, and he'd been transferred to the psychiatric unit. There was never any reason given for the isolation. That evening Evelyn and Inger were allowed to visit him for fifteen minutes after all. He was sitting up in bed when they came, with alert eyes.

"That was close," he said.

They went over to him, hugged him, he was back! Evelyn gave him a pair of pajamas she'd bought, because he didn't own any pajamas, and he couldn't stand them. Now he took the package eagerly, unfolded them, and wanted to put them on at once. There he sat in his new stripes, like a child on Christmas Eve. "Tell me, how in the world did I end up in the hospital?"

"You had to have a tooth pulled."

"A tooth?"

"Yes? You know, you had to have that tooth pulled." "You don't extract teeth in the hospital!" "But it wouldn't stop bleeding!" "But?" he said, "when did we leave Oslo?" "Oslo?" "Yes? You remember we were in Oslo. How did we get back from there?"

Evelyn and he had been in Oslo two weeks earlier. It soon became clear that from that point on he couldn't remember a thing. Now he began fussing that he didn't have anything to offer them. "Wouldn't you like a coke?" he asked Inger. "And I'll have a beer." And then they could sit down. Wasn't there anything to sit on? Sit down. How nice of you to come. But wouldn't you like a coke, honey? I'd like a beer myself. Can't I have a beer?" He kept on like this, and the orderly came. "You've already been here much too long. You were supposed to watch the time." And then they were escorted out.

When they came back the next day, he was sitting up in the

bed, crying. Tears rolled down his cheeks, like a little boy who'd gotten lost in the woods. Evelyn put her arms around him. "Are you crying, Ørnulf?" "Yes," he said. "Why?" "You took so long!"

He sat here waiting all day—for fifteen minutes' presence. After these fifteen minutes—where he mostly begged them to get beer—they were shown out again. But when they got home that day, they decided to disobey. They went back the same evening. "Inger?" Ørnulf whispered. "Can't you take a cab over to the Nordheim kiosk and buy a little beer?" "It's not allowed." "They might not see it. You can just . . ." He kept on like that, and that was the only thing he kept on with.

We'll come tomorrow, we'll come tomorrow, yes, I'm already looking forward to that, but remember to (lower) bring some beer.

That evening the hospital staff found the bottle of white wine in the closet. It was unopened, and he'd only brought the one bottle. But the head of the psychiatric ward, Dr. Topp, didn't know that. He immediately assumed that Mrs. Holm had smuggled in an unknown number of wine bottles for her husband, that this was the explanation for his condition and it was also the explanation for the large amounts of barbiturates that had been found in his liver. He immediately telephoned her and bawled her out. "Here we are struggling to save your husband's life!" he hissed at her through the phone, "and then we discover that you are bringing him alcohol behind our backs! Do you realize that one glass from that bottle is enough to kill him in five minutes?"

"He had that bottle with him when he was admitted, and he showed it to the doctor on duty in internal medicine," Evelyn said, and she was unusually clear.

"I refuse to accept that!"

"The bottle was there from the beginning, Dr. Topp. You must believe me! I am an honest person."

"I don't believe that. Substances have been found in his liver that cannot possibly be due to the controlled doses he's gotten here in the hospital. Therefore it's perfectly clear that you are lying, Mrs. Holm. You are lying! And furthermore, you've been here twice, instead of once, and the last time you went in over the protests of the duty nurse. From now on there will be no visits."

That was the way a head doctor at Fredrikstad Regional Hospital reprimanded a dying woman—a woman whom they'd had under treatment just six months earlier and given up on—for something she hadn't done. The fact was that the hospital itself had pumped Ørnulf full of barbiturates. He hadn't had a chance in hell to swallow anything at all since he had his tooth out.

This was clear, and Inger ran up to the hospital. She ran the whole way. This had to be cleared up. She had to talk to Dr. Topp. But Dr. Topp didn't have time to talk to her. She didn't give up. She was then led into an office, where she was allowed to speak with Dr. Topp on the in-house telephone. "How old are you?" he asked. She was twenty-two and in shock. She was barely able to hold onto the telephone and she could hardly stand up. "You must not speak to my mother in that way," she said. "She's not healthy either! And it would facilitate the treatment if you believed what we said!" "There's no point discussing this back and forth," Dr. Topp said. "I've had many disappointments in this field, and I've been in it for years! We've had the experience of opening an orange—an orange, Miss Holm!—and finding morphine inside! The patients always want something, and in nine out of ten cases the family smuggles something in. Good-bye." Then he hung up.

When she got back, Evelyn was on the phone with Dr. Topp. "Yes, we do apologize, Mrs. Holm, but you know, one can't always depend on the duty nurses. It was all a misunderstanding, and for that matter the quarantine has been lifted," he said, and suddenly his voice was smooth as butter and sunshine, and he continued: "By the way, we need your signature on some papers. Just a formality. But Dr. Holm wants to go home, as you know, and we're not allowed to keep him here against his will . . . ."

Evelyn had serious misgivings. But both Inger and Lisa advised her to sign, otherwise he would take a taxi straight from the hospital to Fredrikstad Brewery and come home with five cases of beer in his luggage. Evelyn went up and signed a paper permitting the hospital to hold him for treatment for three weeks.

And three weeks it was. Twenty-one days. "Twenty-one days?" Ørnulf thought. He went straight down to the garage on the Thiis Wharf and retrieved his Cambridge. Then he drove slowly down Nygaardsgata to *Det glade hjørne,* he rolled down the window and waved to the right and to the left, he drove down Farmannsgate and back through Storgata, where he stopped in at Ileby Florists and bought a bouquet of gladioli, he stopped at Anton Olsen's Bookstore, he stopped in everywhere. "So," he said when he got home with the flowers for Evelyn. "Now no one in this city will think I was in jail for drunk driving. Then he put on water for coffee. Every day he drank coffee and put away a large quantity of marzipan chicks. The Easter marzipan had just appeared, and he ate it with his coffee, and next he got a wild desire for dates. Evelyn rushed downtown and bought dates. He sat in his corner and drank coffee and chewed on sweets. And he was as gentle as a lamb.

"Not another drop over my lips—in *this* life," Papa said.

AQUAVIT AND OLD PREJUDICES

The cupboard doors in the kitchen of 1310-14 had—under threat of eviction—just been painted back to their dull, drab gray-yellow color. The two who did the job settled down at the kitchen table for a smoke, and one of them said casually to the other: "Papa just had delirium tremens. He nearly kicked the bucket."

The words grated in the air, and she was immediately sorry. It was as if she wanted to spare her. One Papa more or less—what difference did that make? She felt an odd sort of guilty conscience. She ought to be lighthearted and happy—not dragging along all sorts of things inside her. She was always trying to force herself on her with something private and terrible.

They talked about something else. They went up to the coffee bar in the Tower Building, and here they ran into some big shots in the Socialist Student Club. It was Tore Grasvoll, the misguided candidate for the chairmanship of the Labor Party Student Club, tall Peter from South Africa, who expressed everything ironically with great casualness, and Jens Utgard, whom everyone knew. He was a handsome boy with a high forehead and dark eyebrows, and he stood right in front of Inger with his half-liter of beer and said in his western Norwegian dialect: "Do you come from a good bourgeois home in Eastern Norway?"

She was flattered that he'd bothered to ask her a question, since everyone knew who he was, even though it was this one. "No," she said. "You're not?" he said. "But where are you from, then?" "Fredrikstad." "And what is your father? Lawyer? Lumber baron? Granite King? Ship owner?" "Doctor." "There you see!" Jens Utgard smiled meaningfully and toasted.

That was the first time she'd ever heard the geographical designation "Eastern Norway" used to prove something. Besides, Jens Utgard was going to be a doctor himself, and so was his friend Tore Grasvoll, and the tall Peter from South Africa. It amused the boys to hear that the two of them had just joined the Women's Rights Society, a lively discussion arose, but Rose Mary and Inger were in a not-give-a-damn mood, they'd already drunk two half-liters of beer, and they went with the big shots up to their floor, because there was more to drink there, aquavit, to be precise. Their spirits rose and Tore Grasvoll took Inger and picked her up. He was big and strong and she squealed and kicked her legs as he carried her down the hall to his own room. "Rape! Rape!" she shouted, and when she caught sight of her own silk-stockinged legs in the air she felt that at last she'd managed to behave correctly. Never had she looked so much like a lady. That was why she rushed out with Grasvoll, the medical student, after her and repeated the performance several times, until Jens Utgard decided it was his turn. She embraced him on the sofa where Rose Mary was already sitting with Peter from South Africa, and Tore Grasvoll had to concede that the battle was lost, and he disappeared.

So there they sat, each of them in someone's arms, kissing them, the two boys in the middle of the sofa, the two girls on the outside. How meaningless. Here they ended up in the arms of some boys they barely knew. But after her desperate charade Inger was in a completely keyed-up mood, and she disappeared into Jens Utgard's kiss. Then Rose Mary took her hand.

Her hand lay on the back of the sofa behind Jens' back, and Rose Mary's arm lay in the same place, behind Peter's back. Her fingers took hold of hers there on the back of the sofa behind the boys' shoulders. It was unmistakable. They were holding each other.

That was how a touch should be. Now, said the touch. Now is now. Now has always been now. But never before had it been as now as now. It was good to be alive.

And in this position Jens Utgard from an unknown home in Western Norway got the most passionate kiss any boy had ever gotten from this doctor's daughter from Fredrikstad.

They kept it up like that quite a while, and it was perfect. Because Rose Mary continued to hold her hand without the boys seeing it, but suddenly she exclaimed: "NOW I'm going to walk to Ullevålseter!" Inger laughed ecstatically, it was so funny. But she'd laughed at something awkward as well, just now. The boys laughed uncertainly, and Rose Mary repeated her remark approximately every other minute until she suddenly put her money where her mouth was, at any rate she disappeared out the door with Peter from South Africa at her heels.

"Aren't you going to get undressed?" Jens Utgard said. She got undressed. There she stood, naked and drunk on the floor. So did he. He lay down on top of her in the bed, stroked her, was handsome. The light was on, they could see each other. "Turning off the light is just an old-fashioned idea," he said. "You're turned on," he added, and he wanted to make love. She felt embarrassed. It was true. "Not unless you have something to protect yourself with," she said. Because you knew they never did.

But Jens Utgard wasn't going to become a revolutionary doctor from Western Norway for nothing. He jumped up, pulled out the desk drawer and put on a condom. This was an impressive complication, and she made love with him. But just when it started to feel good she started to cry.

He stopped immediately. Turned over on his side next to her, stroked her. But she couldn't stop. "What is it?" he said. "Why are you crying?" She saw how bewildered he was, through the tears. But all the life in the room was gone. It had disappeared with Rose Mary. Was she sleeping with Peter? "Why are you crying, you're such a pretty girl with a beautiful body?" he said. She peered in amazement at the body he characterized like that. Pretty? Beautiful body? To her confusion she saw that perhaps that was true. When? How? What do I want with this body? Will it just lie around forever without being enjoyed by anyone? What a waste! "Just think if you had to walk around with a leg like that!" Jens said.

Then her tears stopped. Was it possible that a boy preferred her to the most beautiful girl in the world? How could that be possible? How was anything possible? "I have to go," she said. "Really?" he said, and didn't try to stop her. "No. Don't go," he begged. He wanted to do it again. Wanted more. Kissed her. Was sweet. He was a sweet boy. "Come on!" "No," she said abruptly, in the middle of the new kiss, and stood up, dressed, quickly, silently, and left the room.

The next day she was hung over. The aquavit and everything else from the previous day surged through her body in the wrong direction, it was first-class wretchedness, and she was invited to Lisa's for chicken fricassee. That was why she had to run an errand to Majorstuen. The errand for Lisa at Majorstuen was always the same, and for that reason had no other designation. It involved buying a bottle of Brandy Special. The thought of this errand sent her straight to the toilet again. But at last she stood in the line at the liquor store at Majorstuen, a physical trial of dimension, because there was no toilet here, she finally made it out with the bottle, into the streetcar, but here the waves started again, and when the streetcar doors finally opened at Ulleval Stadium, the gush from the waves of aquavit flew straight out in the air through the open door.

After having performed this revolting and pitiful scene right before the eyes of an overflowing Saturday streetcar, she felt a little better, and had to laugh. But the chicken fricassee was an impossibility. She sat in Lisa's large, old kitchen and picked at her food. Lisa had been slaving away half the day on this dish, she was a good cook, and she had made this just for her. "Lisa?"

Inger said, quite meek and unsteady, "I think I'm a little sick." "What is it?" "I guess I just can't eat anything. . . I . . . I've got a hangover!" "No, do you have a hangover?" Lisa shouted, as if she'd just been told that she'd won the lottery. "Tell me everything!"

And Inger told her. Lisa listened enthusiastically. At last Inger was telling her something about her inner life. And Inger knew that Lisa, like Mama, longed for precisely this, but she just sat and picked at the chicken fricassee and longed to tell the truth. "Are you in love, Inger?" Lisa's voice was close and warm. "Yes," Inger said.

Now Lisa was more eager than ever, she took away the chicken fricassee and opened a bottle of beer. "Drink!" she said. "You'll feel better." "I can't face anything with alcohol in it." "I promise you'll feel better. Just take a little sip." Inger took a little sip, and felt better. "Are you really in love!" Lisa said. "Yes." "That's what I've always thought. Just wait until Inger falls in love, I've thought, then she'll get thin. That's how it always was with me, too. The whole last year I've been think-ing—that Inger must be in love. But I haven't dared to ask you, you know. You're so blessed quiet. Just think, you're really in love!" "Yes," Inger said. "But not with him."

This answer enraptured Lisa even more, if possible. "Not with him? Not with the medical student you slept with? Who is it then, if I dare ask?" "With someone else. Someone who was at the party." As soon as she said this, she drank the whole glass of beer. "There you see. It helps? Doesn't it help?" "Yes." "Tell about the someone else." "Well, I've been in love with the other person for a very long time. But . . . ." Here she stopped abruptly. Because the next word she was about to say was a personal pronoun in the third person singular. And she didn't dare. She didn't dare now, either, even though for a moment she'd imagined that she'd dare, that she had to, she could tell Lisa, who'd loved her ever since she was bald and full of red spots at the hospital. "But what?" Lisa said. "Didn't he want you?"

"No," Inger said, overwhelmed with relief and disappointment at the same time. Everything sank. Before it had even risen up.

A few days later Jens called and asked her out. He'd gotten an invitation to some friends, and they were all supposed to bring girls along. Did she want to go? She knew she should say yes to this. This was a clear and proper invitation. From a boy she liked. He hadn't just had her, and then disappeared. He wanted to see her again. "No," she said.

She could tell she'd hurt him. He tried to persuade her. And she could only say "No" again, without explanation.

Without explanation, without explanation, she went through life without explanation. She wished she could tell him right there on the telephone exactly what it was. That it was no use. I liked you, Jens, but it wouldn't work anyway! I'm not for boys, can you understand that? You were great and I felt good, but that's not what I want! Because I want a woman. I want a woman, just like you do, Jens—no matter how strange that is! and I have no idea why, I was either made like that or I've become like that, or both, I have no idea, but I am made and I have become.

The fact of the matter was that Rose Mary was definitely not going anywhere that evening. She was going to stay home. And Inger couldn't stand the thought of letting this opportunity to be with her get away. That's how it was. How long would she continue to arrange her life according to her? When it wouldn't ever be any use anyway? Nothing would help. Not a boy, not a girl. No one. I have to live the rest of my life with no one. Where was someone else? Where was there another no one? Was there no one who also was no one? And how would she ever manage to find her? And why should she try to find her when the only one she wanted lived in the next room? I have to go to her, it's making me crazy. I've gone crazy. Am I crazy? This is driving me crazy, I'm just driven around the room in here, and am crazy, and I can fight it and fight it, but no matter how hard I fight, I'm forced out of my room against my will.

She needed comforting! That was what she was searching for. She'd explained that to her, too. Comforting was what she needed, when she came like that. Nothing else. It had nothing to do with sexuality. She wasn't horny. She was in despair! She went straight into her room and fell on her knees.

This time Rose Mary sat right up on the sofa and put her arms around her and stroked her hair. As if it were an agreement! It filled her with sadness. Suddenly she felt sorry for her. She gave her what she'd asked for. Comforting.

But in the middle of the comforting came the desire. She wanted to lie down next to her, feel her body against hers, it was absolutely clear, an urge. An urge? Am I controlled by urges? She was ashamed. She left. This wasn't going anywhere. She'd always leave her without accomplishing what she had come for. The thoughts came in her absence. But in her presence there were no thoughts. There was nothing she wanted to say. She didn't come to say anything at all. She'd never come to her to say anything. Not even the first time. She wasn't interested in saying. It was something quite different—that didn't have anything to do with saying—that she was interested in.

It was strange. It was awful. What shall I do? Is there no one who can help me?

It was Jean-Paul Sartre who helped her.

Sartre had said that life was a choice. No matter what you've chosen in the past, in the future you can choose something else. You are what you do. That was existentialism's great hope, that Christianity did not give. Christianity said you were a sinner, and had to spend your life washing yourself clean. But according to Sartre, things were only good or evil when you did them. You always had a new chance.

Inger made up her mind that life was words. By putting words to her love it had become more real. It persecuted and tortured her and never let her be in peace. Once—a long time ago, when she sat in her lonely room in Edinburgh—she'd made up her mind to put words to the truth. Because this was the only way, she thought, that she could fight it. And she'd written down the names of all the girls she had loved.

Now she decided that all this writing had just made the love more real. And the only way she could fight it was by being silent.

It was a choice. She'd quit writing endless outpourings of her emotions. She'd stop filling her notebooks with yearnings and cravings that would never lead to anything. From now on if she wrote anything it would be restricted to: 1. History notes. 2. Articles for *Dagbladet*. 3. Completely fictitious stories with no foundation in reality. 4. A record of her expenses.

This program was carried out. Inger wrote and wrote. She wrote herself out of her urges. They came back. She wrote herself out of them again. They came, and soon they radiated from the paper. She wrote about absolutely everything. Except the urges.

She took a soup job. And it was May. It involved being a secret agent for DE–NO–FA/Lilleborg, and going out on Roald Amundsen Street and saying to innocent passersby: "Excuse me, my name is Inger Holm. I represent Norwegian Gallup Polls. Would you mind coming in and tasting our soups?"

There were two kinds of tomato soup and two kinds of minestrone soup, and while the interviewees ate their way through the samples of soup, they were to answer twenty-five questions about their soup habits. When Inger thus had established herself in the world of market research, she invited Rose Mary to come and taste. Then she spent the day in a state of constant preparedness between soups because Rose Mary might show up at any moment, and when Rose Mary did show up she got a shock. Shocked, she asked Rose Mary to take a seat, gave her a sample of soup, and said:

"Do you like the soup, miss?"

"Yes," Rose Mary answered, "the first tomato soup and the second minestrone soup were best."

"How often do you eat soup?" Inger asked. "Every day? Two or more times a week? Just occasionally? Never?" "Just occa-

sionally." "Do you like prepared soups?" Inger asked. "Oh, *jo*,"
Rose Mary answered. She seldom made a mistake. But here
was one of them. In discovering the Norwegian word "*jo*" she
used it at random through her own "*ja*-hole." "Do you use
soup cubes or a package mix?" "Cubes! Absolutely!" "Do you
ever make your soup from scratch?" "Never!" "Miss! Can you
tell me now what association you have when you hear the expression 'Blue Ribbon'?" "The Titanic!" Rose Mary said.
"Thank you. That's all. You may go now, and thank you for
your assistance."

Rose Mary left, and that was how Inger got an outlet for her
urges, and as she walked up Roald Amundsen Street after fin-
ishing her job this warm spring day in her jeans and a baggy
khaki shirt from the M. O. Schøyen Bus Company, she thought
about Rose Mary and the minestrone soup and felt quite happy.
At the same instant she was stopped by a man. "Do you have
breasts?"

The man, who was walking in the opposite direction on the
sidewalk, stretched out an arm in the unmistakable direction
of the body parts he wanted to determine the existence of.
Before she could gather her wits, he reached his goal, too.

She pushed his arm away, and stared into the face of a young,
unshaven and narrow-faced man with uncombed hair. "Do you
have a dick?" she asked.

This question left the young man at a loss for an answer. She
didn't stand and wait for one either. Even less did she accom-
pany the question by making a grab for the body part she'd
mentioned. She walked on up Roald Amundsen Street and
caught the two minutes after the quarter hour streetcar in a
very flustered state of mind.

She was hurt. That was the truth. Hurt! That a complete
stranger and totally unimportant male had doubted the existence of her breasts. But there was something else—that was
worse than the question and the hand that came. And that was
that this man—from one second to the next—had succeeded
in tearing down all her thoughts and completely changing her

state of mind.

The streetcar rumbled through the tunnel. People sat around her, not looking at her, reading the daily newspaper, which she also had with her. But she couldn't bring herself to read it. Here everything was safe. Seemingly. There was no one here who looked like they might suddenly grab hold of her right breast and say: "Do you have breasts?" Absolutely not. But of course there hadn't been on Roald Amundsen Street either. That sort of person came from the moon. Absolutely from the moon. From idiot land. Why did she live in idiot land? Was that necessary? Suddenly she burst into ringing laughter. It rang out through the whole Sognsvann streetcar, in the middle of the streetcar silence. Several newspapers were lowered, heads turned, a couple of faces brightened up in uncertain amusement. But most of the faces pretended they weren't equipped with ears on the sides. What if she invented a country? It was up to her. She could invent an idiot land, exactly like the one she lived in. She could send a quite ordinary Norwegian boy there. His name could be Per, because he's supposed to be completely normal. He wakes up outside of idiot land one morning, he doesn't know why, but he starts walking in toward a city, the capital of idiot land. He sits down on a bench. Immediately two people of the female gender sit down on the bench and start poking him around the crotch. "You got anything down there?" they say. "Get your hands off!" Per howls, furious and normal. They slide closer. "How 'bout some action tonight, baby?" they say then. Then Per discovers, to his horror and disgust that all the males in the city are walking around with erections. They have their tool raised up in a sheath! That's why the women on the bench wonder if he has anything there. He should have been wearing a sheath!

The men in idiot land wriggle down the street in colorful, flowing clothes. The women are dressed in a sort of uniform. By now Per is boiling with fury. He stands up from the bench, because the two disgusting ladies won't give up. He leaves angrily, while the two ladies make mirthful and loud comments about him, referring essentially to his rear end.

That was the reason for the laughter that rang out on the Sognsvann streetcar that summer day—so apparently unmotivated, and Inger went straight home and wrote the first chapter of her new novel, *Feminapolis*.

It was completely consistent with Sartre and her decision. It was about something entirely different. It was totally invented. But then she ran into problems. Because who would her Per fall in love with? It wasn't very likely that he'd fall in love with one of the aggressive, uniformed women. It would be more natural for him to set his sights on one of the colorful men.

But he was supposed to be normal! The whole point with Per in idiot land was, of course, that he was supposed to be a normal young boy. But of course she didn't have to give a damn about that. She was writing a book. She could simply not give a damn about everything. It was up to her.

But she knew as soon as the dilemma reached a climax: She knew she'd never dare write a book where a boy falls in love with another boy. And writing a novel without a romance was unthinkable. All human beings fall in love, and in novels they fall in love twice as often, that was the whole point of writing novels. Why did this always have to enter in and ruin her whole future authorship? Were there any authors who lied? What did they do if what they wanted to say was what they absolutely did not want to say? And if she just didn't give a damn and wrote what she wanted anyway, how could Per get involved in a romance with a sweet man in idiot land without any scruples? He'd have all kinds of scruples, coming from the other idiot land as he did. Because of course he was already from idiot land. He'd just come to a new one. The book would have to be about scruples. And who could write a whole book about scruples? And why did you have to end up with a book about scruples, when you actually had intended to write a book about idiot land?

How would she manage to write the book?

"Mama," she said. "I've got an idea for a book."

"Oh? What's it about?"

And so she told Mama about Feminapolis. But she neglected to tell about the romance problem.

But Evelyn put the last plate in the dish rack and peered out the kitchen window. Then she said with all the strength and laughter that were left in her:

"Yes, you write that book, Inger!"

Then she laughed so hard that tears rolled down her cheeks.

And Inger never forgot this request. It remained in her like a promise, that she didn't keep until many, many years later. The book became more popular than she ever could have imagined as she sat on the subway and thought it up, and she received countless letters from perfect strangers who confided in her and told her what the book had meant to them. That was when she remembered a lady named Iona Fairchild on the M/S Braemar.

Spring arrived with intensely hot weather, they drank and partied through the days, it rained cats and dogs over the dormitory, and they went out in it wearing nothing but Kelly coats and underwear, they got sopping wet, floated back to the whiskey bottle, The Weavers sang, "I am a-lone-ly and a lonesome traveller," and they drank from a beer keg they'd ordered—with a tap—and in the middle of the general tumult Rose Mary took Inger's hand and said: "Do you doubt that I love you?"

Then the world tipped completely over so that the North Pole ended up where the South Pole was and vice versa. But Rose Mary wasn't sober. That was why she didn't give up until she'd gotten an answer. The answer was yes, of course, and terrified she answered no. But the remark remained inside her like a plateau, an active, sparkling, living plateau that dwelled inside her wherever she went and held her precisely one-and-a-half feet off the ground, over Sognsveien, over the lawns between the buildings, over the floor in 1314, look, look! she said exuberantly to the dark lady, who soon would have witnessed all the moods it was possible for a human being to be in. "Do you doubt that I love you?" said the weather, and one warm day in June she stood on Fred. Olsen's dock to watch a boat leave.

She was going to watch a boat leave. You had to believe what you saw. The girl who was leaving hugged all her friends, who stood in a half circle around her. Then she cried. A moment later she appeared in a porthole, quite a ways down the side of the ship, there was her pretty face in the opening, and it wept and looked at them, and the boat sailed out.

You had to believe what you saw. And it was sun and June.

Before Rose Mary left she said to Inger: "I've told Frida. About you." Inger felt betrayed. Rose Mary said: "I didn't tell her. She guessed." Inger thought: It meant more to her to satisfy Frida's curiosity for a moment than to keep the most important promise any person has ever made to me. But she didn't say anything. She was incapable of reproaching her. Rose Mary said: "The days after you told me, I think were the most difficult of my life. I don't think I've ever been so confused."

She felt Inger's mute accusation, and she was reproaching herself.

Then Inger looked at her with a surprised expression. It had never occurred to her that Rose Mary could ever be confused or anything like it. To be Rose Mary, was to be in ecstasy. To live in it no matter where you set foot. To have it, like the air around yourself, pure and clear. Now ecstasy shone around the M/S Blenheim until it disappeared like a white dot in Oslo fjord.

They walked down the dock, Frida and Inger. And for a long time they said nothing. They walked in the sun and pulled themselves together. Inger had never opened her mouth to Frida about what she knew that she knew. But now she said quite simply: "This is the worst thing that's ever happened to me."

Frida walked a little ways, quick in her movements, as always.

Then she said: "Inger, now that you've finally been through something like this, just be glad it was a woman. Then you can be rid of that damn prejudice that women can't be friends."

When Inger got home to the dormitory, Lidia came and invited her into her room. She sat down in front of her on a low stool—with her elbows on her knees and looked at her.

Over the past few months Inger had forgotten about Lidia's existence. She'd seen her every day, heard her sounds, heard how she played Beethoven's Seventh Symphony through the door. A new girl had moved into the suite. Inger barely knew what she was studying. She'd completely lost contact with Elsa. Marit Heimstad from Lisleby walked by now and then, she'd moved down to building 1, they chatted, and said: "We'll have to visit each other sometime!" But they never did. Now Lidia sat in front of her on the little stool and offered her a glass of white wine. "Do you feel like something has died inside you?" she said.

Inger nodded.

THE SUMMER OF 1964

The well was below the house at the lowest point of the field right next to a steep rock wall. It was an old well, the barn-red well-house had a steeply sloping roof, and it never went dry. Even in the summer of 1955, when all the cisterns were empty, there was still water in the well in August. All around it stood buttercups and clover; the blackberries were in bloom, but the buttercups shone. Had anyone ever seen a more radiant flower?

The dark surface of the water was disturbed by the bucket, which slowly filled with water. It was the summer of 1964.

Every day Inger went to this well. It was the first summer since she graduated that she hadn't been away. She'd always longed to travel, but this year all her longing was gathered here, and there was nothing she could do about it, but stay where she was, and long.

The house at Ekekjær was theirs now. It was a large house with living room, dining room and drawing room downstairs and five bedrooms upstairs, alcoves and three-season porch. It was being painted. It shone white and large in the landscape with its white gables and trim. On the other side of the yard was the bungalow, which Emilie had built with the insurance money the time the barn burned down, and called it the "gardener's house." Its fate was still undetermined. "You have to buy it, Lisa!" Evelyn said. "Then I won't be alone here!" "I'd never be able to afford it!" Lisa said.

The dark surface of the water was disturbed by the bucket. Does she think she's going to live? Have a life—where Lisa would live in the bungalow? Life was lived as if she'd be alive. Ørnulf established himself in the living room with a guest book. Then he beckoned everyone in so they could congratulate them. Lisa installed herself in the brown room that faced east. Every room had its own color. She withdrew with her little miniature pinscher, Birgitte, and a bottle of port, and played solitaire, every time the waves in the living room got too high. She never said good night. She just vanished, quite soundlessly. Evelyn went for walks with Ellen. They saw lions and tigers on the road, that they came home and told about. There was especially one spot behind a knoll.

Inger saw them coming across the yard. She'd entrenched herself in the blue room on the west side. She had a stack of books with her. She became engrossed in them with all the passion that previously had been applied to listening for footsteps. For every line she read, she had thoughts she could write down and mail to a girl in south London.

And she got replies. In thick letters that landed in a mailbox by a boat slip, right by the marina, where it was so pretty. It was pretty everywhere at Tjøme. And written on the envelope in blue ink was Inger's name. Her eyes met the ink, and because they did, she went on living.

She longed to talk to Mama about this. What would Mama say if she told that her life resided in that blue ink? This might be the last summer I have her.

"Mama, I'm going to go to Spain next summer," she said.

"Oh, no!"

"Oh, yes!"

"But then I won't get to see you?"

Next summer. Next summer?

"You'll get to see me all this summer and on every vacation, but I have to go to Spain because . . ."

Because that's what I live for.

" . . . because I promised."

"Are you going with Rose Mary?"

"Yes, we're going to go down and visit Frida. We agreed on it before Rose Mary left."

"You like her . . . ?"

"Yes, she's really . . ."

She's really, she is so really, how could she possibly say how really Rose Mary was of everything it was possible to be?

". . . great," she said.

Then she went up and entrenched herself in the blue room. She plowed through the stack of books. *The Bells of the Kremlin, Marcus Thrane, Father of the Labor Movement, The Rise and Fall of the Third Reich.* Everything that could get her to understand history.

History was the one subject she'd always known she would take. Ever since the revelation she had in the closet room in Edinburgh, when she saw the man under the stars, history had been at the center of everything. But actually this center had come into existence long before. It was when Anna Karlsen had come with the blue book, *Our People,* and they were ten years old. "Olav was only six years old when word of the battle of Svolder came to Ringerike," it said. For some unknown reason the sentence stuck in her memory. History was people who got word of great things and understood their destiny. But history had always been so kind before. The grandchild came to the grandfather in the beginning of the first history book, and the grandfather told how streetcars had been pulled by horses before, and that he remembered when the first lights came. Unjust things had happened; Joan of Arc should never have been burned. But when all was said and done, history itself had agreed with these people, and now she saw that it wasn't like that. That people everywhere had suffered in vain. Marcus Thrane! What had he gotten out of his struggle? There he'd sat in prison, been sick and suffered. A role model? What good had it done him to be a role model, he was dead. And the prisoners under Stalin, the faithful Communists, when did they get their due? And they could never even be a role model. And the Jews, who were just crammed into boxcars and gassed to death with Syklon B. Who could nullify the hole that Syklon B had come through? She read *The Scourge of the Swastika* by Lord Russell of Liverpool.

That book changed everything. It told all about all the barbaric and scheming methods the Germans had used, against Jews, against Russian prisoners of war; scientific experiments, how they'd lowered them into ice water and into boiling hot water to see how much cold and heat a human being could endure, how Jews were crammed into trucks and a hose was run from the exhaust pipe straight into the trucks where they were sitting. That was before Syklon B came. When they discovered Syklon B, they deceived millions of people into going into some rooms where they thought they were going to have a shower.

She'd always heard about this, both at school and at home. But she'd never read about it—so concretely. As if she herself were sitting in the truck. She knew that Jews had been persecuted and killed, that they'd been imprisoned in so-called concentration camps, where they died of hunger and Typhus. But where in history hadn't they learned about killing? Everyone killed everyone in history, and which ones ended up as heroes, depended on who won. But what was this? A history so gruesome that no textbook had told about it. The history book at school ended in 1939.

There were books, she knew that. *Among Living Corpses* was the name of one. The survivors had told their stories. Lord Russell had captured their voice, and he'd gotten in trouble. The British authorities were afraid that his book would damage the good relationship that was being established between England and Germany. But he staked his position on it, and wrote.

Inger thought about the Jews. After Lord Russell of Liverpool's book it was impossible not to think about the Jews.

She let the book rest on her knee, she took it with her to the beach, and sat between the pine trees at Emilie's old sunning spot. Ellen crept close to her. She came with her small body and the hope that she'd soon be done with the book. "Can't you tell me what's in the book?" she said. "You see, it's not a book for children." "No, but you don't have to read it out loud. You can just tell me what it says." Not a book for children! But Syklon B hadn't spared the children. Little Ellen! How much too small you are—to experience what you must! She put her arms around her. "Well, it's about a man with a little black moustache named Hitler. He tried to control everything that happened on earth." "Did he do it?" "No. That is, first he managed it, at home in Germany where he lived, and everyone shouted with joy and waved at him and threw flowers at him wherever he went, even though everything he said was completely mad. But they didn't realize that. Or they pretended they didn't realize it." "But what did he say then?" "He said . . . he said . . . Inger tried to think herself into the trunk of the pine tree. "He said that all people who weren't exactly like he wanted them to be, shouldn't be allowed to be there. There were some people called Jews in Germany, they came from lots of different countries, and settled down, and had lived there a very long time. Then Hitler's people came and chased them out of the houses where they'd been living and put them in prison and lots of them died. But the people who lived next door to them pretended they didn't see them being hauled away. And that was why he could just keep doing it for a very long time. But then he tried to get people in lots of different countries to glorify him, too—and to not look at what he did. But they did see it, and fought against him, so in the end he had to give up." "Oh? What's he doing now?" "Well he's dead, because he didn't get his way." "But you can't die from not getting your way, can you?" "No. But he got so angry that he took his own life. He took some of those pills, probably, that you ate when you were little, you know? And that are very dangerous if you take a lot of them. And then he died."

307

Inger and Ellen sat looking into the pine forest and thought about Hitler. Then they chased him away, and Ellen said: "Can't we go out on the air mattress now?"

They went out on the air mattress. Ellen was like a dolphin. They splashed and laughed, and the longing was in the splashing, and the sea gulls screamed, but Inger couldn't stop thinking about the Jews. And suddenly the walls came crashing down. The walls in the living room where Mama and Papa's history was.

Mama and Papa had gotten married in Potsdam in 1937. They'd walked down Kurfürstendamm, in love. They'd made Helga on a street named Uhlandstrasse. There was a picture that was brown, with Mama and Lisa standing at a *U-bahn* station with throngs of people in SS uniforms.

"Mama!" she said. "What did you think when you walked on Kurfürstendamm and saw 'Jude geschlossen?'"

They were sitting on the porch steps in the evening. Ellen had gone to bed, Papa was in Fredrikstad.

"We thought they'd be sent to work camps and be retrained and learn a trade." "But they had a job! They had a store!" "There was terrible propaganda against the Jews. It was said they didn't work. Stories were published about Jewish film-makers who raped young girls." "But if that were true, then it wasn't because they were Jews, was it?" "No, but that's how it was represented." "Well, did you believe it, then?" "No. But actually we looked at Hitler as a kind of comical figure who couldn't possibly be in power for long. And when his screaming got too bad, we turned off the radio." "But didn't you know what happened when the Jews were sent away?" "No. We didn't find out about that until after the war. And at first we didn't believe it. But then we realized it was true. And then we felt that the world had gone back to the Middle ages."

There was no reason not to believe Mama. There'd never been any reason not to believe her. Even so she felt that Mama and Papa should have been able to do something to stop what was happening, instead of walking around and being in love.

She just couldn't stop feeling this way. There was something dead wrong with the whole business. "After the war," Mama said, "I thought: I'm never going to be interested in politics again!" "But, Mama! You *have* to be interested in politics! You just can't not be. Things have to be organized. They just can't not be organized. And then you have to have an opinion as to how. Otherwise there'd just be a big mess, obviously!"

Mama sighed and cleared her throat, she had such a distinctive little way of clearing her throat. "You're right," she said, "that's what I used to think, too. But the war ruined that. I made up my mind that I would not ignore my mother on the street. But then I was despised and threatened with liquidation. We sang "God Save the King" at a meeting of the Actor's Guild, and afterwards Werner Gislo came over to me and said: 'If it comes out tomorrow that we've been singing "God Save the King" here, you won't be alive the day after tomorrow!' The war brought out the best and the worst in people. When you were born I lay next to another woman who was having a baby. She chatted and held forth and said: 'There's no such thing as a good German!' 'Excuse me,' I said then, 'but my mother is German.' When the nurse came in she asked to have a screen placed between our beds. And every time she had a visitor, she whispered to them: 'There's a traitor in the next bed. Watch what you say.'

"That's how you spent the first days of your life, Inger. Behind a screen."

Mama told. "There was one night in Oslo. It was dark, of course, there was black-out everywhere. We'd been at a party, and came trudging down Ullevålsveien. There on a corner two uniformed Germans came toward us. And as we passed, we realized that one of them was Reichskommissar Terboven. When we turned the corner at Collettsgate, Papa said: 'If I'd had a hand grenade now, I would have used it.'"

Later Inger often thought about Papa and the hand grenade. If he'd used it, and managed to get away, he'd have been a hero. No matter how racist he might have been, and that in his heart of hearts he'd been on the German side. He'd have been a hero anyway. He wouldn't have had to sit in his chair at home and be in the wrong for all eternity. He wouldn't have had to drink himself into bitterness, and torment Mama with how right he was. Maybe their whole life would have been different if only Papa'd had a grenade that night.

Actually it was impossible to imagine how it'd been—to have been young when the war came, and have so many things destroyed that you'd dreamed about. You weren't even allowed to stand on the steps with your student cap on your head and a catastrophe in your breast. The catastrophe was all around you, and destroyed everything inside. It was so easy to sit here later and be the next generation and say: This is what you should have thought and done!

"When the war was over, there was just one thing to hope for," Mama said. "And that was you! Sometimes I think that your generation is the most spoiled one in the history of the world."

Inger laughed. "If that's so, then it's not our fault!" "No, I don't think there's anything wrong with that! I've never understood what it meant—to spoil children. You *encourage* them! What people need is *praise!*" Mama said.

They stayed sitting for a little while on the porch steps, looking out at the hazelnut bush and the blue evening sky. When Mama was little she'd had a porcupine family in there.

"Sometimes I think I wish I were you," Mama said.

"Oh? Do you think things are so good with me?"

"Yes, I do, actually."

Inger smiled a little at this, and was amazed. Of course Mama had no idea what it was like to be her. And even so in the same moment Inger suspected that she was most certainly right.

Because what was it like to be Inger when the alternative was to be Mama? Then things were unbelievably good with her, of course. And then and there an intense defiance awoke within her, that just grew and grew as time passed—that she would live her life so that her mother would not have lived in vain.

No one would ever have her under his heel. That was the only way that the meaninglessness that was happening to her mother now would have any meaning at all. Mama, she thought, I'm going to be the way you want me to be! What else can I do with the fact that you are dying and will never get to see it?

On many evenings during the summer Inger and Evelyn sat like that, talking on the steps. When Papa was in Fredrikstad there was room to think.

The attack of delirium tremens had transformed Ørnulf totally. At first he was like a child. Then he became like a juvenile who devoured sweets. Then he became like the papa Inger knew from her childhood, full of energy and fun; the papa who'd taught her to fish and row, taught her to swim, so she was never afraid of deep water. Then once again he became the papa who sat and drank.

It happened on a Sunday outing to Arvika, across the Swedish border. They'd gone there over Pentecost, and he hadn't had anything to drink in over two months. He was in a marvelous mood, the sun was shining, they drove through Rakkestad, "There's no place in the world as beautiful as Rakkestad!" Papa said. That was what his club buddy in elite bridge always said, Bjørn Mjelster, because he was born there. And the place really was beautiful, too, surrounded by green hills and a river running through it, but when they came to the City Hotel in Arvika Papa ordered a Mellan Swedish beer.

It was a quite ordinary, yellow sparkling beer. It was placed on the table and Papa drank it in one gulp, standing. "Aaaaah! That hit the spot!" he said.

Then it was as if everything sank. In the little glass of beer, that disappeared down Papa's throat, sunshine and green hillsides, joy and hope all sank. She'd believed him! She'd really believed him when he said he'd never drink again in this lifetime. Now she knew that he'd drink every day until he died.

He arrived at Tjøme with a cardboard box. In the box was hell. It was a brown cardboard box with nine corrugated cardboard dividers, and in each of the spaces stood a bottle with a gold cork and golden contents. And that was what the summer's hell looked like.

Mama held her own. She went for long walks with Ellen over the meadows, and in the evening she squeezed oranges. But her body was swollen and yellow. And at night screams were heard from the living room. They sounded like death cries. Inger could lie listening to the yelling through the old wooden walls, and she knew it was about nothing more than a glass of milk or an ashtray. He might have been sitting for a half an hour asking her to remove the ashtray, and she might perhaps have said, when he asked her about it the first time: "It's not quite full yet." Then the hell from the cardboard box came out in an endless argument about the ashtray, and whether Mama maintained that she had not refused to empty it.

Inger lay listening to the death cries and read about the chilling of Russian prisoners of war in scientific experiments, and knew that this was what the screams were about. Sometimes she went down.

"It appears that Mama thinks she has to go upstairs to get out of the house," Papa said.

It was true that Mama was in a daze. She'd been drinking now anyway. She had a glass of white wine in front of her. She didn't respond to Papa's assertion. "Do you deny that you went upstairs to go outside?" Papa said. Mama didn't reply. "Answer me!" Mama didn't answer. She sat there, almost motionless.

"You promised to quit drinking!" Inger said. "Now I know I never can trust you again!"

"Who're you going to trust?" Papa said calmly. "You'll never get another papa."

Mama sighed deeply now and stirred in her chair.

"Where're you going?" Papa asked. "I'm going . . . to the bathroom," Mama said. "Remember you don't have to go upstairs to get there, you dizzy dame," he said. She left without answering. "*She's* dying!" Papa said, as soon as he heard the door close behind her. Inger never answered this. She sat—stiffly—in Papa's terrorism-air. It was as though he owned the air in the living room. Mama came back. She sat down. "Now . . . I'll have a cigarette. And then I'm going to bed." The words were vague, hesitant, flat, almost, in the certain knowledge that everything she said could be disputed.

"You can't go to bed before we get to the bottom of things."

"We'll . . . never get to the bottom of things."

She'd become apathetic—in his presence. She just shut herself inside herself, sat motionless, completely unlike the way she'd been before, when she'd always protested and finally exploded. When he was in Fredrikstad she livened up. But when he came, she just sat there.

"You can't go to bed until we get to the bottom of things," Papa said.

Then she shouted loudly and fervently:

"Ørnulf! We'll *never* get to the bottom of things!"

That left him speechless. For a moment he sat there pretending that he wasn't. Then he said. "Until that paper is destroyed, we can be regarded as separated." "Dr. Topp said it was merely a formality." "That's bunk! You signed a paper saying I was insane! If you refuse to declare that paper null and void, I'm going to court."

It was approximately the fifteenth time he had said this.

"Good Lord, you were sick!" Inger said. "Mama had to sign, she didn't have any choice. If you'd gotten out of the hospital then, you'd have drunk yourself to death immediately. Do you realize all you talked about was beer!" "That paper must be destroyed! There it says, black on white, that I am insane," "There wasn't a word on the paper about you being insane, Papa. But, damn it, there should have been!"

"So! You think you have an insane father?"

Now he was enjoying himself. He was truly in his element. Not the least bit angry. He relished the commotion that followed. He poured himself another cognac.

"You'll never find a man, Inger," he said, "you love me too much. You'll be lonely! Carry that with you like a ball and chain."

After the cigarette, Mama left, as she had said.

"Night, night," she said, and closed the door behind her. They heard the sound of her footsteps on the stair. "*She's* dying!" Papa said. "And I can't live without a woman. I want you to know that. Do you understand?"

His voice was gentle now. Friendly. Inquiring, actually. It was a question. He wanted her approval. "Yes," she said simply. "I understand."

From now on every time they sat together in the evenings and Mama went out for a moment and closed the door behind her, Papa said to Inger: "*She's* dying!" And then he wanted to discuss with her the fact that he wouldn't be able to live without a woman. That was how it was that summer, and also throughout the fall, the times she was home in Fredrikstad, and that was how it continued as long as Evelyn lived.

FRANK

Frank came. He'd resigned his commission and settled down in a minimal, old apartment on Grønnegaten in a ramshackle building with an enormous chokecherry tree outside. "The building's supposed to be torn down," Frank said. "But that probably won't be necessary. I have the feeling that if I sit in the bathtub, I'll end up in the basement." He looked at her: "Has Rose Mary left?" he said. "Mmm." "That must be a terrible loss for you?" "Yes."

He wanted to take her out. "There's something on your mind. There's a door that must be opened! What is it? What is it, Inger? Why won't you tell me what it is?"

He never got an answer.

She never imagined it would be so awful. She sat in 1314, still listening. For the sound of her distinctive, uneven footsteps. But all the footsteps were even and quick and not the way footsteps were supposed to be. All her movements existed for her. And she was gone. Her voice wasn't anywhere, and was everywhere in the walls. In the pictures on the walls, the kitchen table, the window facing the flagpole. It was impossible to live in it. She was dying.

She was still walking around, but she was dead. She had a toothache. It was in a molar, it had to be taken to the Dental College. She took the tooth to the Dental College, because the tooth was alive in all of its agony, but the feet that pumped the pedals did nothing but pump the pedals. I've abandoned all the people I know, she thought. She took out her address book and figured out that she knew fourteen people. The only proof of my existence is the appointment reminder from the Institute of Odontology. On it I can see that there's a person named Inger Holm.

Frank came. "Do you want to go to Berlin?" The word Berlin awakened a life inside her. Mama and Papa's life. She'd always wanted to go to Berlin. No one in her family wanted to go there anymore, but despite the city's terrible past, this was where her own short history had begun. "Yes," she said. "Great!" Frank said. He beamed, there was sunshine in his heavy, warm face. The brown eyes looked at her with gratitude and love. "I'll buy the tickets."

The world is made up of the people I've abandoned for the love I didn't get, Inger wrote. What kind of beginning was this? "She went to have a root canal." Inger looked at the paper. Not bad. You have to wonder how it will go. Don't you? According to E.M. Forster one ought to wonder how things will go. Otherwise you're not interested in reading on. This was a surprising beginning. In the next line she had the heroine take her life. Without having had the root canal.

That was certainly a short book, she said out loud to herself. She went down to the minimal apartment on Grønnegaten. There sat Frank with tickets, and a pile of small, printed calling cards. On these was printed: "Inger Holm Rasmussen," in small, neat, black letters: "Inger Holm Rasmussen," "Inger Holm Rasmussen." "You realize we have to get married," Frank said. "Otherwise we won't be able to stay in the same hotel room." All right, Inger thought. Why not? It's fun to get married. It must be, since everybody did it. Isn't it fun to get married? If she got married, she wouldn't be unmarried. And if she didn't get married, she'd never manage to get divorced. Better divorced than unmarried. And since she could never have the one she loved anyway—much less marry her—she might just as well marry Frank. He loved her. And he didn't touch her until she wanted him to. And that was never. She decided to say "Yes."

But then she thought about Papa. Papa would think it was terrible. He'd be furious, despairing and jealous. If she got married, she'd just be doing it for the fun of it, because it was completely crazy and ridiculous, and she was a free person, she was free to do completely meaningless things. But was it right to hurt Papa so, just to accomplish something meaningless?

"No," she said. "Why not? Ørnulf doesn't control us," Frank said. He'd guessed approximately half of her reasoning. "For once he'll have to realize that you're a grown woman!" "I'm too young, Frank," she said.

So they departed unmarried. They took the ferry to Kiel, where a beautiful, middle-aged woman offered herself to Frank for 50 kroner, which *she*—it should be noted—would pay, it was refreshing to see that there were other perversities in the world; they flew to Berlin from Hamburg, because Frank didn't want to take the train for one instant over Communist soil.

Coming to Berlin was like coming to three cities. There were still many ruins, both in the west and in the east, and one of them had been elevated to a monument—in the middle of the glow of neon signs and modern office buildings. "This is what the Americans have built up," the taxi driver said, "with *our* money!" he added. But everywhere there were little things that Mama had talked about. *Ubahn*-stations, grape juice and free rolls with the goulash soup. They went to see the Wall. The amazing thing about it was that it was a wall. Simple and terrible. Frank and Inger stood and peered over at the third Berlin.

"I want to go to East Berlin," Inger said.

"Out of the question! You'll get sent to Siberia!"

"Pooh!"

"Communism is unnatural for human beings," Frank said.

That was what he'd always said. That was why as a young man

317

he'd joined the Norwegian Nazi party. But when the Germans shot the ten hostages in Trondheim, he quit. From then on he went around in fear of being liquidated, both by Nazis and Communists, and he fled to Sweden. But at the border he was turned away because of his past, and he had to flee back to Norway again and live in fear until the end of the war. That had never left him.

"But I want to go there," Inger said.

They left each other in a bar near Checkpoint Charlie. On the other side of the wall they were celebrating the fifteenth anniversary of their existence—*Für Frieden und Sozialismus*—and there were pictures of Walter Ulbricht in large glass cases everywhere. The red banners and picture of the dictator seemed like some kind of gaudy, newly manufactured backdrops hung on the facade of a city that most resembled Oslo during the war. Time had stood still. All the women wore skirts, and there were lines everywhere. She stood in one of them and waited for a half an hour, so she could accomplish the secret mission that was the reason for the whole excursion. Buying a postcard and sending it to London.

When she got back, she sauntered by the wall in the direction of Checkpoint Charlie until she heard a fierce bellow behind her, and there stood a man with a machine gun. Oh yes, she thought and turned. This is where you usually get shot for walking. She showed him her passport and received a salvo, but not from the gun.

She didn't tell Frank about this particular incident when she met him in the little bar on the other side. He was dead drunk. He'd convinced the bartender and all the other customers that she was on her way to Siberia to dig coal for the rest of her life, and he had to be dragged home. At the hotel he wept. It was a strange weeping. So full of anger. He wanted to tell her how terrible war was. It was something he'd lived through then. It was still inside his head. But it wouldn't come out.

Inger had to live with Frank's secret just like he had to live with hers. The next day they walked arm in arm down

318

Kurfürstendamm. Then she noticed it. The air! How mild it was. So she put her arms around Frank's shoulders and began dancing with him in the street.

"*Das is die berliner Luft, Luft, Luft!*" she sang, and faces turned toward them and smiled. They stopped in front of a bookstore and looked, Frank ready, as always, to buy anything she pointed at. Suddenly a title flew into her eyes and obliterated all the other titles in the window. *Die Homosexualität der Frau*. It was written in black letters on a white background and it was a large, thick book. A whole book had been written about them! Just about women! In D.J. West they were nearly all men, just like in the sneering language at parties, too. If such an enormous book had been written about them, then there must be many others! Where were they? Where were all these women that the book was about? It must say—in the book. In the book she'd find out where she could go. If she could only get a chance to open it, go into the store, page through it a little, she'd find all their hiding places, the secret clubs, maybe it even gave the names of some of them?

"Is there anything you want here?" Frank said.

"Oh no. It's just always so fascinating to stand and look in a bookstore window," Inger said. And she made up her mind that as soon as they got home to Oslo she'd go right back to Berlin again and buy the book.

Once Lisa had told her that she and Papa had ended up at a Berlin bar where all the women were men and all the men women. Maybe they were still there? When evening came, she said: "I want to see the prostitutes now." She figured that where there were prostitutes there'd be homosexuals, too. They got in a cab. "*Wir wollen das schlechteste was gibt!*"[1] Frank said in his Trondheim German. "*Wie bitte?*" "*Das schlechteste was gibt!*" Frank repeated.

They came to a saloon. It was an absolute dive. But if there were any homosexuals there, they were dressed up as prostitutes. Or as the fat bartender behind the bar. Or as the married couple in the corner. But they always were, weren't they?

A dark-haired woman in a dress with a split skirt wanted Frank to come with her into the back room. "No," Frank said. "I'm with my wife." The woman sat down next to the wife and looked at her. And she sat not even a fraction of an inch away. She sat right up against her so she could feel the whole arm along her arm.

"*Is* that your husband?" she asked, when Frank had gone to the men's room for a moment. "No," Inger said, frightened. And the whole time they were in the bar the woman never stopped looking at her.

That was an experience she never forgot.

Frank and Inger went back to the hotel "*Zum wilden Löwe.*" He put his arm over her in the double bed. The hand drove Rose Mary out of her dreams, and she pushed it away. But it came again. All night long the hand came and disturbed the one thing she'd always had in peace. Rose Mary who came and held her, because she could do that freely even though she was in London. Finally she took her comforter and lay down on the sofa so she could have Rose Mary in peace. There was a knock at the door and the breakfast was brought up and the tray placed on a little table by the sofa, and Frank came over and wanted to lie on top of her. She got so desperate that she used a trick from Blazing Arrow.[2] Blazing Arrow was always being forced to the ground by some devilish pale-faces, but he gathered his legs and braced them against the stomach of the pale-face, lifted him up and hurled him away. This was what Inger did to Frank. He flew backwards across the room, and in flight he took the whole continental breakfast with him. Coffee and tea and soft-boiled eggs and hard rolls and butter and marmalade lay strewn across the beautiful carpet. Frank got furious. "Pick up after yourself!" he shouted. And Inger picked it up—without a word.

It took some time before they got over this. But they got over it. They went dancing. When they got to Hamburg they danced the twist there, too. That fall everybody was dancing the twist to "A Hard Day's Night" sung by an entertaining, dark-haired group of boys called The Beatles. "I apologize for what I did," Inger said. "But I hadn't gotten any sleep all night." "Sometimes it's just too much for a man," Frank said. "He overflows." Hmm, Inger thought. Frank said: "I think I'm the only man who can save you. Why don't you give me a chance?"

When they got back to the minimal apartment on Grønnegaten, she lay down in his bed and let him have the chance he asked for. "Will you come to China with me?" Frank said. That summer he could show her China and Japan. That was tempting. But she couldn't travel that far without becoming his. "I'm going to Spain," she said. "What're you going to do in Franco's Spain?" "Well, it's not exactly Franco I'm in love with, you know," she said.

One evening after they'd been to the movies Frank came inside with her. He always walked her home, and turned around at the door, but this evening Inger asked him in. They had a beer, and Inger put on a record. It was *Joan Baez in Concert II*, and the first tune was "Once I had a sweetheart, and now I have none," and Frank held her close, and wanted to kiss her, but as his face came close, and Joan Baez's thin, ethereal voice resonated in the room, she began to cry.

He held her, let her go, held her again, because he didn't know what was best. "What's wrong, Inger? You have to tell me what's wrong!"

I miss Rose Mary, she thought. The words were clear in her tears. These alone, and no others. She didn't answer his question. That is, she began to say quite a lot. She was depressed. She wasn't getting her life together. She was nervous. All these things were blatant lies. Not because they were lies, but just because they weren't this one and absolutely only thing she wanted to say.

"I love you, Inger," Frank said.

1. We want to go to the worst place there is.
2. A reference to Edward S. Ellis' *Blazing Arrow: A Tale of the Frontier.*

MARIT

A movie was showing at the Ullevål Movie Theater. It was a film version of Johannes V. Jensen's novel, *Gudrun*, and the sweet young heroine by that name ran happily and lightly down the stairs on her way to her beloved. But with her door open a crack, her landlady, Mrs. Bruun, with short-cropped bangs above her approximately sixty-year-old mystery novel face, stood watching her. This scene was repeated several times, always with the same dramatic irony, as the heroine never noticed the eyes on her back. Finally she was invited in for tea. Mrs. Bruun looked at her over her teacup with the same mystery novel look. "Watch out for men!" she said. "They've never accomplished anything but ride on us!" And next she took Gudrun's hand, fell on her knees before her and begged her to put her in chains. "Call me Karen!" she shouted, and Gudrun rushed out, terrified, into her lover's arms.

Marit Heimstad from Lisleby and Inger walked up Sognsveien with this film behind them. For a long while they walked without saying anything. Then Marit said: "It's like it's so fashionable to have these *lesbian* elements nowadays. . . ." She trailed off at the end, as if the sentence weren't quite finished. "Yes," Inger said. Then they walked a long while without saying anything again. And when they spoke, it was about something else.

Throughout the fall they visited each other often, and the visits always ended in a discussion of the post-World War II treason trials. Marit's father had been a prisoner at Sachsenhausen. He'd told very little about what he had lived through, just about the white busses. But Marit herself had read the depictions published right after the war, she'd grown up with them expressly because he'd been silent.

"The traitors got the punishment they deserved," Marit said. Nothing could budge her from this conviction.

The conversations shook them both up. They sought each other out again, just as uncompromising as before. "Do you know what it was like to grow up learning that your parents were swine?" Inger said.

She realized that this was the first time she'd ever dared discuss this with one of her peers. That was why they sought each other out again and again throughout the fall, and never settled their argument. "When King Haakon said no to the Germans, he was saying yes to life," Marit said.

Inger had never met a more patriotic person. "A Norwegian spruce tree!" Marit might say, as if it were a deep confidence. "When the Germans came and saw all the Norwegian spruce trees, I don't understand why they didn't turn around and go home again!" Inger preferred pine trees. "Oh, no!" Marit said. "A spruce tree!" "But pine trees are Norwegian, too," Inger said. "No," Marit said. "Not as Norwegian."

One evening, for once, they ended up in a discussion about the Labor Party. Neither one of them was planning to vote for it. "The Liberal Party looks after Norwegian interests best," Marit said. But Inger was still planning to vote for the Socialist People's Party. "I think you should vote Liberal Party," Marit said, "because all your views actually agree with the Liberal platform." "In that case you can just as well vote Socialist," Inger said, and they sat like that, squabbling—in quite good spirits, and Inger put on *Joan Baez in Concert II*. "Frank says that Goldwater is a breath of fresh air in American politics," Inger said, and hoped with that to be able to bring a little harmony into the room. It worked. "But he wants to bomb Hanoi, you know," Marit said, and looked at her hard. "Are you going with him?"

This was a question completely foreign to their usual discussion topics. But it was late, and Joan Baez was singing. Besides, Inger had lighted a candle. "With Goldwater?" They laughed. "No, with Frank?" Inger lighted a cigarette. "I couldn't imagine going with someone I didn't agree with politically," she said. "Hmm," Marit said. "I always see the two of you walking by." "A-ha. He wants me to marry him." Now she wondered if she should tell Marit about all the printed calling cards, and she began: "The last time he was here he tried to kiss me, but then I started to cry." "Why were you crying?"

This was not at all what she had intended to say. She tried to get out of the awkward situation by starting to tell about the trip to Germany. And when she'd kept it up a while, Marit said: "But why did you cry?"

Inger was silent. Of course I know perfectly well why I cried. It doesn't take much to say it. Four words. I missed Rose Mary. But Marit Heimstad from Lisleby was the last person in the world who would approve of grief like that. "Why did you cry?" Marit said. She was sitting in the chair over in the corner and Inger sat on the sofa, and Marit rolled one cigarette after the other, and she had just one question, and she repeated this question for an hour.

Inger sat on the sofa and heard the voice that kept asking and asking. Why didn't she give up? Obviously she was never going to answer anyway. Marit was not an especially tolerant person. She didn't accept the sufferings of the traitors. She had no desire to admit a single wrong that had been done to them after the war. How then could she ever accept a wrong that was never even talked about? You can just keep on asking, Marit. You'll never get an answer! "Why did you cry?" Marit said. "I missed Rose Mary. You see, I think I'm homosexual," Inger said.

It was quiet. Marit sat there and had heard it. For the second time in her 23-year-old life Inger had uttered these words to another human being. And she sat in silence. And she was scared to death.

Then Marit said—and she said it with a calm and slow voice, with her distinctive way of trailing off at the end: "You aren't the only one, you know . . . ." Inger looked up. Wasn't she the only one? She looked at her. Who? Who? Who in the world did Marit think was the other one? If she wasn't the only one? If she wasn't the only one, there'd have to be one more. Where? "As a matter of fact, I've thought the same thing myself," Marit said.

You!? Inger thought. How in the world can you be homosexual!!? You look completely normal. You're even from Lisleby. You have blond hair and blue eyes. And you walk with quite normal steps across the lawns at the Sogn dormitories. You're wearing a checked blouse and a light blue jacket. How in the world can you sit there and claim to be homosexual?

But she'd said it. And there was no reason at all to believe it wasn't true.

There they sat. Two young women. In the same room. Alone. And both of them thought they were homosexual. And there were ten feet between them.

They remained sitting. The candle burned its way down, and they took turns picking it up—because they'd run out of matches—to light their rolled cigarettes. And when these were smoked up, Marit went home. But the next day, when Inger woke up, she thought: Marit. Here I am. And there she is. Now we are two. And then she went down to her room.

As soon as she was inside the room, she put her arms around her. Marit pulled away. "We have to get to know each other better first," she said. "Know each other better? But we've known each other since we were twelve and met at the skating rink!" "Well, yes, but we don't know each other." "Yes we do," Inger said. They put their arms around each other, they leaned against each other and began to kiss, they stroked each other's backs, a comfort that soon became desire. They shut the curtains and turned off the light, but that didn't help much, because it was broad daylight, and it was very strange to see a female body, like that, with another female body, they definitely didn't dare to look at it, they waited until it got dark.

When it got dark, and they definitely couldn't see each other, they lay with each other and didn't have to see what they were doing. But in the morning it came to light. "Close your eyes," Marit said, and they closed their eyes, and got up and opened their eyes and ate breakfast; their hands found each other, and soon they were in the narrow bed again, naked, with the curtains drawn, the door locked with a pair of pliers over the door handle and through the key hole, and it was in the middle of the morning, and so the days went.

They never got enough of this. How could it be that when they'd made love the day before, and also three days ago and the night before that day, and even before that, that they should also make love now, at twelve o'clock?

It was incredible. She never thought it would be like this. That another person's body could be like that. That body and soul fit together. They fit together! There was no difference. You did what you did, and your soul was part of it! But why were they never finished?

She'd imagined that passion, this peak of pleasure created by the fusion of two bodies, was like a kind of heavenly meal, an absolutely and completely spiritual meal, and that—when it was over—you'd gotten what you wanted.

Instead she found that she'd never been so restless. She went to lectures as before, she gave English lessons to housewives, she bought frozen pea soup with two boiled potatoes at the grocery store at Sogn (and with smoked sausage), she made the bed, she read about Frederick the Great of Prussia, but she always had a restlessness in her body, in her legs when she walked, in her arms, in the pit of her stomach, in her head, when she walked up Sognsveien, she could never walk fast enough, the road up from the streetcar, past the Kassa Restaurant, up to the Ullevål intersection, up past Konvallveien, it was just an endless road of impatience that wanted to get to Marit.

And she laughed. For two weeks she laughed at everything in the world there was to laugh at. And it certainly wasn't because she hadn't laughed before. But now any conversation, any chance meeting with the girls in the apartment, clerks in stores, streetcar conductors, housewives she was teaching English to, possessed of an unceasing and immediate sense of fun, she rushed wittily about spreading laughter and a completely improbable good mood, where on earth did it come from?

"I feel completely crazy," Inger said.

"I love you," Marit said.

"I love you, too," Inger said.

These were the first days of their lives. For twenty-three years they'd had to wait for them. Until their bodies were alive— with their soul. They confided everything in each other and were always together. They always stayed with each other at night and always ate breakfast together, went for walks together, read their books together, smoked together, looked at the view together, went to the movies together, went home together, slept together. And it was only the times when they were each supposed to go to their own classes, or Inger was supposed to teach, or one of them absolutely had to do something or other that wasn't possible to do together, that they weren't together.

So that all of this sudden togetherness wouldn't seem suspicious to the girls in their apartments, they did everything to conceal their overnight visits to each other. They took turns staying in one's and then the other's apartment, and the one who didn't belong there snuck out to the bathroom at night only after it was absolutely quiet in the apartment—and with pounding heart. In the morning they whispered or pantomimed. When the coast was clear, the one who didn't belong in the apartment opened the door soundlessly and snuck out. Five minutes later she came back and rang the doorbell. And the one who belonged in the apartment didn't open. "Is Inger home?" or: "Is Marit home?" they'd inquire. And then the one paraded into the other's room, and they ate breakfast together in broad daylight.

Luckily they lived on the first floor. If there was an exceptional amount of traffic in the hall and in the kitchen in the morning, they jumped out the window instead, and went around the building and rang the doorbell. Then they cooked two soft-boiled eggs.

They went for long walks. When they'd gotten far enough into the forest, they held hands. If someone came along, they immediately let go. But one day they let go too late. The hiker in the knickers had seen them. When he'd passed them, he stopped and shouted at them. They turned and looked at him. Then he shook his head sadly and said: "Yes, the war's to blame for a lot of strange things!"

They had to laugh at this. They laughed and went on. They put their whole life in each other's laps. And that to someone from Fredrikstad! Inger thought. If I'd heard that when I went to The Yellow Institution I'd have refused to believe it. But there she was. A Fredrikstad girl, large as life. Actually a Glemmen girl, even. But now Fredrikstad and Glemmen had merged. "Fredrikstad and Glemmen have merged!" they said.

"Do you remember Stina Weidel?" Marit said.

"The one with the braces on her teeth?"

"Yes, but she got rid of those. And then I fell in love with her. We were together our senior year."

"What happened to her?"

"She was born again," Marit said. "Then I was born again, sort of. So I went with her to Bethel. She said we were going to find God together." "And did you?" "Yes. Yes, we did. But I didn't like the meetings at Bethel. Of course I just went there so I could sit beside her. And hope that she'd come home with me." "Did she?" "Yes. Sometimes. And we'd sit and pray. And once, after she left, I sat down right where she'd been sitting, and stared out in space for an hour."

Inger thought about Stina and Marit. Then she told Marit about all the girls she'd loved.

"Didn't you ever go with any of them, sort of?" "Go with?

No, are you crazy?" "One time Stina and I lay and held each other all night long!" Marit said. "We were up at the cabin." It was awfully wonderful to think about it, Inger thought. All night?

As they walked along talking like that, Inger suddenly saw her room in Edinburgh. It was a warm day, they'd been outside playing badminton in the garden. How had they ended up in her room? Were they going to play badminton there? Inger couldn't fathom why they were standing inside the room. And they weren't standing either. Without her having any idea why, they were suddenly lying on top of each other. Sheila on top. What was the excuse for lying down like that; it was just an ordinary afternoon. It had felt so awfully good. So good that it was embarrassing, even now. "One time I ended up on a bed with Sheila," she ventured. "Oh? Tell me about it!" Marit said.

Tell? Tell, tell. When had anyone ever said "tell" before? All her life it had been *tell*. Her whole life had involved saying A and not B. Finally, finally, Inger could say B. She took Marit by the hand.

As Marit and Inger went on their long walks and put words to all this, suddenly they were also terribly angry. They were not alone! They weren't just Marit and Inger. Since they were Marit and Inger and their stories were so alike, there had to be others. Where? They'd grown up together, they'd stood on the same steps and been photographed. How many others were there, all over, who'd stood on similar steps in front of historic buildings in their city with a catastrophe inside them? And what good was the catastrophe? What was the deeper meaning of them being driven out into the world with scorn and insults like the ugly duckling? When would the ice finally break up so they could see themselves, look at their reflection in the water and see that they were magnificent? When would a group of children stand on the beach and shout at them: "Look! There's a new one!"

There was a new one. They'd come to each other. Just then there was an article in the *New Statesman* devoted exclusively to homosexuality in women. On the basis of this article Inger wrote a long letter to *Dagbladet* under the pseudonym "Martha Q" with the title: "Female Homosexuality—a Non-Existent Phenomenon." Here she accused society of doing its utmost to prevent homosexuals—and especially homosexual women—from finding each other.

The Swedish doctor Lars Ullerstam, "Martha Q" wrote—had struck a blow for "the erotic minorities," given lectures in the Student Association and written a book. Director of Health, Karl Evang's, comment had been: "Sexuality is not a sport."

The article was given a lot of publicity and was printed as a feature article in the Easter edition. But the headline had been changed. "Female Sexuality—an Endless Hell," in bold-faced type on the front page. See page 3. It stimulated no debate. The only reaction came in the form of a short article in the Andøya News. Here it said: "What viewpoints are too dirty to be printed anymore?" (But Inger didn't know anything about this article, since it had never occurred to her to subscribe to this paper. But the so-called Association for City and Countryside received it through the Argus news-clipping service, where it was clipped out in deep secret.)

"Martha Q" did, however, receive three letters—forwarded to her by *Dagbladet*—from ladies who thanked her fervently and warmly for the article. One of them wrote that "Martha Q" mustn't believe she was writing to her because she was homosexual. The other one wrote that she preferred to continue living her life in loneliness and self-denial, but she had her violin. The third one waited three years to send the letter.

Frank came as before, and Marit said she wanted him to stop coming. "Why?" Inger said. "I won't stand for you to go around with an admirer." "But what am I supposed to do?" "You'll have to tell him you don't want to see him anymore." "But I've known him all my life. Since I was three! He's like . . . an uncle! You don't break up with an uncle!" "Yes you do,"

Marit said.

Inger did as she said, and he never got any explanation. "I don't want to see you anymore," she said. Because she knew that was what one said in such situations.

But this was not such a situation. It was a completely different situation. I've tried and tried! And all the time while I've been trying I've known it was a completely false experiment. Do you know what it's like to live your whole youth in false experiments?

What would Frank have said if these words had been uttered? She never got an answer to that question, because she hadn't dared to utter them. The conversation would have been a relief, no matter what he said. She longed for it, and she'd never be able to forgive herself for how awful she'd been.

Frank came, desperate and drunk, and was turned away. He went down to Fredrikstad. He asked where the hardware store was. He wanted to buy an awl, he told Evelyn. And he was going to use this on a fair-haired young woman. Evelyn and Ørnulf couldn't understand what he was talking about, other than it had something to do with Inger, and that he was crazy. He didn't go to the hardware store. He went to a florist. He bought two orchids. He sent them to the Sogn dormitory with the words:

> You will I tenderly in rhythm bind fast!
> you will I deeply and enduringly preserve
> in poetry's young alabaster forever last![1]

1. from "Metope" by Olaf Bull.

331

"WE WILL OWN THIS LAND"

Now and then when they were down in Marit's room a little squeak could be heard from the room next door. "What's that squeaking?" Inger asked, because now she was sure she'd heard it. "Oh, that's just Urdahl's guinea pig," Marit said. For some reason she always referred to her apartment-mates by their last names. "Poor baby!" she added, and her voice got small and babyish. "Poor wittle Per, now he's all by his lonesome again. Tsk, tsk, tsk," she said. "Inger?" she said and got out of bed. "I'm just going to go and check on him a second."

She put on her robe and disappeared. Inger heard her rummaging around in there, and how Per's squeaks got more and more eager through the wall, clearly she was feeding him, while she talked baby-talk to him the whole time. It was against the rules to have pets at Sogn, and Per was clearly a deep secret.

But after the first disclosure, it happened again and again that Marit interrupted what they were actually doing, and went into the next room wearing a bathrobe and sympathy.

Why'd she feel so sorry for him? A guinea pig was a guinea pig. Inger was irritated. She made up her mind not to be irritated. But every time Marit started in with her Per-talk, she was even more irritated than the last time. At the same time she pretended to be just as interested in Per's health and welfare as Marit was. And in his loneliness. Because Urdahl was often out. That is, she spent most of the semester down in the basement watching television.

So Inger saw to it that they were in her room more often instead, so that Marit's attention wouldn't be absorbed by Per's squeaking. But Marit's relationship with Per was clearly of a telepathic nature, because suddenly she might say: "Poor wittle baby! He's hungry now. I promised Urdahl I'd feed him." "If you go down to that guinea pig, don't bother coming up again!" Inger shouted.

The shout astonished them both. A little spasm crossed Marit's face, as if she'd been struck. I don't love her, Inger thought.

Marit went. Without a word. No, I don't love her, Inger thought to the door. If I loved her I wouldn't get jealous over a guinea pig. We have to break up.

When you loved someone, she radiated out into the room, unlike all others. She could be wearing a gray coat, have medium blond hair, colorless skin and a pale mouth, and she radiated even so—it was no use, she stepped out of the crowd, and you got a shock. You got a shock, even though you knew she was supposed to come right at that moment, you'd even agreed on it, and she'd come right on time, and as she appeared, the whole place was changed. She transformed every last thing in the room, and if she opened her mouth, everything she said was worthy of comment. She simply *could not* say anything uninteresting, she was unable to make a single irrelevant movement, and she was completely incapable of being anything but beautiful.

Why wasn't it like that with Marit? Why didn't she ever get a shock when she saw her? Where was the longing?

Inger missed the longing. She, who'd been sick of it all her life, suddenly missed it, and she thought: I have to tell her. How?

After three hours Marit came up. She was wearing a red windbreaker and she'd obviously been crying. "Get dressed now and let's go for a walk," she said. It was the Lisleby voice talking. The one that knew what was wrong and what was right.

They went out. The weather was mild and there was heavy snow on the tree branches, and they walked along the roads up in Gaustad Woods, and there, where no one could see them, they sat down by a spruce tree. "We can't be together any more," Inger said. "because we don't love each other."

Marit cried. She didn't cry with tears or sound, but her face cried, over the red windbreaker. She looked out over the snow, through the trees, and Inger thought: Now it's been said.

"We're the same age," Marit said. "We're the only girls we know of, who feel *like that*. We have the same background, and even come from the same place. We can discuss, and we like being together—*that* way. Don't we?"

"Yes."

"So that's why I think we should stay together," Marit said.

Inger was silent. Everything Marit said was true. How would they ever manage to find anyone else? Where was the girl Marit should be with, and where was the girl Inger should be with if they weren't going to be with each other? Where?

"But we don't love each other!" Inger repeated.

Marit didn't answer. She just sat against the spruce tree as before, and Inger sat there close beside her. The sleeves of their windbreakers rustled against each other. A blue one and a red one. Their knees in their stretch pants bumped into each other and stopped where they bumped, one supported by the other, the other by the one—in the cold snowy air. But Marit didn't answer.

They walked down to the dormitory again. They didn't say anything. The whole way they walked, and they didn't say anything, and they weren't together anymore. When they got down to Building 1, they went to their own rooms.

The world was as sad as only the world could be. Where would they go? They each sat in their own rooms and looked out on the completely transformed, sad world, as it appeared through the square window opening. They said to themselves: I must *not* go to her! And so they sat, separately.

What kind of separation was this? What kind of a notion? They could only be together, obviously. Then everything would be fine again, and the square with the mournful window world would be pure and clear, and they would laugh. Laugh at themselves, who'd brought such sadness on themselves.

They'd been sharing life for fourteen days. That wasn't long. And it contained their whole life. No one knew anything about these fourteen days, and what they were and how they'd forced the whole world to justice. Whom could they go to with their grief over this? To whom could they say: It's over! We're not together anymore. And I'm grieving. Who?

There was only one person on this earth they could tell, and that was the person they were grieving over. They sought out this one person, and told about their grief. They mourned together, this day and the next. They saw each other every day, slept together, snuck in and out of each other's doors, went for walks, read and talked, and suddenly they realized that the only difference between before and now was that they weren't together anymore.

Inger made up her mind that there would be one more difference. They should stop saying that they loved each other. They stopped saying that they loved each other. They loved each other as well as they could. They slept with each other to the notes of *A Hard Day's Night*. In the middle of "I Should Have Known Better," Marit said: "I want us to buy rings."

"Are you crazy?"

"Yes!" Marit said. "I want us to buy rings. I want our relationship to be just like all other relationships." "But I never would have bought rings if it'd been a normal relationship!" "I want us to get engaged," Marit said. "I don't believe in engagements!" "Then you don't care about me," Marit said. "Yes, I care about you." "Then we can buy rings." "No. You know I never wear jewelry!"

They put on a little record. It was a song recorded after the liberation on a 45 with a blue label, called *Norway in Red, White and Blue*[1] with Jens Book-Jenssen. To this they made love again. They loved each other in red and white and blue, they loved each other with a blue-eyed faith in their country and with bold and blond-banged foreheads, and when it was over, they put on the flip side, a no less patriotic song called "We will own this land as it is!" also with Jens Book-Jenssen, and to this they kept on loving and tried to own the country behind their locked door.

"I want us to buy rings," Marit said.

"I already said no."

"Then you don't care about me."

"Ohhhh, can't you just forget the rings?"

"I want our relationship to be completely normal. The same rules should apply for us as for them."

Inger kissed her and hoped she'd forget the rings in the kiss. But Marit didn't forget the rings. They loved each other through the few records they had, again and again, but Inger didn't want to buy rings, and Marit wanted them to buy rings, and this always came up in the most passionate moments. Finally they went to David-Andersen jewelers.

It was a sunny day in February with slush downtown and white-clad spruce trees in the hills, and Marit had taken care of the order, and David-Andersen had probably never gotten an order like that before—or had he? had he?—because here came two young ladies, two ladies with quite ordinary appearances into his store on the corner of Karl Johans gate and Akersgata and picked up two rings with each other's names inside. The lady behind the counter pierced them with her horrified and absolutely patriotic gaze while she acted like nothing was out of the ordinary and wrapped up the rings.

They took the streetcar up to Frognerseteren. They ordered apple cake with whipped cream and Coca-Cola. Then they unwrapped the rings and put them on each other's fingers under the table.

Here is an engagement. Secretly, secretly above Oslo they celebrated it, the view was beautiful as always, the apple cake was good, they found a symbol of their devotion, their unity, their faithfulness, they just found a small thing, the thing everyone else found, but what should they do with their hands when they went down again? "Do you think the girls in the apartment have understood anything?" Marit said. She always used this expression. "Understood anything." "I don't know," Inger said. "Lidia said the other day when we were going out: 'You act like her date!'" They thought a little about what this could mean. "Urdahl'd have a cow," Marit said. They thought about this a little, too.

"The last person in the world I'm going to tell is my mother," Marit said. "Oh?" "We never talk about feelings at home." They thought some more. "Do you think you'll tell your mother?" Marit asked. "No, my mother is sick. She's going to die soon."

She hadn't said that before. She hadn't managed to say it. The words refused to come out.

Marit was completely silent. To her amazement Inger saw pain in her face. Marit didn't know Evelyn. No more than everyone in Fredrikstad knew each other. The sudden sympathy took her by surprise. Sympathy was something older people did. "Do you want to meet her?" Inger said, taken aback, almost as if to comfort her. "Yes, I would—very much!" Marit said.

---

[1] Also known as "Where'er you go in hills and mountains", a patriotic song celebrating the liberation of Norway in 1945 from five years of German occupation.

TO THE FOUR WINDS

"Listen to this record, Mama!" Inger said, "Marit and I always play it." Mama thought that Beatles-music was just noise. Even so, she was the one who had given Inger *A Hard Day's Night* for Christmas. But Inger wouldn't give up. "Listen to this one!" She put on:

> If I fell in love
> with you
> I must be sure . . .

The two-part harmony filled the living room, Mama listened. Inger looked at her in anticipation. "You *have* to admit that's good, Mama!?" Evelyn nodded. "Oh yes," she said and smiled. "Marit and I play it all the time," Inger said eagerly.

But her nerve failed her. It failed her.

She brought Marit home with her. Evelyn liked her. But after every time she was there Evelyn forgot her name. "Marit and I," Inger said. "Marit?" Evelyn said. "Is she the blond, cute one?" "Yes," Inger said. "And she's studying history. We discuss things and it's really great being with her."

But her nerve failed her.

Every day Evelyn sat with her swollen body and her legs on a footstool and watched television. Ørnulf was grumpy. He still threatened to toss it out the veranda door. Nonetheless he'd just bought a new and more modern set. And so it happened that Evelyn and Inger got to listen to The Eurovision Song Contest. They guessed and commented. This was fun. Then a sweet, young blond girl came on the screen and sang a lively melody:

Je suis une poupée de cire
une poupée de son!

and she hadn't sung more than half a line before Evelyn and Inger shouted in unison:

"That's it!"

That was a moment of celebration. That they said it like that in unison, pointed and laughed, and turned out to be right at the end of the evening. They were alone. Ellen had gone to bed. Papa was at the club. "Marit and I," Inger said.

But her nerve failed her. It failed her.

Easter came. Mama came toward her in the hallway, her face yellow. Even more yellow than the last time. Small eyes, where the part that should have been white was yellow, too. She came with her big, swollen stomach—with her arms and with her joy at seeing Inger again, and Inger thought: She's going to die soon now.

She's dying. Papa's terrible words would soon be true, she could just see it, in Mama's face as soon as she came, and paralyzed, she asked herself: Will I live all the years I will outlive her without knowing what she would have said?

She made up her mind. She just made up her mind.

Not for a moment had Inger imagined that Evelyn would do anything—the day she herself dared to open her mouth—but listen to her and understand her. Ever since the evening she had sat in bed and been seventeen and Mama had suddenly asked her if she was happy, she'd known. She could have answered! And Mama would have been glad. Not at the answer, because of course the answer was no, but because she answered. Ever since that time she knew that she'd been able to come to her with the truth, and for all these years she had been nervous—only about her own fear.

"Mama," she said. "There's something I have to talk to you about."

They went into the living room and sat down, and Evelyn sat in Papa's chair. Something she usually never did. Ellen followed them in and sat on the sofa. "Ellen," Inger said, and it hurt her, because Ellen had missed her, too. "I need to talk to Mama a little alone."

Ellen left, and when she had closed the door behind her, and Inger heard that she was in the little bedroom, she said: "Mama? Well, it's just that I think I'm homosexual."

Everything went black. But it was said. There was a silence.

Mama stood up. She walked across the room to the mantle and picked up a pack of Seven Seas. She opened it with her slender hands, took out a cigarette and lighted it, as she stood. Suddenly she was the wide awake, young Evelyn. Full of life. Full of the Evelyn who'd once stood on the stage of the Carl Johan Theater singing. She blew out the smoke with a little straightening of her body. Then she looked straight at Inger: "I think you're bisexual, because that's what I am."

Mama was speaking! And this was what she said.

Bisexual? Inger thought. That was a word she'd almost never thought about. "But, but," she said, "have you been in love with girls?"

"Yes," Mama said. She walked across the living room floor and sat down again. In Papa's chair, as before.

Mama told. She told about how she and Ragnhild had played together in the garden and had a wonderful time together when they were children, about how she'd longed for Paula in Germany for many years, and thought about her and written letters to her about everything she was thinking, and how she'd fallen in love with her all over again when Inger was in Edinburgh. And how she'd laughed with Rita on a weekend at the cabin, after she was grown up and married, and memorized all the capital cities in the world, while Helga and Inger had been asleep in the bedroom, and the capital of Honduras was called Tegucigalpa.

"But were you going together, then?"

"No. But you just know in the air that you're in love."

"Yes, don't you?"

"That's why I think you're bisexual."

"But then I would have fallen in love with some boys, in the air! You did. You were in love with a boy named Knut in junior high. And later you fell in love with Papa. I just fall in love with girls! That's not very bisexual, is it?"

"No . . ."

"Haven't you ever thought about it?" "Yes. I thought about why you never had a boyfriend in Oslo. You're an attractive, young girl." Mama flicked the ash from her cigarette. "I thought about you and Frank. But I never thought about that as anything more than a friendship. Was it?"

"No . . . no, it wasn't, from my side. He wanted to marry me, but. . . ."

"I thought you were going with Rose Mary."

"Did you think that?" "Yes." "But I wasn't." "Why not?" "Well, she didn't want me." "She didn't want you? Why not?" Mama was indignant.

"Well, she wasn't homosexual." "Hmm."

"Have you thought about others, then?"

"Tove Midtbø," Mama said. "You really liked her a lot when you graduated, didn't you?" "Yes. And others?" "There was one you got to know in high school. What was her name? She was sweet, but a little quiet. She lived up on Kapellveien."

"Oh, yes. That was Beate."

"And when you were in Edinburgh, weren't you really excited about Sheila?"

"Yes."

They thought a little more.

"I still think you might be bisexual." Mama said. "It took me years before I got any enjoyment out of being with Papa. I thought it might've been because I'd done it so much myself. I guess I don't think you should give up completely. I think you should try talking to Papa about it."

"But I don't want to talk to Papa."

"Why not? He doesn't have anything against homosexual women! It's just homosexual men he can't stand."

"He didn't have anything against René, who was in love with him at Sauda Lake."

"No. When it comes right down to it, he probably doesn't have anything against homosexual men, either. I think you should talk to him."

"I'd rather tell Lisa. Do you think I can tell Lisa?"

"Lisa? Yes, I guess you can." She hesitated a little. "Yes, of course you can tell Lisa. But I think you should talk to Papa, too. He's not so dumb about this sort of thing."

"No, maybe not. But I don't want to. You mustn't tell him. Do you promise not to tell him?" Evelyn gave in. But reluctantly.

"I've started going with someone now . . ."

"In Oslo?"

"Yes. But she's from Fredrikstad. It's Marit. From Lisleby."

"Marit? The blonde girl? The sweet, blonde girl who was here?"

"Yes."

They went out into the kitchen. Looked out the window. Stood there by the radiator where they'd stood so many times.

"Mama? You understand, if turns out I am homosexual, then I'll end up with another girl. Because I don't want to live alone!"

"No," Mama said. "I can certainly understand that."

Mama went into the bedroom and lay down a little. Inger brought rose hip tea in to her and sat with her. She put her arms around her and said: "Mama? I love you so awfully much!" "Do you really?" with emphasis on the do. Surprised, almost, happy. And this was the last conversation Inger and Evelyn had.

. . .

342

What this conversation was, Inger didn't know at the time. She only knew one other homosexual. That was why she didn't know anything about what happened when young people came home and said they were homosexual. She didn't know anything about tears and scenes and threats of being sent to psychiatrists, about orders not to tell aunts and fathers, about fear that people in their town might get wind of it. She didn't know anything about mothers who collapsed and thought that their whole life had been in vain. Nothing about family members who threatened to take their lives or take to their beds for months. She knew nothing about families who washed their hands of their children so they disappeared from their home forever and cut off all ties.

She only knew that she had a mother. She wanted to have her blessing for the life she knew she would live. And she'd gotten it.

Marit came on the Thursday before Easter. They played bridge, and Mama explained the rules to Marit and gave some good advice. "Remember, you should play through your opponent's strong suit and up to the second opponent's weak suit," she said. "And if you don't know what to lead, you should lead with the high card of nothing." But after each time Mama talked to Marit, she forgot her name.

On Good Friday Inger was up at Marit's house. Papa phoned. "Inger, you have to come home. Mama has to go into the hospital."

Inger came. Now Mama was in bed all the time. It was the first time. "I don't want to go to Dr. Axelsen," Mama said. "But you're in the best hands at the hospital," Papa said. "I don't want to go to the hospital," Mama said. "Good Friday is the longest day of the year." "But Dr. Heyden is there, too, Mama. Don't you want to go see him?" "Yes," Mama said.

The ambulance came and got her. All three of them went downstairs with her. Inger got into the ambulance with her, and held her hand the whole way.

Lisa came during the night. Ørnulf took a taxi into Oslo and picked her up. Inger and Marit sat up and waited. They came at one-thirty. Lisa sat right down in the entryway in her black fur coat and pulled off her boots. "What blasted awful weather!" she said, and fussed a little with the curls that had suffered under it, and the whole apartment was transformed.

But her face was full of the pain over what was happening. And her footsteps into the living room. Pain over Evelyn, her little sister, now she'd come to share it.

They went up to the hospital in the morning. Evelyn was in a room with three other patients, under the white comforter, yellow, but pretty, smooth. It was a young face lying there. She smiled a little when Lisa arrived, put her arms around her, Lisa sat down by the bed, put her head on her breast and held her tight.

"Evelyn?" she said. "Can you hear me?"

"Yes," Evelyn said weakly. Her slender hands held Lisa's shoulders.

"I'm going to buy the bungalow," Lisa said. "Do you hear me, Evelyn. I'm going to buy the bungalow. I've made up my mind."

Inger stood over them and heard her. Looked down at them, down at the two sisters who were holding each other. "I'm going to buy the bungalow," Lisa said again. Held her. Wanted to be sure she heard it.

"Are you really?" Evelyn said and smiled faintly again.

"Yes. Then we can be out there together. You'll have me. You'll always have me nearby."

"Then I won't have to be afraid at night."

"No, because you can just come over to me. Or I can come and stay overnight with you, in the house. If you're alone there, when Ørnulf is in Fredrikstad."

"And there's a thunderstorm."

"Yes. When there's a thunderstorm we'll sit inside and count. Look out through the window and count between the lightning and the thunder clap. And neither of us'll be afraid, because we'll have each other."

"Yes."

"Yes. You'll never be alone in the house, because you'll have me right next door."

"I'm so homesick for Tjøme."

"We'll be there together. We'll always be there."

Suddenly Evelyn moved her head to the side. A large mass of blood ran out of the corner of her mouth, dark, half clotted. A nurse was there instantly with a white, banana-shaped basin and held it under her chin.

"Did I make a mess?" Evelyn asked.

"No, no," the nurse said and wiped her mouth. The basin was completely full.

Lisa and Inger went out. They went to the lounge at the end of the hall and sat down. Then Inger burst into tears, and took Lisa's hand.

"You'll have to be our mama now," she said.

And Lisa held up. She was about to lose the person she loved most of all in the world. Beyond all others. Beyond love and passion for men she'd had, beyond the love for her own mother—the love, that was inside her, for the child she'd never given birth to. Evelyn had had that love. Now she held this love in her daughter's grasp.

"You're not going to buy the bungalow, Lisa, are you?"

"No," Lisa said.

But Inger knew that this lie was beyond the realm of lies, a place where both lies and truth are erased. Lisa had entered in there with Mama.

This was the Saturday before Easter, and Inger went to visit Mama again. "Time goes so slowly," Mama said. Inger sat down by her. As soon as she looked at the white comforter she noticed that she felt like fainting. Things started spinning around in her head, and she had to stare out the window at a tree so that she wouldn't fall off the chair. "Does it?" she said. "Do you want me to come tomorrow?" "Yes," Mama said happily.

But Inger didn't go to see Mama the next day. She couldn't bear to. All day she thought about Mama who was waiting, and the time that wouldn't go. She thought about her as she lay in the bed, and she thought about her promise. And she didn't go.

She'd regret this for the rest of her life.

No matter how much she thought about it later. And how many excuses she might try to give herself: she was young! she nearly fainted! losing Mama was the most painful thing that had ever happened in her life! it was no use. She could never forgive herself for not helping Mama pass the time on the last day she was alive.

The next day Inger and Ellen sat in the wide bed in the bedroom. They had two large pillows behind their backs and were reading a picture book. The telephone rang. Inger waited until she heard that the receiver had been hung up. Then she got up. "Just wait. I'll be right back," she said.

Out in the kitchen Lisa and Papa stood by the window. They were both crying. They were each looking out the window in different directions. But when Inger stood in the doorway they turned toward her. "It's over," Lisa said.

Inger stood there, bewildered. "Should I tell Ellen?" she said. Lisa nodded, bit her lip, met her eyes. Turned her head away. Inger went back into the bedroom. Ellen was still sitting there with the book in her lap. Inger sat down beside her, put her arm around her, and said: "Ellen? Mama is dead."

"She is?" Ellen said.

Then they turned to the next page.

But on the dresser was a little package. It was wrapped in white crepe paper with a red bow, and next to it was a drawing of flowers in many colors, they danced around the words which were written with a new color for each letter. "To Mama! Happy Birthday! From Ellen."

Because Evelyn died, strangely enough, on her birthday. It was the day after Easter that year. And she was forty-seven.

Inger looked at the package and thought: I wouldn't have had to tell her that I was going to Spain. I did just the opposite of what Lisa did.

They kept on reading the picture book. What else was there to do? Maybe it was wrong. But what else was there to do? Ellen is eleven years old. She's only a little older than I was when Helga died. Mama will become a life inside you, which in the beginning is so strong that it's almost as alive as your own life, and that you think you'll never forget. But as the years go by it will get farther and farther away, because you grow. Things happen, the city changes, you yourself change. You ask: Would she have recognized me now? Here I am. What would she have said about that? Look, now I'm graduating. I've gotten my student cap. I'm standing on the steps being photographed. But you'll always have to shout over greater and greater distances.

But I can't say that now. What can I say now? Why is it so hard for me to talk to her? I should be the first one to know what it's like to be a child when someone dies. Maybe that's why I keep turning the pages and reading? Because I remember how I sat reading *Donald Duck* while all the grown-ups cried. And suddenly I shouted that I was looking forward to the new issue coming in October. Then I realized how small and childish I was, and that children just weren't prepared to experience a death. Maybe it's because I remember how I stood, one October day, by a hole that had been dug in the ground. Everyone stood around the hole and it was nasty and cold and the pastor read some words from the Gospel of John. Then he took the green urn and lowered it into the earth. Then I said: "Mama? Is Helga in there?"

Then Grandma burst into tears and turned away, and I realized I'd said something terrible. But I'd only asked because I was surprised. The urn was so small.

How am I going to reach Ellen? Is it wrong, what I'm doing? What should I do?

The road past the hospital lay gray and April wet. The bare trees in the Seaman's Park stood out against the sky and longed for the tiny leaves they would soon have. But it was still too cold. Ellen and Inger walked down Ferry Landing Road, they didn't say anything for a long time. They just walked there and were sisters.

"Are you cold?" Inger asked finally, because Ellen wasn't wearing a cap, or a scarf either, stubborn as she was on some points. "Oh not at all!" Ellen answered. "One doesn't get cold now that it's spring, you know, madam!"

"Oh, it's you, madam! How do you do, how lovely!" "Yes," Ellen said. "But it's so dreadfully sad, also, you know. I mean, Mrs. Bollerud . . ." she said.

"Oh, yes," Inger sighed. "I heard she was ill?"

"Yes! She's very ill." "How sad!" "Yes terribly sad. And how have you been? You're well, I trust?" "Oh, yes, indeed. I'm well! My husband has just invented a new super vitamin and . . . ."

For an instant they turned toward each other and looked at each other with large, surprised eyes.

For the next several days there was a terrible racket in the back yard of Bjørnegården Apartment. Men arrived with ladders and power saws and started in on the old elm tree in the corner. One by one the dark brown, gnarled branches fell to the ground, each the size of a young tree. "They're cutting down the elm, Papa!"

"Yes," Papa said. "I've been thinking about that, too. . . ."

Slowly he stood up from the corner and stood behind her at the window and put his arm around her waist. Together they watched the tree fall, and a short, heavy stump was left, its fresh-cut surfaces shining.

Ørnulf and Inger took a taxi up to Fredrikstad Central Hospital, and stopped in front of an entrance. A nurse came out to meet them. Ørnulf and Inger got out of the car and greeted her. "Would you like to see her?" the nurse said. Ørnulf pinched his lips together and shook his head. "Don't you want to?" Ørnulf stood looking at her. "She looks so pretty!" the nurse exclaimed. It was as if she were imploring him. But Ørnulf just shook his head and said nothing.

Then they drove behind the hearse to the crematorium in Borge. When they arrived there were lots of people standing outside waiting for them. Everywhere Inger saw faces wet with tears. When she met their eyes they burst into tears again.

Ever since then she was filled with gratitude at the tears. She could call it up, see a face dissolving in tears. And it felt good to think of them crying! Because she herself could not.

The crematorium in Borge was filled to capacity. Everyone who'd known Evelyn came, everyone who'd known her as Dr. Holm's wife, who walked through the town in her leather coat and long, black pants, and who'd comforted them over the telephone, taken messages, maybe even saved the youngest child's life once. Neighbors in Bjørnegården Apartment building came, who knew that Mrs. Holm hadn't always had an easy time, that she'd been sick for a long time herself, but that she never said anything about it, was always willing to listen to what other people had. She wasn't any ordinary Fredrikstad person. If they told her something, it didn't go any further. They knew that, and that was why she heard a lot about how people in Fredrikstad suffered, and what they had to struggle with, behind the facade that Fredrikstad always demanded. The salesgirls on Nygaardsgata, hair dressers, seamstresses, maids they'd had, waitresses at Bjørnen Cafe, everyone came here who felt she was part of their life, even if just a little. But there were also a few who hadn't known her as Mrs. Holm, the doctor's wife, but knew her as she had once been: Evelyn

Gjarm. A fair young girl, full of playfulness and jokes, a young woman who viewed the world through humor's never-failing magnifying glass, and never stopped finding things to laugh at, even if it was only a man walking down the road. They'd laughed—with Evelyn Gjarm, and later with the Evelyn Gjarm who survived within Evelyn Holm to the end of her days.

Everyone came to the beautiful crematorium in Borge in the clear spring weather, the sun shone through the high windows behind the altar, shone on the white casket, sent pillars of light toward the unfathomable. They all came with their own grief. They came with precisely what she'd meant to them, and filled the chapel.

Way up in front sat Evelyn's brothers and sisters, all arranged by age. Now they were just five. The youngest was missing. They'd been six for so many years that the number seemed unnatural. They thought: Who will be next? This doesn't obey the law of fairness. They thought strange thoughts, all kinds of thoughts, each their own thoughts, and one thought in common: the man sitting farthest to the right in the front row had himself to thank for the fact that he was sitting there.

The young girl sitting beside him was not thinking this. She was thinking: Mama's dead. How was that possible, when she was so bright? Just as bright as the streams of light shining in over the altar now. As bright as the casket itself and all the flowers.

Pastor Hornfeldt stepped forth. He knew that Evelyn had never been a believer. Could he stand there and condemn her to eternal damnation according to John 3:16? No. He couldn't. Because he was no ordinary Fredrikstad pastor. He was a very unusual pastor, and there was a time he'd been made to feel that. Now he stood by Evelyn's casket and said: "To believe? What does it mean to believe? To believe—is to have an open mind."

And it became a sermon of the open mind. Because he knew that was what she'd had, and he knew she knew that when she died, her earthly remains would be lowered into the earth, become earth, become grass and flowers, which in the end would be scattered to the four winds.

"If only her openness toward others—her insight!—her rare ability to understand other people's pain—if only that ability could be spread! spread among all of us sitting here, who have benefitted from it while she was alive—yes if only this could happen, and we could drive away the terrible moral cowardice that makes us guilty of turning our backs to other people's pain—if only this could happen—yes, then we would have a better world."

On the bus into London that summer Inger heard a song. The bus was full of foreign and Norwegian students and it was heading toward King's Cross. Suddenly, in the back of the bus, a boy stood up. He had long, dark blond hair, jeans and a baggy jacket, and blond beard stubble. And he began singing a song.

It turned out that most of the foreign students on the bus knew this song, and they sang along. But Inger had never heard it before. It repeated, then a new verse, then the same again. *When will they ever learn?*

Then a new verse.

It was catchy. It was easy to learn. It was a wonderful song.

It was about war that always begins again. And about life that always defies it.

Inger sat there—on the way to the person she'd loved. She was hearing this song for the first time. She didn't know what would happen when she saw her again. Would she still love her? She sat there riding onward, yes, when she sat like this on the bus with this song in her ears, it almost felt like that.

She'd just watched her mother die. For many years she'd witnessed her father deciding his own and her mother's fate. She had seen how they loved each other. And now she was sitting here and had just said good-bye to a girl.

This girl had stood beside her through the most painful time of her life. She'd cried with her, held her, been. Marit had been there, and now she was bringing a little mascot from her along on the trip. She didn't know how it would go. She didn't know if they could still stay together, and if there would even be a world for them to stay together in, and if it was possible to create such a world. But she was sitting there, listening to the song, and soon she was singing along, it felt good to sing, it was the kind of song that never came to an end because it ended with the question it began with, and suddenly she had an intense feeling of future.

Someday the catastrophe would disappear. And she had a feeling of how it could happen.

POSTSCRIPT

Three and a half years later Ørnulf died of grief. He was found alone in his apartment with blood stains through all the rooms where he'd crawled and tried in vain to get up on the bed. After many years of drinking his blood refused to clot, and the doctor who came to the scene recorded hemorrhaging. Since the day Evelyn died the expression on his face had changed for good. In a ceaseless attempt to find her he drove from Fredrikstad to Tjøme and from Tjøme to Fredrikstad. That was how he made his infatuated flight so many times—to her, and as long as he was en route, waiting in Moss, sitting on the Bastø ferry, he could make himself believe she was there—at the end of the journey. But she was never anywhere. How could she die and leave him behind? At times he was furious at her for that. He found other women. He didn't love them, and they knew that. They stayed with him anyway—until they fled from him in fear. He drank and drank, he got nearly up to the level he had been at before his attack, but not quite. People around him tried to help him. He didn't want help. He knew that all doctors were idiots. And he had no desire to live. "The only reason I don't take my life," he said, "is that I don't want to give other people the pleasure of outliving me."

Then one day they did. And finally he had peace.

About the Author

Gerd Brantenberg was born in 1941 in Oslo, Norway, and spent her childhood and youth in Fredrikstad. After obtaining her arts degree in English, History and Social Science at the University of Oslo in 1970, she became a high school teacher in 1971, teaching in Copenhagen and Oslo until 1982.

She has been active in the feminist movement since the early 1970s, working in particular with the Women's House in Oslo and the Refuge for Battered Women. She has been a board member of the Norwegian Writers' Union and is a recipient of a State Scholarship for Artists and Writers.

About the Translator

Margaret Hayford O'Leary received her Ph.D. in Scandinavian Studies from the University of Wisconsin. She is Associate Professor of Norwegian at St. Olaf College, where she has taught courses in Norwegian language and literature since 1977. She has published several articles on Norwegian women writers and coauthored a textbook in intermediate Norwegian, and she is a member of the board of the Norwegian Teachers Association of North America.

Welcome to the World of International Women's Writing

An Everyday Story: Norwegian Women's Fiction edited by Katherine Hanson. $14.95. ISBN: 1-879679-07-8 Norway's tradition of storytelling comes alive in this enthralling anthology. The new expanded edition includes stories by contemporary writers, reflecting recent changes in Norwegian society: immigration, the artistic and cultural renaissance of the Sami and changing family structures.

Under Observation by Amalie Skram. With an introduction by Elaine Showalter. $15.95. ISBN: 1-879679-03-5 This riveting story of a woman painter confined against her will in a Copenhagen asylum is a classic of nineteenth century Norwegian literature by the author of *Constance Ring* and *Betrayed*.

Unnatural Mothers by Renate Dorrestein. $11.95. ISBN: 1-879679-06-X A compelling Dutch novel, by turns hilarious and heartbreaking, *Unnatural Mothers* explores the oldest bond in the world: that of mother and daughter.

Two Women in One by Nawal el-Saadawi. $9.95. ISBN: 1-879679-01-9 One of this Egyptian feminist's most important novels, *Two Women in One* tells the story of Bahiah Shaheen, a well-behaved Cairo medical student—and her other side: rebellious, political and artistic.

Unmapped Territories: New Women's Fiction from Japan edited by Yukiko Tanaka. $10.95. ISBN: 1-879679-00-0 These stunning new stories by well-known and emerging writers chart a world of vanishing social and physical landmarks in a Japan both strange and familiar. With an insightful introduction by Tanaka on the literature and culture of the "era of women" in Japan.

Wild Card by Assumpta Margenat. $8.95. ISBN: 1-879679-04-3 This lively mystery is set in Andorra, a kingdom between France and Spain. *Wild Card* tells the story of Rocio, a young sharp-witted woman who devises a scheme to beat her sexist boss at his own game.

How Many Miles to Babylon by Doris Gercke. $8.95. ISBN: 1-879679-02-7 Hamburg police detective Bella Block thinks she'll find some rest on her countryside vacation, but after only a few hours in the remote village of Roosbach, she realizes she has stumbled on to one of the most troubling cases of her career.

Originally established in 1984 as an imprint of Seal Press, Women in Translation is now a nonprofit publishing company, dedicated to making women's writing from around the world available in English translation. We specialize in anthologies, mysteries and literary fiction. The books above may be ordered from us at 3131 Western Avenue, Suite 410, Seattle, WA 98121 (Please include $3.00 for postage and handling). Write to us for a free catalog.